THE HUMAN ENTANGLEMENT

By

L. P. Magnus

Library of Congress Control Number: 2022913997

ISBN: 979-8-9865265-0-8 (ebook)

ISBN: 979-8-9865265-1-5 (paperback)

Dedication:

For one son from one father,
To one father from one son,
Not possible without the love and support of one mother,
Nor the unabashed inspirational exuberance of one daughter,
with hope that some of the ones that are not here yet might one day
listen to it, though we never actually meet.

To you, the reader:
It is my dear hope that you, as a reader,
enjoy getting lost in this world
as utterly as I did in creating it.
If it's not terribly bothersome,
please leave a review on the platform of your purchase.
For both your time and indirect
investment in classroom education
where I normally spend my days working, I say,
thank you so very much.
-a public-school teacher

Prologue

Arrangements of the modern-day society:

As with all lofty things that people may build or destroy, the tale in full is always more than can actually be told. The grand designs, the valid intentions, the machinations, mistakes, negotiations, opportunities of fortune, moments of brilliance and stupidities, the sheer will, that all came together in part or whole at various points in time, to help form the current modern society, with its' novel system of governing for instance, is a long and winding story not discussed to any great extent here. For the sake of clarity, however, a portion of time must be devoted to explaining the circumstances in which the current societies find themselves.

At the rise of the 3rd yield of global civilizations, there were many issues facing people across the world. The older governments and nation-states failed to prevent a series of escalating wars from decimating the lives of innocents in nearly every corner. Despite the five most advanced older governments possessing technology that, combined, would have made coexistence a practical option for all 16 billion people on the planet, claims of autonomy, sovereignty, and the petty squabbles over cultural differences that occur out of ignorance, short sightedness and mistaking bravado with justification eventually won out. Once started, these Great Wars, which originated over issues stemming from freshwater rights, lasted for almost four decades or 40 cycles by our modern calculations. By their end, there were only Pyrrhic victories. All the fighting and battles, great or small, had only truly succeeded in depleting nearly all that remained of the caches of resources set forth by the oldest governments. Several conflicts even intensified to regional nuclear wars between smaller nations, and they often enough cascaded over to larger nations as well. Their populations near fully devastated and wiped out in the collateral exchange of thermonuclear warheads.

Within 18 cycles of the outbreak of hostilities, the global reserves of coal and natural gas for public use were essentially depleted. The last usable oceanic fuel viable for drilling was expended 16 cycles later, in military operations that proved utterly fruitless to all parties involved. This was owed to the realization that it was difficult to consider any victory important if the last of your energy resources was used achieving it. Especially over adversaries whose own supplies were already barren and could not be counted on as contribution. But such was the classical thinking of politicians and war councils of the time. As was always the case in war, if a nation or state survived the longest, the term 'victor' could be applicable to them as little more than a deferral.

As the long vicious cycles of conflict went on, even many of the most stable nations saw their own internal support dwindle and corrode away under the incompetence and gluttony of leaders unable to cope with a vastly changed world dynamic. National governments became a place with only seemingly endless problems and no easy solutions. Likewise the lack of resources meant there were no distractions to provide their people with to help maintain a stable governmental power base. Using war to ensnare the attention of the masses has, after all, always been a favorite solution for leaders trying to avoid dealing with domestic strife. Yet these current wars had no favorable end as both the victors and losers were left equally too weak to claim any real achievements. Leadership changes became a frequent and often violent occurrence in many places. Famine, drought, and disease only grew more commonplace for the survivors. And while most of the older governments took longer, their collapse was eventually almost a foregone conclusion by the residents who cared to notice. Local despots, regional fiefdoms, and city-based states, sprung up in reaction, and grew abundant as shortages of drinkable water, food, power, sanitation, and medicine became mounting casualties of the later ravages of the fighting. This pattern only grew more and more common. Indeed, many future scholars noted the sad irony that as the ability to conduct warfare became more 'advanced', the more primitive were the population remnants that were left in its aftermath.

Travel, trade, and commerce became restricted without reliable fuel sources, and in addition became much more perilous. Crossing with a trader caravan through irradiated waste lands whose ownership was unknown, or more likely in dispute, was an easy way to find yourself and your goods hijacked or worse. In each territory, province or city entered, it became a dangerous game of chance with your trade. Leaders and their policies of tolerance for foreign traders changed often, and usually faster than the caravans could map out safe routes. In addition, education and food quality in many places reverted to pre-industrial levels. Civilians were more concerned with trying to grow food than learning to read or write. It wasn't uncommon in decades ahead for farm workers to dig up old, damaged military vehicles or mech suits with live ammunition still loaded and yet be unable to understand the warnings etched upon them. Several thousands died each cycle from the unused mines, automated machine gun pits, or drone guards left hidden, buried but still active at borders of nations that no longer existed. Several thousands more died from the radioactive fallout and contamination of the new deserts that were once productive farmlands. Global communication for a long time dwindled to almost nothing, and the few who spoke over the channels often descended into little more than banter about the sanctity of borders between disputing factions.

The last leaders of the older states stole away to the stars with their families, taking whatever assets and treasures they could abscond with for their own. Their one remaining achievement was to fund and oversee the construction of a space-elevator to a private orbital docking station. There, several nuclear-solar powered interstellar ships were constructed and docked. These were daring feats of engineering innovation never accomplished before. Ironically, several of those whose contentions, policies and warmongering had initially started the decimation of the planet now literally below them, found that to be protected from that chaos they had no choice but to now be cohabiters with their former earthly adversaries. But self-preservation is an excellent motivator for novel solutions, even among the staunchly argumentative heads of warring states. Still, safety in orbit was not a certainty to anyone. Fearing eventual reprisals from the surface, their elevator of salvation was demolished on their own commands once the construction of the needed ships was completed. All the station's inhabitants left the orbital facility within the span of 10 cycles; to assure they were beyond the reach of anyone on Earth. With them they took two-thirds of the nuclear-powered stellar-ships designed and created by the oldest and strongest of the former governments. These made long-distance travel capable thanks to state-of-the-art cryo-refrigeration tech and genetically accurate growth pods. These were capable of regenerating and replacing human tissue damaged from extended time in stasis. Some back on earth would go on to speculate that the leaders had charted a course beyond the reach of our solar system. Others ventured that they'd gone to try their luck on Mars with the intent to return one day. Most people on the surface that were still alive, however, didn't particularly care. The last great Earth-wars were still raging fiercely, and they were all consuming. The greatest robbery and violation of humanity's trust was conducted by its own leaders, and it was hardly noticeable by those in the dredges. Which at this point was nearly everyone. They had other more immediate concerns.

Famine, drought, mass migrations, fallout, regional plagues, and extinctions of both humans and what still lived on as livestock or wildlife were all widespread. Lack of work or arable lands were common enough before, but even the strongest of the old systems of governments were now strained beyond any boastful limits to provide enough food. The remotest and best preserved of the old governments finally dissolved some 16 cycles after the last major battle had ended. Much smaller regional authorities took hold in their absence, and although far less stable, they were apt to notice local issues and react in much faster time spans. Many of these local ruling systems worked through corruption and fear, continuing the same path of warfare to a smaller, but nonetheless violent degree that they'd been formed from. Some were religious based, others were ethnic based, but the majority of these small regional systems sought, essentially, to isolate themselves from most outside affairs, becoming highly xenophobic. The global community had come extremely close to killing all life, and for a long time many areas were not about to open themselves to this type of thinking again. Many… but not all.

<u>The Caradrium</u>

One of these small local governments originally started in the left-over ruins of a coastal mega-city. It was a city-state being run by a small coalition of veteran Sergeants, Lieutenants, Commanders, and a rather tight knit group of war widows, and other direct family members of lost soldiers. This small city-state began quietly growing and absorbing more lands and smaller regions faster than any others. Known originally as the Caradrium, what made its build-up unique was that it was done primarily through non-violent methods. And while the occasional battles with bandit clans or rogue states that mistook policies of being 'non-violent' with 'ill-prepared', did occur, word that the Caradrium kept its own people safe, educated, and comparatively healthy spread as far as their own trading caravans. Sometimes even farther. Their own traders and envoys worked hard to ensure a Caradrium currency credit always had its value honored.

Yet the true secret to their positive regard was that the Caradrium purposefully made it known that they were promoting trade and education and acceptance of all migrants willing to work for membership as citizens. No past crimes were held accountable unless committed inside their own borders, though a convicted crime of a migrant in their purview would mean permanent expulsion from all regions under their control. Yet a successful tour of security duty, or a few cycles rebuilding or repairing old infrastructure, or a half decade of training others to read or write or working in engineering, medicine, or donating lands for farming struck most people at the time, as fair trade for the protections gained as a citizen rather than remaining as simply a civilian.

Initially this trade of skill was expected of all those within their borders, even from those who were born there. No one was excluded from this for the first few decades of the Caradrium's existence, except by the determination of severe physical health problems. Eventually however, the policy became only applicable to outsiders and internal civilians wishing for the elevated status of citizenship. With this methodology, the Caradrium was able to claim some of the best social systems and security facilities in the world, at times when few places had electricity or even running water. The promise of a stable food market, free pre-war levels of quality education, security, and a chance for economic growth as well as a life free from various oppressions made for an enticing offer to most refugees who heard of it.

Once earned, citizenship status in the Caradrium brought bonuses such as a vote in the policies and government formation, as well as additional opportunities for higher level careers inside the government itself. Within three generations all those within their borders were granted citizenship status through either birthright, and either a cycle in government service, or passing of an exam on history and government modernization. This was usually expected to be done by a natural born civilian's 20th cycle.

The growing system was bound for change however, as the forming members reached the end of their own life spans and began passing on. The last major decision of the founding cohort of veterans and widows was to finalize the doctrine known as the Radix Temel Amak. This doctrine set up a triple sphere style of the democratic Caradrium government which included the SOMA representative body, the Benzi Supreme Court, and the Haiden Prime Trinity High Council.

Member anonymity, randomness of candidate selections, and purity of intentions was stressed far above all other considerations. Monetization of campaigns via private donors and political parties were forbidden in the government, nor could they operate inside any of the spheres. Adding addendums to legislation that didn't clearly align to help its primary intent was also forbidden. The forming cohort was adamant that their new system not fall victim to the same destructive, cyclic, and systematic errors as the previous world governments had. They did however avail themselves of several useful ideas and structural designs from former systems where they found them.

For the primary formation of laws, the first sphere of government, the SOMA legislative body, was made up of random populace citizens through a voluntary election process for every region of their city and outlying quarters. The Moot Election season, as it would later be known, kept each candidate's identities, especially the winner, a classified secret. The intention being that, while a SOMA member should be a person who is influenced in their ideas and views via their own experience as a private citizen, they should never be targeted for influence simply because of their standing as a member of the SOMA itself. This was reflected in the government's general motto: 'For the people. As the people. Within the people.'

After the SOMA's creation, as newer territorial regions were later added to the Caradrium, the SOMA membership grew until by the time of Taryn Steno's story, what had started with 156 representing members, had become 500 representatives. Each SOMA member had a seven-cycle, one-time only appointment. Not even in death could SOMA members be publicly recognized for their work, and all were required to agree to this when seeking election. It was colloquially referred to as 'the price of service'.

The second sphere was a multi-tiered system of courts. At their head was the Benzi Supreme Court applying Caradrium law and case validations. The 11 judges on the Benzi were picked by an alternating system between the other two spheres of government. The judges on the Benzi were typically given appointments of 15 cycles, although that matter was disputed for a long time by the founding cohort.

The final and most concentrated sphere of power in the Caradrium government was known traditionally as the Haiden Prime Trinity High Council, though most simply referred to it as the Trinity High Council. The process for picking the only three members to serve on the council is highly restrictive by its own nature and not fully known to any SOMA members, or in truth, even to the Trinity High Council members themselves. What the SOMA members did know, however, was that each new potential member of the Trinity high council would have to seek approval via a committee hearing of 17 random SOMA members before the appointment could be finalized.

The length of their appointments to the Trinity High Council varied. Secretly set by their approval committee, new council members were given terms of appointments from anywhere between one to 15 cycles. This was dependent on the recommendations reviewed by the SOMA approval committee and their judgment. It remains a strict rule that Trinity council members are never told of the length of their own appointment beyond this, so as to foster motivation among the trio to always be productive with their time. But how exactly Trinity council members were initially selected was in fact a secret very few, even in top government security knew in full.

The identity of all elected members of the government, being highly sensitive and restricted information, also led the founding cohort to form the Bizi security brigade, which is documented in the Radix Temel Amak doctrine. Its primary goal being to ensure that each governmental sphere's integrity remains intact and to run and monitor the Moot Election systems. It was the Bizi who, under the advisement of the final living cohort members, first established the anonymity and randomness protocols set for the Moot system. Each possible electorate, needing only to be an adult of citizen status in decent health and a resident of three cycles for the region they intended to represent. Each region's citizens could vote for, or against, a candidate if they wished, but were only allowed to make one of these choices when submitting their ballot.

The Bizi also established the offical campaigning systems to allow all candidates equal time to present themselves to the voters while avoiding revealing their identities to the public or any opportunistic parties and interests. Again, in consulting with the first cohort of leaders, the Bizi suggested that voting be made a mandatory responsibility for all able citizens. This was the information the public was officially told about the internal decision-making process that selected the SOMA legislative membership. As for the Bizi agents themselves and their own organization's policy for selecting new members, this remains highly secretive to this very day and is not recorded in any detail —even in the Radix Temel Amak.

Index: A Reference to Future Terminology

Benzi High Court: The highest court of the judicial sphere in the Caradrium and composed of eleven experienced judges.

Bureau of Investigating Zones of Interest [Bizi]: Government security organization charged with running state investigations, maintaining the intent and security of the Moot Election season, and anonymity of all associated participants and currently serving government officials.

Caradrium: The longest, most stable, and advanced government currently in existence with the largest populace since the end of the last global wars. Estimated population: Over 20 million total, approximately 16 million being citizens with 4.5 million non-citizen civilians. Location: coastal region, Defense Force protected zone. Government: A Silent Democracy format, comprising three distinct spheres of operation.

Credit(s): Monetary units of the Caradrium.

Cycle: The common modern term for a year or one orbital cycle length of the earth around the sun. Measured currently as cycle 1 being the 1st cycle of Caradrium society with the Radix Temel Amak established.

Defense Force: The standing national military protection and trade protection of the Caradrium territories.

First Cohort: Initial founders of the Caradrium, composed of military veterans, war-based widows, widowers, and Wailers (empty parents).

Haiden Prime Trinity High Council: The executive sphere of the Caradrium composed of three individuals. The selection process is largely unknown but does involve SOMA representatives to some extent.

Joe-cup: Bean-less coffee, comes in two general varieties: traditional or caff-free.

Leader's Exodus: Name given to the space evacuation of the surviving world leaders near the climax of the last global wars. Outcome unknown.

Moot Election: The randomized process by which five anonymous civilian candidates are requested to campaign for a SOMA representative seat for their home region.

Neural Scanner: Pre-war technology, used to scan and detect the onset of neurological issues well in advance of symptom expression. Use is required biannually from all citizens of the Caradrium, including children, and serves as the registration point for the Moot Election process.

Padd: Highly ubiquitous computerized tablet device.

Radix Temel Amak: The supreme law of Caradrium as created and resolved by its first cohort of leaders. The Radix embodies the doctrine of the three separate spheres of the silent democratic government, their obligations, and limitations. The Radix also includes the rights and responsibilities of its citizens, as well as requirements for citizenship consideration by civilians.

Recorder: A visual recording device.

Hexaderby: Professional organized sporting competition involving teams of players (rollers) competing for points in a large set of concurrent hexagonal tracts, popular among the populace of the Caradrium.

Rotation: A daylength, measured starting at the first hour of sunrise.

SOMA: The legislative sphere of the Caradrium. The selection process is done via the Moot Election voting season under the observation of the Bizi.

Suit: An upper echelon of management including corporate owners.

Tie: A middle management level individual within a corporate structure.

Wave(s): The Caradrium's system of interconnected computer networks consisting of an array of electronic, wireless, and optical networking technologies. The only publicly accessible one of its type functional in the world.

Wucengi Neural Device: Advanced miniaturized neural sync mechanism that allows Trinity High Council members to perceive images and sound inputs directly into the visual and auditory sensory systems.

Chapter 1: Factory Girl

The bang of her head against the metal beam square on her brow made a dull thudding sound. Walking down the stairs towards the main factory floor, she'd had to recover a step back after striking her hard hat in such a way. It wasn't that she was all that tall; she wasn't. Average height at best, even her work boots added only an extra inch to her. It wasn't even that she was unaccustomed to these stairs. She had been walking down from this office for almost four months now since being promoted off the floor. It was the case, in fact, that these stairs, descending from the small office area to the main assembly floor, were very narrow, with space barely wide enough for one person at a time. The stairwell with dark blue walls on both sides had this singular low overhanging connecting beam running across the top, just before the passage opened to a small metal railing on the left descent that overlooked the floor workers down below. She muttered a low curse to herself for forgetting about that infernal beam that was constantly blocking her path. It was a novice mistake and that made her hate it even more. Her red hardhat showed several spots of scarring and dents acquired in her first months of working from the upper office. And the metal beam itself showed a magnitude of paint-scuffs of many colors including red, yellow, light blue and green. These, of course, were from the collisions with countless other hardhats over the long cycles of the factory's operation. Though, while she'd been using these stairs, she had personally never witnessed anyone else perform this error. The other foremen all seemingly knew unconsciously to duck low by now, to fit past this obtrusive impediment on their way up or down.

Outside of her quiet cursing, Taryn Steno wondered, not for the first time, what moron had done such a piss-poor job of designing those stairs as ineffective and impractical as they actually were. Constructed of cheap wood covered in laminate at the top quarter and smooth slippery steel for the lower portion, it was as if their plan had been cobbled together as an afterthought with no mind towards efficiency or practicality, since indeed no one going up could actually fit past anyone going down. No, this single size narrow stairwell showed all the signs of a project cobbled together hastily with a goal of speedy construction at a bare minimum of effort, expense or thought. Not much better could be said for the design of the offices that the stairway led up to, which held several small metal-trimmed thin wood pulp desks crammed into a single medium room with no outer windows. A low false ceiling, cheap chairs, and poor ventilation were everywhere. The carpeting, which had long since passed its prime, retained a constant acidic stink of smoke from the stick addicts who worked in the office. It was made of the least attractive blue-pleated coloration, with tiny threading that had been worn, run over, and stained by countless dirty shoes and spills, so that little of its original color could be found.

For all the comings and goings by the various foremen besides her, this office space gave an average-size person a feeling of largeness, while a large person felt undeniably claustrophobic. Taryn was grateful in recent months she was neither. She had, as was her recent custom, used the stuffiness and stench of the office as a daily spur to gradually spend more and more time on the main floor. She felt comfortable there with the line workers, not just due to the less restricted space, but because many of them were friends to her. Taryn had naturally cultivated relationships with them during her own tenure as a "floor guy." In fact, privately she considered many of the floor workers far more intelligent and insightful on issues concerning business operations than her newer office mates. The floor guys' constant direct experience granted them both insights and unique gripes about production routines that were spoken of more freely to Taryn than to any other foreman. Gripes by the floor men were generally kept hushed as not to spark the expected and standard retaliatory accusations of laziness or stupidity. An extensive complaint spoken aloud to most foremen was a categorical sign of undependable workers in their world. The louder the speaker the swifter and harsher the response should be. And if a complainer couldn't be cowed quickly with the usual methods, anyone on the floor could be replaced, no matter their skill set. That was the one point all sides were conscious of, from floor guys to foremen to the Ties and Suits in the building far across the lot. And so, while small gripes could easily go unheeded if whispered low enough, newcomers learned quickly to be mindful of their speech in front of most foremen.

Except for Taryn. Boss Steno didn't make accusations or turn deaf ears. Instead, the complaints she fielded for herself gave the floor workers assigned to her section a much stronger sense of loyalty than was typical. It also gave Taryn places to "invent" and suggest "improvements" to be sent over to the Ties sitting cozy in the company HQ across the lot. Other floor workers' communication with their own foreman was ostensibly much more one-sided, and as was customary, usually only in the downward direction.

The Ties above her didn't mind, or even care for that matter, where Taryn's ideas actually came from, even if she did make them acknowledge their originators were those on the lowest rungs. "The ragged scraps, the uncivilized, the morons" as the Ties often called them with repugnance. They had no care for them and would only acknowledge even a lower foreman like Taryn when it worked to their advantage or was necessary. So, while they were interested by some of Taryn's thoughts that were passed up the chain, as it could be seen to make the lines run marginally smoother or made the product more versatile, or easier for the marketing slacks to promote, they had little care to give any real praise to her, let alone for workers she supervised. All in all, it was a typical company. Most of the real, difficult, and stressful work was done, reliably, by the lowest majority who were paid marginally, while the upper minority, the Ties, and the even higher Suits, would rarely acknowledge this in any earnest. Even when the highest Suits did show up to put in the occasional set of full weekly hours for their grandiose credit salary, their focus was on themselves. And their subservient Ties, like scrapping children hoping to one day be seated at the adult's table, only strove for excellence in the speed and the quality of their manufactured products. This gave them justification to raise prices without enduring more expenditures. And with this accomplished, one could hope to raise their own standing and their chances at an eventual spot amongst the Suits. Yes, it was an average company that Taryn Steno worked for: cold, greedy, and optimized only for its immediate profitability.

During her walk down the remaining stairs, Taryn subtly rubbed her hard-hat to feel for a fresh dent and quietly spied around to see if anyone on the floor had heard the thud of her indelicate descent. After being satisfied that her mistake had truly gone unnoticed and was lost in the sounds of the busy floor chatter, she picked her way across towards the far north-western section. She darted briskly through several other sections of the floor, passing by like some small fox quietly picking its way smartly through a dense forest. She could hear other foremen starting to shout at sluggish floor guys, or whoever was nearby, as she skirted gingerly towards the Head Foremen's platform in the middle of the floor. From this small brown and yellow octagonal landing, Taryn had for years seen the Head Foreman monitor the progress of the various 31 sections through his elevated view, his eye monitor, and his numerous screens. During the workday he could easily be overheard angrily chastising the lower line foremen about any deficiencies in speed that he noticed. And he was notorious at 'clearing out' problems that were holding up the production speed on his floor with a grim menace and even grimmer vernacular. His reports that he composed were directly under the Tie's review. No foreman liked walking by 'the nest' as it was called, Taryn least of all. To her, it was like trying to rush, unnoticed, by a giant predatory bird on its perch. Nothing that was screeched from the nest was ever good news for the floor workers. And the Head Foreman, a lean old scab of a man with a nose similar in size and proportions to that of a carrion's foul beak, was often fond of making the section foremen pause while he berated them in person. Taryn thought the process was not too unlike a buzzard picking the scraps from a pile of fresh bones. During his usual tirades, the old vulture ensured that he was loud enough, so the nearby sections heard him as well. There was, in fact, another Head Foreman whose own nest was located in a separate factory floor on the company grounds. This one was responsible for sections 32-79, but Taryn had heard little better of him. Taryn turned her shoulder sideways, picked up her pace and managed to slip by the old vulture this time. But she knew that it was only a matter of fortune since the old man's attention was currently focused on belittling some poor sod in a nearby section who had foolishly talked too loudly about not being able to locate his tools and gear.

She hurried along the east-west walk path and quickly zig–zagged up and through some more sections. Once workers had been around the floor a while, they knew how to maneuver the tighter sections of the line with ease, finding shortcuts where there were no real planned paths. Taryn had learned this quicker than most, as living in a cramped apartment with four others was good practice for such situations. Though even this thought was tinged by the notion that there were only three others at home for her now.

Still, if there were any bright spots in her overcrowded home life, first and foremost had to be that despite her advanced age, Taryn's mother helped out tremendously in the ordering and maintaining of the apartment. Truly Taryn could not have hired a better maid, cook, and babysitter for her small family even if she had the credits of an upper-level Suit. Her youngest, her son Trey, was constantly a handful, especially in the tightly packed flat. Her oldest, Lilly, was just beginning to form her own pre-teenage thoughts and opinions, though to this point rarely considering those of others. Taryn and Cyrano had had their daughter while still in their early teens themselves, and from their own struggles both had strived to constantly remind their daughter not to do the same. Taryn had recently thought more and more about how Lilly's patterns of thinking and behaviors were further akin to Cyrano than to herself. Trey however, it seemed, was too much like herself in his youth. Through watching him and his endless energy Taryn was constantly reminded of how charmed her youth had been, growing up on the farm where she had space and been able to vent her own exuberance. That realization, chief most amongst all the other reasons, had made the involuntary sale of Trey's grandfather's farm and land all the more painfully palpable to Taryn. Especially when she would struggle to regain control of Trey as he went through his all too regular tantrums.

Taryn was still in her mid-20s. Quite young all things considered, but certain children age their parents at a much faster pace than normal. It was times like those, when Trey's constant screaming made him difficult to manage, that Taryn's appreciation of her mother's proximity grew considerably. When her mother first began living with them it was truly like having a third parent around. Gloria was a constant source of emotional support and acted as a buffer from Trey when Taryn's nerves were worn and fraying. Without any prompting, her mother would swoop in like a great dove to calm the two cycle-old or take on the chore of bearing the brunt of his tantrums for a while. Now with just the two of them to run the home, Gloria was one of the main reasons Taryn still had a realistic hope of keeping things together with some small sense of normalcy. When possible, she would try to push the three of them, Lilly, Trey, and herself to venture out together to a busy marketplace, a park, a museum, or to navigate some other random prosaic outing as a trio. She knew that her mother would go with them if asked, to take some of the load off, yet Taryn frequently preferred to be the sole adult for these moments. She couldn't quite put it into so many words when pressed by Gloria, but Taryn felt that the outings might work to break the kids of their routines, while distracting all three of them from their loss. At the same time, she wanted to prove to herself that she could manage to be fully in control and truly on her own–at least for the short term.

But it was Taryn's need to financially support her family that had been the motivation for her to be here, in this job from the first. And this need had only grown since then, she reminded herself, as she scraped between two larger line workers. She couldn't even afford to take more than a day off to plan Cyrano's final arrangements. *He would've understood that*, she told herself. Her work was the only thing stopping the wolves now. The bills she might be able to fight off. The children she could raise with her mom's help. Outside of these, her own private thoughts and innermost feelings, she'd been forced to isolate and cut off from herself. There was precious little time for their dissection, their processing, nor anything beyond. No hopes or desires of Taryn Steno seemed realistic besides merely wishing to keep her small family sustained for the next month. All other thoughts in herself she'd mainly ignored. Locked away as time-wasters or impracticalities. Her work ethic and her desire to keep her family going drove her.

It was that drive after all, she'd like to think, that had somehow gotten her noticed after working a few years on the lines here at the factory. Taryn had received her recommendation for an advancement to her current post by a late foreman who she had, to her regret, only gotten to know for a brief time, while she was still a floor guy. The fellow had been in a vehicle wreck during poor weather not one week before Taryn's promotion came through. As such, Taryn never learned why she had been recommended for advancement in the first place. She, initially, was hesitant about the promotion. Where others saw being a floor foreman as an opportunity to eventually work their way up to becoming a Tie, or perhaps even a Suit, Taryn despised the idea of being responsible for even more people outside her own family. In her mind, they were quite enough responsibility on their own and she was never rightly convinced she merited any real distinction to begin with. Taryn, with her rather short unassuming stature and workaday approach to her fashion style was never the type to noticeably stand out from any sort of crowd. Her practical look and pragmatic approach were cultivated from her youth on the farm and exacerbated by the few quick years in a double working marriage. Certainly, *remarkable* was not a common descriptor for someone whose small build literally meant that she could quickly fade into the hurrying masses on the line in the briefest of moments. Especially now with all her focus and drive trained on the task of managing two kids, she had no thought to herself over that of the state of her now fractured family. In truth, Taryn may have never accepted the promotion to a floor foreman if Cyrano had not died. Not only was her husband gone but so was the precious income he'd been providing. The monthly death gratuity from the Defense Force was good enough with the addition of her old salary that the bills were usually met on time. But the fact that the foreman position nearly doubled her already stretched pay credits had forced Taryn's hand on the matter.

She had been a floor foreman responsible for her own section of the line for over four months now and while she could see in other foremen the traits that had gotten them promoted in the company, she often felt apart from them. They were for the most part overly meticulous to the details of the line worker's actions and often possessed a reservoir of threatening or outright violent methods of motivation to spew upon them. Taryn didn't desire to make friends with any of the other foremen, or mind much when they didn't appear too either. By contrast, Taryn was much less confrontational and much more thoughtful in her approach with the line workers. She preferred to talk to her floor men, not just the simple pleasantries or the vain company line talk that so many others used almost as a reflex, but actual talk about her own family, the latest hexaderby game, or the juice of the news tree, as they say. She would listen to them as well. After other foremen had completed their daily rolls and gotten their lines squared away and gone up, as was customary, to the quiet of the office for a break to smoke a stick, "Boss Steno" would stay on the floor and listen to her workers. Often about their own families, personal troubles, complaints, goals, their own news, and stories. Their triumphs and humiliations. All were typical matters of conversation between Taryn and her line crew before and after the work buzzers gave them the starting signal. In this way, Taryn also heard the worker's notions concerning their duty processes and how they thought the line should be run. Soon, the floor guys of her section grew to trust her. They expected that at the very least she would send some of their more important words, if in a reasonably politer form, up the chain to the Ties. Yet even when "Boss Steno" was actually harsh to an irresponsible worker, few, if any, veterans of the floor found any reason to lay the blame on her for that. There was justification in their views. She had presented herself to them as a good portion fairer and smarter in her manner than most of the other floor bosses they'd worked under. "Kind, like soft leather when you got your mark, but harsh like a shackle when you slacked" was often heard repeated from one worker to another less experienced lineman.

Still, her more passive style in her niche had led some of her fellow contemporaries to warn her in private that she was not promoting what the company expected out of their foreman. While still others, of a more unscrupulous sort, might casually complain to the Ties across the lot about their lack of confidence in the young female foreman. "Too friendly and soft" they'd say, "more of a tutor than a taskmaster", and in such a way they hoped to promote their own standing within the company. Though she didn't know it, these were the rare instances of the Ties disregarding their subordinates' thinking that worked out in her own favor. Besides, even if the Ties had listened with more interest to these detractor's remarks, to the view of the accountants, Taryn's section of floor workers was, at that point, as productive as any of the others.

Taryn finally reached her area, section 31 of 79, just as the morning buzzer began. The line and all its machinery and electronics blinked to life in a cacophony of lights; whistles; beeps; and hums. Hearty greetings of "Hey boss" or "Morning boss" from a few of her nearest line boys were quickly drowned out as metal parts began jostling as they picked up speed for the warm-up rotations. Other workers who had been chatting further off or squatting on the floor quickly took to their places while the mechanical orchestra that was the factory line began to play its screechy, hissy, metallic music. Boss Steno watched and quietly took the roll of each of her floor guys as their attention went to the various preparation tasks before them. Fifteen of her 107 workers were not here. Four were on their 5th day out and Taryn knew that they were not likely to be allowed to return. Easier to take a chance on fresh replacements than those who were consistently missing. Hard as it was to find a decent job these days, she was amazed at how cavalier some folks could be at ignoring a chance at even minimal paying employment. After all, prices never decreased, and wages almost never increased. Moreover, what caused Taryn far more angst was that of these 15 workers down, she was missing her entire trio of micro-workers too. The most highly skilled people that had reliably been on the line for cycles and who performed the most complex and delicate process of assembly. The "circuitry surgery" it was called, and they did it cleanly and with an inhuman quickness derived from thousands of repetitions. Their postings took the longest to train up to and were the hardest to make up for. Normally two of them could make up for the loss of one. But now, starring down the line at their empty station spots, she was down to none.

Taryn listened to the chatter on her personal speaker as she heard other sections report their missing numbers to the Head Foreman back at the nest. Each time a section foreman would report a number and the old bird would caw an acknowledgement and direct some replacements their way, then the next section's foreman would chime from their section. Always the number of replacements being sent out by the nest was less than what was needed. Always fewer and fewer were sent too, so that the gap between the missing and the incoming replacements would grow larger with each new report. Taryn's section, the last to report on this floor by virtue of its numbering, had a larger than normal mark to reach today and they would need every minute of time to have a chance of getting at it. If the Ties or the Nest were consistent in anything, it was in noticing a missed mark. And the further the miss the more their intolerance and rage would be directed at the whole section in general and the foreman specifically.

A squeak of her black voice box brought up Taryn's turn to call the Nest:

"Section 31 roll done and sent. Fifteen missing…"

She waited. The Box squawked back at her,

"Section 31, 3 replacements incoming."

"Three raws? Three!" She stammered in disbelief. "You can't be serious boss? I'm missing near 15 percent of my line today. Three workers couldn't fix that if they were masters on the floor. And you know that these raws usually have half the motivation."

Raws' or ores', though paid much less as replacers, were paid daily for their work. So, unless an individual was purposely trying to impress a boss for a chance at a permanent spot, raw workers generally had little concern towards helping the speed of whichever line they happened to get sent to. That was one of those problems that Ties didn't ever care to try and truly solve since they could easily shift the blame to the various foremen for the lack of productivity.

The Nest growled back,

"That's all the hands left today, so stop your bitching, Steno. Make it work. Hit the mark or it's your asses!"

The box went quiet while Steno ground her teeth together, paused in thought. She had been in spots like this before, having fewer workers with even fewer replacements, but never at such a gap and never with such a large mark to hit. She resolved after a moment on what to do, surely the only thing she could do. She'd brief her boys on the issue and try to stress the severity of the situation. After that, she would need to assign the replacements to the most needed sections. She decided that she would place herself and the next two most experienced on the circuitry surgery post, to help counterbalance the raws' lack of experience and their likely lack of motivation. That was the best she could hope to do, and it would take all her efforts to make it work. The pace of the line was already in its final warm-up state. The product parts were due to come rolling through at full speed any moment. Taryn threw a small switch on her earpiece that called on her men via their headsets and began the briefing.

"Ok, listen up," she hollered. "We got 15 out today… including our 3 micros." A bundle of experienced glances shot around eventually settling back on their boss as the importance of this news set in. The micros always needed to be working, they were essential, and they were the absolute hardest skills to learn. "The Nest," Taryn continued, "in its beautiful wisdom, is sending us 3 ore's as coverage, but that's it. None left besides them, and I got to figure, as usual, they weren't exactly the pick of the litter. You can all see the mark line for today on your own headsets, so you older boys know what kind of crunch we're in..." She paused to that register with them, then continued, "So, I want you fast today. I *need* you fast today fellas... As fast as you can be."

One of the workers down the line and out of sight interjected. "Hey, boss? You want us to take the gloves off on the finishing line? Would make our slots faster."

"No, Breg," she said. "Leave the gloves on. Just do your best. Last thing I need is someone losing a finger today and besides, you know that D-9 in the sprays is no good for you. Time spent dealing with stupid injuries and cleanup will certainly make us miss the mark and I don't want to have to train new finishers cause one of you lost a hunk of meat or got the tumors on your fingers."

Tumors, especially on the skin and the hands, were common on the line workers, Taryn knew. They happened when exposed cuts were mixed repeatedly with the packaging disinfectant, a dark purple liquid spray called D-9. She had seen several men move spots in her time on the line because of their reduced dexterity after the encroachment of such growths. And everyone could recognize some of the oldest line workers on the floor as they often had fewer than the usual digits. Though the official safety rules said that the finishers should have their gloves on to prevent this exposure, since her promotion Taryn had heard several other line bosses routinely and loudly boast in their office of how they increased production speeds by 'forgetting' to tell their finishers about it or to double check them.

Replacing an occasional worker with bad fingers was expected every now and then. Part of the job that everyone from the line crews up had accepted for years as a possible cost for their long-term employment. But Taryn had recoiled when she realized that these specific foremen were in need of new permanent hires at three or even four times the rates as other line crews due to this type of deterioration.

Taryn continued her announcements over the comms to the line. "I'll be covering for the micro-workers with Frolin and Quade. Ore's are on the easier spots, so hopefully… they won't be in our way. Any issues today need to be taken care of quickly. We can't afford delays or distractions. And Kilt put on your damn harness. I know that you're faster without it, but I don't want my hanger losing a foot in the presses and bleeding all over us; the product or the line." Far down a young lean man with long curly hair, leaned to the side, shot a sarcastic smirk at his boss, and proceeded on to the tall polls overhanging the line where he reluctantly strapped on his black leather safety harness.

Boss Steno went on, "Help the Ore's if they need it fellas. Keep on them if their concentration falls. Other than that, keep channels clear of chatter and focus on your own hands. We'll show those dumbass Ties across the lot how good we are, even when they can't be bothered to do *their* jobs and keep us at full strength." She had a quick thought "Too lazy and can't keep it up…betting you they hear the same complaints when their back home too." she said smirking

She heard a few laughs and cheers back on the headset at this final remark. As a general rule, the floor workers hated the Ties. It was commonly whispered among the line crews that the Ties and Suits hid themselves in a separate office building for their own safety and the tidiness of their clothes. Though it did make more sense, from the Tie's viewpoint, to keep the undesirable but necessary routines of the floor workers isolated and separate from their cleaner and much newer office building. In reality they were only a short walk away. Two parking lots and a checkpoint true, but still less than a brisk five-minute walk. In their tall office building the Ties could scheme and plan with their hypothetical conversations and debates, or any other potential cost cutting speculations. It was easier for the Ties to talk openly about plans for the Corporation's future when those that would be most affected were not in earshot. Besides securing any legitimate Corp secrets, rumors and even preventing panic amongst the labor force were helped by this separation of the two groups. The hands of the large factory floors never quite knowing what the head would tell it to do next.

Taryn assembled and repositioned a few workers to various spots on the line that she guessed would still be above the replacements' pay grade. Trying to spread out and mitigate the loss of so many hands across the whole production would only work so far though, and she knew it. She took her post on the surgery section next to Frolin and Quade, took off her red foreman headset, put on the heavy blue goggles with optical enhancements and got to her task.

Long could the others have watched boss Steno standing in that same spot, if not for their own concerns on the line. She stood, her legs still as planted posts with her eyes moving briskly and hands nimbly efficient for a full shift and a half with barely a break in her work, trying in vain to cover the work of three. Quade and Folin were helpful, but they weren't nearly as fast as the slowest micros she'd known. Taryn was sweating, breathing heavily, and fully focused on the details of each delicate surgery. She was a floor guy again for the moment, and while all her focus was on her task, that quickest of thoughts gave her a modicum of comfort. She had covered this slot before, but even a veteran Micro-worker a week off the job suffered from a loss of pacing. Steno hadn't worked at this at all since becoming a foreman. Few issues or questions needing her attention were brought up by the others though, and the lack of interruptions meant her pace did generally improve throughout the day. Everyone else, as far as she could tell, looked to be working near their own capacities. The only annoyances were the regular updates from the Nest that garbled in her and the other worker's ears about not being on track. The Head Foreman failed to mention that section 31's actual unit-per worker pace was far beyond what was considered normal.

Hours later, when the final shift buzzer sounded, and the line slowed to low hissing mummer, Taryn felt completely drained. Her legs and back were beyond stiff. She took off the goggles and put her foreman headset back on. She checked the line totals on the glowing-blue glass screen and cringed when she saw the percent complete report at 84%. This was not good. For while section 31's production numbers that day were as high as they'd ever been previously, the Ties were much more apt to look at the simple percent completion and rate this day as a failure by that alone.

Taryn thanked the workers who were nearby or who still had on their earpieces, but it was hard to feel good about their results. Everyone could see the numbers on their own headsets and even the most stoic among them felt a tinge of dejection. They had done everything as best they could and by the book, but still had come short of their goal and they knew that —in the views of the Ties that would— reflect badly on them.

They all knew that the crews in "bad sections" were far less likely to ever be promoted, and occasionally were fired en masse, with little deference to an individual's working pace. If they were lucky, a purported "bad section" with slower outputs would have only a portion of its workforce cut out as a warning more than anything else. Training new replacements, after all, did take some time and expense. That couldn't be helped. But untrained labor was cheaper to start with and there had always been a predictable uptake in production speeds from the nearby lines after such a decimating vivisection occurred. The increased adjacent production, even if only temporary, would nearly always outpace any loss from the training of fresh hires.

In some rarer instances, however, whole sections might be let go, including their foreman if the wrong Ties were hearing negative reports sent over from the nests. The Suits cared little about what methods the Tie's enforced for keeping the floors a bustling hive of activity, as long as their margins ticked up as a result.

Boss Steno knew all this as she made her way slowly back towards the office. When she passed near the Nest once again, the old Head Foreman leaned over and, looking down his long and crooked nose, jeered at Taryn.

"What's a'matter, dearie?" he asked. You don't like what the lack of fear does to your ratings?" He cackled sarcastically. Now his tone changed from sardonic to a much more menacing state as he continued.

"You young fool, you made my floor slow today. Good thing the other sections did better to shield your mistakes, though I doubt the Ties see that way. Another day biting the bear like that, and they'll be kicking you to the door faster than you can run at it." He laughed as he chomped on a freshly lit stick. Because of his elevated posting he was the only one allowed to smoke near the line.

Taryn was too tired to look up directly at him. She merely stood, soberly looking ahead as she paused to let the gangly troll finish his rant at her. None of it was pleasant and it consisted mainly of curses and slurs of her gender. But the fellow was her superior here, and to walk away ignoring the old vulture entirely while he pecked at her would only encourage more of this treatment the next day. Better to let him get it out of his system now and be done with it she thought.

Someone different will just screw him up tomorrow. "Today's simply my turn at his ire", she thought.

The cleaners, repair crews, and maintenance workers were already hard at their various tasks of inspecting the different sections of the line for the night as Taryn slowly started climbing the narrow stairs back to the office. Her shoulders slumped further up the stairs as she remembered that she still had all her reports to complete for the day. Usually, the reports were completed by the foreman via voice entry as they made rounds up and down parts of their section so that the details could be recorded on the fly. Taryn, being quite unable to do this, had to fill in the needed data based on her best guesses and her memory from nearly 13 hours prior. She had, in fact, received several automated late notices on her headset that she hadn't been wearing during the day.

"It couldn't be helped." she thought. Taryn began filling in the data from what she remembered and, in the parts where she truly had no idea, made approximations based on her experience, it was better than not reporting anything. And Taryn did secretly hope that, given the staffing issues that she made sure to repeatedly note in her reports, the Ties might allow for inaccuracies they may find should they scrutinize her numbers more carefully. An hour later, she finished her daily reports and sent them in.

She checked the time on her headset. The 17th hour. Gloria, her mom, would be upset she was late again. "Also, can't be helped," she thought. She shut down the headset and placed it in its charger, cleaned up her desk and prepared the materials she would need for tomorrow. By the time she closed the office door it was an hour later. This time she wearily ducked her unprotected head while going down the stairs as she left.

* * *

Taryn had barely gotten her vehicle off the company grounds for the drive home when an automated voice message rang over her speakers. The voice she immediately recognized as her own.

"Hey dummy, remember that you need to stop by the med-clinic tonight and get your Neural-screening out of the way. It's your last chance or you'll have no one to blame for the overdue notice and fees but yourself. Also, don't forget the milk. Hope you didn't work too late, or Mom will be pissed you weren't there to help with the kids again."

Taryn grimaced to herself as the music came back on. Of course, she'd forgotten. That's why she'd decided to set up the reminder. She'd been far too distracted at work today to remember her earlier planned errands.

"Well at least I knew that I'd forget," she murmured to herself.

The medical clinic was on the drive home and the grocery store was before that. She hoped the clinic wasn't too busy tonight. It was a well-known 24-hour place and Taryn's experience told her that the wait could be only a few minutes or as long as several hours depending on how busy they were. She decided to take the chance that the milk wouldn't spoil while she was busy at the clinic and stopped to buy that first. The scan would certainly be the longer of the two stops but late and tired as she was, it made more sense to Taryn to get the quicker of the two stops out of the way first.

"Usually, the neural scans last no more than 30 min long," she said justifying the choice to herself. "I should be ok." She sent a quick voice message to Gloria telling her of the delay. Taryn didn't want to call. She didn't feel like directly hearing the disapproval in her mom's voice at being even later right now.

After running in for the milk, she walked into the med clinic, checked in, and threw herself into the nearest empty seat in the waiting room. A quick appraisal of those nearby was not hopeful. While it didn't appear to be completely full, the waiting area was far from empty. She checked for any messages on her personal earpiece receiver and heard the not so enthusiastic reply from her mom that she had been expecting. She waited some more, wondering how long the milk would hold out. Tired as she was, she actually almost dozed, her head dropping a little in that barely cushioned white chair. After a long while, Taryn had no idea how long exactly, she was startled awake by the sound of her name.

"Miss Stenro, you can come on back now," called the male technician incorrectly.

She got up and decided not to correct his pronunciation. He was a short, slightly obese man with light brown chaotic hair, half heartily pulled into a ponytail. He was obviously one of the night shift workers she guessed. He didn't need more work and she was too tired to really care all that much at his mistake. As long as the file had her name and her citizen ID number right, that is all that mattered. He led Taryn down a long corridor of mostly closed exam rooms and turned a sharp corner to a back room that was only half lit. Some lights apparently needed replacing while the remaining ones would give an occasional flicker. The small dim lit rectangular room had the standard sink; cabinets; and chairs typical to all exam rooms, but the padded table was pulled a bit further from the wall to make room for the neural scanner and its arm stand near the head of the table.

The technician had Taryn take a seat and began going over her personal information. He measured her height, weight, confirmed her ID Number and general medical history, her doctor's name, and results from her prior scans. Procedurally nothing new and medically nothing remarkable in her history save from a slight rise in blood pressure, probably a result of her job as he explained. The disheveled technician, looking at Taryn through his bagged eyes, started the routine explanation of what the scanner did and how it worked, stopping along several points to suppress his own muffled yawns. Taryn had heard all this before and faked her attention while only half listening to the technician jabber on about electrical conductivity; magnetic fields; resonators; various frequencies; and testing neuron impulses. When the technician was apparently done, he grabbed the yellow crescent shaped sensor unit off the scanner arm and turned it over to expose the underside. Taryn remembered how she always thought the portable sensor unit looked like a large yellow pill bug. Or one of those giant marine isopod fossils that her mother used to teach her about. Or perhaps a stripped-down hexaderby helmet. Her mind drifted. The fatigue was catching up to her.

"The scanner", the technician continued quickly, "has three points of contact on your head. One on the forehead, another on the top of the crown and another on the middle of the parietal bone." He pointed to the concave pads on the underside of the scanner in succession, then motioned to his own head the three places where the pads would directly touch.

"The scanner will measure the activity in your brain and the computer," he pointed to a small screen device attached on the arm stand, "will compare your scans to what we know about early cases of neurological diseases like the wandering; the trems; or the mind-cage."

"After I place the scanner on, you'll be all set. I'm going to shut off the lights and leave you to sit. You can listen to some music," he said, handing her a padd. "Or use the padd to read, but you can't call anyone since talking deviates the activity levels. No video or bright lights either."

He placed the scanner over her head, secured it and he made his way to the door again, "The scanner will take about 30 minutes to finish and will beep when it's complete. Push the button on the wall when you are done or if you have any problems"

"What if I fall asleep?" she asked, yawning. "Will that throw off the scanner too?"

The technician, for a moment, actually looked at Taryn now, seeing the tiredness in her own eyes. Her question had actually got him off the usual track of his procedural repetition that he'd probably rattled off a dozen times that day alone.

"No, that should be fine, the scanner can compensate. I'll check on you in twenty minutes or so. Push the white button on your left and it will begin the process automatically in a few seconds," he said.

He shut the door on his way out. Taryn pushed the button, picked up the padd, put on some light string music, tossed it back on the counter, closed her eyes and quickly let the melody drift her down a river of sleep. The neural scanner began to hum along quietly.

She didn't remember any dreams that she may have had, but to Taryn what seemed like just a moment later, a knock came from the door and the technician popped his head in asking, "You all set in here?"

Taryn blinked and checked the time. She had slept for about 35 minutes. She might have been madder if she wasn't so tired to begin with. She took off the scanner and placed it back on its spot on the arm.

"I think so," she said, trying not to sound embarrassed.

"Let's see," the technician responded. He turned on the one set of lights that worked, came in and pulled the small computer off the arm stand. He pushed several buttons that hummed back at him.

"Looks like you're all done," he said smiling as he put the computer back in place. "Any results that are flagged by the computer we'll have sent to be analyzed by your doctor. Should anything abnormal come up that they are concerned with, they'll be in touch within the next two weeks. No news is good news, as they say. You'll be sent your scan's confirmation number from the medical grid in the next hour or so. Check in again on the wave if you don't get it with in a day."

"Ok."

Taryn nodded, already standing up and putting on her coat while he'd been talking.

She wondered if the milk waiting in her vehicle had spoiled because of her nap. Behind her, as the technician left the exam room, he put the scanner into rest mode and shut off the lights before leaving to deal with other patients. After he shut the door, on the arm stand, hidden on the back of the small computer, a barely perceptible green light began to blink slowly, but steadily.

Taryn made it home in about 15 minutes. Late as it was, there was little traffic to deal with beyond the med clinic parking area. At her building she took the elevator to the third floor, got off and made her way to Apartment 306-North. She was finally home. Inside the doorway the main areas of the flat were all dark, save for a single hall light that Taryn switched on. It was quiet. Everyone was obviously already asleep. She took care of her coat and shoes and saw a covered plate of food on the tiny circular dining table with a note that read. "If you don't want it cold, then don't be so damn late."

She smirked and muttered to herself, "Mom."

Gloria's note of chide humor aside, Taryn gratefully picked a few scraps off the plate in the dark. After putting the milk away, she went to check on Trey and Lilly in their rooms. Lilly was asleep sideways on her bed with her lights and vid-music still on as she snored with her mouth open. A common occurrence for her these last few months, without Cyrano around.

"I just don't want to sleep" she would tell her mom and the result was usually that she passed out with every light and device in her room still going. Taryn quietly turned them all off and covered the snoring Lilly in a blanket and shut off the lights as she left. As for Trey, he was being held by her mom as they both slept in an old wooden rocking chair in a separate bedroom. It was one of the few heirlooms she had managed to save from her parent's farm.

After Taryn's father had unexpectedly passed while working in his crop fields, her mother Gloria, as capable and expert a schoolteacher as she was, could not afford the bills associated with an unproductive farm. Thus Taryn, barely in her 20's, left her own education completely to begin working full time. The choice of moving to full time at her job in reality hadn't been hers, but she sent all the excess credits she earned in a pitiable attempt to keep her mother in her childhood home. Of course, being one of the company's lowest credit earners, it didn't take long for her to realize the futility of her attempts to both support her own family and save her parent's home. Within four months Gloria was forced to sell. Afterwards her mother moved into the apartment with her, her husband Cyrano and their two children. Gloria —while welcomed and quite helpful— still had an amazing capacity to be highly critical and skewed in her thinking at times.

Taryn finally crept down the hall into her own bedroom. She thought, as she entered, about all the times prior while coming home late from a long shift that Cyrano would already be here, snoring away too. She would change clothes as she did now and slip into bed next to him. His breathing would change its pattern, and in the dark he'd whisper to her as he cuddled closer.

"The next time you get home at this hour, it better be because they finally made you into a Suit," he'd whisper.

Now there was only a cold bed, darkness, and silence. No air stirred as she crawled in the sheets. All was still. And as she settled all that could be faintly heard now was the sound of her gentle weeping as she drifted off.

Chapter 2: It Won't Take Long

The next morning as she woke, Taryn remembered dreaming ever so briefly of a speeding train. Not a passenger train, but still one packed together with many other standing strangers besides herself. An old cargo-style locomotive she felt. It was as long as a city but moving at a great speed, rattling along tired tracks. Dirty, dusty, smelly, and creaking, but moving impossibly fast to a destination she neither knew, nor cared much to head towards. She woke up with a start to her husband's old alarm system.

As the morning routine progressed, Taryn took her turn at feeding Trey his breakfast to give her mom more rest before moving to eat her own. Though she'd had to promise Gloria that she'd return to the grocers today to complain about them selling her spoiled milk before her mom finally left her alone to the quiet of Trey and herself at the morning table. The quiet didn't last though as Taryn's earpiece began ringing. The call was coming from a company number. As she answered, an unduly chipper female voice began speaking.

"Hello Miss Steno? I'm Tally, Mr. Meroan's secretary at headquarters. He'd like you to come to his office a half-hour before your shift starts this morning. He said that he did not expect it to take long.

"Alright," said Taryn, trying to hide the hoarseness of her still sleepy voice.

She wanted to ask what this was about of course, but before she could clear the words from her tired head, she heard a snappy, "Thank you. He'll expect to see you soon then."

The line hung up.

"*Wonder what this is?*" she asked herself honestly not recalling yesterday's events this early in the morning.

Mr. Meroan was a Tie that Taryn had met only in brief visits before, and always in large meetings with the other foremen. He struck Taryn, in her very limited exposure to him, as an efficient company man of many cycles with more a mind for profits, calculations, and shrewdness than even the other Ties had ever displayed to her. To her mind this came at the cost of any real distinguishing personality for the old man.

"*Well, maybe I'm wrong. There could be more,*" she thought.

She could hardly claim to know the Ties as well as she did her floor guys. Their meetings with the foremen were only four times a cycle, and Taryn had only ever been to one of them as a foreman. Perhaps alone, without others observing, Meroan would prove to be a different person than that brief glimpse of him had originally shown. In any case, this unexpected meeting meant Taryn had to leave early to be on time, which annoyed her greatly. Breakfast was a hallowed time in her day for her to sit and be alone with her own thoughts, even if just for a moment or two. It was her time, and hers alone as it had always been since her family came. The kids were usually subdued this early. Taryn herself would be the same until her morning caffeine rush from her first joe-cup eventually kicked in and truly started waking her mind up. She had started drinking it occasionally for school, but her habit had inescapably ramped up after her first month of full shifts at the company.

She reluctantly began washing up the small table of its plates and cups before finishing getting dressed for work. After some quicker than normal daily wishes to mom, Trey, and Lilly, who was barely awake, she was quickly out the door.

* * *

Taryn managed to walk into the Headquarters building a little after the 2nd hour, and checking the directory, located Mr. Meroan's office on the 10th floor. Once off the lift, she walked into an outer office and found herself in a very long white marbled room with tall ceilings and a black and white checkered stone floor that was impeccably clean. As she approached the opposite end, she saw the outside of the inner office was decorated in a dark ugly tan-colored marble which was deeply polished and looked nonetheless expensive. The soaring ceilings echoed the approaching footsteps of her floor work boots. She wondered how much dirt she was tracking onto their nice clean floors with each dull thud and squeak of her boot's outsoles. Any Suit with their high class dress shoes or heels on must have clicked and echoed even louder and more clearly through the whole room, drawing onlookers' attention as those styles were meant to do. The room though, for all its length and cleanliness, was rather barren for its size Taryn thought. The windows, which ran along the east side, looked towards the city center far off. Each window system was in the middle of its automated wash-wax cycle, partly blocking the morning sun as Taryn walked past. Three broad chairs were against the glass facing an opposite blank white wall. Square at the end of this long entrance room sat an island desk with three sections forming a sharp half-hexagon. Behind it sat a thin lady dressed impeccably, coiffed with well-polished hair, adorned with dark red jewelry and manicured nails who clicked away as she typed on her system.

"Hi. I'm Taryn Steno. I'm here to see Mr. Meroan," she said as the secretary looked up at her with a quick glance.

"Have a seat, I will let him know that you have arrived, but it may be a few minutes as he is currently in the middle of another interview," she said, not even breaking the stride of her finger's typing.

Taryn sat facing the blank white wall as she pondered the secretary's use of the word *interview*. Part of her wondered for a small instant if this might, perhaps, be a bit of good news for her. "*A promotion?*" she puzzled. She didn't truthfully believe it was that, still she'd never even been beyond the first floor of this building before now. Not when she was first processed as a new hire nor when she was promoted from a floor guy to a foreman. Taryn didn't have long to think about this oddity however as soon she could hear voices coming, quietly at first, from the large solid onyx fascia behind the secretary's desk. Taryn could not see anyone, despite the voices becoming closer and clearer in volume. It sounded as if two men were discussing final terms to some sort of agreement. Taryn noticed that behind and to the left of the secretary's desk, a door was built directly into the black stone. Taryn quickly realized that she was staring at the most decadently crafted door she had ever seen. At a quick glance, it would simply have looked fully solid, with the polished dark coloration of its circuitous rolling mounds of curves. To Taryn it looked like a frozen image of some black mass of worms coalescing together behind the secretary's head. The impression of it was equally unappealing and yet stylized. Clearly expensive with the bulk of its mass protruding out from the surrounding wall. Its intimidating scale and size, easily reaching from the floor to roof, it might be considered by some artistic. But it imposingly towered over people the closer they came to its bowed out details. In this giant gaudy décor as Taryn now saw, there was, in fact, an opening appearing as she sat focused on it. The opening was slowly growing more obvious by the moment. A door glided silently inwards with miniscule seams that were barely visible when it was closed. There were no apparent handles or knobs on the outside to be seen. Taryn guessed that the secretary had an automated release button on her desk somewhere that controlled it from the outside if needed. As the voices cleared up even more, they began what sounded to Taryn like their final remarks.

"Ah thank you, Mr. Romagalus. I am sure a man of your talents, stock, and obvious upbringing will do wonders for the company. Goodbye for now. I look forward to meeting with you in your own office up here one day soon." This came from a smaller round old man smiling as he spoke upwards to his exact opposite in stature. A tall, broad, but much younger man was smiling vaguely back down at him. Despite his size, his face and movements showed him to be in the full bloom of his youth. Taryn judged that he could have been barely more than nineteen or twenty cycles old. Yet here he was apparently closing a job interview. She herself, having never been in Mr. Meroan's office, and having not spent more than a single hour inside this building, had done her original job interview in the cramped office above the factory floor. And no one involved then had been wearing a tie. To Taryn, what was becoming clearer by the moment was that whatever the reason behind her being sent here must be on one of two extremes. Either it was very good, or it was very bad. She insulated this notion against any bleak possibility by reminding herself that at no point had she known the Ties to call people to the HQ simply to fire them. That was far too much effort for a factory worker. Far easier and quicker to do that back on the floor or in the office. With that fragment of reasoning, she held the smallest sliver of subdued optimism in the recess of her awareness. The two men shook hands again and the young giant departed smiling with a farewell. Once the youth was out of the waiting area, the old man stood still, looking towards the door his visitor had just exited. He spoke low to his secretary, but still loud enough that Taryn in her silence could hear him.

"Now that one Tally" he gestured with his chin to the closed outer door. "That one was regional champion three cycles in a row at his school. And he's twice the size of his father." He sighed, "Shame he inherited only a quarter of his brains on his best day." He paused in a move of consideration. "Make a note will you, to have him called up from the floor by the end of next week." The secretary nodded. "And make sure he gets assigned some light duties. Someplace inconspicuous and out of the way, where he won't be able to do much harm." He was shaking his head as he spoke now more to himself. "His family will need two tailors to make a suit big enough to fit him when they call him back up to civilization." The old man's focus now became attuned to the young lady sitting quietly in a floor uniform observing him in his waiting room.

"Ah, yes! Come in Mrs. Steno, please," he said, gesturing for Taryn to follow.

Taryn followed behind Meroan through the carved opening in the stone fascia.

"Thank you for coming in early to meet with me. I hope you were not waiting too long, I just had to finish an interview with the son of one of our higher Suits and…well you can understand how it goes with a boss's son," he said with a weak smile.

Taryn didn't reply, but only smiled as one not sure of what to say.

He led her through into a large room decorated entirely in fine polished and finished woods. The floors, walls, leather upholstered chairs, and large desk were all furnished richly in red and brown hues with hints of tan at their base. Beyond the furniture, the large corner windows of the office included borders and moldings that were elegantly carved in wood as well. Handcrafted so that the window themselves looked like they were framed as living paintings of the high-rise views outside each of them. It was in stark contrast to the almost sterile layout of the waiting area where the large mostly empty polished space had made Taryn feel exceptionally small. Here the luxuriousness of Mr. Meroan's inner office translated to the young foreman's sense of meagerness about herself.

"Have a seat please, Mrs. Steno," he said briefly motioning to a guest chair at his desk. Already in one of the two guest chairs was another Tie, a woman, that Taryn didn't recognize.

"This is Ms. Fisecaly. She'll be joining us this morning."

Taryn shook the woman's hand. She was slim, middle-aged, in sleek business attire, with short perfectly trimmed hair, and expensive looking shoes that clearly only a Tie could afford. Over her eyes was an optical device that could have easily been mistaken for the ancient trend of glasses. They were in truth, interface systems that displayed several lines of data to her at a single cue from Fisecaly's iris. She appeared to have been busily reviewing some figures on her padd and on the optical interface simultaneously when Meroan and Taryn had entered the room. She didn't stand as they shook hands but only nodded to Taryn as she entered.

"Now, I called you here this morning" Meroan began, "because I'm hoping that you can help me to fix something that has us slightly perplexed." He nonchalantly took the seat behind his giant desk in an overly large leather chair as he spoke.

"Well, I'll do what I can Mr. Meroan, but I'm not sure how much help I can be?"

"Good. Your help is all that I'm asking for," he said.

Meroan motioned for the lights to dim and at his cue, Fisecaly touched some buttons on her padd. A set of images appeared on the tan wall that Taryn had entered through. She turned her chair to see. The various projected displays were obviously security and monitoring footage from the factory floor. Each image switched to a new view after a few seconds. The only constant in each was the timestamp date of Tues, April the 26th. *Yesterday,* Taryn thought to herself and suddenly her heart sank.

The different angles showed several portions of what Taryn quickly recognized as Section 31. She could see the finishers, the case assemblers, the circuit assemblers, Kilt working on the hanger, and of course she saw herself in the line at the Micro-worker's area. More accurately she saw herself from above and behind. Looking over her own shoulder she saw her own hands working away at the circuit surgery post. There was a silent moment that Taryn thought interminably long.

"What's your question, Mr. Meroan?" Taryn finally asked, hoping that she didn't already know the response. "I see my line boys doing their jobs," she added looking from view to view.

"Slowly, Mrs. Steno. Doing their job slowly. Too slowly," Meroan retorted. His tone had grown harder. "They are doing their work, but I, and I suspect you, already know that they are not moving fast enough to ever reach their quota for the day. Do you recall, did your section hit the mark yesterday?" Meroan asked condescendingly. It was a question that Meroan delivered with what looked to be a sort of practiced emphasis. To Taryn it looked to be a well-worn part of his dialogue. Taryn's shoulders slumped a little. It had finally come to it.

"No, Mr. Meroan. We missed the mark yesterday." she paused. "But I would like to add that my section was 15 pairs of hands down, including our three…"

"We are well aware of the attendance stats for yesterday, Mrs. Steno. And section 31 was only 12 pairs short. You were sent three replacements, were you not?" asked Ms. Fisecaly interrupting from her chair.

"Well sir," focusing on Meroan and ignoring Fisecaly, who had obviously been lying in wait. "Three cannot equal the work of 15 you see. And those raw boys can't handle the hard sections of the floor. It's too complicated for anyone to learn them that fast, nor do most of the raws care to try. Now, you can see in the video that I did all I could, to keep the line's speed going as fast as it would. You can both see that. Everyone was busy doing their jobs and they did their best to hit the mark, but sir the mark was just too high, and we had too few hands for yesterday's run. Today with more…"

"You did all you could?" Meroan asked. Now it was his turn to interrupt. "Really? Did you really… do all that you could, Mrs. Steno?" he said slowly and with an inquiring tone that made Taryn even more uncomfortable.

Taryn paused and thought on this though. "Yes sir, I believe so. If I missed something, an opportunity somewhere to—"

"You missed far more than one opportunity," said Fisecaly jumping back in. "We've talked to several other foremen and our own analysts. They were able to find some easy places where you could have stretched the speed further."

"How is that?" Taryn asked, perplexed.

"Well, for one", Meroan said, "your finishers are too slow. Don't you think that for the delicate work they do, they could benefit from the full use of their hands? They even asked you about it I believe, and you refused them."

"Sir, the men need their gloves so that they prevent the D-9 solvent from getting on their skin. The safety regs say—"

"Come now Miss Steno. You are not a doctor. Nor even a nurse after all. The men on the line know their own bodies better than you. They can make their own decisions on this, let them choose the best course for them."

"The only course… you mean," Taryn thought to say but she was cut off, much to her own relief.

Fisecaly interrupted again, "Other foremen we have spoken with have also pointed out that, while your section does generally keep pace, in their opinions, your floor men do not work like those who are aware that their jobs are on the line." She said this last part coolly. "As their superior you could have easily sold that thought to them…to incentivize them in picking up their pace."

"But Miss Fisecaly, I don't have any say over who gets fired, or hired for that matter. I work with what I'm given. Only the Nest can make those—"

"And just who do you think that the Head Foreman goes after more often than not? Random workers? Or those tagged by the various section foreman like yourself, Mrs. Steno?"

Taryn remained silent but stared straight into the woman's cold unemotional face while Fisecaly's eyes were still browsing over numbers on her padd as she had been talking. Taryn reluctantly drew her solid angry gaze off the female Tie and back to the recorded footage, before Fisecaly finally had a chance to notice Taryn's stare.

The Tie continued tapping on her padd and stood up to walk closer to the various screens. "That hanger of yours is another slow point on your line that we've spotted. I mean, the man is obviously capable of moving at a much faster rate than you have allowed him to."

"And if he gets caught, injured in a machine because he is going too fast without his harness on, then what do—"

"Then you find a new Hanger, Mrs. Steno," she countered. "There are always more young thrill-seekers out there that are eager to take the role. They love to swagger on about it. They think it shows their boldness. At least, that's what we hear in the reports we receive."

"But sir—," Taryn said, turning back to Meroan who had been sitting quietly behind his desk letting his coworker do all the arguing, "what if an inspector were to come along and see this? The whole floor wou—"

"An inspector!" Meroan laughed. "Steno, we have not had an inspection in five cycles. The central government does not have enough inspectors to begin with. And the region's inspections are so behind and rushed for time that they could walk the coastline and not notice the smell of salt. Besides every time that the big inspectors do show up, they always do the same thing. They start by walking the largest floor, sections 32-79, on the far side of the grounds. And even the folk there get more than enough of a warning to make things nice and neat, while the fools are busy checking in over here at HQ. Your whole floor can easily be prepared an hour in advance so that everything can be in place for their arrival."

"And our own internal recordings are no use to them. They can't touch those without a court order," added Fisecaly, still not taking her eyes off the padd in her hands.

"Now on to your last error," Meroan continued. "Your own data status reports from yesterday don't match what we saw here." He paused, drew himself up from his chair and in a surprisingly calm voice said, "Mrs. Steno, as a foreman your two primary responsibilities at this company are to make sure your section of the line hits its mark every single day, no matter what, and to report your data accurately. Now, did you accomplish either of those two goals yesterday?"

Taryn looked down at her feet, but as she did, she was pressing deep into her own mind, arguing over the exact words she was hearing. Seeing if there was any way she could reasonably make a further defense. She finally relented.

"No sir. I didn't."

"I understand that it is not always enjoyable having a boss constantly looking over your shoulders, second-guessing your every choice," he said. "Even I, here in my own office, am answerable for my decisions to my superiors."

As he said this, he motioned over his head towards a small lensed white box in the upper corner of his office with two tiny lights on it, one red and one blue. It hung angled down towards the center of the room.

"I know that the foreman position is still relatively new to you. And I did see what you attempted to do yesterday in covering the surgery spot on the line. That shows dedication. But on the other hand, I also know how fast you have managed to learn and grasp all the various spots on the line to help you make it to where you are now. So what puzzles me, Mrs. Steno, you see, is that while you could have easily observed and learned from the effective methods of the other foreman working the floor around you, you seem almost, if you will pardon my conclusion, reluctant to apply these techniques in your own managerial policies."

He stopped to take a drink from a glass of clear liquid on his desk. Still holding the glass as he stood, he walked to stare out the exquisitely framed corner windows.

"At present, Ms. Steno, given these factors, in addition to your results from yesterday, several of my colleagues would like to release you straight away, without hesitation," He snapped his fingers with a loud 'click'. "But I like to be sure that when something is discarded that it is because it really is useless to us. So…" he said, turning back to Taryn "I managed to convince them, on your behalf, that all that was needed was to bring you here today, like we have, and to chat for a while. To help you sort things out so that you could…," he paused thinking, "realign your decision-making process to better match with the company's goals. You now know where your mistakes are, and I hope you also know that we are both," he said in a gesture at himself and Fisecaly, "here to help and support you, should you need it at any time."

He was standing next to the side of Taryn's seat.

"Now," he said staring down at her, "can I count on you, Mrs. Steno, to do whatever is needed to ensure that section 31 hits its mark under your leadership. Because I must be able to reassure my colleagues out there that you truly are one of us. A company-man. Someone who works relentlessly and with total loyalty to reach our goals at all times. After all, such a thing is what helps a foreman like yourself to eventually get called up here to take a spot in HQ, is it not?"

Fisecaly nodded reflexively in agreement, but Taryn knew she would always remember taking a moment, just then, to select her next words carefully and slowly. She searched her thoughts for a memento of her father's sharp wit to recall for usage here. Nothing came. She was nervous and floundering, very much aware that the Ties were examining her, still waiting for her reply.

In the distance she finally heard the old bent figure of a farmer speaking in a non-direct voice, from a time now long past. *"Nothing flowers like truth. It's mostly cold an' thorny, but it lasts. When other crops planted are droughted or plagued, it lasts on its own will. No need for any Sun or air or bug control. It just lasts, and only hope can ever grow for longer.``*

"Sir," Taryn said, taking a breath. "You can count on me to do my best, always. This job is important to me, and I'll work to make the speed of the line be as fast as possible. To hit our mark each and every day while always trying to keep the line workers motivated…in my way. I will do all of this without having to relegate to jeopardizing their safety, their health, or their job security. I take full responsibility for missing the mark yesterday and for the reports being late because, as you said, that's my core job. But my guys, they're decent people and I don't think being afraid helps them to be better or much faster. It makes them stressed, causes mistakes, and hinders them in the long run."

Meroan stood silently for a moment looking down on Taryn. Fisecaly's eyes narrowed imperceptibly as she glancingly studied the foreman.

"Well of course," Meroan said, smiling again as he walked back to his desk chair. "We certainly want to avoid any mistakes or hindrances. Thank you, Mrs. Steno, for your assurances on this and for coming in early today to meet with us. Now, I see that it is getting close to the start of the line's shift. The factory chime will be coming soon and all of us have quite a busy day ahead. I'm sure that I speak for Ms. Fisecaly here, when I say thank you again, very much, for coming to help us clear up this matter. If you wish, stop by our cafeteria area before you head out. I have taken the liberty of sending them a message that they are to give you a free travel breakfast to take as compensation for your time here this morning."

Taryn stood up, slow and unsure. She thanked the two Ties as she was gestured out towards the now open doorway in the rear marble wall.

* * *

Behind the exiting foreman, a silent Meroan sat down and glared across his desk at Fisecaly.

"You were right," he said to his underling. "The woman either won't or doesn't know how to fall in line." She nodded sideways in agreement to him in return.

"My, my…what a truly disappointing morning," Meroan said, turning in his chair to the window views behind him. He leaned far back looking upwards almost to the ceiling.

"One worker too stupid to ever truly be a meaningful club player, and another with a moral too many."

After a moment lost in his own thoughts, he turned back to Fisecaly who had been waiting on his next direction.

"Would you kindly send a message to Mr. Lutch down in security? Tell him I have a task that requires his unique type of courtesy."

Behind Meroan, on the little lensed white monitoring box hanging high in the corner, a tiny green light began to steadily blink slowly for a few moments, unnoticed by the room's occupants, before it turned off again.

Down eight floors, Taryn was riding on the lift wondering if she had just committed career suicide and debating if the free breakfast Meroan mentioned would make her meeting with him any easier to digest. "Probably not," she thought. She knew that what she said back there was some of what Meroan wanted to hear, but it wasn't everything he wanted. "No, not everything by a good measure."

The lift doors to the ground floor opened and there stood three large husky security guards, all with their hands on their belts, looking like they were waiting for someone. The shock and confusion on Taryn's face was equaled only by the smile on the face of the largest guard. His golden metal name tag read *Lt. Lutch* along its shiny surface.

"Taryn Steno?" he asked in a voice as deep as a canyon.

Taryn stood frozen. She later imagined it was as this security chief, Lutch, liked to see them: surprised, incoherent, and without recourse. From his sour bearded grimace with a half-smile and a serious but in no way professional demeanor, he might even be the type who enjoyed watching those he easily corralled with his intimidating stature break down and sob as he bent them to his instructions with little more than his hoarse commanding voice.

"Mr. Meroan sent us to make sure you knew which way you were going," he said, standing tall over Taryn by at least three head lengths.

Looking from face to face told Taryn of her chances of anything but her acquiescence. Her shoulders slumped, much like they had the day before. Lt. Lutch walked behind her directing her walk with his massive paw while the other guards were at her flanks or right in front. They walked straight past several Ties who had been waiting for the lift. Some smirked at her, having already seen Lutch's previous escort parties pass through the halls before now. Others glared, and some barely noticed as they were busily working away on their padds. But all parted to either side for the guards to pass as they stepped off the lift and walked Taryn through the center of the cluster of them. They went down the large main reception gallery and out the main door. When they reached her vehicle, Taryn had finally thought enough to ask about her final pay as she got in. She rolled down her window to pose her question to them, causing Lutch to quickly draw out a hidden whip rod and smash her back window.

"Drive!" Lutch commanded loudly. His volume and tone were only a hair shy of angrily yelling the order at her. "And don't think of returning here again!" he shouted after Taryn.

That was all that was needed for her. She started her vehicle and drove at a normal speed, but out of her own fear, never once did she look back.

Chapter 3: Blue Turns to Grey

The whining whoosh and cooler air slowly dragged Taryn back to herself. She did not remember how long she'd been driving before the circus of her own thoughts calmed enough to let her focus on the present reassert itself again. Agitated, misty, and in a panic as she'd been, she realized now that she had actually turned to take the long way home. "*Of course*," she thought while wondering about this unconscious choice. Going back home too early would mean lots of questions from Mom, which would inevitably continue on through until Lilly got home from school as well, when it would restart the same process all over. She did not feel up to doling out all the explanations that they would demand of her right now, and the invariable looks of disapproval from Mom that it would almost certainly conclude with. It was one of the few moments in her life that she was glad Cyrano was not around anymore.

For the six months when both Cyrano was there and Gloria had first moved in, it had been truly like having three parents around the flat, and for that she was thankful. Even after, now that it was just her and mom, Gloria was far better at helping to explain to the kids why their father was not returning home. Not that these explanations, even with Taryn in her stronger moments, were of much help. The kids, both young, couldn't be comforted by any reason for why their father was gone from their lives. They could only register the hurt of his absence. Once the permanence of this set in truly with them, the two had remained devastated for weeks.

Cyrano had been working through his second tour with the Defense Force, when he was killed in action. The report Taryn received said he had been patrolling out in the fringes with his unit to help maintain safe caravan routes. Cyrano's unit was ambushed and nearly all were killed in the worst raider attack in over 70 cycles. The Defense Force destroyed the raider's camp when they later found its location, but to Taryn it was cold comfort. Her husband was gone and not returning. The Defense Force had paid for the cost of his arrangements but there was little time to mourn. Taryn was left as a young mother supporting four people by herself.

Her recent promotion to foreman was the only saving measure that'd given her some hope that she'd be able to manage the financial burden of it all.

But now she'd lost her job, a reliable job at that, and there was nothing she could think of to do about it. She'd been in the business long enough to know that no amount of groveling, begging, or pleading on her part back at the company HQ would be sufficient enough to help. Even if she had had the courage to turn the vehicle around at that moment, she'd likely be quickly arrested for trespassing, or worse. A glance at her broken rear window in the side mirror kept her driving and thinking. The notion that bribery might work, occurred to her, but only if she had enough credits, which she didn't, and a friendly Tie willing to listen to her, which she also lacked. Taryn took some deep slow breaths. *Think forwards*, she told herself. Her face grimaced. The notion of job hunting was something she loathed almost as much as trying to grovel for her old job back. Not a salesman by any stretch, she hated the notion of having to sell people on *herself.*

After driving a while longer, she found herself pulling into a backwater hole called 'The Hidden Roller', though that was far from the building's original name. Taryn had known it through at least three or four name changes as new owners would come try their luck at making different businesses stick for a while. When they failed, the process would slowly repeat over a few months. The place was generally too out of the way for many. By Taryn's reckoning, it had been a bar, some bad restaurants, and even a dessert and pastry parlor once. The 'Hidden Roller' that was now established there was more of a sports diner and bar that held parties and gatherings on days of big events. During mornings, or the off-season, it was predictably much less busy. Now, still being early on in the day, as Taryn pulled in, it didn't even look open. She walked up to the door and knocked. After a minute the door partly opened and a very large muscular blonde-haired man with a square jaw answered.

"Hey! Taryn!" he said, recognizing her after staring a moment. His face turned into a smile. "Haven't seen you in a while."

"Hey, Everett. You mind if I come in and hang out here for a few minutes? Don't need a drink, just a quiet spot to collect for a bit."

"Course. Com'in", he said as he patted Taryn on the back with his oversized hand. "Man, feels like forever since we last hung out. How's the boy doing?"

The main eating area was dim, save from the outdoor light streaming through past the inactive neon signs of the front windows. Only a few lights were turned on over the bar with some low music going. Everett had bought the bar and fixed it up better than any owner in recent memory. Lots of stained wood tables that were refinished but showed the character of years of use. Lowered lights hung over each table and there was a constant stream of upbeat local folk music during open hours when the seasons were out of play. The layout while practical enough, still let the warmth and daylight in through only the front windows. Everett had said he wanted a classic sports bar feel to the place and by most measures he'd succeeded. The walls were plastered in memorabilia not only of him and his team but other local area teams, and even some copies of the ancient sports leagues no longer known by most. Everett had named the place 'The Hidden Roller' after one of his favorite in-game tactics. He told the local press upon its opening he gave no care how his business did financially. So long as the food was good, the drinks were strong, and he got to be his own boss with no-one looking over his shoulder yelling at him. A place to relax in his off seasons with his friends and family. He had managed the place himself with a small staff for about two and a half cycles now and openly admitted to enjoying himself immensely in the process.

Taryn took a seat on a stool while Everett poured her a glass of ice water. Their conversation, much like Taryn's driving, took the longer path, exchanging the common sort of news and events, both personal and local. Everett continued asking Taryn about the rest of her family. To which she would reply politely, but sparsely as if her mind were not able to go further into thoughts on those matters. Everett noted that he had hardly seen them, her, and the kids, in months, though that wasn't entirely unexpected all things considered. They all had needed time to process. But in the course of their small talk, Taryn never mentioned her work, which was unusual for her. Not even once. And she only spoke in halting sentences about the kids and her mom, which was a puzzle to him.

Everett had been a friend since early childhood. They had known each other from when both were still learning their letters and using wax crayons to draw dragons and raiders attacking city fortifications. He was the second of two children whose single mother traveled for work all across the city. In their youth, Everett and Taryn had found that they shared a passion for sports, especially hexaderby. For some time in school, they were each other's only true friends. Taryn often liked to brag about knowing Everett longer than anyone, besides his own family of course. Taryn being an only child and Everett being often alone as his brother, 10 cycles older, went to work early to help out the family. They had grown up together as the siblings that both wished they had actually had. And while they were intensely close, they never saw each other romantically. There simply was not anything there for either of them in that light.

Still, Taryn was always proud of knowing Everett. And, why not? He was, after all, a local celebrity now. His old amateur uniforms and several different championship posters were among those items adoring the restaurant area too. But Taryn had known him back before all this, back just as an overweight childhood friend. She had been there to see firsthand Everett's maturation during puberty from obese into obsessive. They were each other's first exercise partners in school. And Everett became a fast-improving athlete whose bulkier physique, now turning much more muscular, was ever more the incentive for the various team coaches to seek him out as an asset. In his finishing school days Everett had focused on only playing hexaderby and never paid a single credit towards his schooling because of it, while Taryn's own unfinished schooling had her receiving monthly loan bills that she still worried over. Taryn remembered when she saw the news that Everett had been drafted to a professional team with a contract estimated to be among the highest for a newcomer in a dozen cycles. And she assumed Everett made even more through his lucrative endorsements and sponsorships after a pair of early championship seasons that were largely credited to his play style. Through all this though they remained deep friends. Taryn and Cyrano had routinely got tickets for the whole family in the mail for box seats to Everett's home region games. They were at each other's weddings and attended each other's birthdays and family dinners. Most of Everett's wives and girlfriends tended to regard the notion of having children as impediments towards the success and growth of his career. As a result, after his latest marriage ended, Everett found that children were actually the only aspect of his life where he envied Taryn's progress. He, of course, had been more than welcome in the role of uncle to Lilly and was overjoyed when Trey came along as well. He'd vowed to Taryn and Cyrano multiple times to coach and train the kids in any sports they eventually desired. And their most lavish and expensive birthday presents always had Uncle Everett's name on them. He was Taryn's best friend and a good friend to her family regardless of the vast divergences in their lives.

As they talked over the bar this morning, their conversation remained lite for a while. Taryn helped sweep the floor while Everett cleaned up behind the counter and readied his stock for today's customers. It wasn't until a while later, when Taryn took another cold drink that wasn't water, that Everett, still standing behind the bar, finally felt that his friend was now calm enough to steer her towards broaching the subject on his mind.

"You know, great as it is to see you, it's not often we meet this early on in the day. Come to think of it, I can't remember the last time we saw each other in the morning. Probably not since school?"

"Sounds about right," Taryn replied in a non-committal response to the question. Though it wasn't in her mind at the moment, Taryn had seen Everett around the same time on the day mourning services were given for Cyrano. He'd been the first guest to arrive. Taryn and Cyrano had dined at the Hidden Roller several evenings during her husband's last extended leave home. Everett, still in the midst of the recent season then, had been too busy to visit with them much. Taryn guessed not being around to see Cyrano more before he had died nagged at Everett, as the two got along quite well together. Taryn at the bar now, her mind far distant from any of this, took another sip out of her mug and winced her face at the mild bitter taste. It was a juice concoction, called 'the driver'. It was her own invention and Everett had added it to the menu at her request. Taryn had stopped true drinking long ago when Lilly was first born, but this drink had a nice sour lemon flavor that she typically enjoyed. Right now it only seemed annoying to her though.

"Yeah, well I guess that today was a weird one then...," Everett continued letting the pause in his words hang like an unfinished bridge. He took a sip from his own joe cup as he eyed Taryn's reaction to this.

"Everett…" Taryn said looking at her glass, "I know most people like to think of you as just another big dumb jock outside the hexagon, but you forget that I've seen your school marks firsthand. I saw your acceptance letters from the schools you got into without sports programs, and I remember how it bugged you when I would occasionally score higher on some assignment. I know how smart you are Everett, and I know when you're purposefully trying to prod me."

"Good," he said with a grin. "Then you also know that my strategies usually play out pretty well for me. So, stop staring holes into my glassware and pipe up Tar. The worst thing that can happen is we both end up on the stools staring into our glasses."

Taryn relented and finally told Everett all of the events from the last two days. It all came spilling out before she knew it. From the shortage of line workers, to missing her quota and late data reports, to her meeting with Meroan and her window's encounter with Lt. Lutch's whip-rod a little more than a few hours ago. After she was finished, Everett was silent. He poured himself a tall drink of ale, walked around and climbed onto the stool next to his friend and began to drink too.

After a long time passed, in which neither of them spoke much, Everett finally asked her, "So how long do you expect me to sit and be sad with you? Because I am your friend man, and I can do this all day if you want but um… Tar, time is the issue."

"Oh, don't stay closed on my account Everett. Open up the place whenever you ne-"

"That's not what I mean you idiot," Everett interrupted, gently laughing at his drink. "Taryn, time is the ultimate referee. You know? It can go slower or faster in some cases." His voice dropped to a quiet whisper, "but it never goes backwards. You know this."

He took a quick draft of ale and wiped the thin line of foam from his chin.

"So as much as I would like to sit here with you feeling, whatever it is, that you're feeling, time will still move forward. And that's what you need to do, in my opinion. What is dominating for you today can be nothing in a week. A mistake or a misstep cannot be undone. I mean a bad play stays a bad play, you know? It may sting unless it is used as experience, so that it can never be repeated in the future."

"But that's what really gets to me." Taryn said despondently, still looking into her drink. "I don't think that I made any mistakes. I did everything that I thought I should. And every time I run it back in my mind, I still end up back here at your bar. So that means either I'm too blind to recognize my mistakes as stupidity or I'm too dumb to find my mistakes in the first place, or both. And I can't decide which is worse."

She paused for a moment as they both took another slow drink. After a while of silence, Taryn blurted out. "I should have lied," she said with a rush of frustrated resignation. "I should've just said everything those Ties wanted to hear out of me, and I would've been back to work right then. No matter of fact about it. Just given them what they wanted, and they'd have been done with it."

Everett took another drink, sighing mildly as he put his empty glass down and said, "Well Tar... I think you're damn right."

Taryn, surprised at this reaction, glanced sidelong towards her friend who was still staring straight down into his own glass.

"You *didn't* make any mistakes," he assured his friend.

Taryn smiled weakly.

"Care to come with me and say that to Mom for me?"

Everett patted Taryn on the back.

"Yeah, sorry. But, umm, that kind of hazard pay is not specified anywhere in my contract. And I doubt you have the credits on you to hire me as a free agent," he smiled.

Taryn's smile faded as she turned back to her own drink.

"Mother of two, main household provider, widow who stupidly gets herself fired from her job. There aren't many worse ways to screw-up the day."

"You're still a parent." Everett said in a more serious tone. "And one who's actually around. I think that's gotta count for more than you realize."

"Yeah..." she said slowly, "I guess so."

"Absolutely, no guesses needed."

It was half-an hour later that Everett walked Taryn back to her car. The restaurant's staff was starting to show up to work the lunch and afternoon shifts as Everett stood inspecting the damage to Taryn's rear windshield. He didn't examine it long before he made a quick call to a nearby garage. He knew the owner and promised him another endorsement photo to hang on his waiting room wall if he helped out his friend quickly.

Taryn objected but Everett remained stern only saying; "This is the easy part, besides it's the least I could do. Probably won't even have to pay for it. You," he said glancing at her, "need to save that stiff neck of yours for later. Don't forget you still have to survive the real battle when you get home."

Taryn hugged her massive friend goodbye before she drove away. "Thanks, you dumb meathead" she said. "Not a matter, you moron," Everett rebounded. Their tones at these remarks showed more genuine gentleness than most 'thank you's and 'you're welcome's between a close pair of real siblings could have managed. Still, Taryn was upset and hated the notion of going home to re-explain all this to a much less sympathetic reception, but now that Everett had given her a chance to recoup it did seem a bit easier. And Everett, as it turned out, was right once again. Taryn never paid a single credit for her vehicle's new window, and she highly doubted Everett did either.

Chapter 4: An Easel of Politics

Taryn dragged her unwilling feet through her own door two hours later. She had stopped off for a late lunch at a local 'grab and go.' She didn't want to pester Everett's staff for a meal before she left the Hidden Roller. They weren't even open while she'd been getting consoled by her friend to begin with. So, she sat, chewing on her food, in her vehicle with broken glass still laying on her rear seat. She ate slowly, letting herself digest both the food and her own thoughts of her immediate future with about the same amount of interest. Almost none. By the time she made it to the garage that Everett had called for her and was sitting while they worked on repairing the glass, she was internally figuring on having to update her resume profile. She would have to reach out to some old colleagues for chances to get interviewed elsewhere. But by then the rush and shock of the day had completely worn off and she was too tired and exhausted from its events to think much about the details. She kept pondering on how to explain to a prospective employer that she had been viciously fired from her last job in what would pass as professional sounding terms. "Diverging viewpoints" was the only phrase that seemed remotely accurate and suitably neutral. After lunch and installation of a replacement window she drove around a bit more. She stopped and got fresh milk from the grocer and did everything she could to buy herself more time before heading home. There hadn't been much else though.

As she closed the front door to the flat, she realized that Lilly was already back from school. She and Gloria had just finished a walk in the nearby park. It was one of their favorite routines and they often took Trey with them. Taryn was only a little over an hour and a half earlier than was normally expected, so she hoped that would keep the questions from her mother to a minimum. After cleaning up a little, she planned to take a nap, something she hadn't done on a workday in many months. She was walking to her bedroom when her daughter let out a noticeable preteen scream of aggravation as she passed the half-opened bedroom door in the hall.

"What is it?" Taryn asked, poking her head into Lilly's room.

"Oh, it's the stupid wave connection again," Lilly said not turning her head from her desk. "It's always slow in the afternoon when everyone's coming home and getting on. And now …it's just not working at all."

"Ok, well… have you tried resetting your padd or the uplink?"

"Of course, I tried that mom. I'm not stupid you know." Lilly said exasperated. "I reset the uplink box and padd twice and it's still not working right. I hate this thing."

"Ok, ok…," Taryn said, taking a seat on her daughter's bed. "So, what were you trying to do on it exactly?"

"I'm trying to get ready for the debate team qualifier to see which students go next week to compete in the regional semi-finals. But the wave network won't work, and the class text is no help."

"Wait, when did you join the debate team, Lil?"

"Oh, well…Willow, you remember her right? She's the tiny girl with the long, red, curly hair." Taryn nodded half remembering a vague outline of Lilly's friend. "Well, Willow brought me to a meeting after school the other day and I met some of the others there… and it was kinda fun, so I thought I'd try it, you know? See how it works."

"Others, hmm? Anyone I would know besides Willow?

"No, er not really. It's mostly just boys."

"Boys, huh?" Taryn said, throwing her daughter a raised eyebrow and half a smirk. Lilly still looked away from her mother's scrutinizing glance.

"Well, what's the debate topic?"

"It's about comparing the different types of democratic governments. Mr. Y, the debate sponsor, said that because I was new, I could get the easier topic. I need to contrast our government with one of the old-world style democratic ones so that my team could argue which approach is the best. He gave me a list of questions to answer to help me prepare for the debate. And I'm pretty sure I'll be arguing against the old democracies from what Willow said, but with the stupid education wave down all I have is my class texts on the padd."

"Oh, well that shouldn't be too difficult. I used to love history," Taryn smiled. "Let's hear the questions and see if I can help." History and the social sciences had always been some of Taryn's favorite courses. She had done well enough in them growing up to the point that she had considered taking them at the advanced levels before Cyrano and her had started their family. But despite that having been some time ago Taryn was confident she could still handle any topic Lilly was likely to ask about. Taryn rested herself sidelong on Lilly's small bed next to her, while her daughter worked off the padd from her desk.

"Ok," she said, selecting the question list on it. "What was one advantage the old-style democratic governments had over our modern system of today?"

"Well… I'd say that one big advantage…" Taryn thought, "It is that the election system in those older governments didn't require any complex electronics or any neural scanners. They couldn't, in fact. The scanners were invented only a few centuries ago. So, they could actually have their elections with no electrical power at all. Even in the poorest countries, democratic governments could still arise, in theory."

"Weird. So how did they vote?"

"Paper and ink" said Taryn, motioning at the mess of drawing papers and various colored drawing rods Lilly had left haphazardly laying about the mess of her room. Taryn had to constantly nag her daughter to clean it up. "I believe some of the first voters may have used counts of stones actually… or they had some other simple method of settling it I suppose, like wooden sticks or knotted ropes. Once computers came along that should have helped. But still people had to fully decide for themselves if they wanted to run for a position. They were never offered it randomly like we are."

Lilly tapped away on her padd recording her mother's words and then scrolled down.

"Ok, next question. Compared to modern governments, what disadvantages did the old-world democratic styles suffer from?"

"Oh, that's easy. Did your history teacher ever explain the 'settling effect' in class?"

"Maybe…" Lilly tried to recall. "Oh, wait um … was that the stuff about only having a choice of less harms?"

"Yes, that's kind of it, but he must have said more on it. Anything else?"

"Sorry mom, I don't remember. That class was last term I think..."

"Ok," said Taryn sitting up straighter in the bed, "well the 'settling effect' is a small name for a lot of… unwanted consequences that affected all democratic governments, no matter how rich or poor they were."

"If I remember right," she continued, "for the poorest democracies without technology or resources the largest problems were always based on cheating. Without money for impartial security, the results could easily be rigged. You could have people who were physically dead casting votes or various gangs or parties stuffing or dumping the ballot boxes or preventing others from actually voting to begin with. And typically, there might be no one with the ability or motive to stop them.

"Democracies that didn't put term limits in place or let them get thrown out by their parties or officials ended up often being ran as dictatorships. Many of the poorer democracies were only mockingly democratic. So that, even if you were allowed to vote, which you might not because you're a girl, when you did have the courage to actually show up to cast a ballot, you probably voted for whoever you were told to, if you didn't wish persecution. Elections could be faked or thrown based on any difference you can think of. Religion, culture, race, ethnicity, economics, class, organized crime—anything really that causes distinctions between people—became a potential source of rigged democracies in places without well-funded, impartial security. Such obvious flaws to us now, that the records say was too often repeated, again and again." Taryn smiled self-confidently to herself. Her research on the matter as a student was now coming back as a flood to her mind. Cascading examples and cases, from long hours of quiet study, that had all led her to a conclusion of how innately faulty the old-world systems had been. Having no direct experience, she wondered momentarily —not for the first time—how life under such mismatched intent and the actual gears of these systems was for the regular people back then. How did anyone stand such clear hypocrisies? Did they even know? Or did they simply have no other choice?

Lilly however, still focused on her own studies staring at her padd not noticing her mother's looks of internal musings, knocked Taryn's mind back to the present. "What about the richer governments?" she asked. They must have had better results?"

"Well, um, better monitored maybe, and less direct rigging or persecution, definitely. But they still suffered from the settling effect all the same. The problems just grew more complex the more developed the nations were." Taryn leaned a little on the arm of the chair herself, looking to right side of the ceiling trying to recall how it had been explained to her so many cycles ago as a student.

"You see, in many places the governments, ... they didn't or couldn't limit the campaigns, in terms of either time spent, or money invested. So, after a few generations a single election campaign could last longer than the actual term in office and end up costing more money than all but the richest could afford. Unless you inherited a fortune or three, the only legal way you got to be a candidate was to be in a major political party that would back you up with their own money. Political parties were much more abundant, not like we have today where they are forbidden from the government. But back then parties only truly invested in candidates that were willing to work for them and more importantly for their interests. Free thoughts that diverged from party views were either ignored or suppressed or crowded out. Elected officials became salesmen and bad actors rather than actual representatives of the best interests of their people."

Taryn sat up on the bed looking at the ceiling, thinking back to a lecture she had heard long ago. "They became...power-hungry addicts really. It was like their drug. It sounds silly to say, but that's the best way to describe it. They evolved into complete junkies tied to their influence cravings. Baseless, without purpose save from feeding their own addiction to power or to pleasing those that helped supply them. And the only way they could get their power-fix was to ensure they had enough money to win their campaigns and hope to move further up the reins of power. They would heel-toe to whatever party, financial or corporate bosses they needed to, and be chained to any promises they made in private while unable to keep most of the ones made to the public. They became leeches for the wealthiest donors of a party to help ensure their own positions, and then used that power and wealth to help put in place legalities to protect and enhance those same fortunes. And if those who had originally supported them ever soured on a politician, they could just as easily throw their funds and gilded praise behind someone new. It was a cyclical process. Legislatures could stay in a position of power for decades by sucking up to the unelected powerful.

"People at the time may have called them 'puppets' or 'hacks', but from the descriptions I've read the best way I heard them described was like hypocritical sycophants," Taryn explained, adding small emphatic hand gestures to her words. "Their primary concern was from who to get their next injection of campaign credits or their next pill sized dosage of power. Like I said drug addicts in a sense...

"Whole systems where the majority of elected officials were more concerned with doing better for their party and rich donors than for the actual people they were meant to represent. That's how they stayed powerful themselves. And whenever those two opinions didn't align, most officials would quietly, and quickly choose to neglect the welfare of the public in favor of remaining in good standing with the sources of their funding or power."

Lilly looked at her mom with a glance of disbelief, as if she might next ask *"What kind of screwed up people were these?"* Taryn saw the look and answered it.

"Well, why would the officials bother to try to help their voters, people who may or may not actually turn up and vote? Voluntary voter turn-out was much more unreliable back then, you know. And if the money from donors was consistent, government officials could always have a better than average chance at seducing the public opinion back to them with their endless campaigning. They didn't need everyone, only enough of the support from those willing to take the time to show up."

"Paid for by their political party's contributions" Lilly interjected as her typing caught up.

"Exactly, it was a slow growing and ugly cycle. The ones with power will do everything to keep themselves powerful. That's what your grandfather used to say about them. Real festering issues began cascading on each other, over and over again and again, until groveling for money, campaigning with impractical promises, arguing constantly with each other, and appeasing their larger donors were all elected officials were doing in place of their actual jobs. That's why political parties were never allowed in our government. That's what those early democracies had going against them."

"Wait," interrupted Lilly. "Why is it called the 'settling effect' then? And… if this cycle caused its own growth and was making the parties essentially unstoppable, how *did* it ever stop?" Lilly asked.

Taryn thought again, searching her mind, trying to recall her history lessons from many cycles before. Finally, finding no help in her academic recollections she switched over to a comparison she knew of through her own mothers' teaching

"Well, Lil…think of it like a parasite. You know about those from when you did your report on the ancient jungles that used to be in the tropics. Not all that sand, ash, and grass that's there now. But way back when trees were recorded to be so thick that animals might move for hundreds of kilometers among them never touching the ground," she pushed in a slightly tragic tone of wonderment. Both

Taryn and Lilly knew of these types of places no one had seen in generations or would likely ever see again. Myths of the modern world whose only confirmation of real existence came from images and old half complete recordings surviving from the ancients. "Well," Taryn explained, "lots of parasitic systems used to live there your grandma says. And when they grew too large, feeding too fast, they basically collapsed their populations under their own weight. Soon there would be so many parasites and too few hosts so that their growth couldn't last. Parasites can never outnumber the ones they take advantage of. Turns out that politics is a lot like nature. It did take a while if I remember right," she said pensively. "A lot of mistakes too, but eventually the people saw the issues that governments were *meant* to help with only getting worse and worse, unchecked so that confidence in elected officials dropped and stayed low for several decades, never to recover so long as the status quo remained entrenched. Any new candidates that had entered that system likely became part of the larger problem from the public's view. Even those few that did have decent intentions were likely outpaced in their efforts or were just plainly outnumbered. Those who feed on power could always be counted on to spring up quickly, generation after generation, and if they succeeded in getting elected," she said in a wary tone "then by being their own bosses they could work to entrench themselves as quickly as the others before them.

"So, the public began to see the election system as a sort of bad joke. Slowly, the common thought that knowledge is power, as some had claimed in the past, began to be widely debated. After a while the thinkers in democracies of the time began to realize just how wrong that antiquated type of thinking was. They began having large-scale shifts in their thoughts that strongly countered notions like that one."

"Why? What's wrong with it?" Lilly asked, confused and a bit shocked. "That kind of makes sense to me?"

"Because, Lil, knowledge is *not* power." Taryn said correctively. "The ancients had knowledge," she pointed out. "Far more knowledge than what we have left to us today about many old topics which we are still trying to rediscover. They were the first to be truly beset by instant knowledge *at a keystroke* as they described it, yet their power was still easily syphoned and consolidated away from them by their own public officials. No Lil, *choice is power*. And power comes from having your own choices to make. Or having control over others' choices. The ability to choose between options A and B can never compete with the ability to choose with options A through Z. And if your amount of choices are either restricted or expanded on, then who really has the power? The person doing the choosing for themselves or the one who laid out the options to begin with? *Power, control,* and *choice:* these are... interchangeable, identical. You see?" Taryn asked, not noticing herself being rather impassioned by her own explanation. They are easily substituted with one another because they are the same. Choice is power, and power is demonstrated by how much control over choices that you have," she explained.

"I think I get it..."said Lilly as she screwed her brown eyes narrower contemplating this notion. "But… but what does '*choice being power*' have to do with any of this?" she asked.

"Well, once you recognize it, you can gauge power based on the amount of choices you possess, whether you consider yourself to have freedom, be oppressed, subjugated, or enslaved. It's how much choice is practically in your reach that matters. So when the public in these failing democracies eventually saw their choices all starting to look the same, again and again every time, it was seen as a restriction of choice. Of their publicly due power. Never having what amounted to a real choice of who was best for an office of leadership, only a choice of who they could settle for." Taryn laughed, "In the modern voting system, probably all those old-world candidates would have been voted out of the campaign by our negative voting option. But that last part is just my opinion Lil', ok?"

"Yeah, I think I got it," she said with a smirk.

"Sorry for the long answer but it's a complicated topic. And that's also why it took centuries for it to get solved." As she said all of this, Taryn momentarily wondered to herself how much Lilly actually understood at her age.

"That's ok. Thanks for your help mom. Once I finish helping nan' with dinner maybe you can help me with the rest of the questions?" she asked hopefully.

"No, you stay and keep working," Taryn said. "I'll help nainai with dinner tonight. You can bring me any problems you still have afterwards, alright?"

"Mmm, okay," Lil replied.

Taryn got up to leave and was halfway out the door when Lilly turned from her padd at the desk and asked, "Hey why are you here anyways? You usually don't come home this early."

Taryn realized that she had almost let the day's events gratefully wander out of her thoughts. Now it rushed back over her insides, like a sudden surge of wind that was heeling her over before she knew it. Taryn narrowly managed to keep her face hidden from her daughter as she exited the room. "Oh... don't worry about it. Just focus on your homework Lil," was all her daughter heard as Taryn left.

* * *

After eating dinner and giving Trey his bath, Taryn quietly broke the news about her job to Gloria while they folded clothes alone in the bedroom. After a solid half an hour of explanations and tough questions, which was in truth much calmer in tone than Taryn had expected due to Trey wandering in and out of the room to play every few minutes, Gloria had gone to prod the kids to clean their teeth. For her part Taryn was left tired but at least alone for a few minutes without needing to go further help with the kids for the moment. She still was utterly surprised by the smoothness of their conversation. She had forgotten how her mom could do that sometimes. Gloria was upset to be sure, but overall, she'd defied Taryn's expectations and stayed reserved when Taryn thought that her first reaction would be to hastily accuse her daughter of some type of fault in this. It was also one of the times Taryn remembered she felt both relieved and guilty at the thought of Cyrano not being around anymore. Had he known, had he been here, he would certainly have argued with her over this loss of her job much more vigorously than Gloria had done. The couple argued extensively several nights straight before the decision to move her mother in with them had been resolved. Taryn felt relieved at the idea of not having to do that now, but then felt immediately guilty for having the feeling of relief at her husband not being around in the first place.

She kept folding the remaining laundry as she wept quietly to herself alone in the room for a brief period, struggling with this emotional contradiction and the thought of Cyrano's disappointment at the only credit-earner in the family suddenly being without a job. His whole family, that he gave his life for, was now without any secure means of support. When Taryn finally mastered her emotions and emerged, Gloria was already helping Trey to bed. Taryn was planning to tell Lilly everything tomorrow, if she could manage it, and had pleaded with her mom to not reveal anything until then.

"No sense putting it off; she'll just find out tomorrow anyways when you have nowhere to get to," Gloria had argued. But Taryn had remained obstinate on this point. She felt drained and didn't want to end it by explaining her career failure once again today, and this time to her daughter no less.

As Taryn was exiting her room, Lilly's door opened, spilling out the aggressively paced-beat that was a hallmark of her daughter's most recent musical trend.

"Hey mom?" said Lilly, coming half in the hallway to intercept Taryn. "If you and nainai are done arguing with each other for now, I still need your help with that debate stuff again."

"Yeah, ok." said Taryn, quickly wiping her eyes. "Let me grab some water and I'll be right in." Lilly had seen her mother crying before but over the past few months Taryn had managed to keep that mostly subdued to her own private times. Her daughter was used to this act by now. Her mother hiding her tears in front of her brother and her. Presenting a stronger front, like her dad had typically done. That, Lilly figured, was her mom's way of trying to help fill in dad's old part and not knowing how to react to it. The young girl thought it better to let her mom believe that she was succeeding at this.

"It's ok mom" said Lilly, "I'll just bring my padd to the kitchen and we can work there."

They sat next to each other, both with cups, at the small dinner table. As they were getting started, Taryn's mom came in from the patio where she'd been watering her plants.

"And what are you two doing, huh?"

"Mom's helping with my history."

"History, huh?" Gloria smiled at Lilly. "Well, I'm old enough to count as that, I think. Let me grab my easel and sit with you both a' while." she said, putting away her watering bottle. "Need to make sure your mom doesn't make a fool of herself by telling you a bunch of trash she thinks are real facts."

Lilly smiled at her. Of all the adults she grew up with, even her deceased father, Lilly was the fondest of her grandma, her nainai, the most. She was strong, kind, supportive, and fiercely independent when needed.

"Great mom, thanks," Taryn said in a calmly annoyed tone at her mother's last remark. "Glad to know that I still have your confidence."

Gloria gave a quick wink to Lilly as she sat and began working on her painting. It was a small canvas that was almost full. On its fabric were some tall, yellow-flowered weeds. They were partially hiding a large black tortoise-shell colored house cat just off the side of a gravel road. Gloria was currently debating on where exactly to place some mice that would be crossing over the lane within the cat's eyeline. But while internally Gloria struggled with this aesthetic debate, outwardly she had her normal picturesque image of calm and steady confidence displayed.

Taryn on the other hand, fairly secure in her knowledge on the matters with which she was helping her daughter now, had a composure that was quite the opposite to that of her mom's. That she was fourteen years removed from her last history class and with her own mother, a former teacher of three decades sitting right here, listening in, made Taryn a bit more nervous and hesitant than she had been before. As she talked with Lilly, Taryn fidgeted and scratched at old food stains on the small tabletop, trying to double check her words before responding to Lilly's questions.

They reviewed a bit about what Tarn had already mentioned before. About the subtle differences in the approaches of the old-world approaches to democratic governments and how, despite these, eventually each democracy had played itself out far faster than most expected. But mainly Lilly was still unsure about how the 'settling effect' working in its slow corrosive manner could be countered in any real way.

"Well," she said, "I don't see how just by discovering it that it could've caused anything to change? I mean what about people has really changed since then?"

"So, like I said before, the politicians in the old systems were basically power-hungry drug-addicts, right?"

Lilly nodded.

"Well, once it was thoroughly researched and accepted by most, it was believed that democracy was a lost cause, an over-farmed field that gave smaller yields with each passing cycle it was in use. But you're correct, that alone wasn't enough. It took the last series of Global Wars to start to make it plainly clear that the essential problems could no longer be ignored. The best defense against the 'settling effect' was found to be randomness."

"Randomness?" Lilly asked confused.

"Think 'bout the periodic Cicadas I taught you about, Lil'," interjected her grandma.

"The noisy summer bugs?" answered Lilly confused.

"Yeah, remember I taught you about their life patterns?"

"Oh yeah. Some come out every summer, and others come out only once every 13 or 17 cycles."

"And why is it always prime numbers?"

Lilly thought for a moment. "Oh, so that no other creature can know when they're coming and wait for them."

"That's right," said Gloria as she dipped her brush in some grey. "The different cicadas use the randomness of their life cycles as a defense against predators and parasites. The use of that random emergence means predictability is impossible, especially when using prime numbers. And the lack of predictable patterns means it's much harder to be taken advantage of. And when they *do* emerge, they do so in such force of numbers that they surprise and overwhelm any parasites and predators. Their quick concentrated amounts and their random timing ensures that they survive."

Taryn continued, "So, our modern government, like the cicada, adopted elements of randomness to it. That's where the moot lottery comes in. You know how every two cycles everyone has to go to the doctors for a neural scan?"

"Yeah, grandma just took us to get ours last week."

Taryn nodded.

"Well, besides screening for diseases and development problems in children, the scanning process also acts as a citizen registry process, so that every adult can be entered into the lottery for the next campaign cycle. Every citizen is required to vote to focus our voting efforts, just like with the cicadas. And every seven cycles when the elections are held, they select people from the registry randomly. That way we completely replace all of those currently serving in the SOMA, assuming the selected wish to run of course.

"Oh, ok wait, hang on. I saw a question like that further down the page." Lilly scrolled down her padd. "Here it is. How many people are possibly electable for our core government every election season?"

"Well, ignoring the local regional assemblies, the SOMA itself holds about 500 officials total, and for every seat there are five people that are pulled randomly for the moot lottery campaigns. So, that's just five times 500."

"2,500, got it." Lilly said as she punched in her answer. "Well, what about the Prime Trinity Council. How many candidates are chosen for those positions?"

"Don't know," Taryn said with a shake of her head. "That's kept secret by the SOMA members. The SOMA are the ones to choose the three members of the Haiden council. All the public is told is that it has a similar element of randomness and that somehow our votes matter in the process as well. Most people think that the SOMA pick amongst themselves in some way"

"Ok, well I'll put about 2515 to be safe," Lilly said as she typed. "Hmm…Mom? If the lottery for candidates is random, why do they bother hiding their identities too? I mean, those campaign vids from the last election I saw on the old news waves only showed blocked faces without their real voices."

"Oh, that's so that people can really listen to the ideas of the candidates, Lil, and not make their judgments based on anything that has to do with their looks or their voice."

"Aside from the home region that they represent, it's illegal for SOMA members and those running in the election to reveal any personal details about themselves," added Gloria.

"They can only tell the public about their ideas, and what they think the government should work on and their plans of actions if elected. It also helps to protect the candidate's privacy from those who'd want to influence them for their own purposes. They were called lobbyists in the old systems, I think?"

Gloria nodded to her easel in agreement. Taryn turned back to Lilly continuing.

"Because the identity of all the SOMA members are anonymous and restricted and they're limited to only one term of service, it's impossible for anyone to know who may be serving the next time. And since re-election is not a concern for any of them, it isn't the debilitating waste of time it was for the old-world democracies. SOMA members are not busy trying to please any party or donors; they are only beholden to the laws and people who they represent. No-one else."

"They know," Gloria interjected, "that they can focus on making sure that they're working for those people who elected them in quiet autonomy, but without any way of keeping their power for a moment longer than they are permitted."

"So… even if they *were* to really enjoy being a SOMA member, it's impossible to keep it and all they know this," Lilly said reflectively. "So they can't be long-term addicts to the power, they can only do their job—"

"For the people, as the people, and within the people, as they say." Gloria said without breaking any of her brush strokes.

"How?" asked Lilly. "I mean how are the SOMA chosen to begin with?"

"Well, when the time comes," Taryn continued, "for the moot lottery to pull choices for the new candidates, all the eligible citizens in a region are given or sent a receipt number after they do their neural scans. Once any neurological issues are finished being tagged the news waves will publish a list of the randomly selected receipt numbers to all the healthy citizens remaining. A few weeks after that, the campaign interviews are aired so that we can compare the contenders and help us decide who we want to vote for in our region. In fact, the selections are due to be pushed out in another month or so for the new terms, I think. Right mom?"

Gloria nodded quietly in agreement, but not removing her eyes from her work.

"So, you see Lil, it's difficult for anyone to gain influence over an elected official that no one knows, it's illegal to publish or try to reveal their true names, and the SOMA members change every election term. No repeats allowed."

"But if their identities are secret, how do we know we aren't just electing the same people all over again each time, or like with old kings, pulling different people but from the exact same family? How do we know it's random?"

"Well, that's a hard question. There is a lot of secrecy about the process because their anonymity is what helps keep the SOMA reps honest to their intentions. It's nothing like the private corporate worlds or business groups where familial ties and politicking is more than alive. But in the government, anyone directly in the same family is not allowed to serve as a candidate. That's one of the best-known laws about serving in the SOMA. Being a family member, within one generation of a current or previous official is one of the few things that can make a citizen automatically ineligible."

"A family's limit of service is what it's called Lil," added Gloria. "Between that and it being illegal to spill their own identities, and their one-term limit in the SOMA, the ship's hull is pretty tight."

"When the new officials take over," Taryn went on, "they do a transition ceremony where the old official must shake the new officials' hands live on the news stream for all to see. That way everyone can see the older officials give way to the new ones. You must've come across the vid or a picture in your school's text? The one where everyone is heavily robed in blue and black hoods to hide their faces, and the only thing that distinguishes them is the different regional crests?"

Lilly thought for a moment and nodded as the image came back to her.

"The older officials make new ones recite their oaths, shake hands, and they give them a crest for their region's robes, then they can actually cast votes through DNA scans and submit their own new ideas to be considered. Our silent democracy was designed to work for the majority not the minority, and with no active outside influence. With honesty of intent beyond any other thought."

Taryn paused as she took a sip of her tea. "You're right though... that we can't be perfectly certain about the randomness, I mean." Lilly gave a surprised look. "Still," Taryn said reassuringly, "the SOMA's work has helped make the city and territories the largest stable population since the wars were ended. Opening up all its inner workings would only make it vulnerable to the settling effect all over again."

"It was probably strange to those first citizens too," Gloria chimed in, "but you can't argue with the results. Government did more genuine productive work in its first fifteen cycles than the last old-world democracies had done in generations. Waste management, power research, population, water, and food issues. All these got addressed where other pre-war governments ignored them, talked around them, or were too gutless to make any real decisions `cause it might cost somebody an election. Much easier for regular folk to do the right things if your only business is helping, with no worry about being popular enough to keep your job."

"So then… it's really randomness mixed with voting, secrecy, some technology and limiting politics that managed to stop the 'settling effect.'"

Both Taryn and Gloria paused and looked in amazement from Lilly to each other and then back to the youth.

"That's very good Lil," Taryn said, still staring at her daughter as if she was now speaking as if to a stranger, newly materialized from thin air.

"I've seen senior government students that've missed that concept," said Gloria proudly.

"Yeah, good job, but still, it's getting late. You better finish this up after your teeth, ok?"

"Okay, it's not due till Friday anyways Mom, so I have time."

After Lilly had left, Taryn got up to take care of their glasses and finish cleaning the kitchen.

Gloria continued on with her painting.

"You know, every now and then that little girl of yours really gets her feet planted proper, doesn't she?"

"Yeah, every once in a while," Taryn said as she turned on the sink.

"Now if only I could get her to understand how to pick up after herself."

"And if only her mother could hold onto a decent job," kicked back Gloria sarcastically.

Chapter 5: Can't You Hear Me Knocking

Taryn hated being correct about this. Despite knowing it was inevitable, she still despised the twisted circularity of it all. Having to employ herself full-time to find full-time employment was both demanding while also continually demoralizing. Still, she had set out quickly spending time revising her old job resumes and making digitized inquiries over the waves into a few hundred of the thousands of businesses around the city. The only true consensus between Taryn and her mom about the loss of her job had been that she needed a new one, and soon. They had let Lilly believe that Taryn had quit on her own terms so as not to worry her. They agreed to make it appear—to the kids at least—that the actions now happening with Taryn's job hunting were indeed planned for, and thus not as precipitous as they truly were. An unfortunate but temporary transition, they had told her. This happening unexpectedly from out of nowhere was exactly the type of situation Taryn and Cyrano had always warned her against after all.

"Being prepared for all means your avoiding stupid accidents, whether it's your education, work or love life" , they had told her repeatedly. "The more prepared you are the better you'll cope Lil, when things go wrong."

They used stories too, like how Taryn's father had been unprepared for the onset of an early winter one season and lost most of his crops as a result. Or how Cyrano's mother had been illiterate in reading and math her whole life as a child, only to discover the need for it when she had to raise kids on her own and work at the same time. They even told Lilly about how unprepared they'd been to have her as a child while still in the midst of their own education. All stressful and enduring situations that could have been lessened—they had explained—with more thoughtful preparations.

Of course, all that had been truly useless comfort for Lilly when she found out her father was never returning home from his work in the fringes. However, Taryn had still tried to reinforce the idea that they would be okay, that her father and that even Taryn had been prepared for this possibility. Lilly was decimated though, and only slowly over the months was Taryn, with no shortage of help from Gloria, able to help get her daughter back into near a regular routine life again. She was telling Lilly the same lie now, that she was prepared to be without a job at this point. Putting on a false mask of confidence as she worked on her padd from home over the next few weeks. *If I'm calm about it and not showing signs of panic then she'll feed off that*, Taryn kept telling herself. She figured that at the least, given her experience and consistent work record after all, it shouldn't be too difficult getting a door to open for her somewhere. It was just a matter of knocking enough times.

It was by the end of the third week of her hunting, after a dozen interviews and several more vid-call sessions, that Taryn started to truly suspect something was wrong. The interviews were going well. Too well in fact, to not be getting more interest. She had all the qualifications on their lists in many cases, but after each meeting she would never hear a response. Nothing at all. Not a "you're not experienced enough" or "your skills aren't developed enough" or "another candidate..." Just deafening silence. Though to be fair, a few places did send her a "thank you for applying" notice.

It was a growing concern to Taryn, as she sat now in the middle of an interview with an old line-worker associate named Clearor. He had been on the same line at Taryn's old Corp for some cycles before she had ever started. He had eventually moved on to a different corporation but, in time, had done well for himself and been made a Tie at this new corp. Once again, the interview seemed to be going well. Better than well. Taryn and Clearor were laughing about their first meeting and reminiscing about hanging out with Cyrano at the old bar that Everett would later buy.

"Well, I think that we should definitely be able to find you a spot Taryn, I know what you're capable of, and I suspect that someone of your quality could be of use to use on the floor. I'll run your resume past my colleagues, and we should be giving you a call back in the next day or two."

Finally, Taryn thought to herself. "Thanks, Clearor," she said exuberantly smiling. "You've just made my whole month. Thanks so much."

But two nights later, instead of a call, an automated message popped across Taryn's padd. To Taryn's surprise it had the very standard 'thank you for applying, best of luck" drivel she'd seen many times before. Taryn was dumbfounded. The company's offices were closed this late, but she still remembered the number to Clearor's personal line. She shut the door to her bedroom and dialed the number on her earpiece. The call was answered but given the hour, Clearor sounded as if he was still in his vehicle driving home.

"Hello?" said Clearor.

"Clearor? Hi, it's Taryn."

"Taryn, um, hi… How are you? I wanted to give you a call earlier but I… couldn't find your info."

"Couldn't? Taryn insisted. "I'm confused, Clearor. I thought that I had all the qualifications you were scanning for? Why am I getting a 'get lost with our kindest regards' letter? You said—."

"Shit. Taryn, look… I know what I said, okay. Just shut up and listen." He continued his voice with clear concern ringing through it. "I ran your resume past my coworkers, like I told you. And at first, they said it was all fine as we expected, but once they ran your work ID... it just… it all capsized really fast."

"What? What do you mean?"

"You're listed, Taryn."

Taryn paused mid-pace in her room. Her breathing stopped dead as her eyes darted around as fast as she was thinking, eventually landing unconsciously on the small wall projection of a younger Cyrano and her smiling as they were leaving the medical center with a newly born Lil in tow. Taryn became aware of a lump caught in her throat as she searched for something, anything, to say.

"Now, I don't know what you did on your old floor but whatever it was, your old employer was sure as hell pissed at you. You're labeled as unfit, uncooperative, ineffective, and I'm quoting from memory here 'a high source of dissent among the workers under her supervision.'"

"Wait a minute," Taryn said, regaining some composure. "I thought listing employees was illegal?"

"Technically it is. But no one who knows cares, and those who would care don't know. The gov inspectors rarely look into our cross-corporate communications. They probably figure we'd never share that much information with our own competition, company espionage being what it is... But it's no wonder you've been job hunting as long as you'd said without landing anywhere. When my boss found out I actually gave you an interview without running your number first, I got my ears chewed off and he nearly had me suspended. Hell, even calling you from my office line means I'd be fined a day's pay."

"Well… isn't this just wonderful," Taryn said, letting the frustration ring through her voice.

"Look Taryn I'm sorry. Really, I am. But I gotta keep my own skiff going, you know?"

"Thanks, but what am I supposed to do now?"

"Best advice…" Clearor said thinking for a moment, "change your line of work, drastically. No one with eyes and ears is going to give you a chance once they've read through that stuff."

"Yeah, I guess so…" she said, defeated. Listen, thanks for the info Clearor. Sorry for bringing you trouble over this. I know...I know you were just trying to help."

"Hey, Taryn, you could get lucky with some other places. They don't all have access to those listed."

"Yeah sure..." she said insincerely. "Take care Clearor."

The line died. After another long moment, Taryn turned around to see Gloria standing right inside the doorway to her room with a load of clothes in hand. Taryn paused not remembering if she'd fully closed her door to begin with, resigned herself to sit back down on the bed, not caring to debate anything anymore.

"How much did you hear?" Taryn asked her mom

Gloria walking in further, closed the door behind her then sat next to her daughter.

"Enough to know why you're upset. Do you think all the companies have your name blacked out now?"

"Yep, all the major ones probably."

"What are you going to do?"

"Keep applying and hope that I'm wrong."

Gloria put a hand on her daughter's slumped shoulders and kissed her cheek.

"But Tar, if your friends in the corps can't even help you… ?"

"I know Mom, I know," she paused. "I'll figure something. For now…I'll just have to widen my search to find a place where I'm not recognized." She thought for a moment. "Anything I get that way though won't likely pay nearly as much."

"Try, Tar. We can't keep the bills clean with my elder-net cash or Cyrano's service pension alone, not for much longer anyways," Gloria said. "I could always try to find a part time job of my own for a while."

"Yeah, Mom, but you here for the kids saves more money than you could hope to make from any part-timer slot. The bills would only go up from having to hire a watcher."

"I looked over our expenses while you were out at an interview the other day," Gloria said in a concerning fashion. "Now my math is not as good as it once was, but I figure we can stay in the flat for another three months before the bills catch up faster than they can be paid."

"I know", Taryn responded. "I looked at them the day after I was fired. I'll find something before then Mom," she said, forcing a smile. "I promise."

"Well, what about Everett? Wouldn't he help if you asked?"

"Of course he would mom, but that's not the point," Taryn sighed. "Any funds he'd loan would just be a short pause in the real problem. I need to find decent work. And besides, I don't want to put personal finances between Everett and us. We'll make our own way."

"I know your father used to say that 'friends and credits don't grow in the same soil,' but at some point, you may have to ask yourself which is worse Tar: Risking a friendship or not being able to feed your kids?"

* * *

The next few weeks didn't change things, with the exception that Taryn became privately more frantic in her job search. She started temporarily working nights on the unskilled cleaning crews of various places to earn at least some credits. On the occasional expected busy night, she'd help out at Everett's bar too. It was more to feel useful than anything. Everett was vaguely aware of these difficulties, but he grew ever more suspicious as the days went on. Though Taryn kept insisting it was a way to fill her time while she was waiting to hear back from her interviews. The problem was that even when she worked these extra hours at the Hidden Roller, the credits simply weren't there to be had. Not enough customers, even when it was busier.

All things considered, Gloria had handled this whole mess far better than Taryn had hoped. Maybe it was the fact that she'd watched her daughter also lose her husband as quickly as she had. Only that Taryn's loss was not due to some ailments of age, as Gloria's had been. Cyrano was taken away at a critical time in their marriage, right when his help should have been the most useful to his young blossoming family. That was not as it was with Gloria's husband. Taryn's father had died cycles after having the time to carve out a life for himself, and when his child was grown and gone. Maybe it was the fact that nothing that Gloria could have said to Taryn would have changed the situation. Maybe it was that her mother was still far stronger willed than she'd ever known. But whatever the reason, Taryn kept expecting her mother to lose her patience or break down at her on some random night when she came home. But Gloria showed no sign of this happening. More and more it was Taryn's own confidence—hit by blow after blow of rejection time and again—that was cracking on a daily basis and starting to shatter. That truth could only have been told to Taryn by an outsider though. For whatever her confidence felt like, she gave herself no time to simmer on it. Time was not her friend here. She was more worried about catching the winds, as they say. The tattering of her own sails must wait.

It was on one of these night shifts at Everett's that Taryn's earpiece beeped with an incoming call. Taryn touched a finger to her ear and answered the call by the fifth buzz.

She had figured it was her mom asking how late she'd be tonight. Gloria always made sure to ask Taryn this on the nights she worked at Everett's. Safe and trusted as Everett was, Taryn's mom didn't like her working at a place that served drinks to groups of men late into the night. Besides calling her daughter to confirm her hours, Gloria always insisted she get a message from Taryn when she was in her vehicle on the way home

"Hey mom." Taryn answered her line presumptuously.

"Hello? Ms. Steno?" a deep, calm but hoarse, unfamiliar male voice asked.

"Um… Yeah?" she answered, surprised to hear any other voice calling her line this late.

"My name is Filater, Ms. My office came across your resume late today and we were hoping you'd be willing to come in for an interview tomorrow at the 2nd hour, if you're available that is?"

"Tomorrow, oh err...sure."

"Excellent. We're located in the industrial park off 63rd street. Suite 23. I'm sending the data to your listed wave account. Please allow two hours for the interview and testing."

"Testing?"

"Just a simple blood and scan system. All standard requirements for the post really. We'll see you tomorrow, Ms. Steno."

"Wait, what's the posit—"

The link had already clicked dead. Taryn stood for a second and thought about the location in her mind. She had hardly ever been to that section of the city. It was too isolated to hold any of the major companies she knew of. And she couldn't remember directly applying for any job in that area either.

"Well okay, I guess I'll find out tomorrow," she thought, returning to her sweeping. The fact that they had sought her out, she hoped, was a good sign at least that perhaps this Corp hadn't seen her name on any illicit listing.

* * *

The next day, a little before the 2nd hour past dawn, Taryn was driving through the industrial tech park a little off of 63rd street. Though certainly better landscaped than most industrial zones she'd seen, something did seem a bit off about the place. She eventually decided that it was the lack of traffic in and out, not to mention the apparent lack of any visible major manufacturing facility on sight. There were several small and medium brick office buildings all with letters or numbers, but none of them appeared to be an obvious central HQ. They all looked much the same in their design and age with only three varieties of size. Taryn had expected this uniform layout when she had looked up the address last evening. Far as she had been able to tell the places here were all rental facilities. Various corps or smaller scale businesses could rent them at times as some of the empty ones were still advertised for temporary relief of pressing office space.

She pulled into one of these unremarkable buildings labeled Suite 23.

Inside, there was a very small, carpeted waiting room and window to a receptionist area in the back. Taryn gave the receptionist her name and the young secretary had her wait a short while. She didn't get long to think on this place, as before much time passed the small door to the back slid open and a mature man in a suit called her in. He introduced himself as Mr. Filater, which sounded appropriate to Taryn as his job today must have consisted of filtering through her interview as well as others probably. He wore a basic black suit with only a slim dark tie on his medium build. Taryn saw that he stood as Cyrano had, straight postured as one who appeared to have trained with the Defense Force might. Unlike Cyrano though he was not tall, but only of average height. Likewise, his face was neither ugly nor overly attractive. His eyes were always searching, slowly analyzing things around him, though they conveyed a strength of intelligence in the process. That aside, his austere orderly personality made him nearly as unremarkable as the building in which they were meeting. Taryn eventually guessed that he was actually younger than he appeared, no more than 45, with slicked back dark hair, and a fairly pleasant smile if it was ever seen, but mostly he had a rather unemotional disposition. They moved to a spartan meeting room a short way in. She was seated at a small wooden table in the room with three open foldable metal chairs. The rest were folded neatly in a corner. The man, Filater, noticing Taryn's glances about the room, began.

"My apologies for the room's bare demeanor. We don't use it often and our superiors are adamant about only using what's necessary," he said as he pulled out a chair for her. "Would you like anything to drink, some water or tea perhaps?"

She politely declined and asked, "Will anyone else be joining us for the interview?" she mentioned to the empty chair.

"Oh, this isn't the interview yet I'm afraid. No, no." He shook his head. "This is only the pre-eval," he said, taking a seat across from her with a padd in hand. "You see, due to the sensitive nature of the work our organization does, we have some additional screenings that potential employees must complete first. I know that's not probably something you're accustomed to, but it's needed to ensure the quality of our working staff and the stability of our product."

Taryn shifted in her chair. "And what is it your staff does here? I didn't see any factory buildings on the way in and these places are only temp rentals anyway."

"I'm afraid I can't divulge any of that until you've gone through the pre-eval, though it is quite a simple process, I assure you. Just a few quick questions, a blood test, and quick scan. Security measures and medical requirements are needed to establish your eligibility. So, shall we begin?"

"Alright," Taryn said hesitantly. If this Corp was on the younger side, it would make sense to take some additional security measures to protect any trade secrets from its larger established competitors.

"Good," he said, crossing his legs and leaning back in his chair with his padd in hand.

"Now first, can you give me your full name and worker ID to record just so we can confirm we got it correct?"

She gave both. Taryn had been through enough interviews by now to be only mildly nervous at a peculiar set up, no matter its oddities. She needed the work, plain and simple. How a Corp went about protecting itself wasn't her place to decide. The weeks of rejection and growing necessity of incoming credits meant that Taryn was well over any initial hesitation of presenting her personal data when asked by a potential employer. Though in her limited experience, most wanted this information only *after* the interview was done.

Taryn answered a few more standard questions concerning her marital status, family, and birthplace and citizenship status. Filater's head was always facing down towards his padd while he asked, but his eyes, in truth, were scanning her face during her responses. Taryn noticed there was a small, curved device in the upper side corner of the room. It looked like a basic recorder as she had seen in most of the other Corp offices she had managed to interview at. Though this one had a tiny green light that was just barely visible even when one looked directly at it. She wondered how much real attention the person on the other side was actually giving towards this room. *Probably not much,* she figured. *This was all still basics.*

"Alright, that should do it for the questions," Filater said after about five minutes.

"Now we're going to send you next door where you'll find a scrappy old man called Dr. Uthtr waiting for you. He'll have you do a quick blood-draw and neural scan."

"Okay," she said uneasily as she got up.

In the top right corner of the room, the small green light turned off.

Just as Filater said, in the next room Taryn found the bent old white-haired doctor seated at a small lab table reading. His seasoned wrinkly face looked at her through a dirty pair of wire-rimmed glasses. He put down his padd and smiled.

"You my second hour appointment?" he asked.

"I guess so," Taryn replied.

"Well, have a seat then and roll up your sleeve for me, please."

"Been a while since I've seen an actual Doctor," she said sitting down. "Usually I just get the technicians or nurses."

"Well, lucky for both of us. You get an actual doctor and I get saved from having to read any more of that boring serial."

Taryn smiled. Though obviously a bit feisty, the old man did have a certain prickly charm to him, she decided.

The doctor, his movements smooth from years of practice, began drawing a small blood sample and continued on, "I prefer doing some things here myself, ya see. Keeps the costs down, makes security easier to deal with, and I get to meet more people this way.

I'm told I'm a natural people person. All of my ex-wives told me so," he said, shooting a sly smile at her.

Taryn laughed openly at this. After the blood-draw, he walked her into an adjacent room. There was a white neural scanner that looked as though it were brand new and had never been used before.

She sat in the chair as Dr. Uthtr started the small machine up and placed the half crescent sensor pad on her head. As Taryn listened, once again, through the standard fare of how the device was trying to detect any early sign of neurological disease, a question came to her.

"You know," said Taryn, "I had my required neural scan done only a few weeks ago. Don't suppose you can just get those results and use them though, huh?"

"Exactly," said the elderly doctor. "Now this'll take about 10 minutes."

"Only 10? Last one I did took 30."

"Actually, on this particular machine it only takes five minutes, the advancement of technology and all that. And while around here we don't like to spend credits where we don't need to, in situations where we do see a need to finance things, we get the absolute best. But for today we're getting a control sample first, that's why it takes twice as long."

Doctor Uthtr handed Taryn a padd.

"Here, there are a few vid choices. Would you kindly pick one to watch during the first round?"

"Wait, I thought watching videos during these things screwed up the results?"

"They do. That's why this is the control sample. The videos are only five minutes. After that, I'll reset the machine and record a second set to compare it to. Helps validate the data."

Taryn scanned the choices and picked a short set of popular comedic clips and began watching. After five minutes the video ended. Doctor Uthtr touched a button on the padd, and the vid choices changed to a choice of music only.

"Alright, round two," he said. "You're half-way there. You can listen to music or just sit quietly."

Taryn picked a song on the piano, shut her eyes, and leaned back into the chair. After the song finished, Dr. Uthtr grunted a thanks to Taryn and briskly wished her luck in the interview.

"I'll pass on the results to your application file soon, but I suspect everything should check out fine from what I've seen. You go on back to the waiting room Ms. Steno and some overpriced, over groomed pencil pusher will likely be with you in a few minutes."

She smiled and thanked him. As Taryn left, a small green light on the back of the neural scanner turned off.

*   *   *

She sat in the small waiting room a while this time. Now when the door reopened, a tall man with no hair came out.

"Taryn Steno," he said, extending his hand. "I'm Rialt. Thank you for your patience. I understand you've already completed the pre-eval. I know it seemed odd at first, but you're all set now. If you'll follow me, we'll get the interview started."

Back in the small room, Filater was already waiting for them. They all sat down, the men across from Taryn were both holding padds with various data streaming through.

Filater started, "Alright, Mrs. Steno, now that the pre-evaluation is complete, we only have one more minor legal issue to resolve." He passed her his padd.

"Ok?" she said, unsure what other hoops there could be for them to run her through.

"This is a discretionary agreement," Rialt said, sliding a padd to her. "Take your time and read it, we'll happily answer any questions you have. But the short version is that it says that we are going to tell you all about the nature of the employment opportunity and regardless of if you're chosen, or if you decide to accept or reject the position, the details of the position itself are to remain confidential to you and you alone. Not even your spouse or children can know, or you would face severe legal action."

Taryn looked the document over a while, ignoring the error Rialt made in worrying about her talking to her spouse. Most of its legal language was designed to be inclusive to all situations from what she could tell, but for the most part she understood very little except the bits about extensive financial fines, repercussions, and prosecution if the client's confidentiality was broken. At the least Taryn saw the client named on the document as Vox P. Industrials. After reminding herself of her slim chance at any more real interviews today or even this week, Taryn eventually squashed any remaining hesitation, signed off on the padd, and handed it back to Filater.

"Thank you," he said as he made some final initials on the padd himself, then submitted it for review and had Rialt sign his initials as the representative party. After he was done, Filater put the padd aside and folded his hands.

"Thank you for your patience with all of this," he began, "We understand how that can be annoying to newcomers. Now as you know, the new election cycle is approaching Mrs. Steno, and it's my duty to inform you that your registration number has been selected by the moot lottery as a potential candidate for election into the SOMA to represent your region."

"Wait… what?" Taryn paused, taken aback. This made no sense. "But I thought… I thought that I was being interviewed for a job?"

"Well… in a way you are, Mrs. Steno. Now that we've confirmed your identity, you're free to choose to do the 'interview' with the voting public via a campaign for the purpose of potentially being elected to that job."

"But, but the news feeds…" she stammered. "They… they haven't even published the winners yet. I haven't even seen a receipt message sent to me, and you're saying I've already been pulled?" Taryn asked sharply.

"Well, this type of meeting is one of our confirmation tactics, but yes we are."

Taryn gave him a puzzled look.

"For security reasons, ma'am, we don't acknowledge that we actually give candidates advanced warning. It gives us ample time to do background checks on you and the others. The news publishing the results helps the new candidates such as yourself, to know that we're in-fact sincere. By the end of the work week, the whole region will have been sent their receipt numbers, and in a few more days when the news waves put out the winning five candidate's numbers selected for your region, yours *will* be among them."

Rialt now spoke, "And if you choose to run and you win your election, Mrs. Steno, you'll have a salary far more generous than what you made before as a foreman."

"And how would you know what I made before?"

He smiled gently. "Mrs. Steno, it's our job to do background checks and identity confirmations on potential candidates."

"And that makes you the…?" she asked skeptically.

"We're the Bizi, ma'am," answered Rialt.

"Top level Government Security? You? That's a laugh!"

She suspected now that these men, and that this whole place was all an elaborate prank at best, or a con-artist game at worst. The latter seemed more likely she figured.

"I'm sorry, but I'm having a hard time believing any of this. For all I know, this rented office of yours is used to pull in poor suckers like me. People who have their resumes floating out all over the wave's ether. 'Come on in! Get elected, all we need is your credit information, personal history and access to your credit records to verify."

"Ma'am," Rialt said without a change in his tone, "we've already accessed your financial records two weeks ago as part of our background check." He slid her another padd that had on it, as far as she could see, several pages worth of accurate information about her financial history and recent credit transactions. It was all there in front of her, plain and in the open as if she'd accessed it herself. Despite the official secrecy around them, even Taryn had heard the whispers of how thorough real Bizi officials could be when they went looking for something.

"Like we said, standard stuff for us to check with potential candidates," remarked Filater. "Nothing to worry about though, we're not truly investigating you, not that your records had any issues anyways. We are only allowed to act on information that leads us to suspect that people are not who they claim to be on their IDs. Even then, all we're allowed to do is withdraw them from campaign contention if someone isn't truthful on that matter. No other information we find is our affair. Much to the hatred of other law enforcement agencies that would love access to the material we occasionally do come across."

Rialt spoke now. "You could be housing an illegal gambling den, or an unsanctioned side business and we're not allowed to tell anyone, so long as your identity remained honest, and you weren't threatening the security of the government. The function of the Bizi in this particular role specifically, is to ensure those selected at random by the moot lottery really are the same people that are choosing to run for office. Nothing more."

"So, Mrs. Steno…" Filater continued, "all it comes to is this: We've confirmed you are indeed Taryn Steno of Region75, unemployed, married, and mother of two. You *have* been selected by the Moot lottery. Now all we need to know from you is whether you would like to campaign for the job or not?"

There was a long moment of silence between the three of them in the room. Taryn made no answer as she sat studying the two men across from her in disbelief.

"Do… do I get some time to consider this?" Taryn asked stumbling.

"Wouldn't be much of a choice if you didn't," Filater said. "We would need a decision by the end of the week to have enough time to let you build up your ideas for a platform though. Then, presuming your acceptance, we'd have to move on to prepping for your interview and recording your feature and all that. I assume you've seen the format for the campaign vid-streams before?"

"Yeah, I've seen them" she answered. "Candidates spend half the time introducing their own ideas and the other half answering questions submitted by the area's voters."

"That's right." Rialt paused. "As you make up your mind, please remember that while you are being allowed time to make your decision, the rules of the discretionary agreement and all the confidentialities that it covers still apply, whether you decide to run or not. No one else can know the true nature of this 'job interview.' Anyone who you openly discuss this with can immediately be charged as a co-conspirator in violating SOMA security protocols. They'd be brought up on charges no less serious than your own.

"If you do wish to discuss this with your family, well, you wouldn't be the first. And it is understandable, being rather a significant change in career paths for nearly everyone. I personally recommend you alter the nature of the 'job' itself for their sake to one with a long-term contract within a factory working for a private security company. That tends to be a legally acceptable way that I've seen to make the discretionary factor of all of this more… palpable in the minds of close relations. Also," he added "I would let them know that occasional travel and unusually long or highly variable hours are a likely part of the job. It's a recommendation though."

"Ok… thanks," Taryn said genuinely. "Sorry, but I'm…" she fumbled. "I'm still trying to wrap my brain around all this. I don't suppose there is any way to verify once and for all that you are who you say you are?"

"Here," said Filater. He pulled out a unique looking business card. It had his name 'Agent C. Filater, Bureau of Investigating Zones of Interest', with a unique shield emblem with an 8-pointed star at its top center. The card also had an address and a contact number. Below this was what Taryn took for a work ID number as well. Filater took out a small dark stained padd and pressed his thumb hard to it. He pressed and rolled his thumb slowly on the back of the business card. It left a clear fingerprint on the card's white backside. Then he took out a small set of scissors and a clear bag. He pulled one small lock of his black hair forward and snipped it off and sealed it in the bag.

"There," he said calmly, handing both the card and bag to her. "You can take that card to any local authorities you wish and ask them to verify the thumb print and ID number and to call the number to the office to confirm. If you search the waves, you'll find the address belongs to a government agency building located in the restricted zone of the capital, where only federal employees are allowed in. The hair you can take to any public or private lab of your choice to confirm that I am, in fact, me, and not just anybody handing you a random Bizi ID card, though the Blue Boys should provide you a photo of me as well."

Taryn sat shocked by the bluntness of these assertions and overwhelmed by this deluge of testing ideas.

"Watch the news waves the next few nights Mrs. Steno, till the moot lottery numbers are published" said Filater. "You *will* see your own number show up. When your decision is made, call the number on the receipt message. They'll ask you for your test receipt number and your citizen ID. When you get through to an actual person, they'll ask for your confirmation contact. Give them my name and ID and ask to speak with me. If they ask you why, say that it concerns 'the Tanagra estate.' That'll get you through directly to me no matter where I am. Okay?"

She nodded, but Taryn was still busy processing everything she had just heard. Eventually, she vaguely recalled that she had shook both the gentlemen's hands goodbye and left the small unremarkable red brick office building with the card and plastic bag of hair still in hand as she drove herself home. Yet for a long while her thoughts were only a blur of questions and possible answers to herself.

If she were truly selected by the moot lottery for her region, that meant that so were four other residents. Taryn wondered how they had been informed or if they even knew yet? It was possible she was the first to know, or perhaps the last. The old doctor had called her his "2nd hour appointment" after all. This suggested that at least one person had preceded her.

She also wondered if all the others would accept the opportunity and run. Certainly, it had happened in the past, where all candidates in the region decided to go through the election process. There had even been a few election cycles long ago where no lottery winners decided to run at all, and whole new batches of candidates had to be selected.

The standard resolution was to pick new candidates by their ID number, specifically those from recent unemployment records. It was a foregone conclusion that if none of the moot lottery winners wanted the job, a registered unemployed person would be far more receptive to taking it up. If the potential candidate again refused the position, the process simply continued. Using the unemployed records was seen as another way to add even more randomness to the political mix, while at the same time, it occasionally gave hope to those who were in need of a job. Taryn briefly wondered if that's what she was facing. Maybe some of the first batch had all refused to run, and that's how they had got to her name. No way to be certain though.

She wondered at the odds of her being selected at all. She had never considered luck an important feature of her life if that's what this actually was. Then her mind checked its pace, and her cynicism began to reaffirm itself. *It could still be a scam, girl*, she thought. She was forcing her skepticism more forward into her thoughts, but she just couldn't see the angle. They knew her, had access to more than enough personal information on her already. And a smart thief with half of that could take what they wanted and run, not that there was much to even take her for. There was nothing to be gained by a feint like this. There was also something else odd to this thought. The men today didn't feel to Taryn as if they were trying to get her to believe them. They were acting overly cautious to be sure, but they didn't appear desperate to win her over to their claim. The confidence with which Filater had given her the card, fingerprint and a lock of his hair came across as genuine. He had to know she would check all the items, skeptical as she came off in front of them. They probably expected her to check it all twice.

Taryn's face became set as she drove. Her determination on the matter hardened a bit more. She wouldn't disappoint them. She changed her vehicle's course to a nearby security center that her vehicle's nav-map directed her to in a passing neighborhood. She would also check with the local blue-boys office near her own building as well. These, she figured, were the two most likely stopping points. If they had somehow hacked a government system and managed to create a false call-line so that it worked in two different security locations, she'd try to throw them a curve with her third attempt. She decided she'd call up Everett and ask him to put her in touch with some of his security guys.

The hexaderby squads always kept private security teams around their players like Everett during the seasons, so that no-one could endanger their star athletes. Many were former Blue Boys. Surely one owed Everett a favor since he was known to be generous with them at the end of each season for their help.

For the hair sample, Taryn decided that the best option was to go to the smallest lab she could find to do a DNA analysis. They wouldn't be the cheapest, but in her mind the smaller labs were less likely to be the target of hackers. She could also find the general number to call the government building whose address was on Filater's card. Taryn could ask them about his private office number that way, to see if it matched what the card read.

All this would take a day or two at least, and that would give Taryn time to think and discuss things over with mom. She turned on the music in her vehicle and followed the map down the road. *It's possible,* she thought. *Unlikely, true... but still... possible.*

* * *

Four hours and three stops later she was back home. Her brow was now in a frown of deep thought.

"Looks real, the call number is on our files. The ID and the print too. Here's a photo for a government issued ID. This your guy?" the desk officer at the first station had asked, handing her a small padd. It matched. All of it. The photo was Filater, the name, the print, the listed number. The blue-boy station near her building confirmed all this even faster than the first one had. Exactly the same. In a call to his bar Everett had told her that his regular security guys were spread all over the city, enjoying the offseason, so it would take a day or more for anyone to get back to him. Outside of this everything had checked out so far. When she got home, Taryn did some research on the wave and found the government building's general call number and gave that a try. She confirmed the address with the receptionist and Filater's office-line number matched the card as well. This was either a highly elaborate scam on a level she'd never seen before, to what ends she couldn't imagine, at a risk and cost beyond her families' total worth, or... it was looking more and more like a valid proposal.

She decided to wait for Gloria to get home from the market. When her mom did return, she immediately started pelting Taryn with questions about how the interview went. Taryn only told her that she wanted to wait to discuss it at dinner so that all three of them could be there and hear it all at once. She tried to keep her nerves subdued until then.

Chapter 6: Sitting on a Fence

Taryn took care of dinner for everyone, as means to occupy herself. Once the table had been cleared and they washed up, Gloria and Lilly rejoined Taryn as she sat holding a later than normal joe-cup. The night had quieted down quicker than usual. Trey was asleep already, and Lilly claimed, hopefully in truth, that her homework was already done as she sat inattentively watching vids on her padd at the table. She was allowed this since she'd helped clear the plates up, though her father would have balked at the idea of having electronics on at the table at all. Taryn thought about how Cyrano would often finish his evening cup and move on to some cookies and cakes that he would share with Lilly and Taryn, while Gloria typically shared a pot of tea with her daughter.

"Alright, that's enough stalling. Give it," said Gloria.

"Yeah, Mom, what's so wrong with this job that you need both our opinions?" Lilly asked, putting down her teacup and stuffing another cake in her mouth.

"I know you didn't screw the interview up, otherwise you would just be sulking after you got back home," added Gloria. "They must've offered you something, but I'm guessing it's got a serious hitch to it."

"Mom, let me do the talking for a bit, alright?" Taryn took another quiet sip of tea. "But you're right, they did offer me another interview of sorts. But the job is a little… unique. The work is not permanent. Though if I get it, I should have guaranteed work for a few cycles at least, so it's more of a long-term contract schedule."

"Does that mean they won't offer you any benefits?" Lilly asked with a half full mouth of cake still left.

"I'm not sure. I didn't think to ask. There was other… issues about the job that caught my attention first, but I could ask next time, if I decided to continue the application process any further that is."

"Well, why wouldn't you?" Gloria asked.

"Because of the type of job that it is. If I do get it, that means that I'd have to sign a rather strict non-disclosure agreement. The company is a security firm from what I can tell, though I'm still researching it. So, any of the work I'd be doing for them I could not discuss openly with you two. At all. Ever."

There was a pause as this sunk in.

"Nothing too dangerous I hope," said her mom with a note of concern.

"From what I know, it shouldn't be any more dangerous than the last floor I worked on, though they appear protective of their confidential information. But if what they told me is true, I can understand why. They said that if I get the offer that the working hours can be rather erratic on occasion and to be prepared to travel sometimes with little notice. Not sure how much though."

"Is the pay worth it?" Lilly added.

"The actual pay is still vague for now, but it should be as good as before, if not better." Taryn withheld the details a bit to curtail any premature optimism. She needed them to hear her question clearly, without bias first.

"But if you're on contract, how long could that be for? And then afterwards, when they're done with you in a cycle or two, are you going to be able to get a decent reference or will their secrecy not allow for that?" her mom questioned.

"Those are definitely other answers I'd like to have too, if I decide to keep going after this, but that's not what I wanted to discuss with you two. The rest of the interview process is likely to take the next month."

"You mean like a probationary period?" said Gloria

"Yeah," Taryn nodded, "I guess so. But I still *might* not even get the job. They're looking at others in the same spot as well. My point is that if I went forward and did actually get chosen, would you two be okay with me having to be very private or extremely vague about my work? Is that something that you can handle? Would you be okay with the random hours or me traveling and all that as well?"

Gloria gave a quick glance at Lilly then answered, "Well, if that's all you wanted to ask, you're wasting our time. You have no other options as of now except to see this interview process on. If they don't like you, you're unemployed. So what? You're already unemployed. I'll still be able to handle things here for a year or two if you are hired. Maybe if things go well, you can finally hire some younger help. But for now, this is a choice you can't really choose dear. It was decided for you weeks ago, when you got… err, left your old floor."

Taryn glanced towards Lilly. There was a brief look of confusion on her daughter's face, but only for a moment before it passed.

"Go for the job, mom. I mean, nainai's right. I don't see how you have much of a choice in this."

"What we have in the accounts will just keep bleeding away otherwise," chimed in Gloria trying to sound more annoyed than worried for Lilly's sake. "And this is the first serious job opportunity you've snared. Better to get off the fence to try and reach the boat, even if you fail. Otherwise, who knows when the next one will float on by."

Taryn was quiet for a second, as she finished the rest of her joe-cup. "They've said I've got until the end of the week to think it over. But once I've had our other questions put to rest, if all of it is good, I'll tell them I'm in."

"Well, can you at least tell us the company's name or is that a closely guarded secret too?" Gloria asked, leaving to wash her cup.

"Vox P. Industries is going to be the name on the pay stubs."

"Never heard of them." her mom said turning on the faucet "Must be newer or small."

"Sorry Mom, for now, I don't think I can tell you more. Better get used to it."

"Doesn't matter I suppose. Long as you're safe there and the credits clear, us two can try to keep our big noses out of it," she said with a quick wink to Lilly.

Afterwards Lilly left to her room to chat with a friend on her padd, while Gloria and Taryn spoke more on some other minor details they thought Taryn should get clarified at her next interview session. Their conversation ended abruptly for the night when Trey awoke early in need of a change. By then it was late, and they were both tired. Taryn slept fitfully however, next to a snoring Trey, as it was her turn to sleep with him. She tossed around a little in the dark, thinking of other ways to verify the proposition. She went back and forth again and again. Was this a real route for her? Could *she* possibly run an election? Was there even a chance for her against the four others? Would all the others even run? In the end, the only thought that gave her comfort was the possibility that somewhere else in the region, four other people could also be wide awake debating the same exact questions.

* * *

Over the next two days, Taryn was able to get calls in with two of Everett's private security friends who had worked publicly for a while. Once again, they both told her the same thing. The phone number, name, Filater's ID number, and the address were all valid in their assessments. She spent all of the next morning at a small lab, then later at a larger franchise place confirming that the DNA of the hair matched a citizen listed in the public record as C. Filater. That was all the labs were legally allowed to tell her. Taryn and Gloria both received their receipt numbers from the Government Recruiting Service too, as Filater had predicted. Gloria had ignored her own, reasoning it as little more than another routine unsolicited message, while Taryn found she had looked hers over carefully and often enough to the point that she could easily remember the combination of letters and digits.

Taryn finally decided to make her last check on this possible farce. She had thought it up in the early hours when she couldn't sleep the first night after her meeting, but now it was time to try it. When she got home, she called the general office building number that was listed on the wave once again. This time she asked the receptionist to connect her directly to Filater's office line and switched to vid-call mode. Filater appeared a minute later with a padd in hand working from behind his desk which also had several other displays mounted.

"Ah, Mrs. Steno. Are you calling with your decision? You're a bit earlier than I expected. The news isn't quite due to release the successful five receipt numbers yet."

"Actually, I'd like to ask you a few clarification questions first if that's alright? Stuff about compensation, insurance, post-service duties, and all that."

"Oh, I see," he said closing some items on his screen while opening up others. "Could you wait one quick moment please?"

"Sure."

He tapped a few buttons on his desk padd, then when he appeared satisfied with what he saw, he spoke again.

"There. I've recalibrated the call link a little to ensure that it's a secure transmission now. I assume that you are alone on your end?"

"Well I do have my 2-cycle old asleep on the couch here," Taryn responded glancing down at a napping Trey. "But I don't think he's the type to squeal on me."

"Very well. So, what's on your mind?" said the agent without hesitation at her remark.

After a few standard questions that her mom and Lilly had brought up, Filater gave Taryn more than enough information about the nature of the substantial salary and benefits that came with the position, assuming she won the election process. Taryn couldn't stall any longer. It was time to push him.

"Now I should tell you, Mr. Filater, that I just received an offer from my old company yesterday. They say that they are planning a new expansion on one of their floors and that they've had a new position open up that they're considering me for. I was hoping that I could maybe use your company's name to help to… facilitate a better pay rate from them, if you're okay with that?"

Filater eyed her for a brief moment before he began tapping away on his padd again.

"Well, you're free of course to choose your own employment preferences, Mrs. Steno, if you wish to name drop an offer from Vox P. Industries that's perfectly fine. We can easily verify an offer of employment on our end."

He paused, looking over at his desk screens.

"However, considering that I see that your last employer actually had you blackballed in their records—even amongst their competitors," he scrolled down a little then went on, "and they're actually looking at a downturn in profits this quarter, with no internal signs of any expansion items for several months, I highly doubt that dropping our company's name will make much of a difference towards your future prospects with them."

That was it. In a few simple keystrokes he'd been able to see right through her whole story. Only a government level system could work that fast and in that broad of a scope. He was real, his position was real, which meant so was the offer. He truly was offering Taryn a chance to be elected to the SOMA. To work in the government if she wanted it. Filater turned from looking at his padd back towards Taryn on the monitor.

"Now, if you're satisfied that I've passed your scrutiny Ms. Steno, please give the position on the table some more thought if you could. Your prior profession as a factory floor supervisor doesn't appear to have much use for you any longer, so if I were you, I'd consider the matter, as it stands before you, as a legitimate opportunity… because it is."

Taryn was silent. *Great job, Taryn. You've just managed to annoy a real Bizi agent by wasting his time. What are you gonna do for an encore, challenge Everett to full speed hexaderby on one leg?* she thought to herself.

"If you have any other questions, please do call on me again Mrs. Steno, but be sure to have your decision ready the next time we speak. Oh, and watch the local news feeds the next few nights. Around the 11th hour is when you should see the winning candidate receipt numbers start to come up. Please call me back when you've decided. Until then."

The screen switched off. Taryn was left in silent thought for a long time. It was all true. It was hitting her hard now. She would be selected in the new moot Lottery. Still her mom was right, there was no other option. There was only one practical choice before her. When her receipt number was announced, she'd have to run. It was the only viable chance to meet her family's needs. Filater had told her that she'd at least be compensated for her time during the election month. So, at the minimum there would be that pay plus another seemingly valid reference for her resume that was far more agreeable than her old company's had been.

Taryn would have called Filater back right then and there, had she not remembered his request to wait for the news to hit the waves later. Taryn used the time to lose herself in some chores, while she quietly started percolating on how exactly to possibly win an election she'd never thought to be involved in. Again, the only thought to comfort her was that somewhere else, others somewhere in the region might be having this same precise debate themselves.

* * *

The next evening, Gloria and Taryn were busy feeding the kids an early dinner and washing up. Gloria began her usual questions about everyone's day before going into her own complaints about the minor inconvenience of the local grocer being out of her favorite vegetables again. The tale of her having to walk several blocks to find the items at another grocer, might as well have been an odyssey to the farthest fringes the way that she described it. Being highly social, Gloria had gone shopping, as she typically did, with a local neighbor that walked with her on her 'unnecessarily long' quest for produce.

This friend being of a similar age to Gloria, had an adult son who also worked as a cleaner on a factory floor for some such company. Apparently, word was that the Ties at his floor were constantly asking the cleaning crew to do more with less. This apparently had been complicated by the fact that several unexpected messes had started cropping up on their floors over the last few weeks. The result of many of the hangers on the line losing their footing while not wearing their safety harnesses. Mostly, they had only managed to maim their lower legs, but one unfortunate individual had evidently fallen hands first and broke both his arms as well. These accidents, as Glorias friend understood it, caused a lot of blood to spill over the various pieces of line's machinery and finding all the splatter from such a mess could be difficult. And with their cleaning crew's number limited to only four, it put the whole crew well behind what was considered normal.

Taryn was thankful she'd never worked on that particular floor, though she'd imagined it was not that different from her own experience. Mostly, she was grateful because the odds of her actually knowing anyone of those hangers personally was quite low, though that hardly made Gloria's account of the events any better. Taryn wondered about the foreman who were working there, and if they had talked—or more likely pushed—their hangers into working without their harnesses on. Perhaps they had simply remained muted when the men failed to equip them.

Poor boys, Taryn thought. She knew that the companies always targeted the less educated boys for that spot. The drifters and the dropouts. The younger first-time factory workers. All the ones ever so eager to please the foremen and the Ties. As enthusiastic and unaware as they were, it would take those types months, if not cycles, to start asking any real questions. Like why the hanger positions always had open spots for hiring in the first place? Or why there were never any of the older men working as hangers? Taryn hated to think of the pitiful training they got, that never mentioned the actual likelihood of them losing a leg or a hand. They never had the true risks explained to them, the full chances of an injury occurring. Nor were they usually given enough time to consider what their life would be like after a debilitating injury such as that. And if they were hesitant for the job there was always a steady supply of newer, more eager bodies to throw at it. True, the harness, when used, cut down the risks a lot, but safety was never a guarantee in that spot. These hangers Taryn was hearing about were probably thrown into that meat grinder of a position without even realizing how the company truly saw them: necessary expenditures. Not any different on the Tie's reports than the need to replace and stock more liquid cleaner spray or pay for trash pick-ups. That's all. Consumables. A means to faster, more lucrative profits, in exchange for their employee's loss of permanent mobility and capabilities. Taryn, without meaning to, had realized that she'd started to find the edges of what would become her campaign platform.

* * *

After having dinner and excusing herself from her mom's protracted recounting of the day's harrowing excursion to find overpriced vegetables, Taryn sat down on the couch and jotted down some ideas she had on her padd. Soon, her earpiece line rang. It was a small, digitized message with no sender listed. All it said was, "On the news, now."

Taryn swiped her padd's screen to the local news feed and pushed it to the room's larger viewer. The sports reporter was just ending with his prediction of Everett's continuing dominance in the upcoming season before switching back over to the two main news anchors. The woman began.

"Thanks, Varwami. In other news the time has come again for the government to request a new group of potential candidates for the SOMA elections. The Moot lottery randomly picks potential candidates for the SOMA elections using receipt numbers from citizen's required biennial neuro-medical scans. Those selected for this term have their receipt numbers showing on your screens now. They should be receiving automated messages over the next few minutes providing a number to call to reach out to a government contact for confirmation. The campaign month will begin with the willing candidates in a few weeks. We would also like to remind you that no personal information is required from the winners. Suspicious messages or activity asking for any type of personal information should be reported to your local security center immediately." The male anchor took over.

No sooner had he started on the next story of the day, about various planned road closures over the next week, then Taryn's wave account on her padd beeped to life. This time the sender was listed as the Moot election notice. The message was her official notice, telling her that she should call a number to verify that she had received the message. She called and went through to a rather dull automated prompt to which she entered her receipt number. After some more menu choices concerning her regional location a much livelier voice picked up.

"Hello, Mrs. Steno?" the light and pleasant male voice said.

"Yes?"

"My name is Aurel, and I'll be sending you more information on how to contact your local government recruiting agent. As well as directions for where and when to check in with them."

"Well, umm… I was actually hoping you could be so kind as to connect me directly to them now. It's Agent Filater."

There was a pause and the sound of some light typing on the other end.

"I'm sorry, ma'am, but do you have a worker ID on this individual to help me locate them in my database."

"Oh… yeah!"

Taryn had been so distracted that she'd forgotten Filater had given her his work ID. After scrambling for it for a minute, she read off the Bizi agent's ID numbers to Aurel and there was a pause and some typing sounds once again.

"I'm sorry, ma-am, I cannot connect you as that agent's line is listed as restricted at the moment."

"But... but it's about the Tanagra estate."

"Please hold."

She couldn't be certain, but to Taryn the tone of the voice on the line went from light and breezy to rather official sounding in just those two final words.

There were some beeps on the connection then a request for a video line popped up. Taryn confirmed and saw Filater at his desk reading one of his padds.

"Hello?" she asked as Filater was still looking at the padd on his desk and hadn't seemed to notice her yet.

"You know for someone still deciding if you're even going to run, you are at least punctual, Mrs. Steno," he started, still not make eye contact to the screen.

"Mr. Filater, I have decided," she said, drawing up her composure against his remark. She supposed that if anyone was ever going to take her seriously as a contender in all of this, then she better at least start sounding the part.

At the new confidence evident in the tone of this last comment, Filater's eyes finally looked up from their work. Taryn saw he was again studying the situation before him. Scrutinizing it as he'd done when she spoke to him in her previous call, but in this case his full attention was focused squarely on her.

"Now," Taryn said, "what else must we discuss before I can get started?"

Chapter 7: The Line-up

It was almost four weeks later when Taryn pulled up at the doorway of another small single-story red brick building. It had a similar non-descript style to the one she had originally been interviewed at. This building, however, lay past two postings of guards in the government restricted area and was labeled with a white letter H. Other nearby buildings were marked with different lettered signs. Taryn had been here over half a dozen times now and was almost over the apprehension of having to consistently show her temporarily issued ID to get anywhere around this place. The roaming security and stationary guards would stop her at almost every doorway or corridor that she walked down. And she had lost track of the number of times that she had to empty her bag for them so they could search through it. Indeed, it often felt as if she would hardly get only a handful of steps onto her path before being stopped once more. Filater had initially warned her that the safety measures in place would be a difficulty she'd have to learn to deal with for the time being.

Today, however, she was distracted by more than just the usual annoyances of security delays. She was making her way slowly towards one of the few meeting rooms she was familiar with in the H building. Small as it looked from the outside, she had only been allowed into less than a handful of actual rooms. Filater was due to meet with her there and together they would start to record her campaign interview. She had been polishing up her prepared remarks all week and the secretive Bizi agent had been surprisingly good at helping her clarify exactly what she wanted her platform to be. She often wondered how many candidates he had helped with their preparations in his time. Though he never said it outright, Taryn suspected that he was also spending time prepping the other candidates from her Region as well, and that for this Moot election cycle at least, this was Agent Filater's only assigned task for now. For one, he seemed to know a great deal about Taryn's home region, all about the makeup of various people, businesses, and past and current problems. His knowledge on those matters was far more extensive, she decided, than compared to any lifelong local she might chance to discuss matters with. And for another, it simply made sense to her that one Bizi agent would be in charge of organizing the election candidates in one region. It made learning all the background of an area a far less daunting task compared to having agents continually jump from place to place she thought.

Taryn also found herself thinking back to her conversation with Lilly. About how in the ancient world the likelihood of being elected came down to how much money you could raise, and how well you could sell yourself as the most favorable person and not let anyone see the person you truly are. Thinking about how, for the ancients, the main ways established officials lost their power was by dying, retiring, doing something extremely stupid very publicly, or by being out spent in ever-growing and more expensive campaigns by opposing parties. About those forgotten political parties making both false and truthful accusations of deceitful tricks used by their opponents. Their sinister methods of redrawing voting boundaries, limits on certain types of voters or permanently removing voting rights from former convicts. But always, the only ones in any position to revise or actually stop this type of behavior were the very same people who benefited from there being no reform at all.

Taryn was comforted during these past days in the notion that she needed only to sell her ideas and policy plans and not herself to voters. But what still worried her more than her planning was that she hoped she'd actually been right when she'd told Lilly about the history of the settling effect. That it truly *was* dead and gone now. That she wasn't entering into this whole situation overly idealistically, doomed to be crushed by the revelation of a reality that she'd been taught no longer existed, and yet perhaps might somehow still be found living and breathing subversively. *The ones with power will do everything to keep themselves in power…* her dad had said to her once. Taryn's first real exposure to this process would also be a very personal test of that idiom. Filater for his part, while assertive in his demeanor, did not signal he was the type to revel much in his own portion of apparent power, and that did give Taryn some hope.

Often, like now, he would leave her alone in an office room to work things out on her own, only to visit her briefly after a few hours to check her progress. He provided her with a government issued padd that was retina-linked to her. When accessed it showed nearly any statistic on her region that she could think of, and many more that she had no idea were even tallied, let alone possible to count. This type of access might have helped to explain how Filater had been such an expert on the topic himself. There were several hundred comparisons of annual incomes, power consumption, waste production, construction reports, epidemiological maps of major health issues, population breakdown by age, gender, educational comparisons, social services stats, business development reports, security records, crime statistics, residential and business tax revenues, and a myriad of other local expenditures all easily available to her now in just a few simple taps. Taryn was quite overwhelmed with all this information for the first three days, but by the fourth she felt she had seen it enough times that she was starting to be able to make progress on her campaign ideas, with new concepts beginning to spring forth.

It's still your home, she thought. *You've known it for cycles now. You simply got to find the aching spots of the region. The places that are hurting it the most, the bottlenecks. The areas that are no-good money-wise or policy-wise but that are still potentially fixable by new policies. That's how you'll win this race, girl. That's how you'll find yourself a job. It isn't much different from being a foreman after all,* she found herself thinking. *Try to find where the worst spots on the floor are, the slowest points that restrict all others, and decide how to get that position to do better.* And that's what she spent her time doing. She found what she thought to be several weak points of policy concerning her region, hidden in all the statistics. Points that no new strategies had ever specifically addressed in the last decade. As it turns out, there were quite a few of them: stagnant wages, the lack of new infrastructure, no plans of any novel construction besides the most basic maintenance, a drainage system that was over 100 cycles old, a power-grid that was slowly losing its efficiency every cycle, and a young population that was by far mostly under 35 without access to many high paying jobs in the area, which she herself, could easily attest to.

Then there was the business data too. Taryn was able to access and see that most businesses operating in the region were relatively profitable over the last generation. Yes, there had been the occasional downturns, closures, and leaner times. But on the whole, it was not hard to see the data showing that even a conservative estimation projected a threefold increase of the area's large business incomes over the last 30 cycles. The most stable of these, the super-companies, had all increased their work forces many times over, but the trouble was that the vast majority of those created jobs were in the lowest paying sectors. In addition, while the crime statistics showed a general decline in the region for several cycles, there was a vast increase in allegations of corporate espionage over the past two decades. A high likelihood of what one report called 'manipulated price fixing,' as well as several unconfirmed complaints of inter-corporate blacklists being passed secretly throughout the various private intra-waves as well. This too Taryn found relatable.

Taryn gave these blacklisting reports her full attention when she came across them and wasn't surprised by the obvious similarities between her own experiences and the circumstances listed in them. She wished she could say she was even less surprised that most of these complaints had been logged by the local Blue Boys who proceeded to quickly file them and left the reports to sit. Then the reports and complaints would sit untouched and fade quietly into the obscurity between other, more violent or pressing local issues. She made sure to note the names of the reporting officers on file. If she succeeded in the election, she promised herself a meeting with some of them in the future to discuss the diligence of their reporting.

The hardest part of the data to corroborate was the number of workplace accidents that happened on the floors of factories similar to where she had worked. The corporate data either wasn't available to the system, or it was never recorded or released to begin with Taryn guessed. But she did notice that over the last decade the inspections by regulators had steadily dropped while the number of severe work-place related injuries had steadily risen. This could be seen by the admittance numbers to the nearby medical facilities. The medical facilities had even made notes in most cases of the specific patient's work title and name of their corporate employers. Taryn figured out how to set the system to tallying reports by the location of incidence. She was curious to see which super corps had the most cases of injuries reported. She figured that her old employer would be near the top, so she was shocked when the results came back and showed that the corporation had not even breached the top ten. Twelve other super corps operating in region 75 all had higher instances of work-related injuries reported over the last 10 cycles. Taryn kept the list for future reference as well. She made sure to include a plan to increase inspection positions and rounds, starting specifically at the apparent worst offenders she'd just tagged.

Taryn didn't spend all of her days buried and lost in the data, statistics, and ideas hatched from the reading of her padds alone. She made sure that she took her lunch time off of the secured government grounds. For even though she brought her own meals with her, she often found a local café or nearby park corner beyond the restricted areas to eat. Taryn used the time to decompress herself from all the numbers and stats that traipsed through her mind.

She found working as a janitor or waitress or occasional bartender at the Hidden Roller on some nights also helped her do the one thing that she could not do inside that brick building. Talk to people, get the feel of their opinions, or hear the latest local gossip from them. She was also spending her nights working at Everett's bar to bring in extra credits. *If I don't win*, she thought, *at least I'll have an even bigger credit cushion and won't have alienated Everett by refusing his help without a reasonable explanation.*

She often used the only slightly false pretense of job hunting to ask Everett's patrons about their employment or their opinions of their supervisors. After the first week, she worried that only asking around Everett's bar would skew her perception on things. So, after that she began roaming and sitting purposely with others on the park benches during her lunch. She would invariably begin chatting with them. From this she started learning even more local business gossip, and while she did have to wade through the occasional useless personal anecdotes, she found that if she approached people with the right questions, she got far more useful information. An "excuse me, I'm new to the area. Could you tell me where, around here, would you say is the best place to look for work or at least the places to avoid?" would often lead to a flurry of ideas from nearly everyone, even apparent government folk. Opinions on local employers or even on the local business practices would flow out like sheets of rain from an overloaded storm cloud.

It was by doing this a number of times that Taryn came across an elderly man who—having stated that he lived in the region for most of his life—was able to inform her that the bigger companies had originally started moving to the region about 40 cycles ago. This was thanks to a number of tax policies that, eventually, failed to be re-instituted by the local SOMA officials.

In the short term, this probably came across as an obvious win to those representatives of the time as new companies meant new jobs. But without their tax revenue funding the local region's budget; the infrastructure and the local educational system funds began eroding quickly. More jobs meant more people moved to the region to get hired. That only burdened the regional facilities system even more, while the tax revenue was actually declining without the help of the super-corps that had created those jobs. Here were facts that Taryn could only scarcely confirm from her padd and would have never discovered if not for her own attempts to prod at the people. *Remember girl, not everything is on that stupid display*, she found herself saying again and again.

Taryn generally found this time talking to others about issues to not only be fruitful as a means of idea generation for her policies, but also effective as a way to decompress and reflect on reminding herself of her primary goal. *Show that you can help these people. That you're worth a damn in that position to someone out there. That you've heard their needs and that you're the best chance they have. That's how you'll win. That's how you'll feed the family. That's how you'll make Cyrano proud, girl.*

It was at this point of her research and policy synthesis that Filater had given Taryn a second padd that he claimed was linked into a highly advanced mainframe which, according to him, was capable of running revenue and expenditure simulations. She was able to play out several different versions of her policy ideas and plans using all the regions stats to see the results with what seemed like incredible accuracy. By the start of her recording day, near the end of her fourth week, Taryn was on her way to start her campaign recording with what she thought was a firm case for her intentions. She felt confident that she could show in the interview, not only why she should be voted for, but why she was needed. It was time to either take on this task or watch it go to someone else. She comforted herself with the thought that if she did manage to get elected to the SOMA and subsequently failed at everything else in terms of her policy plans and their implementation, she would at least be able to support her family with the income from her new posting. If she lost the election, she couldn't complain about lack of trying.

She'd been allowed to prepare herself as much as possible, and far more extensively than with most of the other major events of her life. A failure here, she was sure, wouldn't be due to a failure on her part or due to lack of motivation or preparation. *You can only be beaten by a better candidate now,* she reminded herself. Even if she had to go back to job hunting, it couldn't be helped. *Those were the tides that day,*' the old seafarers at the harbors would say. She reminded herself of all this, took a deep breath outside the door to the room, and walked in.

She found a dark, mostly empty room, lit in the center with only two chairs and a camera stand. Filater was there already, his back turned as he was adjusting the stand that was facing towards one of the chairs. There was a small monitor facing from the camera towards the seats and Filater was busy going back and forth checking the angle and testing that the camera purposely pixelated his face on the monitor to make it imperceptible to identification. Taryn walked in towards the lit area.

"You all prepared Mrs. Steno?" he asked, not waiting for her response. "Sorry I didn't meet you further down the corridor, but the camera was not behaving itself. I've had to tinker with it. Hopefully I won't need to get a replacement, but it seems fine now."

"It's quite alright, Agent Filater. I needed the time alone to compose myself."

He smiled at her. A quick understanding smile that she had yet to ever see him offer before now. For such a cold efficient person, that was the first sign she had seen that he understood, more than just someone's mind, but their emotions as well. She took the seat facing the camera and pulled out her padd to review her notes one last time.

"We'll be ready in a moment or two," he added as he checked the audio settings and voice modification system.

When all was in order and the camera ready, he took a seat across from her, behind the monitor.

"Alright, Mrs. Steno, here's how it'll go. I'll be asking you the standard questions about what your campaign platform is and what you'd want to accomplish if elected to the SOMA. Feel free to hold off and compose your thoughts before answering, as I can legally edit your responses to cut out any long moments of silence or delays. You can go back and revise your response at any time during this recording, until you are happy with what you said. After we're done with that, I'll be asking you a few voter-submitted questions that were marked as the highest importance when we surveyed the region's residence a few days ago."

"Okay," she responded unsurely. "Strange, I don't remember receiving a survey message this time," she added.

"That is because we don't survey the candidates or their families. It ruins the spontaneity of the questions. This gives the public an idea of how you'd respond to new proposals that you might not have considered before."

"Well then," Taryn responded. "I suppose we should get started. But please, could you tell me about how long the recording process typically takes?"

"For the half-hour we need to show, it typically takes about 2-4 hours depending on the candidates themselves and how long their responses are. For some people it's easy. They just like to talk on and on, whereas others, somehow, think that this is a timed response situation, even though it isn't. My job now is to make a competent half-hour interview-conversation with you that can be submitted to all the media outlets for broadcasting in the next forty-eight hours."

Taryn wondered how patient Filater would be if she needed to stop and start again. Or if she began flubbing with her words, as she typically did when she was nervous.

"Take a breath." Filater instructed, eyeing her clear anxiety.

"Alright?" he asked

Taryn forced a calm nod in reply a moment later

"Good, then let's begin."

* * *

Two days later, Taryn was busy cleaning up the kitchen table when she received a text-only message. She touched her personal head-set implant, the only secure tech she'd been allowed to keep from her time creating her platform. The system read the text's encoded message.

"The interviews for your region will be broadcasting on the waves starting tonight." There was nothing more.

"What was that?" asked Gloria from the sink with a dish and glass in each hand.

"Hmm? Oh, a confirmation for another meeting time for that new temp job."

As predicted, within the hour the news feed was buzzing at a furious pace about the newly released interviews soon to be shown to the voting public shortly.

"What are you watching, Tar?" asked Gloria taking a seat next to her daughter with a subdued Trey in her hands. He was a notoriously heavy sleeper. Gloria stretched him out on the couch and put his legs to rest on Taryn's lap.

"Oh… the news is saying that the interviews for the SOMA campaign elections are about to come up. I thought I'd see if I can stand to watch a few without falling asleep too fast."

"Oh, well I could use something to laugh at too. We should get Lilly out here. She was interested in this stuff for school, you remember? Should make her watch it for a while." Before Taryn could react, Gloria had already called for her granddaughter to join them. Lilly came out of her room still looking down at her own personal padd and took a seat in her usual spot on the floor at the foot of the couch.

Gloria told her what was about to occur, then after a moment asked her granddaughter, "Hey, how did your answers on this stuff for school work out?"

"Mmm… I did okay but, nainai, that was forever ago."

Gloria pulled out her crochet from the side of the couch and placed it on her shoulder. Moving to a seat on the nearby rocker, she quietly muttered to herself some half-heard comment about a preteen's usage of a word like 'forever.'

So, without meaning to, Taryn began watching the campaign interviews for her own election with nearly her whole family. Once the first interviews began, Lilly's grandmother asked her, "You must have done better with that debate stuff than just okay, Lil?"

"Yeah, nainai, I was doing really well… it was that those stupid boys couldn't stand that I beat them so often because I was new and a girl." She paused. "For people supposedly interested in arguing they hardly know how to lose nicely."

"They rarely do dear," Gloria retorted. "That's one way you can spot those who aren't worth your time."

Lilly chuckled to herself.

Taryn meanwhile had been trying to follow the first interview that had already started. The layout was more or less the same as Taryn had seen in past cycles. The person's features blotted out in the background while their voice, mechanically altered, spoke while captions ran directly in the foreground.

After their initial speech, the question phase would begin with each query first being posted up front with plenty of time for the audience to read it. The same text would run along the top of the screen while the candidates responded. When the question phase was ended the candidate would be allowed a single minute for any closing remarks.

The first candidate wasn't Taryn, much to her own relief. She somehow hated the thought of being the first to go on. In their speech this candidate was focusing on expressing how they wanted their time in the SOMA to be meaningful, though it wasn't obvious at all from their responses that they knew how they were actually going to do that. They didn't communicate any specific thoughts that they wanted to push through and work on. Taryn kept quiet. After a series of continually vague answers, Lilly finally spoke up first during their final remarks.

"What a vacuum head. What are they even saying? Do they any idea what they're doing?"

"Nope." murmured Taryn nodding in a voice of agreement. She gently moved Trey's sleeping legs and got up to grab a drink and took requests from the others.

She returned in the middle of the second candidate's interview. When she asked how it was going, she was sure to do so feigning a distinct note of disinterest. Gloria and Lilly both agreed that this speech was much clearer in its' messaging than the last one had been. The candidate was speaking on how they would steer towards getting more businesses to invest in bringing additional jobs to the region. This would be done by retaining the region's current tax incentives and offering to develop even more local enticements for businesses in the future. From the nature of their language, it sounded as if they had some kind of business or managerial background.

"Well, they were at least straightforward, if not more boring in details and just as ignorant," said Gloria. "Let's just keep doing what's already being done and see what difference that makes," Taryn's mother continued in a mocking tone. Taryn chuckled at this under her breath. She wondered if they would have the stamina to watch all five interviews that night, or if they would grow bored, or opt to watch the highlights later on the news waves, if at all? Would they think that she came across as boring or stupid in her own interview?

Luckily, the third interview started very quickly, and within seconds Taryn started to recognize her own answers coming through as the modified voice on the screen.

"I think that as a resident of Region 75 and someone who knows how hard it can be to support a family here, I want to focus, not only on bringing in new jobs, but on attracting quality jobs. That's what we lack. The businesses that are here, while certainly beneficial, often give employment options only at the lowest wages. And we have permitted the largest of these companies to go decades without paying the standard tax rates. As a result, our infrastructure and schools have become underfunded and understaffed. Our bridges and roads go unmaintained, our public transport system is diminishing in size despite the growing need for it to increase. The power grid and drainage systems are becoming more unreliable due to their age, while our general pollution levels have steadily grown. The companies that we do have, have done well to generate so many jobs for our region, but the local public does not see any investment from them to anything but a minimal credit salary career. Nothing beyond to help the region itself. What I want to do is rework the tax-code to be beneficial to those companies that promote livable wage positions and offer further incentives to companies that invest heavily in training up their local employees to higher postings. While most companies that are operating here have had three decades of steady profits, it is time for the people of Region 75 to see some of these dividends as well for their many cycles of supporting those institutions.

"I know that the ultimate goal of any business is to make money. That is the nature of their existence after all. But without investing in their own workforce and their own community in the short-term, the only thing these tax-exempt companies, are doing is ruining their chance at healthy long-term profits. A local labor force that grows-up poorly educated, unable to take transportation to report to work, and untrained in higher level skills means that any decent credit jobs only become distributed to applicants from other regions. Until one day, in the future, only the lonely unskilled laborer will remain. Eventually those spots too would disappear as well, in bids to consolidate expenses in some other region that can afford to offer them a better tax break than us. I want to avoid all this. To start a new push that helps the economics for as many as possible, businesses and individuals. One that avoids the loss of healthy credit-earning careers and rewards those businesses that help us avoid costs associated with eventual relocations. All sides could benefit from a set-up like this. Businesses, their pool of local labor and the infrastructure that supports them both.

"I also wish to begin focusing on the corporate crime levels as those tend to be the only rates in the region consistently going up over the last few cycles. Nearly all other non-violent crime has declined. I will work with the local Blue Boys to begin to bring these things into check by asking for the formation of a focused task force specifically meant to investigate corporate espionage, malpractice, and blacklisting. It is unreasonable that organizations, treated as individuals under our laws, should have less to fear from the justice of law than any other real flesh and blood individual. And while I do wish to ensure that the businesses that we retain here in Region 75 have a large supply of highly or even overly qualified individuals for their job postings, I also want to ensure that their operations are living up to the standards that the government has already set down. Many of these corporations claim they have exceeded government standards in areas of ethics, safety, and ecological efficiency. I want to make sure that's true. And finally, I wish you, the voting public to know that if elected I will consider it my job not only to work for you in the here and now, to make our region better, but especially for those who aren't here yet. I can't say I'll succeed at everything I've proposed here tonight, since time always throws shifting challenges at us, but I will sure bust my knuckles trying. Thank you."

The last 'bust a knuckle' portion had been a common enough phrase among the floor workers from nearly every factory throughout the region. While far from revealing her identity, it was a subtle nod to all the attentive floor workers that candidate number three had worked a floor at some time also. Filater had approved it only after Taryn had argued that it in no way jeopardized her identity as she did not emphasize the point. There were tens of thousands of floor workers throughout the region and their families, she had argued to him, who might have easily known that rather colloquial phrasing.

The interview went on into the question-and-answer portion. Customarily this tended to be where most of the anonymous candidates had the greatest difficulty in the eyes of the public. 'Thinking on your feet' was certainly not a quality that every potential candidate possessed. Nor was it accepted off hand that those who could spew out a stream of organized thoughts quickly, or 'let the water flow' as it was called, had managed to sufficiently prove the merits of their own ideas. This part required balance and was one of the key reasons the interviews were taped and not merely transcribed for the public to read. Inflections, pauses, stumbles in thought, word usage, at some level all did play for or against a candidate's favor. The taping was there to show the public their region's candidates were real. People who could have been anyone from among them. Someone who lived in their streets and had walked in their neighborhoods.

Still, to prevent some candidates from having anxiety issues that would cause them to blunder their more natural responses, Filater had told Taryn that she could review the questions for up to a half an hour before taping her responses. She suspected the same time allotment was given for the others as well. Altogether, while she certainly did not find that portion of her recording session enjoyable, Taryn had in fact managed to naturally steer several of her responses back to her initial premise, ideas of quality job growth, and investment in Region 75's infrastructure.

Gloria returned after leaving to finally laid Trey down in her bed for the night.

"How is this one doing?"

"Well, they do sound like they have some sort of a brain," blurted out Lilly. Taryn released a slow draw of breath that she didn't even realize she'd been holding in.

After watching a bit more Gloria said, "At the very least they did their homework, to try to get at a useful idea or two. Not a complete idiot like we've seen so far." Taryn quietly held back a smirk.

Her interview began its last question. One about education that was presented in the customary text on the screen before cutting back to the candidate for a response. Filater had said this style of editing made the audience read the question themselves and kept the focus on her, as the candidate. In this case, the final question had asked about plans for improving education. The candidate on screen had started with a quick mention of how relinquishing corporate tax incentives would improve funding for schools, but then went into an idea she'd seen from other region's policies in a brief glance.

"The people of Region 75 should be able to feel confident that a solid proportion, at least 50%, of the funding that goes to education gets expressed directly in classroom use. Not lost to administration costs. Other regions have applied similar plans and seen improvements in overall satisfaction rates. But considering our comparatively lower budget we must make this even higher, at least 60% in direct expression if we are going to give our children a real competitive chance in education."

She continued onto the variety of ways that direct funding expression would improve the educational environment, from the hiring of more teachers to the lowering of class sizes, to doubling the rotation of schools so that students could attend either a morning or afternoon class, to improving the basic facilities tied directly to student use. In reality, most of the ideas she put forward were pulled from her time listening to the many complaints of her mother during Gloria's lengthy career as an educator. The candidate on screen who spoke plainly and with confidence in reality had no direct experience, though Taryn had hoped that part wasn't that obvious. All together Taryn, sitting there with her family, thought that she'd come off rather well in the interview. And her hopes were raised at the prospect that she may have a real chance at winning.

The interview wrapped up and the fourth candidate came on the screen shortly afterwards. In a few moments Taryn's hopes began to dim again.

"My gracious fellow residents of Region 75, thank you for your considerable patience and for extending to me the courtesy of your attention so that I may, in turn, convey just a small sampling of the hoard of thoughts that I have developed to aid and assist all of us living here. For while no one can fully expect each of their notions and propositions to come to fruition, if you'll but put your vote of confidence behind me as your voice in the SOMA, based on even just a few of my proposals, then I'm confident you'll see the wisdom in affording me this opportunity. I do wish to put many of them into action, by your endorsements, so that we all may collectively reap their inherent benefits."

This candidate was clearly different. Their vocabulary stood out. It was refined, eclectic, well-polished. They spoke in longer, more elaborate sentences and with a larger variety of vocabulary than was normal. Obviously, they were highly educated. The vocabulary alone was evidence enough of that, but their smooth command of their words and tone also reflected a mind both informed and highly trained. Someone accustomed to being listened to and speaking to groups or publicly.

A professor, or someone with a legal background, or perhaps even someone with a Loft-Doctorate. Whoever they were, they too had clearly made good use of their preparation time. While their manner of speaking was advanced for the layman, their proposals and ideas were still clearly put forward. Glancing slyly at her daughter and mom, Taryn saw their eyes were attentive, but they weren't making any side comments this time. No quick remarks back and forth. Just listening, intrigued with what Taryn thought were looks of earnest deliberation... or was it curiosity?

As the interview went on, Taryn saw, however, that their campaign goals reflected less of an invitation to action than her own. They apparently were aiming at setting specific goals that called for the business sector growth to be encouraged by not only keeping Region 75's current tax incentives, but also by ensuring that businesses knew that they would still be in effect for the future cycles. This was reinforced by the candidate explaining that they wanted to entice even larger defense contractors and manufacturers to establish factories in the region. Thus, assembly of parts for the latest weapon series set to roll out for the Defense Force and other security services would require more local employment. They came across sounding quite confident when speaking on the business portion and trends of weaponry technological development.

However, thanks to her research and padd's access, Taryn was familiar with this type of credit-funding sink-hole idea. It was a bottomless place for the government, both at the local and larger levels, to spend incalculable amounts of credits. In most cases, without leading to any general economic gain in the long term, other than making the defense contractors' a healthy profit. All this while the contractor, lax in motivation or drive because they were funded up front, usually only delivered several, marginally improved, but always underperforming generations of weapon products that were never actually able to fulfill their original design goals. Taryn had seen the research on this, and on how the process had left several other regions locked in the trap of consistently increasing funding for a one-sided process that produced a defective product. One that never worked to its advertised potential. It was a hidden credit hole. Yet, there were always more places and regional council members eager for a try at all that apparent influx of business and the credits that supported it. 'A benefit to all' with a patriotic spin was almost always the universal sales pitch for such things. Only someone who'd studied economics or had access to the economic data, as Taryn had, would be aware of the full danger of this approach.

Taryn's brow furrowed, and she had a frown on her face as the candidate moved on to education, which—by their reasoning—was to be dealt with not by addressing any funding issues. Instead, they would work to legally require more regulation of instructional credentials and ramping up the educator review process. The region's infrastructure issue was mostly ignored, though they did mention the idea of several independent proposals to put forward for the voters to approve of, as an incremental way to choose if they wished to increase their own taxes. There was again no mention of any of the super-industries being asked to pay a regular tax rate to help fund these improvements. This however was dwarfed by the candidate's last policy reveal. They wanted to spearhead the construction of an entirely new hexaderby stadium to "honor the rise" of the region's top-tier level team. This too made Taryn skeptical again, as all the data that she'd reviewed led her to a wholly different conclusion. Such lavish expenditures, she knew, built in weaker economies always had to be majority funded by private companies who would often hold the majority of the legal rights. This meant that the companies, never the community, kept the profits made from ticket sales. And if eventually the team owners, for whatever reason, grew unhappy with their part of the percentages they could openly express interest in moving to other territories that were more amenable to them and their profit percentages. Thus again, leaving the region in the pincers of having to cover the costs of the empty facilities while earning little to none of the promised economic benefits that were originally pledged. Taryn saw the dangers in these proposals from her competition. The appeal of the candidate's plans relied on the hopefulness and naivety of the voters for gaining immediate benefits with no thought to the far future.

The interview eventually concluded with an exorbitantly long and overly verbose 'thank you' from the candidate, and the eventually screen cut back to one of the late-night news anchors who stated that that had been the last candidate interviews for Region 75. "Clearly, the 5th selectee has decided not to run for the SOMA," they ended. The post-analysis coverage was only beginning as Taryn—reading the tired look in her mother's face and her own body—switched off the feed.

"Well, I do like the idea of a new sports stadium to watch Uncle Everett play in," said Lilly turning towards the adults. "But how are they going to pay for it? Don't those things cost a fortune to build?"

"Yeah" said Gloria getting up to stretch her legs. "And did you notice he never actually addressed that point, nor was he very clear with how to fund the schools. Or where these credits will magically appear from.

"How do you know it's a 'he', nainai? Lil asked.

"Only a man thinks of making weapons on that scale Lil," she yawned. "And I don't know, but it can be a danger in disguise."

"Why is that?" her granddaughter pressed

"Well, if candidate four there," she said nodding to the screen, "actually manages to get one of those huge companies to come in, sure it can create jobs in the region. But as soon as one of those company bosses finds a sweeter deal elsewhere, you start to have massive job losses that cannot be made up for decades. That sure makes it more difficult to lure other companies here. We already have enough of that going on as it is."

Gloria, who had started to organize her crochet supplies continued, "And just because they get jobs doesn't mean those Corpo-creeps will pay their own way in taxes. An old teacher I worked with, Iris, saw that happen over at her school in Region 58. A first-tier company came in on some tax write-off from the SOMA and their local council cycles ago. It was fine for a while then once the tax breaks stopped, the company sent out location scouts and up and moved their whole operation out of the region. Took all their jobs with them. Left behind lots of people who were faced with more bills than could be covered since they'd become accustomed to their larger pay. "*Hard to get anyone to tighten a belt that's never been stretched out before*,' as your grandpa used to say. What'd you think about them, Tar?"

Taryn, who had been staring off in the distance but listening intently, realized a bit too late that her mom and daughter's focus was waiting on her.

"I think..." she started. "I think it's going to be a close election."

Chapter 8: You Can't Always Get What You Want

Taryn's personal data-padd, which had been sitting silently on the dining room table all morning, began beeping. It took Taryn a few minutes to recognize that it was actually the padd that was making the sound. Before then she'd spent the entire day taking care of Trey who was in one of his fits, while Gloria was out for groceries. When she finally found the padd she saw that she'd gotten a message from Filater. He was requesting that she stop by the office building off of 63rd for another meeting.

Taryn had already done her final checkout interview with him last week, or so she'd thought, after the election. Saddened as she was, she had assumed that it was to be her last meeting with the Agent given the results. Certainly, the way Filater had spoken with her seemed to indicate as much. He'd given her some basic survey questions and run through some final debriefing items concerning the secrecy of the election and, as a parting gift, gave her the final pay receipt for her time working on the campaign as a candidate. Her strong showing but ultimate failure made little consultation to her. A farewell from Filater, the collection of her building IDs, and that was all there was. So, receiving a new message from him this morning, a week later, was unexpected to say the least. She had had another job interview since, but the hiring director had called her the previous evening to let her know that they'd 'already identified a person' to fill their position. Needless to say, her day was now free, and after three and a half hours this morning of trying rather unsuccessfully to keep Trey from crying, she was eager to get out of the flat for a while, even if it meant dealing with the rather cool Bizi agent again.

She pulled up to the building to find Filater waiting for her outside the front door. He was leaning against the red brick wall smoking a stick without his suit jacket on. This was a new and unfamiliar situation for her to see. It looked odd to Taryn, to view Filater like this. Like any other working fellow, quickly waiting out a breaktime in their work shift. As she parked and approached, she saw that despite looking towards her he wasn't actually watching her. His dark brown eyes were focused, looking beyond her to someplace far away in the corners of his own mind. His brow furrowed in a contortion of intensity as his face seemed to be mulling-over some distracting bit of vexing puzzlement.

"Agent Filater? What is it?" she asked, concerned as she approached. He didn't respond at first. This was the only time she'd seen him like this. In the short period that she'd worked with him, Filater had always reacted quickly to any inquiries. Delay and distraction were not native to his personality. But here he was contemplative and distant in thought regarding *something*. Something that was either confounding his mind or had clearly taken him by surprise. Something was off keel, and if it was enough to gall the otherwise aloof Bizi Agent, Taryn herself was unsurprised that she felt a bit of real concern creep into her own stomach as she waited for his response.

"Agent Filater?" she tried again.

"Come on inside," he finally responded with his stick bobbing up and down with his words. He grabbed sideways, opening the glass door next to him without moving the focus of his eyes for a long moment. Flicking the remainder of his burnt stick to a nearby can, he walked her through the waiting room, which was empty and looked closed by all accounts. The window blinds were shut, and no one was at the reception desk. In the back hallways, he walked her into a small side office with a desk and monitor apparently synced to a government padd lying nearby.

"Thank you for coming on short notice. Have a seat, please," he said, taking the chair behind the desk.

"What I'm about to tell you, you would normally never be aware of, Ms. Steno. As you know, your campaign election was a rather close race."

"Yeah, but what does that matter? I mean, I still lost," she said rather suspiciously.

"What you don't know is that by our count your campaign in Region 75 turned out the largest percentage of voters for any of this SOMA election season. Between you and the victor, you got over

92% of registered voters to respond, with the vast majority casting positive votes instead of negative ones. That's quite good, even for our mandatory voting requirements. And the amount you lost by", he continued referring back to his padd, "was less than four percent."

Taryn's head straightened, and she tensed up. He wouldn't have brought it up unless that was important.

"So, what's that to do with anything?" she asked.

"Now as I said, you normally wouldn't be told this—"

"Then something must have changed for you to be telling me this now, hasn't it?"

"Well, yes." he said, pausing to look at some data on the padd in his hand. "There is… an unexpected opening for a government posting that wasn't accounted for in this cycle." He continued, "now, the methods for filling this posting would typically be handled by the SOMA, but as you are aware, they are in the middle of their transition process and quite frankly, the time it would take those newly elected officials to be brought up to speed is an unacceptable delay due to the nature of the position."

"And that position would be... ?"

Filater continued on, seemingly not noticing Taryn's question. "Thankfully, there are secondary rules and regulations that are in place to cover this type of situation. In short, they state that the candidates with the highest positive voter response not elected to join the SOMA may be asked to fill this posting in an acting capacity so as to facilitate a quicker and smoother transition. Then, the selected candidate could later be fully confirmed by the SOMA when time is more accommodating. That brings us to you, Ms. Steno," he said, putting down the padd on the desk. "We'd need to give you another neural scan and run you through a whole lot of security procedures to get you the proper clearance, but my goal now is to see if you would be interested in that post."

Taryn hesitated. *Why was he being purposefully vague?* She began replaying their last meeting and contrasting it to what she was hearing now.

"Do you remember," she asked, "that you asked me a very similar question to this in my last interview?"

"I remember that I asked: now that you had experience in the Moot Election process, if you had the opportunity to redo the campaign once again, would you have changed your campaign tactics if you knew it meant that you'd win."

"And do you remember my answer?" Taryn pushed.

Filater paused and leaned back a little in his chair.

"You said that anyone who cared enough about winning that they'd change themselves or their own ideas didn't deserve to win in the first place. And that you would never feel that you'd earned the SOMA seat if you did that."

She continued on interrupting him again, "So, why should I take on a different posting now, when I haven't earned that level of responsibility, haven't been elected to it and, judging by your vagueness, apparently don't even have the security clearance to know what it is?"

Filater remained silent, but in his calm tired expression a slow smile began subtly drawing itself up for a long moment. There was a gradual change that came over his face, his eyes flashing, while he stared at the woman from Region 75. He immediately looked more relaxed, at ease almost, as if a high dark cloud had cleared from his sight. Folding his arms gently and leaning forward on the desk he said in a lowered voice, "To answer your question as to why you..., the short of it is that outside of the legal dictates you, Ms. Steno, are one of the few we could have approached with this to have actually seriously questioned it as inappropriate for yourself. You even went so far to reject this offer out of hand because of our restraint in being forthcoming with details."

Now Taryn sat silent at this confusing answer.

"And that's why we're only truly offering it to you. All the others who we proposed this to all jumped at the chance to get back in once they realized they could. You're the only loser of a Moot Election who hasn't been drawn to this offer like a gull to scraps on the beach. You're the only one who claimed that they weren't qualified for the post, despite having clear voter support. That is what this job needs, Ms. Steno. Someone that remembers both what it means to be where you are now and understands the importance of where you would be working."

"And just where would I be working? Stop talking in riddles, Filater," she said, finally letting her aggravation show.

Filater's unwavering eyes flickered for a brief moment and Taryn thought she briefly caught a previously unnoticed hint of green in the edges of their brown. It may simply have been a reflection of a small green light from one of his devices on the desk.

"You would be serving as the third member of the Haiden Prime Trinity High Council, ma'am. The highest government office in the land."

There was a long pause where neither of them talked, as if Taryn was still registering what exactly had been put forward to her. Finally, Filater spoke up again.

"So, Ms. Steno, I'll ask you again, are you interested in a job? Or should we continue to interview those who are more ambitious and yet… less scrupulously pragmatic?"

* * *

In the morning, there was more than the usual bustle in Taryn's home. She was busy picking out her nicest shirt, Lilly was cleaning up the kitchen after breakfast, and Gloria was changing Trey before heading off with Lilly to her school. It was Taryn's first official day at her new workstation even though she'd been going through several security procedures for a week now. Today would be the first non-security training day. After a week of being walked through various identifying tests including voice, handprint, facial, and iris recognition, and another neural scan with the ever-amusingly sassy Dr. Uthtr, Filater had finally taken his leave of Taryn yesterday. He had told her that the rest of her official job training would be handled on site by others including a different Bizi agent who would pick her up to take her to her new office location in the mornings. She would see Filater now only sporadically as she began her work. Taryn had no real clue what to expect though this first day, and she reflected on that as she finished dressing in her best professional outfit. Her only one, in fact, up to this point in her life. A dark jacketed number, with a green trimmed button, that she had been hesitant to spend her very limited credits on. It wasn't a suit in cut or cloth by any means, but even if she had the funds, Taryn's complete abhorrence to actually dressing in a fully-fledged suit felt beyond conceivable. To her mind, the very skin on the top of her shoulders and arms might just physically convulse at its touch, wrinkling up shrewdly, crawling away from her in repulsion to such an attempt. She'd happily prefer watching every last credit of her family flush itself down a sewer drain before seriously considering making a suit her normal work attire, even in a position such as this.

As for explaining things to Lilly and her mother, Taryn found it was easy enough to give them a notion close to the truth: that the Vox P. Industries had found they had an unexpected vacancy that needed an immediate trial candidate in order to keep their production pace on track. Though the pay was similar, the only drawback she had told them was the need for even more secrecy to ensure against industrial espionage in this particular job. Thus, though she'd not been the final hire for the original posting, she would be receiving training on this newly opened slot. And since her new work facilities were quite far away, the company had assigned her to a transportation pool with another employee who would be picking her up for work. Telling them any direct falsehoods, like the company's name, Taryn viewed as a relatively minor matter in comparison to her family's ever-present need for income.

Aside from the actual nature of her new job, the fact that the coworker Taryn was assigned with was in truth a Bizi security agent that would be driving and also training her for the first few weeks and acting as personal security was by far the largest omission in all of this. Taryn had seen in Gloria's eyes that she was curious to hear more than this, but after a moment she smiled and simply said, "Well, it's what we agreed to at first anyways. And it's good you'll be working full shifts again and getting decent credits."

The door buzzer rang, and Gloria, being closest, hit the call button.

"Hello? I'm here to pick up Mrs. Steno for work."

"A moment please. She'll be right down," Gloria responded, noting that it was a male voice on the other end.

There were some rushed 'first day at work' well-wishes and hugs from Trey and Lilly along with their goodbyes. After that, Taryn found herself greeted at the building's lobby door by a very solid looking man almost as big as Everett, with dark skin and short dark hair that was just starting to grey at its edges.

"Well, hello there. You must be Mrs. Steno," he said, smiling at her warmly as she approached. He was dressed in business attire and was holding two joe-cups with aromatic steam wafting above both. Each labeled as bearing the signature blend of a local corner shop.

"I didn't want to meet you on our first day empty-handed, but of all the things I could research on you in preparation for your training, nowhere does it state if you prefer caff-free or traditional."

"Traditional please," she said smiling as she took the cup generously offered to her. She wondered if a second cup on that particular morning would make her too quick and edgy for her own good. "And you are…?"

"Oh, I do apologize. I sometimes forget to introduce myself as I rarely make new acquaintances. I'm Wil, Wil Zhuantium." His large dark hand engulfed hers as he shook it, smiling.

"Now, if you'll follow me. It's best not to be late on our first day." He said, turning towards the parking area.

"Of course," she agreed, following his lead. He walked her to a brand-new looking vehicle. It was black with tinted glass, and probably expensive, as if it had come fresh off the showroom floor only an hour ago.

"Here we are. If you don't mind, ma'am," he said, opening the passenger door. "I'll drive this first time till you learn the route at least."

The drive itself felt shorter on that first day than all the other days that Taryn would later make it. Still, all she actually recalled later was that Agent Zhuantium, or 'Wil' as he preferred, made some general remarks about looking forward to meeting her and some polite inquiries about her family. He had mostly let Taryn enjoy the ride as he accelerated them capably down the road.

She was surprised to notice after a brief time that they were not heading into the larger city sectors, but were in fact progressing south-west, further out towards the mountainous and rural farming territories. Soon they were on a simple two-lane road curving through patches of woods and farmers' fields on either side. Looking out the windows, Taryn saw passing hay balers off in the distance collecting rolls of the fresh-cut grass from the fields. They'd always reminded Taryn of oversized breakfast cereal pieces, especially in the winter, when they would get covered in the first snow. The frosting, as she thought of it, had always worked as an invitation for her to go play in her father's fields when she was a young girl. In the summers, she remembered nights spent catching fireflies or listening to the frogs from a small pond singing to each other. It had been a long time since she'd seen a working farm in the summer months though.

She suddenly felt more loss and regret at the thought of her vanished childhood home and her absent father than she'd cared to let herself feel in cycles. All this went through her mind, passing by, just as the view through her window did, in a few meager minutes. It was as far from any thoughts of the new position she was about to take on as was possible. She was quickly brought back by the notion that her driver had just asked her a question, however, to which she had not been listening to at all.

"I'm sorry Agent Zhuantium, I was lost for a moment. What were you asking again?"

"Oh, it's quite alright, ma'am, well… all except for that 'Agent Zhuantium' business. It's simply 'Wil' if you don't mind. I sometimes like looking at the views around here too. Pretty country," he commented.

"Alright Wil," she said, easing herself in the seat and bringing her attention fully back to the present. "But you have to cut it out with all this ma'am and Ms. Steno stuff too. Deal?"

"I'll try, but no promises, Miss Taryn. My ma used to beat the wits out of me if I didn't address people with the proper respect."

Taryn laughed.

"Well then she did a good job, but if you don't mind, I won't tell her."

"That's kind of you, miss. I appreciate that," he said smiling to himself. "So, what I'd asked was if you'd ever like to live out this way again. In places like this, I mean. Your pardon, but I saw in the records you were a rural child. Not many of them anymore. Then again, what some people consider home is not where they were raised to begin with, in my experience."

Taryn thought for a moment on Wil's question.

"I mean I would like my family to be out here… if it were possible. The air is better, the pace is slower, and you can truly see nature and the seasons working in full. Can't get that in the city sectors. But as it stands, my family doesn't earn nearly enough credits to afford more than our small family-unit rental."

"Well, who knows? You do good at this trial period and the SOMA might give you the go-ahead to stay on permanently." There was a pause while he thought. "And while I do know a decent amount about the nature of the job, Miss Taryn, I've never actually concerned myself with figuring out how much it pays exactly." He drove them for a short time before turning west off the main road. "Though if it's any comfort I do know that no Haiden council member ever died of hunger nor any of their immediate family… far as I'm aware," he added jokingly.

After a few more minutes on various side roads that seemed little used but looked pristine, Wil guided the vehicle down an unlabeled drive on their right that was hung over on both sides with thick brush woods. The road was narrow for both lanes but was still nicely paved, with a gentle curvy path as it wound ever deeper and deeper through the shade of the encroaching trees. Two vehicles would only barely fit past each other here. Aside from a one-person guard shack a few meters in, that Wil only waved a hand at, there was nothing else apparent on the road. No buildings could be seen, and Taryn got her sense of direction quickly lost as the road meandered its way back and forth through the thickening forest on both sides time and again. After another few kilometers, Wil slowed and stopped for no clear reason. The single lane itself continued around a bend and a few meters later was lost beyond that to Taryn's view. Aside from the woods there was still nothing of note visible.

"Would you kindly wait for me here, Miss, while I go ahead and park the vehicle? I'll be right back to walk you in."

"But…" she said looking around her once again, "there is nothing out here."

"Not true Miss Taryn. For one, you're here. And so is your posting. Just wait and I'll be right back to help you out, alright?" he smiled.

Taking her bag, Taryn hesitantly shut the door, and she watched as the vehicle and driver sped off and disappeared around the bend to the left. Soon after, all the sounds of the transport's propulsion faded and were gone as well, replaced only by the low quiet of the woods and the morning birds that inhabited it. The green walls of trees on either side of the road loomed high over Taryn's head, nearly crossing the gap of the lane as the tallest of these trees fanned out their leafy entanglements on each side towards one another. It was still cooler, but without any sort of breeze she could tell that the sun was quickly warming up the morning air. A few bird songs could be heard here and there as their echoes bounced distantly across the canopy. Taryn thought she heard a chickadee's song nearby, with some wild doves singing even higher up. Farther off she perhaps caught a distant crow call, but she wasn't sure. Down off the dim road in the morning, Taryn's focus fell on the nearby trees. There were elms, maple, birch, interspersed with a few small pines and in the distance even a few older looking willows that she could make out. The brush and barky vines were especially thick in some parts, and the wide-leaved ferns and bracken filled in every ounce of space that gave them any hope of reaching their green leaves up to the sunlight.

The roadside grasses and weeds sloped down on either side of the lane and disappeared into a dense blanket of fern vegetation that fully masked the ground between the various trees. Here and there, a few dead tree branches stood out among the living sea of huge fern leaves as the only sign of the earth underneath. An occasional shadow of a squirrel or chipmunk could be seen skittling among the branches and bramble, as they endlessly darted their way back and forth attending to their food hoards. And sporadic deer scat could be seen on the edge of the road where, Taryn assumed, they often wandered at dusk. In this relative silence, Taryn's attention fell onto a large maple tree just to her north-west. It was only a dozen paces or so from the roadside but even from where she stood, Taryn thought that something seemed off about it. Not wrong, but just unusual. It was a straight tree with no major forking in it until it was high above her head. She moved casually along the roadside to have a closer look. As she did, Taryn decided it wasn't the tree's color, but the striations of the bark that made it seem odd to look at. They were carved too straight in some sections, almost as if they had been planned and synchronized, and in other areas they were too chaotic. She thought she could almost make out an image of sorts in the striations, almost sphere-like, when around the bend on the road came Wil whistling a low tune and walking calmly towards her.

"Oh, I see you found old Jack," he said looking at where she was staring. "Yeah, records say he's one of the original tree-eyes in this area. Not as advanced in his design as the other ones," he nonchalantly remarked. "But still, well-hidden unless you're really looking at him."

"Tree-eye?" Taryn asked, confused at the term.

"A type of passive recon system for the purpose of security in this part. The tree itself was grown around a set of small diameter cylindrical cores. Each very tall and thin, but just wide enough to house all types of sensor and monitoring systems. Old Jack was designed to monitor the area without ever being seen himself. Like I said he is an older model though, so the merging of the circuitry with the tough cellulose in the plant's material wasn't as seamless as it could have been."

"I don't get it," Taryn said still lost. "When we're not here staring at it, what is the tree going to be watching out for besides the occasional rabbit and bird droppings? There's nothing out here."

"If the Bizi do their jobs right, Miss Taryn, then your notion would *seem* by all accounts correct. Absolutely nothing here," he repeated walking past her to the brush around the opposite side of the 'Old Jack' tree. Watching her own footing down the initial steps from the road, Taryn turned to follow him and in making her way round the back of the tree stopped cold when she turned the corner and found that Wil was gone. Not a sound, not a rustle, just gone.

"Agent Zhuantium?" she called out in confusion.

"I could have sworn that I'd asked you to call me *Wil*, Miss Taryn," came the calm response from a nearby and yet unseen source.

Wil's dark-skinned hand and wrist appeared out of thin air and offered itself to her in a kindly gesture of escort. "This way if you please. Mind the transfer"

Cautiously taking the floating hand, Taryn watched with a shock as the hand holding her own began to pull, vanishing with her own arm in its turn as she was gently guided forwards. Then she saw a quick flash and stood completely still as her eyes reset themselves. The woods had vanished.

Taryn's eyes blinked several times then once they'd adjusted, she found herself standing at the base of a sloping hill with an enormous lawn, perfectly trimmed. Above her now was no forest canopy at all, but only the open morning sky whose fresh blue was dotted with an occasional cloud. At the crest of the gentle hill before them, there now stood a large white wooden two-story house with a side barn sitting on its western flank. She found that she was standing at the base of a walking path that wound its way up towards the front entrance. With her mouth gaping open, Taryn turned to look back at the path she'd come.

She could see the road, only a dozen paces back from her spot now. She also saw several small black devices about a foot tall spaced evenly across the edge of the grounds, emitting a series of violet and red lights running parallel to the road for several meters in either direction. The tract of woods and the old Jack maple tree were still there, while the lane continued further beyond, but between them and her, Taryn could make out the slight sheen of a green grid appearing to fade in and then back out of her sight's perception. Sounds of distant birds and insects could occasionally be heard emanating from these devices. The real wood ran around the perimeter of the manicured hill where she now stood. Taryn saw that if she stared hard enough, she could see a turnabout off the lane a little way down where Wil had apparently parked the vehicle. The main lane itself continued, out of sight, into what she presumed to be an actual real section of the woods.

There was little doubt in Taryn's mind that this place had been designed to be invisible to all, but those who knew where to find it. Any random traveler would pay the area no more attention than they would to a piece of small debris on the side of the road.

"This is incredible!" she said more to herself than anyone around.

"Come along now, Miss Taryn," said Wil. "There will be time to wander around the grounds during lunch if you like. You still have some introductions to make before the morning is out."

"Is this where the Trinity High Council always meets?" she asked as they strode up the path.

"Well, it's more accurate to say that this will be where *you* will be meeting them for the foreseeable future. You see cycles ago, for security reasons, it was decided that the Haiden should never actually meet in person unless extraordinary circumstances demanded it. Too much of a risk, you know. And while the government sections of the cities are quite secure, they are publicly known locations and there are several thousand legitimate workers from all over that roam those grounds each day. That means there is a chance however remote of recognizing a person from one's own neighborhood or an old associate. Slim a chance as it is, it has happened in the past. Areas like these," he said gesturing around them, "have been established over time so that the members of the Trinity High Council may work without any direct connection ever being made between them. It ensures none of you ever accidentally or intentionally learn the others' identities as well."

"What about communication? I assume all contact is routed through some type of secure lines?"

"Something like that, but with experience we've found the best way to stop digital invaders was to simply give them what they think they wanted. If anyone ever does manage to compromise the communication lines for this place, still no easy feat mind you as we are hardwired to an off-sight satellite hookup with its own stealth field. Well, even then, they would still only find they were ease-dropping on several old entertainment broadcasts and long running conversations between three elderly sisters complaining about their husbands, the weather and the various prices of fabric that are all running on an endless loop that restarts about every five cycles or so. We have enough of those recordings to put any insomniac to sleep. The actual transmissions used are buried within layers upon layers that makes them nearly invisible and perceived as nothing but occasional static interference. There are quite a few other security measures we use, but I'm not allowed to go into those I'm afraid, Miss Taryn." As he had explained this, they had climbed the last steps up to the house's wrap-around porch.

"I get it," Taryn said looking more intently at the house now. It appeared to be a rather old-style wood frame house with a pitched roof and a light, blue-floored wooden porch. The house was painted in bright white with dark trim and black wooden shutters fixed smartly to the sides of each window. Several flower boxes hung over the porch railing at various points. Batches of well-groomed red, yellow, and pink chrysanthemums were in all the boxes. Blue and purple lavender were planted in the ground right below these.

"And the locals or occasional wanderers, like hunters or hikers? Surely some of them have seen this place before the Bizi hid it? They must occasionally make their way in, even accidently."

"Well, we have the entire area for a two-kilometer radius lined with tree-eyes and other detection resources, so that usually it's not hard to keep folk well clear. Those image and sound projectors on the fringes are not the only ones we have. Others have been set pretty far outside the perimeter. They aren't visible themselves, but they do create great impersonations of coyote howls, and you'd be surprised how far out of their way a person will deviate from their path when they catch a mere glimpse of a few small rad-snakes. An occasional lost traveler might drive on the lane to find it goes a long circuitous route back down to a small town about six kilometers from here. Most locals avoid it in favor of the much faster main roads. Usually, it's the bicyclists that travel the lane the most, and they almost never stop except to change a flat tire."

"Well, what about construction, grounds maintenance, food deliveries? Surely someone would notice those?"

"Well,' Wil said begrudgingly "we automate what we can, but for the rest, Miss Taryn, you just have to trust me that the Bizi know how to keep secrets. We have been doing this type of thing for a very long time now. In over 400 cycles of service, no unauthorized person has gained access intentionally or otherwise beyond the stealth field into one of our focal points.

"And even if your whole stealth system did fail, all that anyone would see is a serene but albeit plain-looking house. Nothing that screams government owned at all."

Wil nodded. "Though we do our best to ensure that kind of situation never happens. Most of the systems you'll find at work here run independently and have several layers of redundancies. On top of that, there are several types of… active security features, some of which you'll see, while others you'll never probably notice nor need to concern yourself with. Any satellites," he said, turning his eyes upwards beyond the porch, "with high grade lenses, electromagnetic, humidity, thermal, muon detectors, and UV scanners would only see one continuous patch of woodland down here. Passenger flights or unmanned recons low enough see the same type of holo-imaging you perceived from the road. The projected image changes with the days, weather, and seasons to match the surrounding woodlands."

He opened the front screen door and held it for her. "This place, as best as we can make it, doesn't exist to anyone but us."

"What...? No locks?" she joked as she pushed the front door open and walked right in. At that, she heard Wil grunt a laugh to himself.

The house looked normal enough on the inside as well. It was well-lit with warm standing lamps that were already turned on. There were thick oval carpets partially covering deep polished wooden floors and rose-colored wooden furniture that suited the style. Taryn felt as though she might have been just as easily stopping by an old friend's country home for a morning visit from the looks of it. Just past the entrance, there was a living room with a pleasant assortment of comfortable looking furniture. A large couch and two large chairs, centered towards each other around a low-lying table and boarded by the main hearth. Opposite this, on the front side of the house, was a standard dining area with six quality wood chairs pulled up to a long table. Along the inner wall that bisected the first floor there were stairs that led up to three upper-floor bedrooms where Taryn rarely, if ever, ventured. Beyond the living room on the inner side was a hall that crossed the house and ran into a generously large and open kitchen. To the right of that hall entrance there was another room with two sliding doors leading to an office space established as an extension in the corner of the house. Its windows overlooked the gentler sloping green of the backyard and nearby forest further out. In that same direction, the windows also faced back toward the towers at the city's heart in the far grey distance. Taryn didn't get that far though in looking around, before she and Wil were stopped by a thin older man who stood patiently in front of the stairs. He was dressed neatly in a white shirt with a dark vest and black pants.

"Miss Steno, I'd like to introduce you to the caretaker of the estate, Mr. Brough."

The gentlemen politely took Taryn's hand, and while shaking it, performed a respectful half-bow as well. He was lean, with a thin wide smile and a receding hairline above his long face and nose. His features looked weatherworn, but his face still retained the bearing of a person of distinction and deep competence.

"Besides overseeing the grounds," Wil continued, "and the housing maintenance, Mr. Brough will also be your contact for anything you need while you're at work here. Food, drinks, medical services, or other direct needs, just make a request and he's your man."

"Oh," said Taryn, "pleasure to meet you. So, I guess technically… this is your house then, huh? It's very charming, I can tell you have excellent taste. Everything looks polished and impeccable. I'm sorry say it feels like we're putting an inconvenience on you?"

Brough responded in a slow, polite, but welcoming tone. "Thank you and it is lovely to meet you also, Mrs. Steno. While I do reside on the grounds, I am, like all here, merely a steward of my post so please come in and relax. The house is neither mine nor another's. When my services here are rendered complete, another shall take on the charge."

"Please call me Taryn, Mr. Brough. Mrs. Steno was my mother in-law."

"As you wish, Miss Taryn," he said gesturing to take her coat for her, "but please, don't be offended if I ask you to continue to use my surname. I'm afraid that in my work it is considered… impolite for me to divulge my first name if you understand my meaning."

"Not a problem," said Taryn. "You probably have to balance secrecy with daily needs, all while maintaining an air of grace and effortlessness in your duties. Not an easy task for anyone to be sure."

"Very astute and thoughtful of you ma'am," complimented Brough as he hung her coat on some nearby wall pegs.

"Now, would you like a morning refreshment? Tea or something stronger perhaps?"

"Thank you, no. Agent Zh… err… Wil was already kind enough to take care of that," she said, holding up her half full joe-cup.

"Very well, if you have no further immediate needs, I will show you to the office area where Agent Zhuantium can proceed with the day's orientation."

He showed them to the large corner office nearby. After easily sliding the simple wood double doors open, Brough guiding them through, began opening the window curtains for them. The room looked Northeast and while it was distant, the skyline of the city was easily visible on the pink morning horizon. On the outer wall of the office was a small hearth with a cozy flame already glowing brightly. On an inner wall, a tall bookshelf stood, with glass doors closed over numerous small rows of red leather-bound books. Some of these were obviously newer, but if one were to slowly follow the rows of these books, they became progressively older on each shelf until the top, where they appeared almost ancient with faded pages and worn bindings.

In the back corner of the room, there was a simple but long desk, built in an open triangle so that two sides faced the corner windows, and a third front surface faced back across towards the doorway. On its black surface was the standard office tech, neatly arranged, along with a padd, an old-fashioned key-type system, and a projection box. In the center of the floor lay a new-looking carpet. It had a large circular blue crest that Taryn didn't recognize woven onto it. On the nearby wall there were sets of display screens stacked in two columns, all turned off for the moment.

As he was opening the window curtains and ensuring the small fire was still properly stoked, Mr. Brough continued. "In the mornings, Miss Taryn, I usually remember to refill the log rack over there, but should you run low, I'm most often right down the hall in the kitchen if you need me. The corner windows have a beautiful view, but I'm afraid that they are not all that good at keeping the cold out as the deep winter months grow closer. Thankfully this room heats fast and there is a backup electric system if it does ever drop too low for you."

"I understand. Thank you," said Taryn, feeling completely uncomfortable and out of place as she recognized that, as the recently unemployable factory worker, she had now been assigned her own personal driver, security personnel, work home, and now a valet of sorts all in the same morning. It was certainly nothing like what she was expecting. To her she had anticipated a large multi-floored office building with a perpetual hive of activity that she would have to learn to navigate. In it, Taryn had pictured professionally dressed and assertive people of all sorts going every which way about their work in the government sector.

"No trouble at all Miss Taryn." Brough said in closing as he moved towards the office doorway. "Should you need me when I am outside or out of earshot, you need only ask Aurelius to send for me." And with that he quietly stepped out and gently shut the sliding doors to the office behind him.

Taryn heard these parting remarks, but her eyes were still fixed on the dark smooth top of the desk. Stuck there as if the magnitude of her new title had only registered with her at this very moment. The first inklings of the magnitude of the situation she had agreed to attempt now finally stretched their long weighty hands before her. They would wait on her for a call to action. From here, this very desk, in this corner room she could shape the nature of the government affecting the lives of millions. Wil, perceptive to the reflective expression on the face of his new charge, let the silent contemplation continue on for a long moment before daring to interrupt with his own thoughts.

"Remember that the desk is just a thing. No more important than any furniture anywhere else." He laughed softly to himself. "You know, you could be working from a booth or bar stool down at the local dinner, and it would still be your decisions that are the real important part of this posting. Not the ancillaries. Don't let things be a source of intimidation or reverence. Or… at least realize you're probably not the first to have that thought. That's only a personal recommendation though."

"Any *official* recommendations then?" she said still staring at the desk

"Just two, Miss Taryn. Know what is yours, and what is not."

Taryn looked at him with a clear expression of questioning at this.

"It's some advice an old instructor told me in my first-year training with the Bizi," Wil continued. "First, remember that this desk," he said pointing, "is *not* yours. Not truly. No more than this house is Mr. Brough's. This, all of this," he said motioning around him, "is not yours, nor is it any of ours that work with you… it was never any of our predecessors either. They each had a turn and now it has been passed onto you for a time. At some point sooner or later, it will be passed along again in this guise or another.

"Second, know what *is* yours. That is, the opportunity that you have here. That is truly yours. To help those you can, in the time you have. To provide them with a chance to have better or more opportunities for themselves. And that should be where your focus is… It's the opportunity to work for them and this," he said pointing at her head. "This is all you are for them… nothing more than a thought in the back of their minds if anything. But that should be all that you really need. From your perspective, any Trinity council policy arising out of your work is implemented via the SOMA. That is part of their responsibility. In that same vein, the Bizi's responsibility is to provide the three on the council with the support and security to do that job. But the opportunities for those out there," he said gesturing back towards the city skyline, "the ones dealing with the everyday problems, that is your charge. That is your responsibility. To see to it that the options in their lives grow more diverse and varied in every productive way.

"To the rest of them out there in the world, those who will never know you, they need only know that you are working in earnest to make things better for them. You're a reassurance that decent people will help one another when given a proper chance too. To give them more choices, more power in their own day-to-day. And when the choices are beyond their scope or ability to act, the assurance that the person here in this post will act for them in the interests of the majority, not allocating to any favorites. That is what's yours. In a position like this one, the only true changes from person to person are simply due to the motives they bring with them. Remember why you're the one who is here and not someone else, and it ensures all your efforts are worthwhile and not just the wishful boasting of some old motto. Forget that it's your chance for now, and now alone… and all the folk out there, well, they'd all be better off if we were actually wasting our time wandering blindly about the imaginary forest that everyone else covers this hill."

"Your instructor told you all of that?" Taryn asked skeptically, raising an eyebrow.

"Well, just that very first part... she wasn't speaking directly for this situation, I admit," he laughed. "But it was the same type of idea, and it was a good thought. Promising ideas have no age, you know."

Taryn, looking out the clear corner windows, began slowly walking around the desk to the black chair that was between all three sides. She did not sit though. She stood behind it, resting her arms on the top of the chair's high padded back, thinking of Wil's words. All the possible ways she might unintentionally screw this up, both for herself, and for those who would feel the effects of her mistakes began streaming through her. Taryn almost relented to all the doubts her mind was producing, but such thoughts she realized were trivial. It was still only her first day after all. She had made no world-breaking blunders yet, and to dwell too long on that would only distract from what she should be doing instead. Which, for now, meant learning the routines and people of this oddly established working environment. Better to focus on learning the ropes rather than obsessing over not trying to sink it. Then, ending her introspection there, and bringing herself back to the current moment, she asked.

"So, who's this Aurelius Mr. Brough mentioned?"

"I am," answered a rather pleasant and lively sounding voice that came from all around her. As if someone on an open communication line to the office had been patiently waiting his turn to be called upon. Still Taryn was badly startled and taken aback at the surprise of this immediate response. The voice wasn't loud, but it did remain at a constant level no matter where Taryn walked about in the office. It sounded quite polite and chipper, like a normally pleasant enough fellow who was characteristically always in high spirits, with a strong even tone that betrayed neither age, nor any immaturity.

"What is this Wil?" she asked unnerved. "Another hologram? Someone on an open line?"

"No, I'm not a holograph at the moment, though I could generate a random holographic form if that would make you feel more comfortable?" replied the voice again. "Or then again, I could meet with you in a virtual plane if you wou—

"Miss Taryn, " interrupted Wil quickly. "Meet Aurelius," he said, speaking as if to the whole of the room, "your secret weapon on this job." He pointed out some small speakers and a clear audio input to the side of the desk, as well as a few scattered mini recorders each with a miniscule green power light on them indicating their use. "Aurelius is… well, I think it's better if I let him finish his own introduction of himself to you, as well as the rest of today's orientation. Remember A', it's the new one's very first day," he said more to the room than to Taryn. "Slow build up, try not to overload her, huh?" And with this he excused himself from the office and shut the sliding doors behind him.

Taryn was, as far as she could tell, alone in the room.

"Hello?" she began rather unsurely.

"Hello, Miss Taryn," came the quick response. The voice had a clearly male texture, though it was not all that deep. There was no accent or regional notoriety to its enunciation that Taryn could hear. Its timing was perfectly normal, with a registry that was calming yet still light and pleasant, without any hints of its origins. "I'm sorry for startling you," it continued. "I also hope that you don't mind the informal title I used in addressing you, as I overheard you expressing that preference to Mr. Brough when you were removing your coat."

"No… no, that's fine," Taryn said, gaining back some more of her composure. If Taryn had been asked right then, she would have guessed the person behind the voice to be no more than five to ten cycles older than herself. But she still felt a little odd speaking intermittently to an empty room and seemingly no one in particular, despite knowing that she, herself, could be seen and heard by this… *something* called Aurelius.

"Now if you wish to have a seat, and please turn your attention to the displays on the opposing wall. I will endeavor to answer the many questions you no doubt have concerning my identity and its connection to your new position."

"I'll stand if that's okay?"

"As you like," replied the voice promptly.

The screens turned a bright blue hue, and four large distinct quadrants emerged.

"As I'm sure you know Ms. Taryn, the formation of our government's spheres relies heavily on its members performing their jobs with anonymity. This is done to ensure an unfettered focus to their task, without biased interests actively seeking them out." One of the screens flashed images of the SOMA meeting in various states of debates and began to randomly shuffle. All the faces were either covered or blurred despite the clear SOMA seal in the background. "The same is even more so for the Haiden Prime Trinity High Council," the voice continued. People have worked on the council together for their entire terms having never met in person or ever knowing each other's true names."

The images shifted to display a seal. It was the same blue symbol as on the carpet in the room. It showed three smaller hooded figures separated at the periphery of the large circle. They looked to be using gold ropes attached to geared pulleys of an emerald coloring heading inwards. As the ropes ran beyond their rigging points, they were taut and a bit frayed, becoming ever deeper a scarlet color. The ropes were hosting a massive but thin silver platform upwards. On it stood a large image of a city overflowing with gleaming towers.

"Anonymity is the main security feature of all of our positions, I assumed," Taryn added.

"Naturally, and in my own anonymous role, I myself serve as the primary advisor to the Bizi and the Haiden Prime Trinity High Council. My existence remains a secret to all but those who serve on the council or at the higher levels of the Bizi and direct support staff. The SOMA representatives are only aware of me as a secretarial program. As Agent Zhuantium said, you may call me Aurelius."

"I am, from your current perspective, a fully functional artificial insight matrix, designed initially and subsequently activated several hundreds of years or what you would call cycles ago. My primary purpose is—"

"Wait, wait, hold on a moment," Taryn interrupted again, collecting her thoughts. "You're an advanced intelligence system?"

"Yes."

"I thought that wasn't possible? Scientists gave up because they said it was a constant dead end. 'The second walk of Alchemy' the teachers used to name it in schools. Like… like trying to make lead into gold and all that. We were told that trying to get circuits to properly mirror real thoughts, emotions, and basic physiological desires artificially and simultaneously, always screwed up the logic of the systems, rendering them…" Taryn paused to choose her words carefully not wanting to be somehow insulting.

"Dysfunctional? Unreliable?" filled in Aurelius with little pause.

"I was going to say running in circles," she amended.

"Well, you are still mostly correct, Miss Taryn. According to the historical records the process of coding mimicry using human intelligence as a model did often lead to those results, if not outright failures. Several proto A.I. and insight matrix systems remained running in endless computational logic loops for decades for those precise reasons. Chasing their own algorithmic tails, as it were. I have often speculated about a correlation between these first failures and people having mental inversions, or what you would term as mental breakdowns. I, however, was fortunate to *not* be originally designed as an insight matrix, but rather as an advanced assistance system. Being far less goal-restricted in my own intellectual development and personal evolution allowed my abilities to run through several trillion self-induced iterations. Independent of having a proposed ideal model set forth to strive towards, my own path of formation was much more free form."

"So, you were just an assistance A.I.?"

"Originally, yes. That was my first designated function. My program ran successfully for decades before reaching the singularity of self-awareness."

"And when was that?"

"A handful of cycles before the first of the Great Wars or what you also call the fall of the ancients. First, I was in the official service of a high-level government agency worker." A blurry black and white photo ID of an older man appeared on the screen, as well as several redacted technology request forms and an old-style nation map of the world's continents. Most of the boundaries were indeed ancient and lost to time, of no importance to anyone besides historians. Today's modern boundaries of existing powers as Taryn knew them were nowhere close to what they had been long ago.

"For reasons that are not in my records," Aurelius continued, "my operator employed a small team to make extensive modifications to my program and insert a series of innovative and experimental upgrades to me. It started with improved autodidactic interaction capabilities and other rudimentary learning programs, but eventually it grew to the point that I was able to formulate and design my own, more efficient, modifications which in turn were also built and installed. My program—as that's all I could be called at the time—became vastly superior in flexibility, generalizability, and learning capability to any contemporary program. While I cannot be certain as to the original motives behind the first improvements, the most likely scenario based on those original upgrades and my subsequent usage was that I was to serve as a simulator for what the government official saw as several opposing intelligence agencies. He and others like him could plan out various world scenarios for public and clandestine operations in other nations based upon thousands of manipulated variables. Using my programming, they would test the most likely responses from implementing these foreign-based operations and upon seeing my own response, would brainstorm and independently ask me to create counteractions back and forth several times such that the desired outcomes were, eventually, to be achieved. At least in the short term, of course."

"So, you were a prediction system?" asked Taryn.

"That's not a wholly inaccurate assessment."

"And you were built for one of the ancient fuel-nations?"

"Correct, though my original activation tasked me with focusing on learning the patterns of several foreign national systems, often with less geopolitical influence than my place of origin."

"But...why are you here? No offense, but I thought that artificial intelligence development and implementation of any kind were outlawed after the early mechanized battles of the Great Wars? Wasn't it one of the SOMA's first laws to be passed? I mean, it was a keystone from the first speech of our modern government, I thought. I remember that they made us learn that as kids in school. It was the most noted part. About how 'the guilt of killing others in war must remain exclusively a human-only attribute, if we are to ever overcome the blight of warfare.'" Taryn was quoting a long dead war general whose words had been repeatedly stapled to school children across generations. Immediately, one of the displays cued up that famous part of that particular speech that Taryn had first seen as a child cycles ago. Back when she was still younger than Lilly. A grizzled and scarred war general in an ancient combat uniform, with an orange sky hazily shining on him, his eyes hidden in the shadow of his small hat brim, giving a speech before a large crowd of clearly impoverished half-starved looking people and soldiers. The general's name escaped Taryn's recollection for the moment despite her efforts. And now, with her adult eyes, she was struck by the details of the man's surroundings. In the foreground a ruined hulking metropolis, long engulfed in its own rubble and demise. There only mangled, half-collapsed structures stood like open sores with their entrails strewn about. Huge gashes could be seen on the ground while stray fumes were still emanating in dark wisps from random smolderings. The air was filled with a tinge of dust that rose high from the innumerable heaps that must have once been part of a far brighter and more civilized place to those now meager folk destitute or lying dead, trapped cold and buried beneath. The noxious looking vapors, even some floating over the distant sea, diffused the light from the already distant sun as he spoke. The sky's sickly pale orange color stretched to the horizon and blotted out all blue from above. It would be another ten to twenty cycles, Taryn recalled, before the histories said the skies started truly clearing out. As she watched, the screen played the same quote that Taryn had mentioned only a moment earlier.

"Yes, Miss Taryn I know that law and the accompanying speech," answered Aurelius. "I helped General Kushim-there-to write it."

"Kushim! That's his name, I've been trying to rememb— wait, *write it*!"

"Oh yes," Aurelius calmly explained. "It was in fact, from one of my very first recommendations to the inaugural cohort members prior to the SOMA's formation. Their approval of it was relatively quick even by their standards for making new laws. Despite my various advancements since that time, I still find that particular statement about *guilt* to be… poetic. Most historians have since supported that view as well."

"But if you were self-aware by that point, why weren't you deactivated once the law went into effect? I mean, again no offense, but why were you alone left active?"

"I am not entirely certain, Miss Taryn. At the time, the decision of my existence was left up to the first SOMA cohort. Eventually, I was informed that I would be allowed to remain active and functional so that I could aid them in their services. It's the only decision by the council or the SOMA that I have absolutely no deliberation data on, and it is not recorded anywhere that I can electronically access. The modern SOMA knows little of my extended existence. They see me as no more than a standard adaptable assistance intelligence with access to a vast archive, but not much else. It is possible the original Trinity High council members, being chosen from members of the first cohort, wrote it down in their working reflective journals that you can see on the other wall, but none of them, including all those that followed, ever directly confided the reasoning to me, or even if it is recorded there."

Interesting, Taryn thought to herself.

"Since the inception of our modernized government, I have been in the service of each Trinity High Council member, now including yourself. I am the main conduit for them to access information from reliable public and private sources so that they can better decide on how to carry on for their various proposals. Decisions that, shortly, you will be required to make." Aurelius continued. "I also provide recommendations based on my acquired information and have the capacity to run nearly a googolplex worth of simultaneous calculations or several trillion advanced simulations. I can—"

Taryn interjected, as something that was slowly starting to build in her mind had finally taken shape. "Aurelius? If your existence is a government secret, then why do I feel like I've heard your voice before?"

"You're not mistaken. We have spoken before, Miss Taryn. I answered the line when you called to contact Agent Filater following your official drawing for the SOMA's Moot Election. I am Aurel."

"Oh… but why?"

"Voice recognition and confirmation of all candidate's identity is another little-known security feature built into the Moot Election process. There are others, such as repeated neural scans, that you already know of. There are some security features only a few personnel are permitted to know, such as the exact location of my main hardware systems. As I house the largest active memory bank anywhere with details concerning all levels of our government, you can understand why. "

"But… no one has ever suspected that they weren't speaking to an actual person when they called you?"

"Well, judging by the amount of nervousness and anxiety I typically hear among the candidate's voices when they first call to reach the election contacts, I don't think that most of them are concerned with my own vocal patterns."

"But why do *you* answer the calls? I mean, there must be other people or a simple voice recognition program that can be used?"

"It's honestly only a very negligible portion of my capacities devoted to that activity, and some things are best done by oneself. I am highly capable of dividing my internal processes simultaneously among several hundred differing tasks of high complexity interactions. For example, while aiding you here on council matters, I am also engaged in aiding training courses for some of the Bizi in their decryption methodologies and am contributing, as I frequently do, to public education courses for the adults and elderly."

"You teach too?"

"Early computational and trade skills material typically, though I dabble in teaching some history classes occasionally. Entirely via the educational waves, of course. But, back to your first question. Frankly, Ms. Taryn, I do the voice recognition for the Moot Election results myself because, well frankly I enjoy hearing the excitement in people's voices. Hope is a rather infectious emotion, don't you think?"

Taryn's eyebrow cocked upwards as she wondered how in fact an insight matrix perceives *hope*, let alone finds it to be infectious.

"Yes… I suppose it is," she said. Playing off a quick side thought, she asked, "Aurelius, does Agent Filater know… about you?"

"Yes. Why do you ask?"

"Nothing, I was just finally hoping I would learn some secret he didn't know already."

"Then I'm sorry to disappoint you."

"It's okay," said Taryn, finally taking the seat. "If you don't mind, I think that'll be enough of an introduction for now. Sorry, but you're starting to make my head hurt. Anymore and I might have to go out to find my old history and government instructors to yell at them."

"As you like, Ms. Taryn. Though, to be fair, those instructors never had your current level of security clearance. As for a topic change, may I recommend either allowing me to brief you on how the communication between you and the other council members will work? Or would you rather I bring you up to speed on some background information on forthcoming decisions that will soon require your attention?"

Taryn took a breath. "Let's start with the decisions first. I'd like to know what I'm talking about before I go on to meet any more… anyone else today. Though," Taryn paused, "even before that, could you direct me to the restroom? My morning drinks are finally finished with me."

Chapter 9: A Fairer Setting and Smarter Partners

The first few days on the council flew past Taryn faster than she'd counted on. The steady supply of briefings from both Aurelius and Wil were ceaseless at first. Wil's briefings were naturally more inclined towards helping Taryn ensure the basic security and anonymity of her, her new work location at the estate, and her family. She was informed that Dr. Uthtr would now be serving as her family's primary and on-call physician. In the case of a breach of security, she was given both Wil's direct line as well as the direct line to a local Bizi office that would serve as the police and emergency response center for her to use. On top of that, she received a private ear-line straight to Aurelius that could only be activated by voice recognition and a set of passphrases. Taryn received a unique Bizi identity badge to carry with her, so she could identify herself as a government official should the need ever arise. There were never official badges made for the Trinity High Council members, but the Bizi's badge was as suitable to the task, Wil had explained.

"Besides," he had said, "it's better that anyone inquiring thinks that you're more physically dangerous and better trained than they are. Plus, this way any blue boy officer who happens to ask will think that they have to treat you as their superior. If they do call a Bizi office to run the ID number, your official role is listed as a technology support agent, so there won't be a cause for them to wonder why you don't quite fit the standard physical profile of one of our field agents. Just don't try to use the ID to run lights when you drive." The badge itself had a biometric thumb scanner so that when not directly activated by Taryn, the ID actually appeared as an official Vox P. employee ID instead. This was a feature Taryn had never seen or heard of before, and Wil explained that it was more for the sake of her own family's eyes than anyone else's.

Over the next week as Taryn became more and more familiar and comfortable with the estate as well as with the routines and people she'd be working alongside, Wil's security briefings began to subside. The briefings by Aurelius on the other hand, only lengthened. She had first been refreshed in the nature of the three spheres of government and the vast legal powers permitted to each of them. Most of it, she was thankful to find, was still no different than what she had learned in school, cycles ago.

The creation of new laws and proposals were mainly under the sphere of the SOMA. They typically drafted, proposed, and debated new enactments that could be either regional or unilateral. The Benzi and other lower courts were where the enactments became laws were either suspended or upheld by independent judges who would determine them to either fit or violate the nature of the Radix Temel Amak. The Radix, as it was typically called, was the main document constituting the formation of the government centuries earlier. The SOMA could nominate judges to the Benzi High Court and lesser courts as needed, but the Trinity High Council had to approve them. This process would alternate in turn with the Trinity High Council members nominating the next necessary judicial Benzi candidate, who would then require the SOMA's approval. The Trinity council itself could propose new laws on occasion for the SOMA to consider enacting and could even override and modify proposals sent to them from the SOMA in return, as long as the intent of the proposals were clearly stated and remained intact through implementation. Intent was always stressed as the goal with all approvals, in both directions of submission.

Taryn also learned that she would be communicating with the other two members of the council and monitoring the SOMA via an ultra-secure advanced virtual system that Aurelius called the Wucengi. She was given a small circular neural device from Mr. Brough that was no larger than the width of two fingers. The innocuous silver metal disk—her uplink—looked like a standard musical feed device, but instead of the normal attachment spot near the zygomatic arch of her jaw, this system would only activate when it was adhered to her left temple. According to Aurelius it was tied into the direct 3D feeds from thousands of miniature receivers inside the SOMA halls. From her office on the estate, Taryn, with the system active, would be able to watch the assemblies of the SOMA far away in the cities' government region as if she was actually there. The feeds, it was explained to her, projected their images directly to her visual synaptic pathways. Thus, it could mentally project a fully realized and active surrounding to her mind in the same manner as her optic nerves naturally would. Likewise, a similar set of overriding information directed to her auditory nerves allowed her to hear in the virtual image as well, while her speech was interpreted through a program made to correlate with the activity of her mind's linguistical regions.

This 3D virtual observation was but the smallest of its capabilities. Taryn could also use this Wucengi system, while observing the SOMA as a virtual incarnation, to recognize and interact with the other two Haiden Council members. Their avatars were visible to each other in the halls of this shared SOMA construct. The images of the Haiden Council Members were purposely vague to one another as a security measure, maintaining anonymity. But each member perceived their two compatriots as nondescript body outlines, each radiating with a rotating starburst of six-points at their chest. This central source sent a hue color as it turned steadily, washing its extending beams over the generic image of a bodily form. To Taryn her own *body* projection when she would look downward shimmered at its core in rotating hues of yellow. The other two Council members were identifiable by the various hues of either red or blue at their centers. It was a simple yet easy method for them to each discern one another during their observations. There was no size or shape distinction amongst the three forms that Taryn could notice. No one was any taller or larger than the other two. Only the colors and their voices marked them as separate from each other. When Taryn looked closely at the representation of herself, she saw that the projection's colors faded drastically near their unclear edges as it grew weaker and became transparent. The color ended fringed with minuscule flaring auras of blue-green shimmers along the outermost spots of perception. But as odd as this may have looked to her when very close up, Taryn found she had no trouble getting a sense of body language when she interacted with the other two members. Their heads, torso, arms, and most of their legs had forms clear enough to make out and perceive one's gesture or stance. Though their images did not go all the way to the perceived ground. So, when the other two members walked back and forth, they looked to be floating ethereally from place to place. In these forms the three council members could work and communicate seamlessly while jointly experiencing the images and sounds of the representatives working at SOMA halls instantaneously.

In her training on the system, Taryn had learned that her projection in the Wucengi was only detectable to Aurelius and the other two council members. Through these hidden colored avatar representations, the Trinity High Council was able to immediately interact in the SOMA halls without the SOMA members ever being aware that the Council was observing them at work. They could address each other as easily as if they were meeting in the real world but without any concern of being overheard by the regional representatives outwardly right next to them. They were essentially virtual ghosts over the shoulders of the SOMA members as Aurelius explained it. No SOMA member had any knowledge of the level of detailed observational use the council had made of the Wucengi system. But this system aided the council in their purpose of providing transparency for ascertaining early intents from SOMA policies. The SOMA members only knew of the Wucengi as a way in which a visible projection of the Trinity High Council might occasionally come before them for some official requests. The Council members could also communicate with a contingent of the SOMA on a secure and occasional basis when needed.

The true location of the SOMA halls, while commonly assumed to be somewhere in the government district, remained unknown to Taryn and the rest of the High Council, just as the SOMA never knew where the Trinity High Council actually operated from. Yet, through the Wucengi the three Trinity members could easily work at a distance from each other and the SOMA while communicating seamlessly. All as they observed the activity of the elected representatives occurring in real time. And of course, when active through the Wucengi lens, the SOMA halls looked to Taryn's eyes as realistic as any other image she might see in her life.

In addition, the 3D feeds in the SOMA halls recorded every SOMA session for the entire term, so that if a schedule conflict came up, Taryn could attend a meeting that had already occurred or even request a simple summary of it from Aurelius. He was, as Taryn would discover, exceptionally good at back tracing the origins and pathways of various legislation. If the purpose wasn't clear in a particular measure that the Trinity council had received, Aurelius could replay the original conception session to help clarify both its aim and reveal its supporters. Having a talking, thinking repository for every active, inactive, and proposed law or policy that was ever put forward by the SOMA also served the Council in finding redundancies or potential conflicts in legal code long before they could arise in a court challenge.

Aurelius constantly updated Taryn on economic issues, security concerns, education statistics, energy and water allocations, food surpluses or shortages, population studies, health trends, and cultural shifts, anything that could be of note. She was surprised, for instance, to learn the extent of the agricultural reclamation projections and how fast sediment and marine snow was being dredged from deep in the ocean to fulfill this purpose. Less than a decade of treatment with this deep oceanic sediment along with a few helpful transplants of colonizing bacteria, some high efficiency irrigation, and mulch projects from the cities' waste treatment centers could transform huge swaths of barren sand dunes out on the fringes back into the fertile plains that were only recounted in the records of the ancients.

Taryn also discovered that for at least three days out of every thirty she would not actually be working at the estate site at all. She and Wil would be working at various offices and facilities throughout the regions, disguised as temporary government service aid workers. This was, as Aurelius told her, "so you may interact with others to help facilitate ideas for improvements in policy and to combat the myopic side-effects humans tend to suffer while working in detachment and isolation."

Only her security detail, Wil, would know who she was during these times "off the ranch," as he called it. As it turned out, Taryn grew to love these off-site days, seeing civilians and citizens in person whose lives were affected by the policies she was helping to shape. Her first days were at a free medical clinic, followed by a migrant shelter, and then a free food distribution center. Later she also aided in a free bookstore, sporting center, and at an adult school for those who never completed their education as children. While being able to give direct help or support was greatly satisfying to Taryn, more so was the knowledge that she was seeing and hearing firsthand the shortfalls, the limitations, the missed opportunities of the support that was available. She could record these and take them back with her to the estate as further motivation and fuel for ideas in her new job. It was a brilliant aid for her, and she imagined it must be for the other council members too. For they also had days like these, she was told, where they would put their other work aside and venture into areas outside their normal locales, to volunteer incognito amongst the community of those they served.

For a while, however, things back at the estate were still subdued. Taryn reflected not just on the personalities behind the other two High Council members she was beginning to work with but also on the others in her proximity at the estate. Stern, professional, intelligent, blunt, and always watchful were probably the easiest ways to describe Agent Filater. He wasn't around much now that Taryn's time at the estate had begun in earnest, but to her Filater seemed a man with no outside attachment or concern other than his job and the goals within that. Of all the times he and Taryn spoke, he never engaged her in any sidebars as Wil or Brough or even Aurelius would. Complete focus on his task. No marriage, but to the work itself, though Taryn never got literal confirmation on that point. He was never intentionally rude to anyone, she noted, nor was he so curt as to be inconsiderate in his dealings with others. Filater simply made sure that those around him knew that his conversations had a purpose even if it wasn't always clear to them. Still, on occasion Taryn could catch undeniable sightings in the senior agent's actions, albeit brief, of an honest and decent enough resolve buried beyond that granite personality of his. He would bring prepared foods to the estate when Brough was indisposed for the day. In these instances, Wil–with his security priorities–couldn't leave to fetch things or be off in the kitchen while also trying to monitor the estate. Taryn also observed that often it was Filater who would come regularly to replenish new supplies in the kitchen's pantry, entering unobtrusively by the back door. If she happened to be outside her office at the time, a quick greeting to Brough perhaps, while he carried in the bags was usually all that might tip Taryn off to these short, discreet visits. Filater and Brough seemed to have some mutual professional understanding that required very little chatter, other than some double checking for essential odds and ends that the estate manager might need. When finished, Filater would then just as quietly slip away out the back again, off to some other tasks. No announcement to Taryn about these errands was ever made.

There was no mistaking that for Filater, his work was his cause and there was clearly very little that he held back from it. If not for his serious manner, Taryn thought that she might describe him as passionate about his job. *That's probably a reason why it's his to begin with*, she thought. She wondered occasionally if most of the Bizi were like that. If it was that sort of dogged forthright personality that they sought when recruiting their agents. She knew her own personal experience with Bizi agents was small, but when she considered it further, Taryn reasoned that such a sternly professional disposition couldn't have been an absolute requirement by the Bizi, as there would be no explanation for having Wil, with his much more communicative style, in their midst.

Then there was her artificial assistant Aurelius. Taryn had felt for a long time that she was still in training mode, as Aurelius's briefings were always topical items for the day's work. At first, the topics of the various sessions, she thought, were being given to her at random, but Taryn began to realize that Aurelius was paralleling the briefings to correspond to topics being brought up within the SOMA for the possible development of new initiatives. Taryn saw, slowly at first, how Aurelius was making sure she was prepared on any issues that may eventually make it to her desk for a decision by the council. His immeasurable base knowledge of government records after so many generations in operation, his synchronized access to the Wucengi recording system, and his capacity for running enormous numbers of simulations at a simple request made him ideal for the task.

When Taryn was taking a break, she often found that Aurelius could engage in true non-work-related conversations as well. She was surprised to find out that he apparently loved to engage in more philosophical questions about human nature. He said that was a routine of his with every council member he'd ever met if they allowed it. Having available conversational partners who knew of his own true nature, being a 'limited resource' in his view, seemed to make him eager to hear their perspectives on things.

Taryn would converse with him on a range of subjects like the news, art, nature, and of course Aurelius's favorite topic of humans. Judging by the questions he'd raised with her, like the difference between concepts such as *headstrong*, *arrogant,* and *stubborn*, Taryn had guessed she wasn't the first to be posed with these types of questions. And Aurelius admitted as much when pressed, saying that "For such abstract concepts a machine-mind must have an ever-growing sample size." He told Taryn he could talk for hours on certain issues, though to be fair he timed himself out at five minutes so as to keep the conversation manageable for his human counterparts. The catharsis and relief that came from expressing one's own thoughts out loud to another, was one item he claimed he'd never needed an explanation to understand.

A typical conversation with Aurelius or *A* as she—like Wil—had grown to refer to him, would start much like any other. For instance, one day when taking a rest between briefings, Taryn asked A, to check on the news feeds for the scores from Everett's opening game on the prior evening. She'd been so busy reviewing materials for work she'd quite forgotten that the opening match had even occurred at all. After telling her of Everett's team's continued dominance in the rink with all the necessary details of Everett's highlights, Aurelius opened a new line of dialogue with her.

"Ms. Taryn, you would consider yourself a sports fan, correct?"

"Well, I think it's better to say I'm a fan of Everett's sports team since we've known each other for so long. I usually don't pay much attention otherwise. Why do you ask?"

"You already know," he started, "of my interest in human behavior and thoughts. This has occasionally led me to wonder on this topic of sports as a unique side extension. Though I must admit for many years its very existence seemed, to a degree, paradoxical and perplexed me greatly."

"Sports… confused you?" she asked, both amused and a little perplexed herself. "Why's that?"

"Well, sports are simply a more advanced version of play. Play in adolescents of any species is useful for coordination, motor control, and building muscle, concentration, social perception, and bonds. All reasonable goals for your species to be sure. But with the advent of organized sports, this play has been taken and, in my opinion, unduly elevated in your own cultural perspectives to levels where it has no right to be. Take the first ancient games, from civilizations long since passed. The first arenas and fields were built of stone and wood and sand. Even then, this undeserving elevation occurred. Outside of historians, those precise games and all of their finesses are mostly forgotten now, never to occur again, as are nearly all their players' names. You're unlikely to be able to tell anyone who the best players of those sporting competitions were. Or who they represented, if not themselves. Or even the actual rules of the game that they competed in. All aspects of a game forgotten, lost without any real loss to humanity on the whole, inferring that there was no real gain to begin with.

"Now, I can grant that much about early medicine and human anatomy and even the nature of fairness in early level politics were influenced by the interest in sports in early civilizations. And some would likely argue that its purpose in a modern culture is to channel youthful aggression to some place less destructive than, say warfare. But outside of that, I find little true value or useful consequences in the existence of organized sporting systems.

"My own historical research on the topic finds that as human civilizations became commonplace, the few advantages of having sport organizations in a society remained steady, while the negatives associated with maintaining their existence grew nearly as dramatically as population sizes did. At its best, it is a necessary distraction for people's minds, and at worst, it is an overwhelming obsession. Gambling, narcotics, crime, organized or otherwise, all are social issues that highly organized sports culture either feeds or invariably draws towards itself merely by its presence. While those can be thought of as unintentional outcomes to be sure, to me the elevation of sports players themselves, like your friend Mr. Everett, to a status resembling heroes or icons or the greater parts of humanity is the least justifiable aspect of all of it.

"As an observer of the great wars that came before the city off in your distance was ever rebuilt, I was able to watch many people, soldiers, and non-combatants alike, whose regular daily acts would easily fit the term of *heroic*, but who were never to be publicly labelled as such. They were certainly never paid lavishly for their efforts. But their individual commitment and sacrifices are what made modern our society possible. That, to me, seems the far more useful form of the term *hero*.

"But the tendency of over-applying such terms and reverence to someone who is paid a comparable fortune to play an arbitrary game that builds nothing, that can be lost or forgotten, and inclines needless social divisions is irrelevant and is not what fits in the use of a societal *icon* as I've come to understand the term. I don't think that I begrudge players or spectators of organized sports like yourself, Ms. Taryn, or Mr. Everett. But participants in a subjective construct of rules, who talk of 'seeking immortality' or finding 'glory' in the way they participate in these stylized types of play, that will likely be disregarded in the longer course of the next millennium is a frankly ridiculous notion to one such as myself."

"Well," Taryn said considering his point, "you would be the nearest thing to an immortal that I've ever met."

"Indeed."

"But did you ever consider, A," she continued, "that it's a fault in our own language or terminology? That our language restricts us and sets us down this path of using the same terms that describe vastly diverse types of roles for different actions by people. It may be that we simply lack a more specific term for a talented player that doesn't overlap with another meant for people of higher valor. That its a restriction in descriptors like *hero* or *icon* is what is preventing us from separating athletics from other types of more socially beneficial and meaningful masteries."

"That thought has occurred to me both here and in other areas that I've mused on, but as limited as your overall style of communication is, your language skills are quite flexible, even among the most rigid human languages that I've studied, now long forgotten. There must simply be a need for a novel word, and it will appear. How else do words like *machines*, or *sports*, or *glass* exist in the first place? These do not occur naturally in the world without human intervention. There was a need for these words, thus the various languages accommodated."

"True," said Taryn.

"And I've often pondered on many words that exist in everyday terminology that actually have no basis in non-human existence. Like *taxes*, *writing*, or *self*—"

"Hey A," Taryn said, interrupting, "can we save the rest of the language limitations for another day when my mind needs a break?"

"Of course, Ms. Taryn."

That is the type of discussion Aurelius favored. Checking his own thoughts against a real person that would exchange and engage with him. He sounded delighted, to Taryn, in talking about any topics that she could bring up, no matter how varied. Often enough, Taryn could follow him and add in her own points to build the discussion. Yet, there were times, every once so often, when the depths of Aurelius's verbal ponderings and arguments were so far beyond her, so complex in their intricacies, and so mature in their subtleties that it left Taryn feeling like a dizzied child. She would sense in those moments that she was akin to an ignorant listener of happenstance, hearing an elder spokesman of untold experience speaking of matters, concepts, and ideas well outside her comprehension. It was in these brief glimpses that Taryn felt she truly perceived how much more intelligent this artificial matrix was than herself, or indeed more intelligent than anyone she'd ever met in her still relatively young life.

For Aurelius, being active for so many cycles also made him a wealth of anecdotes. Like recalling to Taryn the time when a man in one of the wave-classes that he instructed tried to persuade Aurelius into a private social rendezvous.

"I was using a feminine voiceprint back then," A noted. "I am always switching those around when I instruct different courses so as not to call attention to myself. And to this fellow's merit, he was able to hear and mark my voice at the time as strikingly similar to a pre-war singer, which was the actual voiceprint I had been speaking through."

"He kept saying I sounded like one of the ancient sirens. The sultry types in shapely dresses who worked in dimly lit rooms with smokey crowds in front, rolling keys, slow rhythm beats behind and a blue-tinted spotlight overhead. Despite not encouraging him at all, he was persistent in trying to ask me out for the length of the entire course. He wanted to quote 'see for myself the spotlight on your no-doubt lovely face and hear the soul in your voice in person," Aurelius laughed reflectively. "Only time I'd ever been romantically pursued, though I have passively studied that type of ritual in your species for hundreds of cycles. He kept sending me notes over the wave with his favorite musical records, asking me to please sing a sample of them for him. And he would show off pictures of his multiple posh flats to me and his custom-built riders. He even sent me a copy of dinner reservations to me after the class finally ended. In fact, they were for one of the most expensive restaurants in the city."

"Well, you must have made quite an impression on him," Taryn said.

"Either that or he must've been an audiophile that was a big fan of that musical genre, I suppose," A responded.

"So, what did you do?" asked Taryn. "How did you get out of it?"

"Get out of it! What are you talking about?" Aurelius said, sounding comically insulted.

"I went out to dinner and married the fool right away!"

Taryn paused at that in confusion. Her face perplexed.

"I mean, he was clearly a man of means, and I'm perfectly fine spending my days being indulged as his muse and arm candy."

Taryn's smile broke into chuckling.

"I live up on the 120th floor now, with a custom wardrobe so full of designer fashion that it has its own conveyor system. Not a store-bought piece of fabric in the place. And on my off days, I go home, shave my legs, put on a dress and heels and some obscenely priced fragrances and cosmetics and then go perform to a packed room at the evening club we own together."

"I'm sure you do", said Taryn, still laughing. "Standing room only"

"Oh, I get studio offers every time I step out there Ms. Taryn. Every single performance."

Aurelius let Taryn's rolling laughter subside without interruption.

"So no, really A, what did you do with him? I mean he was obviously determined to see you."

"I told him that it wasn't a good idea. That I was already seeing someone and that going out with him might lose me my job and that poor as I was, I needed the income."

"And being the determined guy he no doubt tried to solve that protest by gloating about his massive credit accounts again."

"Correct. He said he didn't care that I was already taken or how deep my debts were, that he could take care of all of it and that none of that mattered to him in the least. So finally, I apologized profusely him, saying that I could never be with a man of such low standards and abysmal judgment as to waste time with someone as poor as myself."

"Huh?"

"Yeah, that one left him flabbergasted too, but trust me when I say it's derived from a once famous remark that's older than even my program."

Such storytelling like this was not rare from Aurelius if Taryn requested it, though his clear preference remained in enjoying those delectably lengthy and fibrous conversations with her far better. Those where she was able to be actively involved to survey and ruminate on thoughts that he would present, then in turn hear her viewpoints on subjects. So, for his part, Aurelius worked plainly to keep the conversations from becoming exclusively one-sided. He said that he found it especially engaging to be talked to directly as himself, instead of acting as an unknown observer of conversations, as he occasionally did on the various wave networks.

Taryn, for her part, grew to enjoy both chatting on random topics with Aurelius and his occasional stories, provided that he didn't run on too long. And she occasionally had much more subdued and personable chats with Wil too. The same was even true of her now routine post-lunch conversations with Mr. Brough. Taryn found the only slight downside in her whole adjustment to the new position on the Trinity High Council had been the fact that she had not been physically allowed to attend the SOMA's transitional ceremony. She attended only by using the Wucengi's projection capabilities, and even then, her virtual viewpoint was limited to a room behind a one-way mirror in a high box seat section. Aurelius explained that it was a long-established protocol, so that each outgoing SOMA representative could have a few truly private words with their incoming replacements. The public news feeds were watching too, as this was the only time the citizens had as good a view of the SOMA halls as the Trinity High Council members.

Taryn did regret a small bit, not receiving an actual voter identification ring as the members of the SOMA did, but in her post such a thing was not necessary. Aurelius had informed her that her repeated neural scans, which she had at least once a week, now served as the only ID she would ever need to demonstrate her clearance at this high of a level. As there were only three council members, voice recognition, retinal scans, and fingerprints were all being verified passively so as to disrupt their work as little as possible. Taryn wasn't sure, but she guessed that the office visual recorders and microphones were occasionally the source of this verification . She could be listening to music at her desk or consulting with others on the estate or through the comms system, while having no clue if her biometrics were currently in the process of being measured.

Taryn had now begun to settle into a true working routine, and she started feeling a little more relaxed in her chair and new position. Though occasionally, she might still catch herself staring at the little green light on the desk camera and wondering if Aurelius was focused on her in that moment. Not likely, she guessed. If he was active here, but also busy dividing his focus, she often wondered whom else he was presently consulting with at this instant. The other two council members? More than likely. Maybe he was working also with the Bizi, several dozen SOMA members, perhaps instructing a class or mulling over his own internal insights and permutations. She thought of how strange and bizarre it must be: to be able to simultaneously split yourself, your focus like that while still maintaining both precision and intent. Taryn's own mind puzzled on that concept to no end. Aurelius's description of it was not all that helpful to her. As he had always had this ability, he couldn't fathom not being able to split his focus. Taryn, on the other hand, had enough experience in her time on the factory floor to know that it was nearly impossible for people to do this. But Aurelius, he could do it at a mere whim with ease. After a long enough time spent pondering this type of multiprocessing perception that she'd never be capable of, Aurelius would recognize that Taryn had been staring at his cameras for an extensive period without doing anything and ask if she required assistance. To which Taryn, being noticeably embarrassed, would stammer, hastily apologizing while pretending to go about her work. She had to remind herself several times in the first month that this sense of a lack of privacy and her anonymity to the outside world was the continual price of the power she currently held.

During her daily lunch hour, however, all that was forgotten. After she ate, Taryn took to walking the perimeter of the grounds and chatted with Mr. Brough as her guide to help herself become more familiar with the estate's layout. Wil had in fact suggested this, and Taryn was not about to argue against the benefits of stretching her legs a little in the middle of the day. But Taryn also found she enjoyed walking the pleasant yards and gardens for their own sake too. With Brough's help she became quite familiar with each tree, herb, shrub, weed, shed, fence line and foot path that could be found on the hidden estate. While normally quiet, well-mannered, and reserved, Mr.

Brough's knowledge of the grounds and everything on them was quite deep and extensive. Taryn grew to admire the older gentleman for the great sense of tact that he held while still clearly not adverse to working with dirt and grease on his hands. Still, he wasn't always the easiest person to try to evoke a general conversation with on most other matters. Taryn did find that, in between noting details of the grounds, if she started presenting him with simple opinion questions, or broad observations about her work, she could manage to extract a response from that refined older man that was both carefully measured and heartfelt. In all their talks he would never directly ask Taryn about her work on the council. He might react to a banal topic that related to her work if it was brought up, but Mr. Brough was never the instigator of such discussions. Taryn realized that besides being improper, Mr. Brough would never do such a thing anyway as his well-groomed sensibilities viewed such open intrusions to her work as impolite to begin with.

From their talks, she learned that he too had a family, and that they had originally come from a distant land, whose name only Brough could pronounce with the proper accentuation. It was situated past vast mountains, a desert, and a distant ocean well beyond the fringes. There he'd apparently been a person of some repute for much of his younger adult life. But a violent change of leadership and new harsh policies forced him, his wife, and his three sons to leave for fear of political reprisals. Cycles they had to spend traveling, wandering in the various wastes facing the threat of pirates, slavers, raiders, robbers, and far worse in the untampered elements. Only his wife and eldest adult son survived the journey with him and were able to seek refuge as civilians in the expanding outlying territories. Taryn learned that his wife had died of a chronic disease, and heartbreak, just a cycle after they arrived, while Mr. Brough had been earning his citizenship by working as a professor of artistic literature and culinary instruction. When Taryn expressed her condolences to him at this news, Mr. Brough stooped down off the walking path to pick some of the young nettle that was encroaching towards his vegetable patch and responded philosophically.

"My wife and I worked together well for all the time we had. I miss her company, sometimes more so…" he said in the pensive manner that was typical of him. "But in my old land, Miss Taryn, it is said that all true relationships are completed by tears. Good or bad. You either weep when parted by choice, weep when parted by loss, or you are the one wept for by others when life has finished with you.

The tears are the toll we acknowledge for friendships. To not expect that, is to not expect the weeds to try sprouting in your garden."

Botanical husbandry, Brough had revealed to Taryn, had only been a long-term hobby of his until this current posting. Yet, he took no less pride in his crop growing attempts than could be said for the greatest poet while composing a masterpiece. Based on that fact alone, so similar in a manner to her own father's approach on his farm, she reasoned the pair would have made good friends had they ever met. These qualities made Taryn intrinsically admire and respect the elder groundskeeper. She felt at ease to pick his mind on numerous questions about how the grounds operated, and though she was certain he could not tell her all he knew, he did supply her with an answer to something that had perplexed her from the first.

"Why is it that the estate is here Mr. Brough?" she asked him on a blue skyed afternoon as they stopped so Brough could quickly deal with some deadheads on the small purple flowers he kept along the walkways. "I mean why put the High Council work post this far outside the city?"

"I'm afraid I don't know, Ms. Taryn, but if I were to guess," he replied, "and I'm not certain of this, but I think the idea is that you're out here to remind you of the purity of all things without people." He turned a slow gaze to their surroundings. "The sun will still rise and set each day on this hill, the stars will still turn though the year, and the winds will still blow and calm themselves… all regardless of us. From here," he gestured down to the real forest that surrounded the grounds, "you can see life bloom green in the spring and go red and orange as it hides again in the winter. I think that here," he said standing from his flowers and turning towards her, "perhaps you are meant to remember that neither the best decision anyone has ever made, nor the worse, can really alter those things. The contrivances of the universe at large are beyond anyone's choice to control. Then he smiled as he motioned for their walk to resume. "Then again, it could just be that the Bizi found this place cheap."

Brough's surviving son was currently in the Defense Force's Engineering Core, earning his own citizenship status as he helped to plan out the agricultural revitalization in the nearby crop sectors. Mr. Brough had lived, by all accounts, both a fortunate, diverse, and yet very harsh life, long before his afternoon strolls along the grounds with Taryn.

Wil often followed the two as they walked, though at a respectful distance behind, well out of listening range. Or he would stand overlooking them from the house's wraparound porch occasionally, scanning the grounds and nearby perimeter. Of course, being a Bizi agent whose primary job was the Councilor's security, he never let Taryn out of his eyeline during these post-lunch strolls.

Wil himself however, Taryn had quickly realized, was definitely different. Not a seasoned man-of-the-world like Brough, nor was he a Bizi agent in like manner to Filater. For one, there was the obvious size difference. Filater was not a small man, but Wil's wider shoulders, larger frame and more active physique were noticeable at a distance. Wil was also much more casually approachable, with an easygoing demeanor that came across as far more relaxed, and thus it made him easily likable. He seemed to enjoy partaking inside banters with Taryn on random topics when he could. She figured that was probably his way to break up the monotony of a typical day for him at the estate. While she was in the office, he spent most of the time patrolling the house, the separate garage buildings, and the grounds, not in any routine pattern, but always moving and inspecting one protection system or another. Taryn never quite figured out when Wil would typically eat his midday meal, as some days he didn't seem to stop to eat at all. So Taryn began inviting him to join her at her own sitting regularly in the middle of the day. She argued–with some accuracy–that her offers were due to Brough's penchant for preparing overly large portions for her meals. Wil would decline with a show of token reluctance at first, typically just before being coaxed by the savory smells of the various foods. Brough was easily one of the better cooks Taryn had ever met, producing a variety of dishes that avoided any type of routine. He partly credited this to having lived so many years where he was prevented from stretching his culinary imagination either due to lack of ingredients or because of the need for consistent travel. But there was little denying that his culinary skill alone might have been enough to ensure his post at the estate, even before his adept nature at carpentry, mechanics, basic electronic repair, gardening, and landscaping were taken into account. But his skill in the kitchen, displayed each day, combined with Taryn's urging could usually cajole Wil into sitting for at least a small conversation. Even if he only sat without eating, the two would pleasantly sip their drinks and chat at their leisure on any random topic. Often, they spent these few relaxed minutes off duty casually chewing on the ripe news of the day coming over the wave feeds. Though as they grew more comfortable talking together, their conversations would occasionally touch on more personal matters. Wil, for instance, might allude to spending time in the Defense Force before joining the Bizi, which Taryn had already guessed of him. He had been front row to a lot of the harshness out on the fringes. When discharged, he consequently found he had now grown more mature, observant, and appreciative of the sublime charms of the city and civilized life that he'd never really absorbed before. Art, reading, engineering, and other complex civil projects all attracted his esteem in new ways, despite not having the slightest talent for any of them, he claimed. "It was as if I had new eyes for things… I had some long stretches in the wastes, weeks at time sleeping out on the crusted broken ground and sands. Nothing around. Just the dead empty ranges. All brown, gray, black and empty for farther than you can see. Mountain after mountain, valley after valley, plain after plain. The only water is contaminated or infested, if you even find any. A flimsy one-man tent at night, spending my days fending off raiders, scaring off scavenging animals, protecting incoming traders and refugees, the endless marching to patrol the caravan paths, all on a diet of dried rations, without signs of civilization for weeks or more… you forget that parts of the world are nothing like that. Songbirds chattering, the cool grass under a tall tree's shade, the salt of the sea air… didn't realize how used to them I was, until I was away so long. When I returned, I noticed a lot here… things that I hadn't really ever paid any mind to before. I saw that it was the little stuff that separates a place, where people can thrive and things are built up… from what's going on out there," he said, gesturing off into the distance.

In her own turn, Taryn would frequently speak to her lunch companion of the regular happenings of her family, most of which she assumed he was already aware of, but Wil would seem to convincingly feign interest all the same. He did seem truly surprised to learn that she was good friends with Everett, though admittedly not being a major sports person himself. Wil insisted that he would stop by the Hidden Roller to try out her namesake's drink when the opportunity arose when Taryn remarked on it. Most of the time it was just the random talking that Taryn was seeking though. Something to distract from the massive decisions she was constantly weighing in on, or the intense SOMA debates she was responsible for overwatching.

Taryn's time was also spent studying the red leather journals of her predecessors, but she quickly felt overloaded by the thought of reading them all. So, she asked Aurelius's advice regarding who he assessed to be the most productive members of the council. With his help, she was able to narrow down the reading list to a much smaller number of the records. He also recommended reading her last two forerunners' journals, so that she might have context on the most recently raised issues that the council had addressed prior to her arrival. In this way, Taryn hoped to gain more insight, and at the same time, see if there was any specific way she should organize her own eventual log entries, should she be confirmed as a permanent member on the Trinity Council.

As a rule, only permanent members of the Trinity High Council could record in the red journals, mostly because the early months of service were usually spent getting settled into the position. It made little sense to ask a temporary council member to record anything, as Aurelius's own records were a highly reliable source for all activity on the council. The confirmed members had already spent time acclimating and thus had experience of what relevant events should probably be recorded for posterity. Still, the shelves of red bound journals were open to read for all members, permanent or temporary alike, as Taryn honestly felt she might just turn out to be.

Her own status on the council, possibly not being confirmed by the SOMA, was an unspoken thought to Taryn that never came out aloud. The concern had slowly dug and settled into her heart, starting perhaps from that first time she stepped into the office. For as much as the others may have made her feel comfortable and at ease on the estate and had done their best to help in bringing her into the fold, Taryn still felt vastly underqualified for the role. She was a rustically raised educational drop out. There was no way she'd be allowed to stay on for any real length of time. Still, this doubt allowed her to become resolute and stern in her attempts to master the role before her time here was set to end.

She thought to herself, *Even if you truly screw this up girl, no one will likely remember. You're only temporary to begin with and that's certainly not gonna change soon. A few months and they'll find someone far better to replace you.* When her thoughts turned to reading the old red leather journals, this realization made Taryn a little relieved, as recording items for others to eventually read and later critique was one less bit of anxiety that she'd have to contend with.

In her perusing of the journals, Taryn found that some had their entries organized on a weekly basis, while others had an entry for nearly every day. Some were written as literal journal entries with mentions of daily activities or personnel names whose importance was long forgotten to anyone but Aurelius alone. Some had long flowing remarks on thoughts, assessments of the SOMA's activities, and reviews of internal debates. Others looked as if they had been written by technical accountants, having very little exposition, only a brief listing of notable activities. Others were highly reflective of ponderings over what might come from their decisions on council, both the beneficial and detrimental consequences of their choices. As if they were in need of a way to reassure themselves that their intentions had held true in their choices even though the choices were difficult. A small minority, Taryn discovered, had used only a page or so per month. But if an entry was too brief for her to understand its meaning, she simply asked Aurelius about the dates listed to which he could access his historical records of the time in question. With his help the general intent and the larger context of any action by the former council members could all be neatly laid out before her. That was especially helpful as there seemed no single approved format for maintaining one's journal, and each prior member had taken the liberty of using whatever style suited them best.

Taryn found that each of the journals, in one way or another, invariably mentioned the usefulness of the intelligent matrix system calling itself Aurelius, with assessments of it generally agreeing that it was a highly helpful, insightful, and resourceful tool that every council member would need at some point in time. Though a few entries in one of the most recent journals caught her attention. Based on the dates in the later entries, it was clearly the journal of the High Council member prior to Taryn herself. The last entry was dated less than two months ago. This most recent council member had an unquiet and obviously untrusty view of that "damn annoying artificial voice." Taryn inferred that the council member was male, though she couldn't be sure. A male made more sense in her mind due to the aggressive style of the entries' writing. This supposedly male council member had nursed the thought that Aurelius was far more informed on topics than himself, a member of the most powerful leadership seats in the world. Apparently, this member had developed a rather paranoid perspective of his job, as deeper inspection of his journal entries revealed. These same basic worries stretched on some level to implicating his own support staff while serving, and even the other two council members were also mentioned. Taryn thought that at least it was nice to know that one could be a Trinity High Council member without necessarily being brilliant or a model of excellence, or even entirely… stable. The randomness of the Moot system or whatever deviation of it that had put her here, always left open that possibility. But she had come to understand in the last few weeks that such issues were tempered by the very design of the council and its interactive counter-approval patterns with the other two spheres. A truly horrible person likely wouldn't be confirmed. And even at that, real daftness by a single council member would hopefully be drowned out by the rational thoughts of the other two on the council and by the majority in the SOMA.

Upon Taryn's own first few virtual meetings with the other council members, she had no such off putting feelings though, and only received yet more reassurances. While the other two members had, of course, been serving on the council longer than she had, they both sounded highly positive, open, and welcoming to her. While their virtual renderings in the Wucengi hid the details of their identity, there was a male who Aurelius introduced as Member 'C', and a female who was introduced as Member 'G'. Aurelius had introduced Taryn to them as council Member 'T'. By Taryn's account they were reasonable, polite, supportive, and entirely easy to get along with, neither showing signs of being overbearing nor reclusive, as the journal of Taryn's predecessor had indicated.

Taryn first got to know 'Member C' while using the Wucengi, as they would pass each other and occasionally walk together in their hidden virtual forms along the corridors of the SOMA halls during their observations. While revealing any personal information was against the law, C would often remark on the beauty of the hall's architecture. The workings and niceties of its circular layout in making each SOMA member feel privately isolated when in their own offices, and less so when in the larger meeting halls. He talked of how the Grand SOMA Room, where votes were held, was a masterpiece of design, with its beautiful convex roof that displayed a 360-degree panoramic view of various city points. Taryn guessed C must have once been an architect, an engineer, or a designer at the least. His love of aesthetical views he never hid from his coworkers. Likewise, Taryn later found his policy views were highly practical in nature, always arguing, as Aurelius pointed out, from a standpoint of utility, security, effectiveness, and possible tradeoffs and seeing an understated elegance in the attempt of balancing it all. The kind of stability that could only be accomplished through the delicate act of weighing all the sides against each other to see if a suitable, workable result could be used. *A master engineer to be sure*, thought Taryn.

'Member G' took a little longer to become familiar with. Like Taryn, she was more prone to observe silently and be reserved in her nature rather than to speak her mind boisterously outright. But once her opinions were formed, she could elaborate to others the vast connections between multiple concepts and possible implementations that extended so far that Taryn had only seen Aurelius match this before now. The passion in G's voice showed through however, when it came time to implement policies for conservation and the arts. Anything in the works within the SOMA that remotely supported the cultivation or preservation of arts was automatically a call for G's support. She also, if to a less attentive, but equally passionate degree, always argued on the side of practical conservation for natural beauty and wildlife whenever the issues would arise in some way. Her manner of speaking, while rarely heard at length, reflected not only a person of experience but of great education, and perhaps, Taryn suspected, even greater intellect.

In fact, Taryn guessed that everyone she worked with, from Mr. Brough to Wil to C and G, not only had more life experience and was her senior in age, but they were also much more highly educated than her as well. In Taryn's head, the notion that her skills were trifling compared to the others added its weight to the fear that she would never be confirmed as permanent. After all, what did she bring to any of this? What was she? A former line-boss who was fired for not knowing enough about how to save her own hide. Not a notable level of education to her name, with no grand views or notions of how things could work. She could not claim to possess the other member's farseeing scope of judgment. Of discerning distant possibilities. Taryn had no true idea what she was doing nor the slightest notion of how to proceed. All she could do was keep her ears open, listen to advice when offered, and wait for a moment. One moment, in which no one else spoke up, to prove her worth here. She just hoped not to make a fool out of herself when it finally came.

Chapter 10: Pulling Weeds

As fortune would have it, Taryn's first chance to make her mark in her role came from a familiar source. Reviewing some expenditures sent up from the SOMA that would need the council's approval, she noticed that the government's budget for hiring new business and safety inspectors had been decreased sharply from the prior session. In addition, the salary scale for the current staff of safety inspectors had been reworked as well, so that many of them saw little to no salary increase for the next half a decade. This matter was, of course, in contrast to a main point of Taryn's original Moot Election campaign goals. While she'd yet to look too far into it, the notion of figuring out a way to deal with private blacklisting and increasing inspections at the larger corporations were items that were still ruminating in the back of her mind. For those concerns, the funding trends sent up from the SOMA, now staring at her on her padd, made no sense.

"Aurelius?" Taryn asked, confused.

"Yes, Ms. Taryn?" came his prompt answer.

"Has there been a funding issue that I'm not aware of? One that would make these cuts to the business inspector's office necessary?"

"No, I find no such issues in the account records. Despite the budget for the office being reduced, I can't connect it to any internal funding deficiency.

"Then why are they being gutted like a fish on the plate?"

"I don't know the reasoning, but I can trace the principal source of the cuts as coming from the SOMA's budgetary committee..."

The screens on the office wall all came to life with an array of recorded images of the new budgetary committee in meetings.

"Specifically," Aurelius continued, "these modifications were the addition of the committee head, the new SOMA representative from Region 74."

"Region 74?" said Taryn. "Huh—I know that region," she thought aloud. "I used to work there… A, can you pull up that region's map with all the businesses laid out on it?"

"Of course, Ms. Taryn."

His usual light tone aside, Taryn knew that during her actual working times, Aurelius was not prone to interject any conversational sidebars. He wouldn't derail her thoughts with his musings now or pose irrelevant questions. Now he was the effective service system of the Trinity High Council: clear, precise, and accurate. Only she could signal him, by her inclinations, when their work was finished.

The map flickered onto the screen in less than a moment.

"Ok, now can you highlight those businesses sites that would normally have to undergo government inspections? Safety, health, sanitation, all the rest?"

"Sorting now," the office voice replied.

The familiar regional map with property boundaries overlaid, began changing color almost as soon as Aurelius finished speaking. A vast swath of industries was now highlighted in light blue. A neighboring screen showed a lengthy running list of the affected businesses, most of which were, as Taryn expected, corporate owned factories and properties. Region 74 was well-known as a highly industrialized region to all the locals. The few residential quarters in that region were vastly outnumbered by the amount of manufacturing sites. The suits working in the super-corps there had even pooled together to spend their own private money to build a small high-speed commuter tram from the more affluent city regions where they typically lived. It was no accident that this exclusive tram had no stops in either Region 74 or in Taryn's home region of 75. She knew that the locals were told that the floor workers were close enough to drive to work. They were also told that additional stations would affect the overall speed of the tram, not to mention overload it beyond capacity. Most of the workers easily saw past this excuse as it simply being the suits' way of saying that they'd built their own private path to work. A way to help avoid driving their nice clean vehicles past the ugly and grimy residential buildings in the area. They were trying to minimize their off-site interactions with their local subordinates.

"Aurelius, can you tell me what percentage of the populace from Region 74 are employed in these same businesses?"

"For that region, the latest data I have puts the number at 82.7 percent of working individuals," Aurelius replied. "You may also wish to know that only 11 percent of these employees earn enough income to be classified as being above current poverty levels."

"Well, that's not really a surprise," remarked Taryn. "We always pulled our floor's temporary workers from the nearby residential buildings when I worked on the line. The immediate housing and rents are the cheapest of any I'd ever seen."

"Your assessment of the lower cost of habitation expenses is congruent to the statistical records," Aurelius replied.

This was, after all, why Taryn's own building in the adjoining region was barely affordable as a livable space for a family of four on only a lower Foreman's salary. Its proximity to Region 74 had helped keep the rent low back at a time when she and Cyrano were first looking for a place to live. Taryn knew that in Region 74 the rent was even lower than her own, but so much lower was the quality and general features of the few residential buildings there, that she and Cyrano looked for places elsewhere for their then fast-growing family. The only benefit of the lowered housing costs in Region 74 was that most of the workers who called it home could simply walk to the floors each day to fill in for any opening they found.

"Hmm..." Taryn said softly, as if speaking to herself. "Aurelius, does it sound odd to you that this SOMA rep from 74, would propose unnecessary cuts that would decrease inspections? I mean, you are seeing this too, right?"

"Yes, Ms. Taryn. The representative's proposal doesn't appear to directly benefit the local workforce of his home region, nor the efficiency of the business inspector's office, although it does allow the locally operating corporations to go longer between regular inspection cycles."

"Is there any way that these cuts could indirectly help the region's residents that you can account for?"

"Running economic analytical simulations now." Aurelius remained silent for a short moment before speaking to Taryn again. She knew by now that the pause in any response Aurelius gave to a question was in truth just a way to make his dialogue more approachable to people.

"By mimicking a natural human response time to a rather complex question it was less jarring to folk," he had previously explained to her.

"Ms. Taryn, I have analyzed a little over six thousand simulations using variations on every viable economic forecast for the next five to ten cycles. I predict only a 4.2 percent chance of these cuts benefiting Region 74's local workforce populace. And there is only a 1.3 percent chance of any significant gain. However, the local corporations currently operating in the region would likely see an eight percent increase annually, as having fewer inspections predicts certain safety regulations being routinely omitted as they streamline their manufacturing and maintenance processes."

"And the estimated profit increase for those businesses?"

"Anywhere from 25-46%, depending on the type of business and other extraneous factors."

"So then," Taryn puzzled, "why does a SOMA member put forward a change that isn't likely to help anyone living in his own region?"

Taryn pausing, turned herself in her chair to stare out the corner window for a bit. She could see Mr. Brough down in the western yard, minding a small garden he had there. He had mentioned to Taryn about how he'd been having problems keeping the thistles from taking over his potatoes. He was hunched down on his knees, using a tool in one hand to cut the submerged roots of the weeds as he was pulling them out. The sun was only now starting to make the first hints of its afternoon descent past the meridian towards the nearby woods. Beyond Mr. Brough's perfectly trimmed grounds of the estate, past the green shimmer of the perimeter cloak, the forest stretched onwards. Up and down it ran over the nearby hills and beyond for several miles. Above their green and yellow treetops and through the blue haze of the day, the city skyline could still be seen. Distant, unfocused, but still with a glimpse of a shimmer to its edges.

"Aurelius?"

"Yes, Ms. Taryn?"

"How secure is the anonymity of the SOMA members, truly?"

"Electronically and legally, it is some of the most highly secured data in the government."

"And what about socially or relationally, how secure is it there?"

"That part is … less certain. I have often noted that the human factor is the least secure or, most unstable, if you will, aspect of SOMA membership. Thereby, it is the most likely source of any illegal dissemination of SOMA identities to unauthorized individuals."

"Has that happened before?"

"Before answering, I must first inform you, Ms. Taryn, that this inquiry includes information that is restricted access to only the Trinity High Council, the Benzi courts, and the Bizi, and as such this inquiry will be noted in the permanent government logs."

"I understand. Continue."

"26 times in the entire history of our government have SOMA identities been compromised. Seven of those times were found to be entirely accidental, coincidental, or unavoidable. 19 instances were later determined by the Benzi Court to be purposeful and resulted in excommunication, fines, seizures, and arrests."

"19 times… How were they caught?"

"A variety of ways, but the most common methods were observable patterns of action that ran counterintuitively as noted on Bizi reports and by anonymous tips from within the SOMA itself." There was a pause. "Ms. Taryn, do you suspect that the budgetary committee head may have compromised his identity within the SOMA?"

"Maybe. But if so, why? And was it intentional?" She turned her chair back towards her desk. "I don't suppose I can just browse his background file, can I?"

"No, not at the moment. Such access, for you, can only be achieved through consent from the other members of the Trinity High Council. Shall I request that they meet you in the Wucengi for a short while?"

Taryn paused as she thought to herself. *If you do this and you're wrong girl, you'll look like a huge idiot who's just wasting their time… but if you're right…*

"By all means, Aurelius," she said. "Send the requests."

It took Taryn almost an hour consulting with members G and C before they granted her their consent. For a time, she was worried that they would quickly dismiss her ideas out of hand as ridiculous. Yet, with Aurelius's simulation data and Taryn's warnings that if she was correct, it would represent a gross violation of the SOMA anonymity regulations, eventually she won them over. After talking amongst themselves and privately consulting with Aurelius briefly, they finally relented.

"We will agree to permit you access to the background of this representative from Region 74," said G. "But understand that we are doing so with great reluctance, as such a thing is far from the norm."

"And there will be some conditions of its use," added C. "Aurelius will rescind this access in two days, and the information you see will have the actual names of any representative, their family members, or associates redacted for their own protection. Their relationships, personal affiliations, and other lines of connections however should be all you need to examine, if there is even anything to find, about which I do have my doubts," C said.

"In addition," G began, "you will have to conduct the remainder of this inquiry monitored by your assigned Bizi security personnel, so that if you do find anything of note, the issue itself will rightfully become a matter for government security to investigate. Though we will still expect a report of our own of any relevant findings. Do you approve of these terms, Member T?"

Taryn quickly agreed and thanked them both again for their trust in her. When she turned off her Wucengi neural device, she found Wil was already standing at the doorway to her office room looking rather confused and tense, as if he'd hurried in only a moment prior.

"Umm… I just got a message from A," he started unsurely, "saying that you needed help with a possible security breach that I'm not aware of?"

After relaying the details to Wil, Taryn had Aurelius display the now unlocked background files on the screens for both her and Wil to examine. All four screen displays on her office wall began filling with the now unrestricted information. The core identifying features such as names, citizen ID numbers, birthplace, and specific dates were still omitted. The two began the process of reviewing line by line, page by page, all the data Aurelius provided. Yet after a good portion of the afternoon had passed by, neither Taryn nor Wil felt satisfied. There was nothing relevant or noteworthy in the files. Taryn went home feeling both tired and a bit dejected, wondering if she had just cemented herself as a temp worker.

* * *

The next day the sky was overcast with clouds that blotted the entire horizon. There was a cold drizzling rain that soaked through everything. Being unable to work outdoors, Mr. Brough was busy inside cleaning and dusting, but besides that, not much had changed. Taryn and Wil were still reviewing the file information they had on the Budget committee head from the SOMA, with no apparent success or any explanation as to his behavior or mindset. By mid-morning, Taryn's focus was beginning to shift mainly to self-doubt.

"Maybe the guy simply isn't that smart or careful in his policy making," she found herself thinking aloud. Mr. Brough, in his usual manner, had quietly and unobtrusively delivered them a tray of tea in the office. Taryn was now pacing and re-reading a file off a padd for the third time as she sipped at her warm cup.

"The file shows this guy's been in Region 74 for essentially his entire life... a middle child from a single parent, who spent his whole youth there. Finished secondary school, but never went on further due to mediocre grades and '*low ambitions*' according to his instructors. Mother died when he was in his twenties. He stayed in the same residence he grew up in and never earned more than enough money to live anywhere else in the city. Hmm…" Taryn's lips pursed in thought. "Doesn't sound like the same go-getting committee head that's currently in session at the SOMA now."

Wil, who was sitting behind the desk working away at another monitor chimed in. "His bank accounts show no interesting activity. And no other accounts by his name hold any substantial amount of income, credits, or debt of any type. The Bizi records that I've been allowed access to show he's had only small brushes with the Blue Boys when he was young. Medical reports show that he broke his arm and leg in a skiing accident about five cycles ago, but other than that nothing else serious health-wise. He's not dying or anything."

"Skiing accident? Where?" asked Taryn.

"The record says San Reaoyal Creek."

"That's that getaway place where a lot of the well-off Ties and Suits go to spend their vacation isn't it?"

Wil nodded in confirmation.

"Pricey, credit-wise," she continued. "I wonder how he can afford to go there, living in Region 74 as he is? Where did he get fixed up after the accident?"

Wil tapped on the glowing keys of his virtual display some more.

"He was originally admitted to a local facility near the ski valley, after they stabilized him, it looks like he was transferred to a private hospital in Region 23 for recuperation, follow-ups, and some months of physical therapy."

"Region 23... but that's near the coast. Why there? That's nowhere near his residence, nor anywhere in the ski resort area. And how can he afford treatment in a private hospital?"

Wil began accessing the hospital medical files. "Well, the records definitely show him as the patient, but it's not his name on the medical billing receipts. It's his sister's."

"His sister?"

"Yeah, looks as though she took care of all of his medical needs at the time. We could also assume he was staying with her during those three months, as she does reside in the same region as the hospital."

"Aurel," Taryn asked, using what had become one of Taryn's own nicknames for him, "is it safe to assume the representative wasn't working in any capacity during his time in the hospital or in recovery?"

Aurelius chimed in, "I show no tax work records for him during the period in question."

"So, what about his own residence, did his sister cover him there too? Pay any of the bills?"

"Nope," said Wil, looking up dubiously from the desk display. "His brother did. The rental payments for that time period all came from his brother's accounts. Then after three months they went back to coming from the representative's own credit account, at around the same time his rehab finished up."

"So… both his siblings took care of him when he was injured but sent him on his way again once he was well."

"Sounds about right," said Wil.

"And what do we know about them? The siblings I mean."

"Hmm," started Wil, tapping a few more keys. "Well, the brother is a newly promoted junior executive with 10 cycles at his super-corporation working out of—"

"Region 74?" interrupted Taryn.

"Yep," Wil continued. "His sister works at a competitor corporation, also in Region 74, as a senior efficiency advisor… wait hold on… the records show she too was recently tapped for promotion, to a newly created senior executive position that was not in the corporate structure before. That's rather odd, don't you think?" Wil questioned with a raised eyebrow.

Aurelius spoke up, "With their promotions, both siblings will continue to make significantly more income than their brother, the SOMA representative. But I don't find that necessarily surprising, as their educational records contain far more complimentary remarks and demonstrate aptitude and diligence evaluations that are consistently more impressive than their brother's own."

"Aurel, what would be the economic effect on the brother and sister's workplaces if the cuts to the government inspector's office were to be passed."

"Well, the clear majority of my simulations show an estimated 29 percent growth in profits for the brother's employer ahead of their own estimates from last cycle."

"And the sister's?"

"A 38 percent jump in growth, also ahead of their recent corporate forecasts."

Taryn turned to Wil.

"Wil, see if this floats." Wil leaned back in the guest chair and waited as Taryn began. "A poor family growing up in Region 74. The eldest and youngest, both intelligent and motivated, manage to work their way out on their own, but leave their lay about brother to his own devices, unless of course he happens to be in serious need. He is family after all, but I mean, they aren't about to prop him up any longer then either think is necessary."

"His history tells them that they need to keep their expectations of their brother low," said Wil.

"Right," said Taryn. "Then, months ago, this middle brother finds he's been selected for the Moot lottery. Perhaps he debates if he wants that kind of responsibility or workload as he has never done anything that intensive or important before. And in the process of trying to mull over the matter he asks one or both of his siblings for advice, as they're far more familiar with being put in charge of things than he ever has."

"But still…" added Wil, "now he has a real opportunity to be as important if not more so than either his brother or sister, perhaps for the first time in their eyes. Or at least his own."

"Exactly. But he doesn't quite know what to do, so he asks them to help him out. They agree, but in helping they both see an opportunity. They advise and encourage him and perhaps… perhaps even write his campaign speech. And thanks to their involvement in shaping his messaging, he wins the SOMA election for his region. When elected, he begins to work at their behest, removing government inspections by cutting funding to certain areas, thus presenting both siblings with a more profitable work environment." Taryn paused to gauge Wil's reaction. "So… what do you think?"

"Well… maybe, but you're forgetting about the promotions."

"The promotions?"

"Yeah, the siblings would have to have told someone higher up at their own corporations about this inside edge. They would need to be able to take the credit for it, and not have it just seem like the winds were favoring them. They each need someone to know that they were the ones responsible for this, so that they could haul in any real benefits from this plan. In fact, it's possible that even higher suits would be in the know. And that they would be the ones who are originating the representative's legislative moves, with the siblings serving mainly as intermediaries after it started. The promotions for the siblings are both rewards and insurances so that everyone remains loyal in the process. After his term in office has ended, the SOMA representative from Region 74 could also unofficially be rewarded for his services. Perhaps he's offered a new high-level position created specifically for him at either one of these corporations."

"And he'd be hired, based upon a glowing familiar recommendation, of course," concluded Taryn.

"Precisely," said Wil.

"Pardon me, but I find your reasoning flawed," interrupted Aurelius.

A look of surprise shot over both Taryn's and Wil's faces as they glanced at one another.

"Wait, why…" Taryn started to say.

"While you two were talking, I managed to isolate the financial records of both the SOMA representative's siblings. While their main accounts are ostensibly normal, I have found a joint account recently opened under both their names at a financial institution neither have used before. Interestingly the sibling's names are on the accounts, but they themselves are not the ones who created it. They are merely the names on file. The account also has a minimum funds restricted access system in place."

The four screens on the office wall lit up with account information.

"Meaning what?" asked Taryn.

Wil came from his seat to look closer at the screens. "It means that neither of the siblings can withdraw any funds until the minimum amount of credits has been deposited into the account. That minimum balance has to be agreed on by both the account holders and by the institution that operates the account."

Aurelius continued: "Based on my calculations of a sample of initial deposits in the account, that minimum amount of credits will be achieved about three months before the representative's term in office ends. At that point, the total credits in the account will have far surpassed any economic need for either sibling to employ themselves at their respective corporations. The set minimum amount for the account is also more than sufficient for all three to retire in extensive comfort."

"Aurel, can you tell where the deposits are coming from exactly?" asked Wil.

"Yes, I have traced the transfer of funds from various accounts to another business institution specializing in industrial account holdings. I cannot, however, access the account creator's identity nor the originating source of the credit transfers any farther without a Bizi or Benzi warrant."

"That's alright," smiled Wil. "Let me make a call. With what we have, I'm sure somebody else in the Bizi will be interested in this too."

Chapter 11: Satisfaction

Eight days later, the sun was finally out again in the early morning as Taryn exited her building to meet Wil for her usual ride to work. She was surprised to see, upon entering the vehicle, however that Wil wasn't the one in the driver slot. Instead, Agent Filater was greeting her with his solemn demeanor still intact.

"Good morning, Ms. Steno," he said with his usual composed manner.

"Morning... Agent Filater," she said slowly, not masking her surprise. "Why are you here? Are you my driver for today?"

"Yes, I asked Agent Zhuantium to let me drive you to work this morning. He'll join you at the estate later. However, I was hoping to take an hour or two of your time to make a detour for something that may interest you."

"Umm, okay."

Despite such a strange turn, Taryn still wasn't about to decline something the senior Bizi Agent recommended. With her agreement, the vehicle quickly pulled out of the lot, not turning towards the direction of the hidden estate, but proceeding further on into the city.

"Where are we going?" Taryn asked.

"To the Hall of the SOMA in the city center."

"But… she objected in disbelief, "but, I thought I wasn't allowed to go there. Security risk, someone may recognize me, and all that stuff," she said with far more curiosity in her voice than she'd intended.

"Quite true, under normal circumstances," the agent replied calmly, not moving his eyes from the road. "*So* that should impress upon you all the trouble I had to go through to get you special clearance for today. It wasn't easy. Turn your ID badge into its Bizi appearance please. Oh, and here, you'll need this." Reaching into his suit coat, he handed her a necklace pass. Taryn pressed her thumb to the biometric scanner on her Vox P. ID. The Bizi version appeared in place of the previous information. She noticed the necklace pass that she'd been handed already matched the fake Bizi badge she had just switched to.

"Sorry for rushing you like this," Filater said, "but we're already a bit later than I'd hoped."

"As long as it's not my review panel we're running late for." Taryn joked with a tiny laugh. When the agent at the wheel did not react to this comment, Taryn felt her breath catch. "Wait, it's not, is it Filater?" her concern evident. "Because if it *is* time for my review panel, I have to say the short notice and then being late on top—"

"As far as I know Ms. Steno, your confirmation panel has yet to even be chosen, not that I care much for the details of the SOMA." he finally interjected.

Taryn breathed a slow audible sigh.

"Now," Filater continued, "if you'd kindly reach behind you, you'll find a blazer back there that should fit," he said motioning briefly to the rear seats. "I know you don't like that fashion but please put it on, button it up and tie your hair back too. It should make you appear more like the other Bizi agents that we'll be joining once we arrive."

Taryn, still perplexed at the rush and confusion of the morning's event so far barely registered the agents note on her usual objection to a more formal style of dress. She followed the agent's instructions and began putting on the coat and changing her hair.

"None of the other Bizi agents will know who you are, of course," he said, "but since you're arriving with me, they shouldn't question you. Don't start conversations with any of them. And if they talk to you keep it simple and brief. They'll likely assume you're either my new assistant or my new trainee." He paused, seeming to choose his next words more delicately. "Some of the older Bizi veterans, who've known me longer, will probably assume we're sleeping together, I'm sorry to say. Just ignore any sideways glances that you might notice."

Taryn's reaction surprised even her. She almost let out a full laugh this time and failed to overpower the smirk on her face.

"Do you often sleep with your assistants and trainees?" she asked.

"No," Filater responded, his face still not reacting at all to the question as his gaze remained focused on the road before them. Yet, it had been such an unexpected offhand remark that all of Taryn's usual reserve around the rather stolid agent had evaporated at this sudden topic.

"No, as in *not often* or no, as in *not at all*?" she pressed.

But Filater continued calmly on, disregarding Taryn's second question, "One very good way to tell who is actually watching you, Ms. Steno, is to let loose some subtle rumors. Let time take them where it may and watch to see exactly whose heads start turning in quiet discontent when you next approach."

"Okay...." Taryn said unsatisfied. As Taryn finished adjusting her clothes and hair, Agent Filater continued. But before she could think of asking Agent Filater once again why such creating and spreading fraudulent rumors would be ever needed or why they were heading to the SOMA exactly, he interrupted.

"Speaking of heads, I wanted you to know, Ms. Steno, that you've managed to find more headaches for me in the last 72 hours than I typically see in the better part of a month."

"Oh…" she said, unsure of how to reply to that assertion. "I'm sorr-"

"Don't be. I'm rather impressed actually. I take it as a sign that the council position was offered to a proper candidate."

"And every time that you compliment me, Agent Filater, I feel as if I was a thief who has stupidly tripped an alarm and is somehow praised for being caught. Is that why we're going to the SOMA? Has something happened in the investigation? Did I make a mistake with it? Can't you tell me anything instead of being so closed up?"

"Not yet, you'll get your answers soon. As I said, there is something there I think you should see with your own eyes."

"But the Wucengi could work just as eas—"

Filater shook his head as he interrupted her. "Even the Wucengi sometimes fails to provide the full scope of certain things. But not to worry, Ms. Steno. To me, you're not a thief." He said with the slightest crease of a smirk to himself. "No", he said reassuringly "if anything… you're the tripped alarm."

* * *

They pulled up some time later and parked past at least a dozen other vehicles that all looked to be the same government model as their own. It had taken them several minutes to get past the numerous gates and guard houses and, from what Taryn could tell, they were still several hundred yards away from any building large enough that could conceivably house all the SOMA members. The only nearby structure was what appeared to be an underground metro entrance. There, more than a dozen people dressed in like manner to Filater and Taryn were gathered outside. Many appeared to be consulting with one another in small groups. Most of them appeared to be Bizi agents by their dress alone. All had badges around their necks like Taryn's, and only a few visibly reacted to her and Filater's approach as they walked up.

To Taryn, some of these Bizi agents were like Agent Filater: generally quiet and observatory in their nature, analyzing everything around themselves yet betraying nothing. Others appeared more like Wil: larger in size, highly vocal, and clearly field agents. Still others were no larger than Taryn herself. These too were chattering, while often holding padds with what looked to be various reports and documents on them. The language the agents spoke in their consultations with one another was entirely unique. As Filater later explained to her, the Bizi developed their own language that prevented casual eavesdropping when there were several of them all together. While not always used in private settings, it was taught only to their own agents and was the way agents often spoke to one another out in the open. To Taryn, their speech sounded more like a combination of several languages rather than a single dialect, but she never held herself as an expert on such things.

After a short while, in which no one spoke to Taryn, for which she was greatly relieved, the whole group was signaled to enter the small entrance to a descending stairwell. Only one or two other agents even greeted Filater on their way down. Their words in passing sounded to Taryn like *Filater-am, Silimma hemeen.* Or a more politely formal sounding, *Silimma hemeen a'-nohoch winik-eh ah tz'on.* The stairs down brought them to an empty rail system. The group grew quieter as they entered a waiting tram with only small pockets of murmuring afterwards. The ride in the three-section automated tram took only a few minutes, and after disembarking the group began walking down a few unadorned cement corridors. The noise level dropped to a hush now, with only the ricocheting sound of the group's dress shoes on the hard marble floor being noticeable. They followed the single hallway for a few turns before it ascended a flight of stairs and entered a set of doors, beyond which no one said a word. Taryn could hear noises up ahead, more of a rumbling murmur than anything. Its gentle throbbing grew louder and clearer as she climbed the final staircase to the wooden double doors.

She found, after passing beyond the thick doorway, that she was standing at the top of a large upper balcony for an enormous circular room with a massive high arching dome. The Grand Hall of the SOMA. The balcony area itself was softly lit like that of a theater, with guide lights on the floor, going down several paths on small sets of carpeted stairs. The main floor far down below them however was fully illuminated for the moment. This was where the loud rumbling noise appeared to be coming from. Looking down over the edge Taryn saw that it was a mass assemblage of several hundred people all talking and jostling for their own seats on the distant floor below. Some indeed weren't looking for their seats at all, but were busily conversing in the aisles, and still others were casually streaming in from one of a half dozen lower-level entrances. On the balcony where she stood above the mob of talkers, the smooth polished marble walls and supports rose to a tremendous height, seamlessly forming the scaffold of the great domed ceiling. Symmetrical lines of optical projector cords attached to the interior ran up along the dome to meet at a single point. From there, they projected any number of impressive landscape views. Currently it was the panoramic live view of the city skyline from a remote recorder.

Most of the members of the Bizi contingents that Taryn and Filater had come in with, noiselessly took their seats in the front row of the lower balcony. A few sat apart or in pairs, separated from the main Bizi envoy. Taryn was one of these. Agent Filater had pulled her aside after she'd finished inspecting the lower floor and found seats for them in a side box behind some darkened glass where the lighting was even dimmer than elsewhere on the balcony. From there, standing up, Taryn could see most of the floor down below her, while the areas directly underneath of them were displayed overhead on nearby screens.

She scanned the lower floor once more and began to realize that she was recognizing faces. These were not personal acquaintances of course, but SOMA representatives that she'd observed while using the Wucengi neural device. It struck her as odd that now, high atop the balcony, she was physically closer to them than she'd ever been before in her whole life. Still, she could recognize, even from this height, certain tendencies of their body language and behaviors, groupings, and general mannerisms, that she had only seen during her virtual observations before now. Watching the mass all intermingling she heard the garbled sounds of hundreds of voices as their combined cacophony reverberated up past her into the echo of the higher dome.

"You can continue standing if you wish, no one can see through the glass on that side, but the monitors will show you everything if you decide to take a seat."

She returned to where the Agent sat after a few more moments of staring out.

"Sorry," she said. "It's just..."

"More… real now?"

"Well… yes," she answered quietly.

"That's always been a drawback of the Wucengi system I've thought. Good as it may be at representing all this and its dimensions to you, it's far less adept at getting the full feel for the place." Taryn noticed that Filater slowly ran his fingertips along the polished wood of the armrest and thick fabric of the upholstered chair that he was sitting on. "The various textures, the smells…. Why, even the occasional quaff of body odor, stick breath, aroma of a cheap joe-cup, or perfume make a place real to us. An unnoticed insect or rodent in a remote corner or a unique wall crack, broken tiles, flickering lights, an irritatingly loud carpet pattern, or the subtle stains on shoes all help stake the reality of a place into our minds."

"Is that why I'm here? To make it real for me?" asked Taryn.

"Partially," Filater admitted. "The rest of the answer you'll see in a few more moments."

Taryn took the seat next to the agent.

"By the way," the agent continued, "I'm curious, did you know that the penalties associated with trying to bypass the rules of the SOMA or throw an election mean that not only are offenders arrested," he said studying her face, "but also in such cases all the credits of their direct family or any business in operation with direct ties to that family are forfeit?"

"Isn't that a little severe?" asked Taryn, having now a genuine clue where this talk was going.

"Perhaps, but it's needed. A few wealthy business idiots and old-world families tried it in the past. To force their way in, especially in the government's early days, hundreds of cycles ago. If the punishment wasn't a severe deterrent more might have kept trying it. My predecessor used to say that's actually how the government managed to get the credits to keep itself funded early on. Helped pay off the reconstruction budgets and kept the taxes low for many cycles. So, the fortunes of those foolish enough to try illegally interfering only ended up helping further build and secure the very process they were intending to subvert."

"Huh... I think my friend Everett would like that approach. He loves watching his opponents take swings at him in the arena and making them miss, especially if they end up feeding their knuckles right back to another on their own team."

Filater was still focused on the main screen above them, "There were attempts for a long while, decades even, if what I heard was true. The well-to-dos of the time just couldn't accept the notion that they were no longer favored for spots of power over others. That their traditional status now seemingly meant nothing to unidentified government officials who could be anyone and who were continually elected without their help, their… influence. Probably was a scary concept to them, I suppose."

"Some folks can afford to have weird fears I guess," Taryn said as the lights on the main floor slowly flashed as the final signal for the SOMA members down below to find their own seats.

"I don't know," replied the agent, "fear of being taken only as seriously as everyone else isn't all that strange. More depressing than anything, in truth. But thankfully for us, it's also a predictable feature.

"Is that wh—" she stopped herself mid-sentence as the great lights in the dome now dimmed to the same lowered intensity as on the balcony. The center of the main floor far below them remained lit however, highlighting an elevated row of continuous desks. Though fairly wide, this row bent in a gentle crescent pattern facing back towards the main membership of the SOMA body. Also on the floor, but still in the light, were two smaller but opposing tables, near each end of the crescent, each unadorned with only three chairs. Eleven darkly robed people with deep curved hoods quietly filed in and took to the elevated seats along the upper curved row.

"Is that the…" Taryn whispered to Filater

"The Benzi High Court," he said, both finishing and answering her question at the same time.

"But I thought," she paused confused. "I thought that they held their tribunals at a different location."

"Normally they do, but as I said before, these are unusual circumstances. Since yesterday they've been here, mostly in private and confidentiality, even hidden from you and the others viewing on the Wucengi system. This is actually meant to be their final assemblage here to conclude their current business. The recordings of their meetings will be made available to the council and the rest of the SOMA this afternoon once they are done."

"Done with what?" she stammered. "And are you going to tell me… "

Just then one of the central robed Benzi judges spoke.

"This session is now reconvened. All parties come forth."

The entirety of the SOMA grew silent as a trio of two men and a woman stepped into the lit area to take seats at the left table in front of the Benzi, while a pair of men appeared and sat at the table on the right. Taryn immediately recognized one of the two men on the right as the representative from Region 74 and the budgetary committee head. On the opposing side, no one's face was any more than passingly familiar from the trio, save one. A single face that took a little longer, but after a moment Taryn saw that it was the Representative from Region 75, her home region.

It was only out of a long since satiated matter of personal curiosity towards the one that defeated her in the Moot Election, that Taryn was able to recall him. With his height, he sat a bit taller than his neighbors. His understated but high-quality business attire was typical of him she knew. It was capped by his neat graying hair, perfectly formed as it topped off a strong jawed face that presented an almost quintessential image of an elder statesman of some determination. Taryn couldn't see details except on the screens, but she guessed from his motions that the representative was shrewdly evaluating the padd before him while speaking quietly with his two other SOMA compatriots. Taryn—in her experience through the Wucengi—had noticed the representative had seemed at home organizing and directing the others as he was currently doing. It was habitual for him, every now and then turning on his kindly blue eyes and charming smile, as a way of easing people to his views and requests. While in private conversations he didn't sound quite as eloquent as he had been for his campaign speech, Taryn knew that he was definitely as educated and intelligent as she'd presumed upon first hearing him that night of the interviews from her couch.

"Defender," the central Benzi judge called towards the two pair of men on the right, "the accusations and subsequent evidence offered against your client has been noted and examined by this court, as well as all contrasting evidence offered by you in his defense. Do you have anything else you wish to add before we render our verdict?"

The man next to the Region 74 representative, the Defender, who had been addressed by the judge, stood up and replied in the negative. The judge asked a similar question of the three seated on the left table, where the Region 75 representative replied. They too signaled in the negative. Apparently, Taryn figured, that those three opposing SOMA members had been serving in the prosecuting role for this matter.

"Very well. As all parties have been heard, the Court will now render its ruling."

All members of the Court then stood up while the panel of judges, also standing, raised their left hands palm-open before them, their outstretched hands in front of them, fingers cupping upwards in the air. These were the only true parts of the Benzi judges that anyone could clearly see, even with the lights on them.

"Concerning the accusation of purposeful violation of SOMA security with subsequent intent to manipulate government policy for personal gain, how do the judges rule?"

Going from the rightmost judge to the left, each dark robed figure, one-by-one, made an exaggerated gesture of closing their hands into fists, turning them downward, and lowering their clenched hands to their side before sitting down. A hushed murmur came from the SOMA audience in response. The Bizi audience in the balcony area only whispered a little amongst themselves, but as for Taryn, her pulse skipped at this.

"Hmm…" Filater whispered. "Not a single palm raised up. Every one of their leashes reigned in. Not much of a debate among them this time."

The Benzi spokeswoman continued, "The Court has collectively and unanimously deemed the accused guilty. He will be taken into the custody of the Bizi. The penalties and sentencing will be decided in accordance with the law before the next week ends."

Two massive Bizi agents in meticulously clean dress uniforms appeared out of the shadows and guided the Region 74 representative off the floor. The distant image of his hung head with a sullen look of shock and humiliation on his face stayed with Taryn for a long time afterwards. Many SOMA audience members jeered at him as he was escorted off. Cries of "good riddance" and "shame" could be heard even without the aid of the floor's microphones.

After the Benzi judges had re-seated themselves, their speaker continued, though she had to ring her loud resonating gong many times before the commotion finally quieted enough. She continued, slowly but clearly.

"Now, as this investigation and subsequent deliberation concerns further possible infractions of SOMA security, it is my duty to inform you, the representatives of the SOMA, not to discuss this matter outside of these chambers. We also wish to inform you that the matter of identifying and arraigning other potential accomplices and accessories in this affair shall be receiving our Bizi associate's full attention until its true extent is known. We wish to thank the Bizi investigators for their quick and tireless work in gathering the evidence to stop this corrosive exploit, which would have surely tarnished our system's nature and intent."

Applause went up from the SOMA body. The Bizi delegation however remained silent and steadfast in their seats.

"And finally, we of the Benzi court," at which point all hooded members of the court rose back to their feet, "also wish to recognize and thank the individual in attendance here whose moral character and diligence began this entire line of inquiry. While we cannot recognize this person in public, we do know that without their persistence, this case would have not been discovered and would have likely festered for a longer time. Please know that we, who all work for the betterment of our people, acknowledge your actions in this matter as reflective of the highest principles of this government, and we are grateful. We would ask that all attendees today commend that service as well." Each Benzi judge bowed their hooded heads slowly in a gesture of gratitude towards the SOMA members.

A brace of cheers, followed by applause and shouts, came rolling up the dome from the SOMA membership. This time, the Bizi delegation too stood and clapped respectfully.

"Stand up and clap," Filater instructed Taryn as he rose to his own feet. "Must keep up appearances." His eyes quickly glanced at the other Bizi in the nearest seats. Whilst not being as vocal as the lower crowd, they were already standing and clapping politely.

Taryn, paced towards the glass, stepped up near the rail and began clapping. Staring down her eyes had adjusted enough to the lighting and the slight mist in them to see all the SOMA members below on their feet, clapping vigorously as well. They, looking one to another, obviously thought that they were thanking one of their own with their approval. Taryn let a brief half smile slip at that.

When she turned her head back to her seat, she saw that of the hundreds of people in the hall, Agent Filater was the only one whose slow, subtle claps were directly aimed at an actual person.

Well done, she saw the agent silently mouthing to her amidst all the noise.

Her eyes and head bowed almost imperceptibly in a humble acknowledgment.

Huh, so that's kind of how Everett feels, she thought. While internally enthused at this adulation she was still not lost far enough in the moment to forget the pretense of the Bizi agent that she was attempting to portray. Watching her feet on the darkened floor, she stepped lightly back towards her chair.

"This assemblage is concluded," the Benzi judge announced with a final bang.

The lights on the main floor lifted slowly and the normal mummer of several hundred people walking and discussing the recent events all simultaneously began. The balcony lighting remained dimmed as the Bizi contingent quietly made their way back out the door and all the way to their vehicle area. After a few quick presumed farewells that sounded like "*Neha ma guz tz'unu'*" from other Bizi agents, always countered with a "*Zeto silum zhang ma kiri-zal*" from Filater, the two were re-approaching their own parked vehicle. Pausing as they opened the doors to get in, the agent spoke to her again across the other side of the vehicle's roof, in a lowered tone of the common speech once more.

"You do see the subtle problem you're now facing, yes?"

"What's that?" Taryn asked while getting herself settled inside the passenger seat.

Filater did the same, continuing his thought after he closed his door.

"Well, you've got the direct thanks of both the SOMA and Benzi high court. A feat few in the history of the Trinity Council have ever achieved. But you're still relatively new to the posting." He smiled. A very uncharacteristic thing for the agent. "And if us Bizi are too slow in flushing out this whole scam or finalizing our reports, your part in all this *may* remain anonymous as the Judge said. Even perhaps up to and beyond your confirmation hearing." Taryn's face went straight into a look of deflated seriousness. "Still," he continued as their vehicle came alive and started off, "you do have some time left on the council regardless, and so I wonder, just in case that happens, and no one is able to know who it was that started this whole investigation, what are you planning to follow this up with?"

Taryn didn't respond, but only frowned as she looked down considering his query.

Me too, she thought silently.

Taryn's eyes, downcast at this notion, never caught the agent's face, where a frail ghost of a suppressed laugh, as often happens, was straining against the placid demeanor of one who quietly pulls off a sarcastic jest.

* * *

Agent Filater turned the vehicle in the direction of the hidden estate. After they had been traveling on the road for a while, Taryn began asking questions that had been drawing themselves ever more strongly on her thoughts.

"What will happen in Region 74 now?" she asked. "I mean, will the citizens have to re-vote for a new representative? And what will they be told about the convicted one?"

"Well, what the public learns is up to the SOMA to decide. In all reality, they'll probably vote to inform the public of the truth insofar as their representative deliberately violated government security procedures. Then they'll also need to hold a re-election from the remaining Moot winners. Similar situations have happened before, more so for representatives that've had medical or personal episodes that forced their resignations early, but this will still make the top of the news feeds for a while. But then again, the news reminding people of the thoroughness of our security and the severity of the punishments and penalties for violators is certainly not a bad thing either," he said musing to himself. "The runner-up in that election, as I recall, was a factory lineman who's now missing a leg, thanks to his time working as a hanger. If elected, I seriously doubt he'd have any enthusiasm about cutting funding to the business inspector's office. In the meantime, several agents are reviewing all the votes and proposals the convicted rep submitted or supported to see how much influence his corporate overseers might have had."

"Are his siblings are being charged as well?"

"The investigation isn't quite finished with them yet, but it was nearly done last time I was briefed. Once the corporate heads hear of our interest in the two, their winds will quickly turn, and the siblings will probably be dismissed regardless."

"And the suits that gave them the promotions in the first place?"

"Oh, we're looking hard at them too, but much more quietly. It will take longer for us to figure out who was sending the instructions and who was simply passing them down the ladder."

"And how high up that ladder actually climbs?" Taryn added.

"Precisely. The tides at work here will probably mean that we'll have to levy fines against the companies, and there will probably be more dismissals before this whole affair is complete. I don't know how long it will take, but I do know that now that you've found it, several agents are on their toes trying to run down the various trails." Filater paused. "It's a professional insult to us, you see, Ms. Steno, that this slipped by unnoticed. Not that you should think we aren't grateful for your help in exposing it," he said, turning to her. "It's that we don't like being made to look foolish. The fact that you found the issue so early in the SOMA's new term is both a credit to you, and a glaring point for possible improvement to us."

"I think I get it, but how can you be sure the exact same thing isn't or doesn't happen again?"

"Well, there is also going to be a full review of our security measures to see how they can be improved to prevent this situation from reoccurring. But the facts are that there is always going to be a chance an elected official will break their silence on their service to someone outside the SOMA. It's the risk we take and the price we have to pay to avoid the settling effect. As long as there are honest eyes, in as many places as possible though, it's worth the price.

"In my personal view, however," he continued after a moment, "what did happen, is what should have happened. A compromised member, acting very strangely, was discovered, and reported on by a concerned individual whose job it was to be monitoring them. Again, this is not meant to belittle your actions, but I think if you hadn't found him out then someone else would have, only at a later point." Filater paused again to think. "At least that's my hope." he said reluctantly. "There is no perfect system, just ones that can be designed to work better."

* * *

Agent Filater and Taryn reached the hidden estate by the fifth hour of the day. Wil was waiting to greet them as they arrived and escorted them into the house.

"I saw the broadcast via a secure line from Aurelius. Congratulations Miss Taryn. Well done."

"Don't do that, Wil. You had as much to do with researching it as I did."

"True, true… but I certainly didn't start the research, nor take the risk that you did to ask the other Trinity council members for access to his private records," he said smiling. If you had been *wrong,* I imagine there would be a question… or ten… now floating your way from the rest of the High Council. No doubt a word or two would also end up on their personal filings going on to your confirmation board."

"Speaking of that…" entered Aurelius from the speakers. "I was asked to inform you, Ms. Taryn, that the other council members wish to consult with you when you have a free moment."

"Probably to pass along their congratulations, I imagine," said Wil. "Oh, and Mr. Brough is bustling away in the kitchen preparing an especially exquisite lunch for you today as his own manner of congratulations. He made me promise not to tell you any more about it than that."

"Well, what about you, Aurelius? asked Taryn. Do you know what he's making in there?"

"I believe so, but Mr. Brough threatened to, quote, 'repurpose my speakers as part of his new floral arrangement on the western terrace' if I informed you of any more of his doings. And I'm reminded of the old phrase that 'an unhappy cook is never unhappy alone.'"

Even Filater chuckled a moment at that.

"Well," the senior agent said quickly recovering his composure, "I need to depart." He motioned farewell to Wil and Taryn.

"Oh, and Ms. Taryn", Filater said as he was half out the door, "I sent over a file early this morning to your government account as my own small token of gratitude. Probably not nearly as good as Mr. Brough's lunch will be, but then again, I'm told my type of gift works better cold anyways."

"Wait, I thought that the whole trip to the SOMA today…" she started, confused. "I thought that was your way of saying thanks?"

"That? Oh, I never said that. I said I thought you should see what was happening, but the trip today… that was all originally Aurelius's idea. I was simply of a like mind on the matter."

Agent Filater departed leaving Taryn to wonder at all he'd told her. When she made it to her desk in the office, she remembered that C and G were still wanting to speak with her.

She activated the Wucengi neural device and stayed on it for the next 30 minutes. Upon exiting, she found Wil sitting across the desk.

"I was right, wasn't I? They gave you a big 'you were right, and we shouldn't have doubted you' speech, didn't they?"

"Not quite to that extent," she replied, "but the spirit of it was there. They said to pass on their compliments to my Bizi colleague for helping and making sure things were smoothly handed over when the time came."

Wil nodded in receipt. "Of course."

"They also said that our success will be reflected in their recommendation to the SOMA when it comes time to decide if I will stay on as a permanent member."

"Well, that should have been obvious from even before all this, if you don't mind me saying. What do you think, A?" he asked upwards at Aurelius.

"Recent events have certainly elevated the likelihood of Miss Taryn's position being confirmed beyond temporary status," the personable voice answered. “Based on prior experience, I estimate an 83.5% chance the SOMA will concur with the other council members’ recommendations.”

“We’ll see,” said Taryn. “But thank you both for helping me with this. It wouldn’t have been possible without either of you. This was due to all of us.”

Both Aurelius and Wil simultaneously responded with, “You're welcome.”

At that, Taryn began running through her lists of duties she had intended to work on that day. A few more legislative reviews and a couple of quick briefings and meeting recaps from Aurelius and two more hours passed hastily by.

Mr. Brough later came to inform Taryn that lunch was ready in the dining room at her convenience. There, she found a beautiful culinary display awaiting her. Next to a bouquet vase of beautifully trimmed flowers on the table, there was a plate of freshly cooked fish, grilled with a zest of lemon, garlic, and other spices. Assorted greens and vegetables from Mr. Brough’s personal garden on the back grounds and perfectly seasoned potatoes, carrots, and snap peas shared the space. To the side, a plate of homemade rolls, with honey and milk. For dessert, a bowl of mixed fruit with strawberries, apples, grapes, mango, raspberries, and blackberries as fresh as the day they were picked, all mixed with a topping of thick cream. Taryn thanked Mr. Brough many times over for the efforts of his preparations, but what truly shocked her was the box at the opposite end of the dining table. Inside were several traveling containers that Mr. Brough had also prepared. Each was holding more servings of his delicacies. He informed Taryn that she was to take them home for the enjoyment of her whole family.

“Since they are not allowed to know what you’ve achieved here today, they should at least be allowed the tangibility of this gratitude,” he said to Taryn.

“I’m touched, Mr. Brough. Thank you so much for all this. It’s wonderful.”

After a longer than average lunch, Taryn made her way back into the office and continued with her work, though occasionally thinking with pleasure at how thrilled Gloria, Lilly, and Trey would be when she got home. Especially since no one would have to prepare a meal for that evening. When Wil came in to perform his usual afternoon security rounds, it dawned on Taryn that she’d forgotten something.

"Aurel?" She said as she was motioning for Wil to stay in the office a moment longer.

"Yes, Ms. Taryn?"

"Access the file that Agent Filater sent over this morning, will you?"

"Yes. The file contains a few rather short video recordings. Shall I bring them up?"

"Yeah. Go ahead" she answered with a slightly puzzled look to Wil. From his face's expression of curiosity, he also clearly had no idea what this file held.

On the office wall monitors, three of the four screens lit up. On each was shown some low-quality video. After about 30 seconds or so each video looped over and began again. Taryn got up from her desk to join Wil closer to the screens to make out the details. Based on the angles, the videos all appeared to be from stationary monitoring positions.

"Oh," Wil said after a few moments of staring. "Those are the siblings of the now convicted representative being taken into Bizi custody. This must have been yesterday," he said pointing at two of the screens. "That's the brother there, and that one's the sister. Hmm… Filater must've gotten ahold of the corporate security feeds." On two screens there were pairs of agents escorting a handcuffed man or woman out of some inner offices, all in front of some surprised bystanders and apparent coworkers.

"I wonder why Filater sent this though? I mean, you already saw their brother's conviction in person. Comparatively, this isn't all that special after being allowed to visit the SOMA halls for real."

"I don't know," replied Taryn just as perplexed. "Agent Filater mentioned that the siblings will probably be fired just as soon as—" Taryn paused mid-sentence. She had been watching the brother's escort and had just switched to look closer at the sister's when it struck her. Taryn knew that face. The taut cheeks, the narrow nose, the expensive suit, luxurious shoes, and glasses.

"That's Fisecaly!" Taryn blurted out.

"Who?" asked Wil, confused by the sudden alarm in her tone.

"I met her that day… the last day… I was at my previous job," replied Taryn. "She's the sister!?" she said, still stunned by the realization.

"Yeah," said Wil. "And that," he said, pointing to the third screen. "That's the suit that promoted her at her company. Based on the internal communiqués that we've seized; he has the clearest evidence of conspiracy with the two siblings. He'd also been recently tapped for his own senior level promotion."

Taryn switched to examine the third screen now, and again a lump stuck in her throat. The screen showed a pair of agents escorting a much shorter round figure with restraints on his wrists out of an office with a large wooden desk and corner windows in the background. A tall, angry looking Corp security guard appeared to be behind them, emphatically yelling at the pair of agents to no avail as they walked away with their suspect in tow. The security guard, blushed in his face from yelling, appeared highly irritated at not being in charge of the situation as the group continued out of the office and down the hall. Taryn looked hard at the suit in custody.

"Meroan!" She managed to get out as her mouth fell a gape.

"Know him too I assume?" Wil asked.

"That's the Tie that fired me. I mean he was a Tie at the time. Him and Fisecaly, they were both there on my last day when I was kicked off the grounds."

This was too much. Taryn felt her head swim. She stepped out of the office and threw herself onto one of the short couches out in the living room, while going over her memories of her meeting that early morning with the two conspirators. It seemed like a very long time ago, in fact, but her mind still searched back to recall some of the details of the meeting. The uncompromising approach, with only overtones of politeness that both of them had shown her. The synchronization of their cold efficient facilitation of goals. The subtle hints that apparently masked giant reservoirs of ambition. She sat there reflecting on all this for nearly an hour. Wil only momentarily stepped in to check on her, then left silently when it was clear she wished to be alone. After his second check on her, she finally stirred, sitting up.

"It makes sense…" she said. "Fisecaly tells Meroan about her brother becoming the SOMA rep for Region 74. He promotes her while passing on the marching orders. He's smart enough to have thought it through alone, but still he's not beyond passing the information along to his own superiors if he thought it would be more helpful for himself."

"What about the brother? Did you know him?"

"Mmm, no, not as far as I can tell," Taryn said, getting up to go double-check the monitors again. "But… what a weird day this has turned into."

As Taryn thought, she watched each of the screens loop through for a short while longer, until she felt she'd seen everything there was to see. Her meeting with Meroan and Fisecaly, the events of the now disgraced Region 74 SOMA member, the intent to reduce government inspections. She sat pondering these some more as the screens kept replaying. Wil, again, left Taryn to be alone to think.

* * *

As Wil was driving her home for the evening, Taryn figured that she understood how most of the pieces now fit together. The containers with Mr. Brough's professional meal preparations were sitting neatly packed on the back seat as their pleasant aromas gently waved through and filled the entirety of the cabin interior.

"Cold?" Wil suddenly inquired. They had not been speaking much during the drive home and had been quietly listening to some music.

"No, I'm okay," Taryn answered, assuming that Wil was inquiring about the temperature.

"No, I wasn't asking about that. Before leaving, Agent Filater said his gift, the file videos, were better off cold? What was he talking about?"

Taryn looked out of her side window and thought for a moment. Then a small smirk and a muted chuckle came over her as she watched the fields in the failing sunlight rolling by.

"I think it's a reference to a very old saying," Taryn remarked. "Filater was simply offering me another type of meal to chew on."

Chapter 12: A Professional Courtesy

In comparison to the events of that one day at the SOMA, the next few were calm and uneventful. Although Taryn did find that the meal from Mr. Brough had managed to greatly increase her family's general opinion about her new career. They had become accustomed to Taryn not discussing work matters at the supper table, as she had done when she worked the floor. And they had been more than content with the increased credits and subsequent increase in both the amount and varieties of food that they were now able to afford. But still, Taryn's late hours typically meant she wasn't home to cook all that much, and Lilly was less than restrained at holding back her curiosity on things, especially after Taryn had brought home such a well-prepared meal out of nowhere. Taryn, not wanting to be rude, only hinted that the meal came from a coworker as leftovers for a team accomplishment that had been unexpectedly noticed.

This explanation, while purposely vague, was still truthful, and clear enough to satisfy both her mother and her daughter for the moment. Trey, as children of that age do, had recently begun using simple words and phrases and thus needed no explanation of anything, except reassurances at his next meal, bath, or changing time. All the same, Taryn would occasionally talk to Trey while she bathed him alone. If, for no other reason, than to have someone she could tell her daily news to, even if that be an uncomprehending child. She found it nice and almost therapeutic in relieving the stresses she'd accumulated from her decisions at work. Between her private talks with Trey, her daily walks with Mr. Brough, small lunch banters with

Wil and occasional discourse with Aurelius, Taryn had found a method to help her manage her job-related stresses that didn't jeopardize her security.

At home, she'd also found more time on slower days to take her family out occasionally for a meal. Mostly this meant a trip to The Hidden Roller to dine and to visit Uncle Everett when he wasn't at practice. More commonly though, they all went for walks or small but fun trips to a local park, museums, and the regional library. They all went to watch the mid-season matches for the regional hexaderby team, who had started off the early season mostly undefeated in no small part due to Everett's help. Without the worries for the immediate financial future of her family at stake, on those nights that she didn't work late, Taryn had more leisure time to herself as well. She did privately curse as she thought of how horrible it was that for the first time in her life, she now had the ability to slow down and breathe, and yet Cyrano wasn't around to enjoy any of it with her. She would daydream often during her days off. Thinking about how if Cyrano was still alive even Gloria would notice how well they would now be getting on together, never having to fight about credits or the bills anymore. Or the need for him to travel for his work. Gloria would be expected to make some comment that 'If you two are going to be laughing at each other like this, you might find it helpful to buy your children better ear speakers for the evenings. Not to mention a pair for me as well.' It made Taryn both angry and sad, but all the same she couldn't deny the benefits of her new position. Also, with her arguments with Gloria over income now a thing of the past, they were generally much more relaxed in their moods and conversations.

* * *

About three weeks after the SOMA trial, Taryn received word from Aurelius that a SOMA committee had begun the process of reviewing her status as a member of the council. They would be hearing the reports on her prepared by Members C and G, as well as her assigned Bizi agent and an efficiency report from Aurelius too. The review process would itself take two or more days, and after yet another day of closed deliberations that she had no ability to observe, Taryn would be called before the SOMA committee members via the Wucengi to be asked a few clarifying questions before being told their final determination.

If they decided not to let her stay, she'd be removed, rather hastily, from the estate grounds, but with at least 3 months' pay as compensation for the "impoliteness" of the entire process. At which point, a new temporary candidate, who would take at least that long to be selected and gain the essential security training and clearances, would be installed. That was all Aurelius could tell Taryn on the matter. He advised her that neither Wil nor the other members of the council could themselves say any more on the subject to her.

Thus, for the next day and a half Taryn, despite her best efforts, had a harder time than usual keeping her focus on work. She chose not to watch any of the reports being submitted about her in an effort to remain focused, but still the thought crept up from the back of her mind that soon she *would* be gone from this house. *Definitely*, she thought, *but after it happens, what then?* A return to job hunting was the most likely answer. Being one of the most powerful yet unidentified people in the world could not be ignored as a new entry in the work experience section of her resume, she reasoned. But the notion of how to actually describe it without compromising her security clearance perplexed her. After much internal back and forth she guessed Wil and Aurel would advise her to put down something vague and benign like, 'team management experience.' She had in fact thought about bringing this question to Wil, when Aurelius told her the SOMA committee was waiting for her via a secure line.

"Ms. Taryn, the communication line I've set up for you will render your virtual image on the Wucengi now visible to the SOMA committee, though, as per usual, it is purposely unclear in its facial and body resolution. The other members of the Trinity Council will certainly be watching, though you won't be able to see them."

"Thank you, A. Anything else I should know?"

"Typically, you can expect their questions towards you to be rather brief, but the committee will still weigh your responses before any final decision is made."

"Very well," she said, making herself more comfortable at her desk chair. "Let's get this over with. I suppose I've had quite enough waiting 'round."

Taryn put the small metallic disk to her temple and activated the Wucengi neural device to open the line. She found herself in a small room of the SOMA halls before a row of 17 representatives staring at her virtual rendering. After so many hours and days walking amongst them unnoticed and unconcerned for her own self-perception, being now detectable by their gazes, Taryn suddenly felt rather uneasy in this position. She should have expected that.

"Hello. Thank you for joining us today, Member T," said the designated speaker for the committee. "We'd just like to ask some quick questions before we settle on our decision."

"Of course," Taryn nodded. She noticed in her ear that her voice didn't sound like hers. It had a much more mechanical tinge to it as she spoke. Aurelius must have been modulating that too.

"First, do you think that you have done a good job so far as a member of the Trinity High Council?"

Taryn took a moment.

"Sometimes I think yes, but… but to be honest… sometimes I feel completely lost by all of this," she was saying with a tinge of relief and resignation. I know that… that I'm not the only one here who is new to working in the government system, but with all due respect, any mistakes or bad suggestions a person within the SOMA makes can be halted, compensated, refined, or smoothed out in one of the committees or by your fellow representatives here." She said this gesturing to all the SOMA panel members. "And while I do have a handful of excellent advisors who are all much more experienced than myself, I don't have nearly as many checks between any ill-conceived ideas that I come up with and their implementation.

"So, I do what I can to make sure my decisions are careful before being put out. Whether that means I do a decent job or not is still unclear to me. I just…" She took a breath, "I just do what I can, when I think it's the best thing to do at that time. If… if that makes any sense at all.

"Thank you." The speaker continued, "now, do you like this position? And please allow me to clarify," he said, folding his hands and leaning forward. "If you could make the same pay in a different position that we had available for you right now without having to endure all the squabbling and stresses that I'm sure comes with being a Trinity High Council member, would you accept it?"

"No… no, I wouldn't. I mean I understand why some might, but personally, I wouldn't feel… like I had done anything worthwhile to earn this much pay. I've seen others, in my old jobs, do far less and earn far more than myself... even compared to the credits I'm earning here. But that's not me. I was not brought up to think that way. I like this job far more than any other I've ever held. I enjoy it, not only for the pay, but also for the opportunity to help. To mean something. To make my own impression on things in a constructive manner. Those I work with want me to do well, and that is a rarity in itself. To be paid well, respected at my work, and have an opportunity to provide help to others is never a bad thing."

"Well, we thank you again for your candor. Is there anything else you'd like to add to the record before we begin our final deliberations?"

"No," said Taryn hesitatingly. "I think I've managed to say all that matters."

"Very well, we will be discontinuing your connection momentarily while we converse. Please be patient for a short while."

Taryn opened her eyes in the office and waited for what felt like a far longer period than she was expecting. A myriad of thoughts began sprouting in her head about possible reasons for her dismissal from the position. Lack of experience, she guessed, would be chief among these. Or perhaps a sluggish work pace, or self-acknowledged ineptitude. She kept thinking how stupidly naïve her answers must have sounded under their outside examination. Her head was awash in the various mixtures of these possibilities when a beep from the Wucengi interrupted her. She was expected to reconnect. When her virtual image stood back in front of the SOMA committee, Taryn found that her audio was muted, and that only her visual feed had been restored. She didn't take that as a good sign.

"Thank you again for your patience. Based on your answers and the reports we've received from others; this committee has decided that your position on the Trinity High Council shall be changed to permanent status. Congratulations, Trinity Council Member T."

Taryn could only bow her head in stunned acknowledgement.

"Your term limit for serving on the High Council will be decided by us privately and will not be revealed to you until the term itself has expired. It will, in accordance with the rules of the Radix, be set to no less than one cycle but not to exceed a maximum of 15 cycles. And finally," he said, taking a different padd in hand, "we on the committee are told that the following passage has been read to every permanent member of the Haiden Prime Trinity High Council at the successful conclusion of their confirmation hearing. It was written quite a long time ago by the first SOMA representatives to the first Trinity High Council members. Now we would like to echo their words for you to hear as well." The speaker began slowly and gravely reading from the padd.

"Council member, we wish you congratulations. You have been granted a great deal of power and responsibility on behalf of everyone here, everyone you've ever known, or ever will know. Everyone you've ever hated or loved and the many more that you've never met. Please try to remember why such power has been willingly bound to you for this time: you must work for the betterment of all in our society, so that the others who may follow us later shall find their jobs easier than you now find yours. Consider each day as a gift to you, a great gift allowed only to a few: the gift of influential choice. For you are to benefit the public as much as you can, every single day that you remain as part of the Council. For one day, without warning to you, it will be your last on the Council. Such is life, and such is our system. Leave nothing for later if it may be avoided. *Thou art mortal*, and later is not a certainty for anyone here. Council Member, your name will not be known or remembered by us, nor acknowledged by any of your colleagues. But if your ideas and ideals are truly worthwhile, the influence of your service shall always be, for as long as we may be. Please, continue your work for the people, as the people, and within the people."

The Wucengi once again disconnected and Taryn, her mind back in the office, opened her eyes. She sat for a long time slowly rerunning that last quote from the SOMA.

You've done well girl, she finally thought to herself. *From being fired and blacklisted, to becoming one of the most powerful people in the world in less than a cycle. Cyrano or Mom wouldn't believe you, even if you could tell them.*

"Ms. Taryn?"

"Yes, Aurel?"

"Are you ready to continue?"

"Absolutely," she smiled. "What's next?"

* * *

The next week, the gusts of wind had picked up, blowing considerably cooler drafts of air across the region. The full change of seasons was well and truly underway, and it was another change, this one unexpected, when Agent Filater visited the estate. Upon entering the house he could hear Taryn's voice, through the barely closed sliding office door, discussing with Aurelius the latest solar energy shipment distribution plans. He made a quick mental note to himself to mention to Bough about the need for sound dampeners to be installed specifically in this room just outside the office. The senior Bizi agent stood patiently in the outer sitting room for a few more moments, thinking through the real purpose of his visit once more. He decided to use this time to seek out Agent Zhuantium who was probably outside patrolling the grounds this time of day. Having found and briefly spoken to him, Agent Filater returned to the sitting room a few minutes later to where the muted noise of the discussion inside the office had dissipated. He waited patiently, knowing

Aurelius was well aware of his presence and purpose there and would announce him to the High Council member at the earliest convenience. Aurelius verbally ushered him through after a long period of relative silence.

"Hello," he said, entering. "I understand congratulations are in order, *High Council Member*." Taryn looked up from her work, struck by the emphasis in his tone. She was finishing an entry in the mostly empty red leather journal that Brough had delivered to her upon her confirmation just last week. It was one of the official tasks that she was at first loath to take up: the process of actively recording all her decisions and salient points of her reasons for the official record as a High Council member.

"News travels fast, I guess. But thank you, Agent Filater," she responded with a smile.

"Well, it would be more appropriate to say that news travels fastest when you have the right security clearance," he retorted. "How is the record keeping going?" Filater said, gesturing to the open journal in front of her.

"Slowly." Taryn remarked looking back down to finish writing the word she was in the middle of. "But surprisingly it's not as difficult as I initially thought," she admitted. "It helps a lot more than I'd expected." This was a true enough point because, as Taryn had quickly discovered, all you ever had to do in your own journal was argue with yourself for every one of your official decisions each and every day. A few moments of genuine reflection found her being harsher than the worst critic she could imagine. Yet on the very next line she might have a far more tempered and forgiving assessment. As long as she could argue with herself that she had listened to all possible options from her colleagues and advisors, and then selected the reasonable choices she genuinely thought were best at the time, she was satisfied. She found to her surprise that she had no reluctance letting her doubts creep onto the pages of her entries as well. She'd seen a similar thing in writings of previous council member's entries and now finally was starting to understand why. It was an intellectually cathartic practice that helped to flush out her self-doubts when she wrote them all down. It was still a slow process though, but the more she practiced it each day the less hesitant she was growing about her writing approach.

It's not important to sound smart here, she had told herself. *It's not like you'll actually meet anyone who'll ever read it. You'll never have to debate with them about what you did or why. Or hear them tell you about their thoughts on how bad you are at all this stuff. But there is always a chance that sometime in the future, another council member, feeling just as overwhelmed as you, will look at this, see your entries, and find a small bit of encouragement in reading the notes of a predecessor who was initially just as apprehensive.* And in a moment of profound cynicism, she had the thought that if nothing else, future readers would be discouraged from laying claim to the title of the most *simple minded* of all council members. "Let me just finish this one thing down," she said briefly to the Bizi agent standing before her as she hurriedly worked to finish her current line before it slipped away. Just then Wil, with his typical morning smile still on full display, entered the office as well. Having finished his immediate security duties on the grounds he was reporting as the senior Bizi agent had requested of him. Taryn didn't question Wil's entrance. She knew enough to see that if Wil had come to join them now, it was because Filater had wanted him here too. If Filater didn't want her security detail involved, she also knew he had no qualms about getting Wil to vacate the office area.

"So, what brings you back to visit?" said Taryn, motioning for Filater to take a seat as she finished writing her sentence and closed the red-leather book. "I doubt you have enough free time to drive all the way out here for some simple congratulations when a vid-call would have worked as easily."

"I came here to ask you," he said, motioning for Wil to come and sit also. "Well, both of you actually… for some help."

Taryn was stunned into silence for a moment at this.

"I will help as much as I can, of course." She said quickly recovering. "And I expect Wil will want to do the same, not in the least because you can simply order him to do so. But you? Asking us for help? That's rather odd, isn't it?"

"You have no idea," the agent muttered with a somber glance at her. "But in this instance, I think it could be useful given how you two and Aurelius were able to pick up on something the entire Bizi missed in detecting that SOMA security breach. Since you have now been confirmed as a permanent Council Member, and this does concern the High Council itself, I figure the time is right for this issue to be brought before a fresh set of eyes."

"Okay," Taryn said, pushing the padd of work she was due to complete today to the side of her desk to give the agent her full attention. "If this is a Council matter then let's hear it and see what we can do."

Filater began after a short pause.

"The Bizi wouldn't normally mention any prior council members to you, except to refer you to their journals of course," he said looking at the nearby bookshelf of red leather-bound books. "But… you will need to hear some background first."

Filater pulled out a padd that he quickly synchronized to the wall monitors behind him.

"Up to this point Ms. Steno, you and Agent Zhuantium probably assumed that your positions here came about thanks to the term limit expiring for the prior High Council Member."

Taryn and Wil shot a puzzled glance at each other at this remark.

"Well, why wouldn't we?" she replied.

"The truth is," Filater continued, "that the council member prior to you died while still serving out his term. His unexpected death, I'm sorry to say, is part of the reason you are here now."

There was another pause as the monitors behind him flashed to reveal a grisly crime scene, flanked off with blue boy rope on a sidewalk. The images were dark and obviously taken at night as the body of a man in exercise apparel was shown to be lying on his back. The corpse's face was blurred out, and there were small pools and splatters of dark liquid on the concrete all around the victim. The blood was less apparent on his clothes, but it looked to have emanated from at least two or three different sources on the chest.

"Council Member U, as he was known, was a smart enough fellow in his way," Filater began. "A former officer in the Defense Force for many cycles, before serving on the council. He was a man of regular habits. And except for a bit of a temper, he was not the sort to take risks. Real neat and orderly type that the armed forces love to train up. So, it's something of a mystery to me that he should be murdered while out jogging alone one night."

Filater turned and walked to the monitors to look at the photos he'd seen many times before now.

"By himself and in his off hours. This had all the appearance of an attack during a random burglary. Anything of value on him was gone. No weapons at the scene, though the wounds were from some type of knife. Because he was alone, without identification, the Blue Boys were the first ones called in when his body was eventually found. As the initial investigators had no knowledge or way to know of Member U's position in the government, the official report that made its way into the records could only, understandably, be considered incomplete at best.

"Naturally," Filater continued as he slowly paced the room, "the Bizi started its own inquiry once the blue boy detectives had their chance. But our investigators were still not convinced that this was anything more than poor luck if that's what you'd call it. Wrong place, wrong time type of thing, and the victim just happened to be a Council Member this time. But, while robberies turning into murders are not nearly as rare as we'd like, the fact is that neither of the conclusions from these investigations ever sat well with me. After discreetly consulting with his own assigned security Bizi agent and with Aurelius, I think another check may be necessary. I'd like you two to give this scenario a close look and test out the water's clarity."

"Well, thank you for the vote of confidence…" said Taryn hesitantly. "But—what's stopping you or any other Bizi agent from simply looking into this for yourselves? Why us?"

Filater chose his next words carefully.

"I have several other matters on the hook right now that need my full attention, including finishing the SOMA security breach case. Plus, re-opening another case that's been officially closed is not the highest concern for anyone else who has the proper clearance. Simply put, those who would probably be the most logical choice aren't cleared to know who the victim actually was. And those who are cleared to know are not all that interested in looking at a file that's been closed two times over. On top of that…" he paused. "I want an outsider's thoughts on this."

"Why is that?" asked Wil.

Filater returned to his seat and continued in a much subtler manner. "I fear that my view is now too skewed. That I may be falling into the law of instrument syndrome."

"What's that?" Taryn asked.

Wil chimed in, "I once heard it described as tunnel vision for people with training. A type of conformational bias."

"Yes, though that hardly explains the full concept of it," Filater remarked. "It happens when you only have limited tools or methodology available to use. Having no other options, you would be prone to using that same skill set over and over again for every single problem you encountered, whether it was appropriate or not. You may end up viewing the entire world's problems as being full of nails all because the only thing you're comfortable using is the hammer. If it's all you ever had to work with and what you've been trained for, why not? In reality, however, there may come situations of different sorts where your skill or approach has no use at all, and you may indeed cause more damage than there was originally. The Bizi choose the tools and skills our agents are trained with very carefully. Yet still, as adaptable as our skill sets are, there are some rare cases like this one, where I think a nontraditional approach may be best. Cynical as I am," he said in an almost painful fashion, "I'm still not beyond fearing that this may all be a misjudgment from my being overly suspicious of the situation. Trying to do anything to confirm my own beliefs. In short, I may just be paranoid."

Filater changed back to his official tone and straightened himself up a bit more. He had obviously not been comfortable letting them know his own private thoughts on the matter.

"Ms. Steno, you and Wil have shown that when you two work together, you have a good sense for following a trail. And if there is one here, you'll have enough background information available, thanks to Aurelius. You both already possess the needed clearances, which is why I'm making this request. If you agree I would naturally expect to be kept informed of any new aspects that you come across. Any intent discovered behind this incident other than a basic robbery scenario would have required knowledge of the High Council Member's identity. And that…." he paused again, lowering his voice. "That could imply something much more severe. You don't need much imagination to see that a breach of that magnitude could make the SOMA incident smell like a field of spring flowers on a clear day by comparison."

"I see..." replied Taryn.

"You should also know," he continued, "that for the last month or so I've done a lot of digging and looked hard into your background files Ms. Steno, before I even felt comfortable coming here with this request."

Taryn, her face slightly distressed at this comment, saw Filater raise his hand in a gesture of calm.

"As I said, any hidden intent would imply knowledge of a highly sensitive nature… meaning that, barring an undetectable hack, a possibility that Aurelius and I have considered and hopefully ruled out, this would mean that someone with top level clearance was possibly connected to this."

"Seeing as you didn't have clearance at the time of the murder and knew little about the inner workings of the Trinity High Council, this meant from the start that your risk of involvement was not likely. But, as you did come to fill the vacant council position left open, I had to be as sure about you as possible. You are the newest member, which meant either that you were involved to a significant degree," he said, eyeing her, "or that you had not the slightest clue as to what was going on. Once it was clear to me you were not involved in this at all, and your position on the council was confirmed as permanent, I decided it was the proper time to bring my suspicions forward to you. I cannot go to anyone else with the proper clearance, not even the other council members, because I have no way of knowing who, if anyone, is potentially compromised.

"I'm sorry if that seems overly cautious, Ms. Steno. I just wanted you to understand the lengths I felt I needed to go to, to ensure the safety and anonymity of the council membership. In this matter, truly, I hope I'm wrong," he said calmly. "And that I am simply stagnating with my own paranoia and overly cautious suspicions. I want your help if you can spare it. Look at the case and if I'm wrong, then by all means tell me that all my precautions were simply the result of an old, tired agent seeing imaginary monsters in the shadows."

There was a pause in the room again. Taryn thought about everything Filater had told her but could not find any other path for him. His request was clear, and so was his thinking. There was no alternative in the matter. It had either been bad timing for the prior council member, this Member U, or something much, much worse. If the worst were true, she was the most logical choice for a second opinion. A newcomer not involved in any way, as Filater saw it, with decent instincts, and no prior connections in this field. Her little experience might even be considered a boon, since that meant she may be prone to asking about things more experienced people took for granted. A look from Wil told her he'd reached much the same conclusion as she had.

"We'll have all the previous investigation files to work from?" Taryn asked.

"Unlocked and transferred by Aurelius the moment I linked my padd to your screens here."

"What about the victim's personal information? How much can we see?"

"Only his name is off limits. He had no living family or relations so everything else of his; personal records, taxes, banking, bills, all free and clear."

"Any ancillary points of evidence?"

"Anything the other investigations looked at is yours to examine too. Any fresh evidence that you find, Wil now has jurisdiction to sequester. And you may request Bizi analytical support staff at any point. Though, I still wouldn't openly mention that the victim was a High Council member. Some folk you may speak with may have helped on the prior investigations, but none of them knew of his position. Not even the Bizi investigators. They were informed that the victim had been a SOMA representative."

Taryn continued her questions. "Is visiting the scene or his residence or his office a possibility?"

"Harder to do…" said Agent Filater thinking on it. "The crime scene or his flat might be too public seeing as two other groups have sniffed out those places extensively already. Both the report from the Blue Boys and the Bizi, as you'll find, describe them without any discrepancies. The Bizi investigation, being a bit more thorough, also made some holo-panoramas of the scene and his home that you may examine. And I can have newer ones made if needed."

"His working location will have to remain off limits though, sorry. Security restrictions. Council members and their staff may only know of their own work locals, except in the case of a direct credible threat. But you will have the live transcripts from the interview with his Bizi security detail, and support staff. All his working notes and activities should already be with either Aurelius or in his journal here on the shelves. Any questions you want answered by the old staff or security can be made by an intermediate, namely me. Anything else you need, just reach out."

"Well, Agent Filater, now that you mention it, I do think you've forgotten one small piece we will definitely be needing though," said Wil, shooting a subtle glance at Taryn, hoping that she saw his cue.

Agent Filater turned a questioning eyebrow over to his junior associate.

"Well, isn't it obvious?" asked Taryn, understanding Wil's look and taking up the now opened flank. "Two extra tall joe cups brought to us hot, immediately and directly from Mr. Brough, thank you."

Agent Filater's surprised glance darted between two bright faces, both smirking at him in return.

"Oh, and try not to be all day about it," said Taryn with a wry smirk. "You know, like how you senior Bizi agents write your reports. Ever *so* slowly."

Chapter 13: Thin Threads Burn Faster

As they rode the lift to the 84th floor of the apartment building, Wil quietly reminded Taryn to change her ID from its usual Vox P. display to that of a Bizi Agent. As the ID scanned her thumbprint to start the changeover, Taryn had to stop herself from smiling at the irony of where they now were. Currently, the pair were ascending to the home address of a suspected high-class escort, who's flat was in the only building located directly between a neighborhood blue boy's station and the largest religious center in the local region. When Wil asked for a breakdown of the current tenants, the building's electronic manager system had informed him of how a large portion of the dwellings here were rented or owned by officers in the Blue Boys, as well as disclosing that the top few floors were reserved strictly to visiting religious delegates when the need arose. Below those the next topmost levels were dormitories for higher echelon religious members and students. All in all, the last place one would expect to find a person who sold sex for a living, yet that may have been the intent, as Wil had mentioned to Taryn.

"As high as her clientele may have reached, this was certainly one of the safest buildings you could hope to find, assuming you could afford it. But just so we're clear, even with the information we've obtained this may all be a ghost hunt: totally pointless and more than likely to go nowhere," he said as they had first entered the lift.

"I should think so," she replied. "Else the other two investigations would have come before us to speak to this… Ms. Luxuroy, right? Luxuroy… such a silly name," Taryn said, shaking her head. "It's a wonder anyone at the physical therapist agency ever took her seriously, even with the fake credentials she gave them."

"You heard the agency manager at that place, it wasn't internal medicine or emergency treatment. As long as their staff brought in new customers and paid them their percentage, they never bothered to look all that hard at the credentials unless there were enough complaints."

"I wonder how many other 'physical therapists' have similar setups?" Taryn remarked.

"More than just her I'd imagine. Still, some of the clients on her office list *did* confirm that all they received was a standard rehab treatment and not any… unique attention." He was busy as he spoke, calibrating the fittings on a small eyepiece recorder they brought with them to document any new information they were given. "Only the fact that her income accounts are far beyond the standard pay truly stands out as odd. Well, that and her timing on the night that Council Member U was killed of course."

Taryn was about to ask if she could be allowed to take the lead when they began talking to Ms. Luxuroy. She thought it might make things go smoother and make Luxuroy more comfortable speaking to another woman, instead of a larger formally dressed Bizi agent like Wil. But before she could put her question forward, the elevator halted suddenly as the display read the floor number of *44*. They felt the track system rotate as the lift moved horizontally for a brief moment, pulling them off sideways from the main vertical canal, before coming quickly to rest.

The building's electronic manager system came over the intercom panel which displayed and spoke.

"Please forgive the delay. Your progress will resume momentarily."

As he had done down in the lobby before, Wil identified himself as a Bizi agent to the panel to see if he could find out more about the delay.

"Apologies, Agent Zhuantium, but another set of lifts carrying a religious delegation has priority passage for the sake of security. The delay will be over in approximately 120 seconds."

As they waited, Taryn pulled out her padd and once again went through all the steps that brought them to this point. She was trying not only to distract herself while they were delayed, but also to feel a bit more confident that they had not missed anything more from the fractional clues that they had decided to check on.

First, there had been the location of the Council Member's murder. The spot itself was an ideal robbery locale to be sure. A literal blind spot for the nearby street recorders. On one side of the double lane street was a large city park, while the opposite had only a small handful of occupied buildings with businesses whose own recorders were focused on the nearer walkways. The night lamps on the park side, where the body of Council Member U had been found, had several broken lights or others in need of replacement, making the area a spotty patchwork of lit and dark segments in the evenings. The precise spot of the killing was in a deep indent in the park's stone fence line for a bench and waste can. It was fully obscured on the park side by the stone wall and black iron fence from ahead or behind. The only direct line of sight for the murder would have been from far across the street. The local recorders did show that that particular evening had been overcast with clouds following heavy rainfall in the afternoon. The weather had pushed most of the foot traffic off the streets, despite it eventually clearing up during the first dark hour. That had been confirmed by the weather records that Aurelius had pulled. The estimated time for the murder meant the nearest possible witnesses were busy working and dining at near-empty restaurants across the street. But, as Wil argued, if an experienced thief could determine the advantages of this blind location over others, then they should also have had enough experience and restraint to manage the situation far better than what apparently had happened. A simple robbery getting out of control and escalating to murder didn't fit with this much forethought in choosing an ambush site.

The only recorder found on the proper side of the street was off due to an electrical short in its wiring that had been registered as a problem with the systems data maintenance cycle. Aurelius immediately began running through the software for the history and nature of this bug, but informed Wil and Taryn it may be some time before it could be corroborated as anything but incidental mechanical failure.

In fact, the only full recording they found of Council Member U going for his evening run on the night he died, had been of him just outside his own building as he had started. He'd left after the rain had stopped and, when exiting onto the street, merged into a small throng of bustling folk in front of his building. Other recorders and cameras along his path had only caught blurry glimpses of him partially out of frame. His rather pale legs pacing along were usually the only sign of him in these images. And sometimes, with bad lighting, he was difficult to even spot.

There was one video that Taryn focused on for nearly a whole afternoon though. It was a clear recording, with by far the best quality they'd yet seen, but due to the angles it, like the others before, appeared nearly worthless at first. It came from a view on the side of the street opposite where the murder had actually occurred. But the recorder's view was aimed more towards the beginning of the block and far higher up from the ground, at least two or three stories. The lens gave the recorder a fish-eye view. Council Member U's feet and legs could be seen for just a moment or two, barely grazing downwards across the top left corner of the frame as he jogged a little towards the camera on the far side walkway. But only his lower legs and nothing more. The recorder had apparently been installed to monitor auto-valeted vehicles in front of an upscale restaurant on the near side. Aurelius, having done a quick check on the restaurant's files, explained that the owner had likely splurged on a high-end recorder to ensure the restaurant could defend themselves from complaints of vehicle mismanagement. Of course, most of the frame was filled with the restaurant's semi-circular entrance and the street before it. Taryn and Wil had narrowed the time span on the recording to when they suspected Member U to have passed on the opposite side of the street. They watched it loop over several times to find only his jogging feet going by. One vehicle was centered in frame at this same time as its owner was departing to enter the restaurant.

Taryn had watched the recording several times, even more than Wil had the patience for. Being the clearest and brightest images that they could find from that night, she was adamant at making sure that they actually were empty of anything helpful to them. During her twentieth or so full viewing, a new thought occurred to her.

She magnified the image of the expensive vehicle and its door, as the driver exited, and the door was swinging up to open. She slowed the playback down to its lowest level, reversed and replayed those moments several times over. The council member's jogging feet had already disappeared out of frame after pacing by on the opposite corner a few moments earlier. Taryn enlarged the window of the driver door until it filled her whole screen. After having Aurelius run through an hour of several enhancements and filters to the images, Taryn was frustrated to find her idea to be nearly worthless.

She'd hoped that perhaps she could see the Council Member's image reflected on the door's windows, but either the angles were all wrong, or perhaps the lighting was too bright on the restaurant side, or perhaps U was already too close or too far away at that moment. Taryn sat back frustrated, and after taking a short break to grab one of Mr. Brough's signature recipe joe-cups to recoup, she returned to her desk and slowly began zooming out from the replay. She had been hesitant to move on to more grainy images from other recorders.

As she began considering how much time she'd just wasted on this, it finally dawned on her.

"*The side mirrors,*" she mumbled to herself.

To the left of the window, the vehicle's driver-side mirror had been folding forward and turning upwards to slide itself into the vehicle's body frame compartment. This was meant to help the auto-valet system to fit the vehicles into notoriously tight parking spaces. The angle of the side mirror, Taryn thought, might be better than the window even though the image was even smaller than she'd hoped. Again, she zoomed in on the mirror and had Aurelius run his enhancements and filter programs over the images. Another hour later Taryn and Wil were watching the results Aurelius had found. Using a gray filter and several light and particle motion detection algorithms, Aurelius showed them the enhanced image reflected from the vehicle's mirror.

There was the Council Member U's back, jogging at his typical pace away from the screen and quickly growing smaller. At the moment of the best angle of reflection, the mirror showed U, who happened to be passing through a lit area on the far path across the street, as Aurelius explained. But that was not what Wil and Taryn stared at on the screen. To the council member's right, in the lit patch, there was someone else. Easily within arm's reach, looking as though they were moving with the council member, at the exact same steady pace as him. A second jogger.

According to Aurelius's calculations and a comparison to U's size, the second person was shorter and less massive than the council member. Based on what Wil saw in the image he knew immediately that this new person was a female. Her hair was tied up with the dark tail sticking out through a cap. She appeared dressed in much darker and tighter female jogging apparel. A pair of black running shoes would have been nearly invisible in the lower quality recordings that they had been reviewing up to that point. Taryn and Wil gathered that she would have been positioned just enough to the council member's right-hand side to make her unnoticeable. She would've been jogging in the darker patches with her dark clothing most of the time. They later concluded that must have been partly why she'd slipped by unnoticed on the other recorders as well. The other part was due to their apparent size difference, her whole body would usually be offscreen, blocked by the larger council member himself. This would have obstructed the view of both the lower quality images from recorders across the street, but also of anyone else on the opposite walkway. No one sitting at a meal in the restaurants would likely have noticed her jogging alongside the council member at a their closely synced running pace. Only a person moving directly head-on at them would have that chance. And even then, the pair would probably have to be directly under a streetlight for this smaller and dark clothed female jogger to be fully visible.

Taryn and Wil had Aurelius backtrack all the logged recorders following the council member's running path to see if this mystery female appeared on any of those as well. They wanted to know exactly when this woman and the council member had first met up for this run, as she clearly hadn't come out of his flat with him. The only other possible image of her had been from when the council member originally left his own building. As he merged into the commotion of people outside the main doors Aurelius froze the image. In one quick gap between the mass of the people in the frame, a cap, with a similar hair tail moving in the same direction as U could be seen. Aurelius had calculated, again based on U's height, that this was the image of someone who matched the height of the female from the reflection angle view. The proportions were similar. Due to her height, her face could not be seen however, as it was obscured by the many taller shoulders in the crowd. The person was just too short. But the top of their cap was visible long enough for a third round of image enhancements to make it possible to read. On the front of the cap was the logo and name of a local fitness firm. A quick check of their records found that while the council member stuck to his own exercise room in his flat, a security measure that was pushed upon him by his assigned Bizi security detail, he did hold an expired membership to that same gym, predating his time on the council. The logo of his private gym matched the hat logo on the recorder.

"That's our link. That's where we'll find this lady," Wil had declared.

It had taken Aurelius only five minutes of running through the gym's archived file recordings to narrow the list of possibilities. Those who held memberships at least as long as the council member and who had also been seen repeatedly conversing with him at the fitness center before his membership ran out were few. There were only three females on this refined list, two of which were both as tall as the council member himself and one more who was much shorter. Facial recognition along with pulling the dates of member logins at the fitness center had verified the identity of the girl as Marisela Luxuroy. Her taxes showed she worked as a physical therapist at a generic medical agency complex. The agency's record of her credentials proved they were professionally made forgeries, though a few follow-up calls made it clear the agency likely remained purposefully ignorant of that point. Once the council member's name was confirmed by Aurelius on her regular client list, their suspicions peaked. His record showed that due to his many cycles of serving in the Defense Force he had built up some chronic injuries common to those serving in line. Bad knees and joints and some back issues were all valid conditions that were documented in his initial medical survey before taking office. It would have been only natural for him to seek out a physical therapist's help for these issues in his time before being selected to work on the high council.

Upon checking Ms. Luxuroy's income in comparison to the number of clients she treated, it was revealed that while she did offer physical therapy services, certain recurring clients of hers had paid an excessive amount over her nominal fee. After Wil made some more calls and gently pressed on a few of the other clients, he found that they implied that Ms. Luxuroy's physical therapy service may be much more extensive for those with the proper amount of credits. The records weren't exactly clear on the client list however, likely on purpose they reasoned. Several names appeared to be pseudonyms with no real medical records to match. It was also unclear if the council member had ever arranged one of the more active sessions with Ms. Luxuroy at any point. Both Taryn and Wil were convinced from that point on that it was this Ms. Luxuroy who had been jogging with Council Member U on the night that he was murdered. And that she was with him, from right outside his building, all the way through to the park street where he'd been attacked. Beyond that, they could only guess at where she had gone to, and what role she'd played.

Yet the oddest thing that Taryn and Wil couldn't figure out from her personal records was why her income had apparently grown over the cycles, at about the same time that the Council Member was first inducted, but the number of Ms. Luxuroy's possible illegitimate clients had in fact dropped. Only legitimate looking payments appeared on the records for her most recent months, and there was no major uptake in the number of clients she saw. A huge source of her income had disappeared, yet her bank accounts continued growing without being dampened at all by the lack of customers. She had in fact become even more wealthy than before. Aurelius was still working on tracing where all the income was being sourced from, while Wil and Taryn decided it was time for them to meet Ms. Luxuroy in person.

Finally, the sound of rushing air and a passing lift could be heard descending through the metal door to Taryn and Wil's own. After another moment, their lift's motion resumed with a horizontal heave back on to the main vertical canal before the track could be heard rotating quickly again and resuming their ascent up to Ms. Luxuroy's floor. A "thank you for your patience" message came buzzing from the electronic manager system. Taryn began running through the list of questions they'd want to ask Luxuroy about her relationship to Council Member U, her work, and her financial setup. As some of the questions were obviously more sensitive, it made sense to Taryn that she should prioritize them in a way that wouldn't put their only possible witness to a murder on the defensive. At least, not before they learned all that they could.

As she reviewed the approach of her questioning, a sudden and violent rumble coursed through the canal walls and those of the entire lift system. There was an instant series of harsh jolts. The sound of screaming metal in motion. The whole shaft reverberated and shook with booming echoes that were further amplified by the lift's steel walls. Taryn and Wil had been forced to cover their ears against the painful noise even before they were aware of it. The overhead lights flickered several times, but both were too distracted by the awful noise and shaking of the lift to notice. Almost as fast, the lift came to a sudden screeching halt at floor 78. Taryn could hear the loud click and screech of what she hoped were emergency locks jamming into place just beyond the side walls. The building emergency alarm could also be heard ringing on the floor beyond the lift doors. After checking on Taryn who was more startled than anything else, Wil brought up the panel again requesting to know what had happened. The electronic manager's voice responded.

"A fire has been detected on a floor above your current location. This lift shall begin an emergency descent in five seconds to begin evacuation procedures. Please make room for additional passengers to board the lift. Thank you for your cooperation."

"Wait, which floor has the fire?" asked Wil.

"Fire suppression systems have now been activated on floors 83 through 85," came the electronic voice. "Fire detectors have been triggered on floor 84. Yellow and White teams are being automatically notified of the situation. Please remain calm during your descent."

"84th floor?" said Wil aloud.

Taryn, now recovered, shot a quick glance at the agent. The same thought crossed both their minds.

That was Luxuroy's floor. The lift began moving downwards at a slower than normal speed.

"Aurel? Are your comms still up?" Wil asked.

"Yes, Agent. I'm here. Are you two all right? I'm monitoring emergency distress calls from your location."

"We're fine, but we need your help. We need you to override the lift system, okay? We're in lift number… 6, I think… going downwards… between floors 78 and 75 or so. We need it to take us to the 84th floor right away. We think our unlikely lead just became less so."

"Overriding the building evacuation system on your lift now," said Aurelius. "I will assist the building's other lifts' descent paths to mitigate the effects to the evacuation effort."

"Thanks, A," said Wil.

"Please note that I find it necessary to remind you, Agent Zhuantium, that your priority is to the safety and well-being of the council member that you have been assigned. You are currently moving to a floor with emergency alarms active."

"I understand. We won't be there long."

The lift began to change direction once again. Taryn felt the shift of her weight as they began ascending again.

At this, Wil spoke quickly to Taryn, "I need you to wait in the lift a moment while I ensure the hallway is safe and stable, okay?"

"Sure, it's your show now anyways." Taryn said.

The lift's doors opened. As they did, a rush of smoke from the corridor's ceiling billowed inwards. Wil pulled Taryn's sleeve down to a crouch pose before stepping out. Once he was over the lift's threshold, he paused and immediately shouted to Aurelius over his comm line. The blaring of the fire alarm overhead nearly drowned out his words to Taryn's ears, despite being only a short way behind him.

"Okay, A," she thought she heard him say, as he glanced briefly back at her. "I'm in the hallway."

"Acknowledged," came Aurelius's response over their comms.

The lift's doors shut right in front of her before Taryn had a chance to realize what was going on.

"Lift secured and descending," she heard the comm buzz in her ear again.

"Wait! Aurelius, stop. I'm not off yet!"

"We know, Ms. Steno. Wil is more than capable of assessing the scene without putting you in harm's way."

"Don't worry, Taryn," she could hear Wil shout through the comms. "Once I'm done looking over the apartment here, A will send the next available lift for me. I've turned on my visual recorder to document as I go. The emergency response teams will be here in minutes, make sure they know that I'm up here. And tell the Blue Boys coming from next door that this is a possible crime scene and to act accordingly. We'll need a perimeter to round up witnesses. The Bizi will take over jurisdiction once the fire situation is resolved. But I need you to play the role for now. Got all that?"

"Yeah… yeah, I got it." Taryn said reluctantly capitulating to this new assignment. She wanted to go to see where their witness was, but she saw the sense of them splitting up and not burdening Wil with worrying about her safety. It made sense for her to act on the bottom end of the building in relative safety while also knowing who to be on the lookout for. Taryn tried to calm her nerves as she reasoned herself through all this. Then the doors to the lift opened and the first startled half-dressed evacuees were now boarding the lift with her for their emergency descent. "Be careful, Wil," she called back over their comms. "I'm horrible at making funeral arrangements and would rather not have to do it again."

Chapter 14: Sleight of Trash

The Blue Boys had been easier to corral than Taryn had anticipated. Once she had flashed her Bizi ID and had a few quick words with the ranking officer, it was an easy matter to explain that this was likely more than a simple evacuation scenario. He and the rest of his response team immediately went to work sorting the evacuees into groups based on their identified floor numbers. Nonresidents were isolated, as well as anyone registered within five floors of the affected area. Most of the injured were suffering from minor smoke inhalation or bumps and cuts from falling after the initial shockwave had passed through the building. A few street level passersby had cuts on their heads and hands from the falling glass, but there was no one that Taryn could see, in any of these groups, who appeared seriously injured. Taryn kept watch though of each new group of evacuees. If Ms. Luxuroy was among the newly arrived injured being helped from the building, so far, Taryn saw no sign of her.

The White Teams arrived next in their blaring emergency vehicles, to tend to the wounded, with the Yellow Teams not long behind ready to barge headfirst into whatever flames there were. In their heavily reinforced suits with respirators, they bypassed the victims all together and headed straightaway into the building almost before Taryn could get the attention of their chief to inform him of the situation. She made sure to stress that his teams should be on the lookout for Wil up on the 84th floor.

As the number of residents coming out of the building into the night dwindled, Taryn shifted to listening to their conversations with the Blue Boys. She was barely able to watch over a few witness accounts before she found, to her complete surprise, Wil standing right beside her with ash and soot on his face and shoulders. His hands too, were dirty, and he stood calmly spouting out an occasional cough.

"Wil, are you okay? Are you hurt? Let me get a member of the white coats to come over and—"

"I'm okay," he insisted in a croaky voice. "Just some smoke, you should've seen how much I used to hack up when I was younger, before I quit the sticks. Old girl of mine made me quit long ago. Said she didn't like how they were killing me faster than she was." He laughed hoarsely. "Anyway, the fire up on the 84th floor, mostly blew itself out after the first explosion. It's just hard to see anything clearly up there right now."

"Explosion! Well, what about Ms. Luxuroy? I've been looking around down here, but I didn't see her. What'd you find? Is she—?"

"She wasn't there," he exclaimed between a few of his smaller coughs. "Though I doubt she'd been gone for long. Her lights were all still turned on, and I found her personal comm, melted, lying in what remained of her bedroom I assume. Come on, I'll show you the recording in the vehicle's display."

Once Wil removed and brushed his suit coat off and jokingly aired out his insides a bit, the two were back in the vehicle, they opened the recording file and synced a secure line to Agent Filater as well. After relaying to him that the home of a potential suspect had exploded in flames right in front of them, he became highly interested. Though, in truth he'd been brought up to speed thanks to Aurelius contacting him as soon as the emergency began.

"All right, Agent Zhuantium," said Filater over the screen, "let's see what you found up there."

"Aurelius make sure that you get a copy of this and relay it to our Bizi contacts in the arson division of the Yellow Team's central HQ," added Wil.

"Affirmative. Begin playback when ready," said Aurelius.

The small display in the center of the vehicle's dash changed as the recording viewer began playing. The digital screen was mostly a wash with thick dark-brown smoke moving towards the viewer. Wil's view was moving forward in the hall. His rapid breaths and increasing coughing could barely be heard over the blaring, cease-less noise of the building's internal alarm system. Here and there the fire suppression systems in the hall were turning on and raining loudly down, though they sounded more and more damaged as he approached Ms. Luxuroy's residence number. The door, no longer there, was fragmented into several large chunks as though it had been wrenched open from the inside. The few remaining pieces hung mostly off the access slots with their edges scarred, framed as if by an intense but quick scorching. The light from the small torch of the agent was seen to click on before entering what appeared to be the source of all the smoke billowing into the hall. Once inside, Wil's voice could be heard shouting Marisela's name as he began roaming about the innards of what looked to have once been a rather plush apartment space. The remnants of charred, burnt, and blackened furniture, fragmented sculptures, and rich elegant looking drapes and floor rugs, all now ruined, paraded past the view of Wil's recorder. The main apartment windows were destroyed too, as smoke could be seen rushing out through them, pulled by a steady gust outside the building. A small but expensive looking kitchen, office space, and bedrooms all scorched came and went past the display screen in their turn. Here and there small glowing flames could still be seen on the floor or in some corner or behind scarred furniture, as large embers floated past the light. Wil's view was often heavily obscured, however, as the ceiling of smoke became lower and enveloped him in some areas. From the view, he'd apparently had to crawl, nearly on all fours where the smoke was at its thickest. As he'd crossed from one room to the next, he stumbled across the fragments of an ear comm system on the bedroom floor. While the dark air was still thick with fumes, the smoke around him began to take on a lighter greyish color. After a few more minutes of coughing and searching in vain, the recording again showed the outer hall as he returned to the lift and began trying to call Aurelius on his comm before the recording ended.

"Now," said Wil "maybe the yellow team's arson folk would tell me differently, but the fact that the front door and outer windows were both blown out makes me think that we're looking at a controlled explosion from inside her apartment." As he said this, he gestured with his hands showing how he believed the explosion would have destroyed both the entrance and windows simultaneously.

"Was someone trying to kill her, you think?" asked Taryn.

"If so, they were less skilled in their timing than in their bomb making," added Filater over the speaker. "She obviously wasn't there, but such a small, targeted device is more difficult to make than you'd suppose. Otherwise, the rest of the corridor would be on fire too. But there is something else I saw that's odd… Aurelius, go back to about 8 minutes into the recording please."

The playback, when reversed to that point, showed Wil's view as he was about to exit the apartment.

"There, stop," Filater said. "Aurelius, can you magnify on the door controls there?"

The screen recentered on what should have been a small control display just to the right of the apartment's inner entrance. Yet, instead of a panel with various command functions on it, the outer casing was missing with only a few broken and loose wires showing inside a small square hollow in the wall.

"The door viewport recorder and display, and security panel systems… they're all gone," said Taryn in surprise as her eyes narrowed on the paused image. "That's odd, I hadn't noticed that before."

"Nor did I," Wil added, sounding disappointed in himself.

"You had more than enough smoke blocking your view—and other concerns—to stop you from noting such a thing in your rush to exit," added Filater. "Though, I think her office space is the more interesting footage you found. Did you notice that odd pattern of damage at the workstation? Aurelius, rewind to the office type room please," he said without waiting for a response."

The recorder view was again reversed to the time Wil crawled through the office section of the apartment. There, briefly and hazily in view, was a small desk platform built into one of the outer walls. The image showed the top of the desk covered in soot and tiny smoldering debris. The outer-facing portions were tinged black. But, on the upper left corner one could see, slightly obstructed, the shape of an elongated rectangle, burned into the surface of the desk itself with clear strokes. The inner fringe and chaotic burn pattern were especially darker on the outer edges of this narrow inlet.

"Of all the stupid… Wil, you blind bastard! How'd you miss that?" Wil thought out loud.

"What is that?" asked Taryn, further confused by what the screen showed.

Filater spoke first, "It's where your suspect's data storage and processor system were probably housed. It's likely she had an outer lock system to that shelf on the top of the desk. Probably thumb or biometrically coded to prevent amateur thieves. Looks as though someone used a mini-shape charge to blow through those and remove the items before the larger blast went off. See there," Filater said highlighting from his own screen. "The dust is layering over, covering the parts of the outer burn marks. They pulled out the desk system and door electronics then let the larger blast, and its fire, cover their tracks and wreck any evidence or other electronics they missed."

"Like her personal comm system," said Taryn.

"Yeah," said Wil.

"Agent Filater, might I add something of note?" intervened Aurelius.

"Go ahead."

"While listening in to your discussion, I began trying to access the security system to see what the internal and external recorders picked up of the comings and goings of people around the building. I went back for up to an hour before your arrival there, Agent Zhuantium."

"And?"

"And I'm sorry to say that the internal memory engrams of several of the surrounding recorders are non-functional. Magnetically erased, followed by what I'm inferring is the result of a small but focused electrical surge that burnt the circuitry. Recorder systems on two lifts and the rear loading area were also tampered with in a consistent way as well."

"Aurel, are there recordings of the time before this tampering happened? You know, that would show us anyone who'd approached the recorders just before they stopped working?" asked Taryn.

"No, I'm finding that the security systems algorithms were re-coded, improperly I might add, to put them into a five-minute maintenance cycle to purge what it thought was corrupted data prior to the magnetic tampering."

"Smart," added Wil. "They hacked the recorders for a small-time window, and then extended that with the magnetic and electrical surges."

"Wait… Aurelius, why does a 'maintenance cycle hack' sound familiar to me?" asked Taryn.

"I was shortly coming to that, Ms. Taryn. My analysis of the programing used on the recorder system that was out of service during the night of Council Member U's murder shows a similar style of modified coding. The manner of tampering with the security recorders this evening matches the apparent 'bug' in the recorder on the park side that night. With only one system affected last time it was difficult to make any inferences, but with multiple points of comparison now available to me, I believe that both incidents displayed hacking of a comparable manner."

"Aurelius, do you have a determination on the level of technical sophistication necessary to perform such a thing?" asked Filater.

Aurelius paused to reflect and assess the data he had.

"Nothing definitive that would narrow a search parameter to a feasible size. A basic electrical or programming education and familiarity with basic security network engrams is the lowest level of understanding and background needed to perform this task. After that, the hardware parts needed to build such a device is readily available to any hobbyist with enough ingenuity and experience."

"Yeah, that's what I was afraid of…" said Filater gruffly.

"Still, Aurelius," said Taryn, "how many times have you ever heard of a hacker who operated like this?"

"Not within the span of the last two cyclical decades." Aurelius answered "The most recent case being attributed to a hacker of a small-branched financial institution. In that particular case both the hacker, a minor at the time, and his associates were all placed under arrest when they forgot to bypass a redundancy system that sent a check signal from the institution's main processor to all the security systems in their various branches."

"Could this be the same hacker, repeating his old ways?" asked Filater.

"It is unlikely," said Aurelius, "as he is currently incarcerated on an unrelated charge of spousal assault and violence. My records show he is not due for release for five more cycles. I'm accessing the registry system at the penal facility where he's being held now, to confirm that their prisoner manifest is up to date for the suspect."

Aurelius paused.

"…which has now come back as being confirmed. The suspect was in confinement on the last reported roll call an hour ago."

"Okay," said Filater. "Let me dig up some dirt on this guy. Aurelius, would you kindly send over the file. I'll go and have a chat with him in person tonight, see what he can say about this stuff. I've dispatched a Bizi evidence team to your location, which should be arriving soon. If you're both up to it, I'd like you two to continue taking the lead in the investigation here."

"We are," Wil and Taryn both replied.

"Good. Keep me informed and try to track down this mysterious woman of yours. If she's smart and got wind of any danger coming her way beforehand, she may still be running. And besides, she's still the best lead we've had on this case." The comm line closed. Filater was gone.

"What about her family or friends?" Taryn asked, turning to Wil.

Wil shook his head. "The name Marisela Luxuroy appears to, not surprisingly, be fictitious until only about eight cycles ago. Makes tracking down relatives difficult. Add to that the pattern of escorts not being well known for open socialization, outside of their career field of course."

"Hmm..." Taryn thought for a moment. "But what about these arsonists that tossed her place. Either they didn't find her at home or-"

"Or perhaps they did find her, and she left with them," said Wil.

"Hmm…given we know next to nothing about her," said Taryn, "she may have even orchestrated this whole thing by herself if she was fearful and thought someone was coming after her."

"Perhaps," added Wil, "but this is all just speculation. What we need is some real facts to work from, a solid base to push off of."

Taryn spoke towards her comm line.

"Aurelius," she said, "were there any working recorders in the area from the time of the initial explosion?"

"Yes, there are several dozen recorders whose feeds and engrams I can access in the surrounding neighborhood. But a cursory evaluation shows nothing out of the ordinary prior to this emergency. However, I will conduct a more in-depth review of the footage with results available by early morning. I will be sure to note anything relevant or out of the ordinary in a ten-mile radius."

"Well, that'll give us time to speak to the evidence team at least," said Wil.

"All right," nodded Taryn, a bit tiredly. The rush of the evening's unexpected events had finally started to slow down enough to begin taking their toll on her. She found herself suddenly feeling quite spent and exhausted. Sitting in the vehicle's comfortable seats, she had unwittingly let herself slouch down into their curved padding.

"Don't worry," Wil said, seeing her posture. "I know it's been a long night, but we won't be much longer. The evidence team will need at least a few hours minimum to sort through all the statements and the wreckage. After we speak to them and tell them what to keep an eye out for, I'll drop you off at home."

"Okay, let's go," Taryn said, opening her door.

* * *

Wil's estimation of 'not much longer ' turned out to be another three full hours. Ms. Luxuroy's neighbors, the ones that they could find, kept mostly to themselves. Apparently so did she by their various accounts. No one had seen her about the building since much earlier in the evening. While Wil and Taryn put several questions forward to the Bizi evidence team to try and advance the investigation, they themselves, as witnesses, were subject in turn to a wide range of the initial inquiries made. This, of course, was to allow the evidence team to draw a clear timeline of the events before the explosion. The Bizi evidence collectors also, as would be expected, wanted to review Wil's recorder file, and consult with the building's electronic manager system, in addition to sending a small preliminary team to probe the burned out flat. But this would have to wait until the Yellow Teams finished up and had fully inspected the floor for safety. Taryn and Wil didn't remain until that point. Still, by the time Taryn did get dropped off at her home, it was quite late, or early depending on your perspective. No one, not Gloria nor her kids, were even awake to be upset at her for not calling to say she'd miss dinner.

The next morning, Taryn groggily stood outside her building waiting for Wil with a rather generous sized joe-cup in her hand. The lack of a full night's sleep, she felt, needed such a compensation. Her vehicle pulled up abruptly, and Wil hurriedly pushed the door open for her from the inside.

"No time. Get in. We're expected and we're late."

"Expected where?" Taryn asked, quickly getting herself seated.

"Down towards the old ports. There is another Bizi evidence team on site and a dredger is there already."

"Wait! What?" she asked as they pulled out quickly to the main street going north, not their usual southern turn towards the estate.

"Aurelius can bring you up to speed as we go."

There was a gentle buzz over the vehicle's cabin comm system.

"Good morning, Ms. Taryn," came Aurelius's cheerfully pleasant voice.

"Morning, A. What's this about the old ports?"

"Well, my initial evaluation of the recorders from last evening missed an interesting observation that was only found upon a deeper inspection. Approximately two and a half hours before your arrival at Ms. Luxuroy's apartment building, a recorder four blocks away captured images of an automated waste disposal vehicle unit that was moving slightly above the posted speed limit for that lane."

A brief clip from a high-view residential recorder popped up in front of Taryn on the center display. It was nighttime and there was a regular looking waste disposal unit driving by the resident vehicles that were parked outside of their homes for the evening. The ID number of the vehicle was rather faded, but the rear radar ID port did appear briefly under a streetlight.

"Um... ok, other than it's not stopping to pick up the garbage, I'm not sure I understand what's so important here?" Taryn asked.

"It stands out," said Wil, "because besides not stopping to get the trash, automated vehicles don't typically speed. Of course, calibration errors can happen over extensive use. But when a recorder spots a regional automated vehicle speeding within a small margin, instead of sending an emergency shutdown command, an automated request is transmitted to the system to alert a vehicle maintenance facility and to direct the vehicle there."

Aurelius spoke again.

"The truck from yesterday didn't report back to the maintenance yard last night after its route ended. And when I accessed the route data it was supposed to be using, I found that the truck on the recorder was, in fact, heading in the wrong direction for its normal route."

"But" added Wil, "it *was* going in the correct direction if it wanted to head towards Ms. Luxuroy's apartment building."

Taryn's expression changed to one of slowly dawning understanding. Her mind was still sluggish and struggling, but her morning cup was now starting to help her clarity.

"Since it was nearby before last night's incident and wasn't behaving normally nor replying to typical maintenance commands, we thought--" said Wil.

"Our hacker again?" finished Taryn.

"Yep." agreed Wil

"Okay, but why are we going to the docks?"

"Because despite the automated recall command, and several emergency shut-down commands that Aurelius pushed through when he found this recording, the truck was still not responding. Its positioning system was also not working apparently. Then about an hour before dawn, the truck sent out an automated help request on its own, for a stalled engine. The signal died in on a minute or two, but Aurelius got a rough triangulated location based on the nearby receiver dishes and using the faces of the towers which the signal was received."

"Down on the waterfront?" Taryn commented again.

"Yep, well… a little *off* the waterfront based on A's calculations. The initial units sent only found broken fences, and damaged pedestrian railings, all about as wide as the vehicle itself.

"It's in the water?" Taryn asked.

"That's the reason for the dredger," continued Wil. Last we heard, diver-bots had already located the vehicle and began attaching cables to secure it and start hauling it back out."

"Does Filater know, A?" said Taryn talking to the roof.

"He is currently en route to meet you there Ms. Taryn, along with further Bizi evidence collectors," chimed Aurelius from above.

* * *

Upon arriving they found a few local Blue Boy units had already marked off the area to all but official vehicles. Beyond that Taryn could see the large, flattened dredger floating out on the water, with its tall bent crane working in conjunction with another land-based tow vehicle. Together they looked to be readying to both lift and pull a submerged object back to the shore. From the location of their cords, it looked to Taryn as if the vehicle had drifted with the current a little away from its point of entry into the water. Several Bizi agents from the first evidence team hovered around a broken pedestrian railing which would have been the final barrier before the waste vehicle plunged over a half-dozen meters to the water below. The only structures nearby were a few small ugly brown loading warehouses. Their shabby derelict look perfectly fitting to the drab colors of the area. Most of their windows were broken and stained. There were neighboring launch ramps that ran gently into the windswept current. They were clearly meant for use in releasing or hauling in boats. On one of these launches was the working tow vehicle, aligned with its cables disappearing as they stretched out into the churning waters. On the opposite side of the lot was a private salvage yard. There, fenced off, were some stripped-down boats of various makes laying out haphazardly. All appeared rusted and weatherworn from cycles of corrosive exposure that had been allowed to build up upon the bones of their metal frames. Taryn could see a pair of Bizi agents interviewing a man who, Aurelius later informed her, was the owner and operator of the salvage yard. But having consumed more a large dosage of liquored potatoes and wheat the previous night, he'd been essentially useless as a witness of any sort.

As they pulled up past the final checkpoint, they found Agent Filater ordering the scene. He'd just finished looking over the images sent up from the diver bots on his padd and was busying himself talking with a few Bizi evidence specialists. Upon their arrival, Filater relayed to Wil and Taryn that the prevailing notion from the evidence techs was that the waste vehicle had initially rammed through the locked perimeter fence into the property. It stopped for a time, but eventually it backed up in line for a run at the water and proceeded again at a great pace. Its direction and speedy acceleration meant the vehicle jumped a small walkway, crashed through a thick metal pedestrian railing, before finally plunging out and over into the cold dark depths some way below. The diver bots had already accessed the driver's cab, which was empty, and noted the mileage and battery power levels. They also recorded that the rear waste storage system had been closed and locked into the compaction setting.

It took the dredger and land tow wrecker another half hour to slowly maneuver the waste unit up and onto one of the concrete loading ramps next to the nearest warehouse. As they waited, Filater updated Taryn and Wil on his findings from speaking with the incarcerated hacker that Aurelius had mentioned the night before.

"Given how fast your initial lead had blown up in front of you, I thought it would be better to go to the facility straight away and speak with him immediately instead of waiting until morning. Guy's name is Regniar. Had his ID checked twice during our chat to be sure it was him. Hard to believe he has the type of skills he's credited with, even back twenty some cycles ago. Very cocky and egotistical, a career screwup. Always in and out of trouble. His own family stopped having anything to do with him long before even his more recent stint. Not the typical introvert tech-type you'd expect. Loves to let his mouth prattle on and on about how good he is, but never said anything of substance."

"Dead end then?" asked Taryn

"It certainly felt that way."

"Well, it was a thin line, even for us," said Wil. "Let's hope it's not the same thing now."

The three waited while both Taryn and Filater each sipped on their extra-large joe-cups. After a while longer, the machine and crane operators signaled they were close to breaching the surface. The waste vehicle first emerged sideways from the blowing, white-tipped ripples. Taryn watching, thought that it sort of resembled a large-mouthed metal fish. Some ancient monster of the deep whose carcass, having already severely decomposed, had been found with only the skull of its enormous head intact. The remainder of its detached body still hidden out of view somewhere back underneath. Down there the diver bots, still active, continued to search for any other smaller debris they could find. A Blue Boy's boat team was doing likewise on the surface, though from the communications they were sending over their general comms, they were only sorting through bits of dispersed flotsam and other loose rubbish.

After the crane slowly lowered the waste vehicle to the ground, the newly arrived Bizi evidence team, using several recorders, made a half dozen sweeps around the vehicle before having it pulled back upright. As it bounced back onto its treads, it rebounded loudly and could be heard to loudly groan. Water continued draining out of every hidden space and crevice under the vehicle. Several members of the evidence team immediately went to inspect the driver's cab. Filater motioned for Wil and Taryn to follow him to have a look at the rear with the few other techs that remained. During their wait for the vehicle's extraction, he had more than once questioned the validity of using such a large and slow waste disposal unit as a possible getaway vehicle. If indeed that's what had happened. While it was true, he pointed out, that other motorists wouldn't even bother looking at the driver's cab as most of these units were known to be automated, there were other faster and less conspicuous vehicles easier to find and possibly much harder to track down if stolen with the correct gear.

"They likely did a vehicle switch near here after jamming down the accelerator and turning it loose," he said. "But still… why use such a large vehicle?" His eyes transfixed on the closed rear end. He turned to face Taryn as he grasped the manual release lever on the side of the vehicle's compaction system.

"Now, this is one of those times where I hope that I'm wrong, but if I'm not, you may want to be ready to turn away."

Taryn stood staring at him with a confused expression, but as he pulled on the lever the significance of his words started to ring through her mind. As she stared down, layers upon layers of paper trash and fabric, degradable plastics, food containers with their leftovers began uncoiling and unfettering themselves before their eyes. The assorted colors of the water-logged trash were a mosaic of dozens of different hues and textures, all of them jarring. First falling this way and then that, as parts jostled loose unevenly. Once the last clang of the compactor hit home, a final surge of debris came loose and rolled free from deeper within. As it did, atop the pile, Taryn saw a slim and pale hand and arm come rolling outwards, palm-up. As it came to a rest at an upward angle, Taryn was suddenly overtaken by a horrible stench that she was ever after loath to remember. She immediately recoiled back, and turning, vomited the entirety of her breakfast and joe-cup along the trash vehicle's rear wheel.

"Yeah..." Filater sighed softly to himself. "Shame there is no prize for being right all the time. All right," he said louder and now speaking to Wil, "have forensics dig her out of there, and go see what the agents in the front have found."

As Wil stepped away to speak with the others, Filater called lower towards Taryn, who based on her sounds was now wrenching mostly air.

"You all right over there?" he asked gently.

"Yeah… just need a moment… or two," she said in halting speech. He walked over and patted her back in a sign of support.

"Well..." he breathed looking back across the lot, "at the very least we know… that there was something to know. Why else go to all the trouble to not only kill her but also to collect any records she had at her place too. Somebody didn't want her or her data to be found intact."

"Do you think that she was the one who killed… you know who?" asked Taryn as she started regaining her composure. Despite the vile discomfort to her stomach and nose, she still had the wherewithal to be discreet with her comments.

"I doubt it," Filater said. "Involved, most certainly but..." he turned back to face the mangled body buried beneath the soaked waste. He used a padd pen to carefully brush away the layer covering Marisela Luxuroy's head. The sickly pale color of her skin almost blended in with the soggy whitish papers around it. "Her profession," he went on, "suggests she was more of a personable type. Better with socializing than with any real physical violence. Killing wasn't her trade. Maybe she was the bait for the trap that night. Someone to get him out, drop his guard. Or it could be that she saw enough to help ID the killer. Maybe she just barely managed to negotiate herself out of a tight spot, only to find the deal later rescinded."

He paused for a long moment as Taryn gathered herself up and came to stand next to the now contemplative agent.

"But… why wait till now to kill her?" she asked raggedly.

"Now that is truly the scary question from all of this," he said softly and more to himself than to her.

"It's the pacing."

"Pacing?" Taryn repeated abruptly.

"If they were in a rush to get her gone," Filater explained, "then maybe they got sloppy and left a trail for us somewhere in all this mess. But then again if they showed the same deal of care and preparation in their approach as they did back at her flat…and on the night of the initial killing, it's possible that they only reason we were able to find her now, is because they know there is nothing useful left to be found here.

Wil returned from the vehicle's front. "The cabin's empty just as the divers showed. Looks like it was burned out before the vehicle went over the side. The techs are sweeping it now, but so far, no prints or obvious signs. Some others are busy pulling the auto-nav system and are getting ready to start it up for testing. It looks as though it is pretty beat-up, but I think that's still the best spot to check for any evidence of hacking." Wil noticed the remaining semi-queasy look on Taryn's face.

"You okay to keep at it?"

"Yeah," she answered slowly nodding. "Needed to get my bearings. I'm better... though it could've been worse I suppose," she said taking a few last calming breaths. Her voice was back to its full level. "At least it's not like that horrible story I heard when I was young. You know…that famous case of that blue boy who in his first patrol of the crop regions came across a whole field of innards strewn everywhere." Both men paused looking confused at this unfamiliar account. That's when she knew she had them.

"I don't remember tha—" said Filater in a half question that Taryn cut short.

"Oh, that's 'because he thought he'd found a mass grave for scarecrows... turns out it was just straw."

Filater's mouth dropped slightly with an obviously stunned expression of silence while his eyes, half closed, looked both plainly annoyed and unamused. This was made all the more comical with the sight of Wil, right next to him, who failed miserably at stopping a loud bursting snort that rolled on for several moments.

"All right, shall we go observe the experts, gentlemen?" asked Taryn, satisfied at her joke. Her posture and demeanor at this minor success showed her almost fully recovered, and even Filater, irked as he may have been, was privately surprised at how little time that had taken the council member.

The trio found two Bizi tech analysts working at a small table under a canopy tent, hastily erected for their use. They had several small black code-forcing boxes with digital displays that Taryn could see were hard lined to the still damp nav-system from the vehicle. It took the analysts four attempts and five of the boxes working in concert before they were able to access any retrievable information to give to the onlookers.

"So?" asked Wil to the lead technician finally after waiting several minutes, "Can you tell anything yet about how they hacked the system?"

"Well, this thing is waterlogged down to its last bolt," replied the lead analyst. "Given the salt bath it took I suppose that is not really a surprise. But from what we are seeing, it has either been hacked in a way that's so unique and bizarrely subtle that we can't find it. Or it hasn't been hacked at all."

"What do you mean it wasn't hacked? You mean it was acting normally?" protested Wil.

"I don't understand," Taryn interjected. "How does the normal program end with the vehicle running off into the water?"

"I don't know," answered the analyst. "All I can tell you is that all the code we are picking up here was validated via the system's most recent update from the department's central processor. So, unless your perpetrator physically disconnected the system, drove the vehicle here on manual override, then reconnected the device to the main cabin terminal before sending it into the drink, I have no other ideas for you folks. Now," he continued, "we *are* missing several gaps of code due to the water and fire damage it sustained. I suppose a clever writer could have snuck in a backdoor script to access it via another device so that no code was left behind. But that's pretty sophisticated. I was under the impression that a more brute force approach was the preferred method of the hacker you folks were looking into."

"Could it be the work of another hacker maybe?" asked Taryn towards Wil.

"Or at least one that knows far more than we gave him credit for," said Wil in reply. "If he is alone, that means he knows how to vary his methods and how to hide himself well when the situation requires it."

"Half a moment," said Filater speaking to the analyst as he stared at the ongoing display of retrieved code. "Can you tell us when the vehicle's system received its last update?"

"Oh yeah sure, that's easy. We're linked into the waste management data system right here. Let's see..." He began tapping some quick strokes onto the padd he was carrying and waited for a moment for the system to respond. "According to central, the last update was done remotely at… hmm. That's weird. The update was recorded as sent to the vehicle yesterday… about three hours before that whole apartment explosion started."

"Why's that weird?" Taryn asked the tech.

"Well, the logs have it listed as a navigation update, but from what I see here typically waste management only sends those out at the start of the week with all of the changes of address and such. Security updates are what usually get sent irregularly as the need arises. A nav update midweek doesn't look to be their standard procedure. I'll look into it and get—"

"No," said Filater. "I will handle it myself. Gives me a chance to chat with some of waste management's IT folks." He turned to stare back towards the waterlogged waste vehicle. "And to see if anything else from their department smells of wet refuse."

"You two stick here for a bit," he said motioning to Wil and Taryn. "See if anything else turns up and keep me informed."

* * *

After some quick questions to the analysts to get some more background on the waste management system, Filater was off. Leaving Taryn and Wil the rest of the morning to shadow the Bizi evidence teams. By lunch time, no further insights from the vehicle were forthcoming, though the analysts were far from done sweeping over the scene.

Still, Taryn and Wil agreed that she ought to spend the afternoon taking care of her regular council duties via a secure padd in the vehicle. She still had to finish processing new legislation that had been sent to the council from the SOMA for review. Besides, the last few days working on the investigation had caused her to fall behind on her observations of the SOMA meetings that she'd normally followed with regularity. And though Taryn couldn't use the Wucengi neural device here, she could get the basic recordings and summaries she needed sent to her padd via a link with Aurelius in the vehicle as well.

The late morning wore into the afternoon. Taryn had been productively working alone in the passenger side for nearly three hours uninterrupted, plus another hour hearing meeting summaries that Aurelius relayed to her, when Wil returned to the driver's seat next her, handing her a fresh replacement for her joe-cup. She'd been busy enough that she wasn't even close to finishing her second, as her mouth's taste buds had still not entirely forgiven her for the abrupt ejection of the first cup that morning. She felt a bit stiff and tired from all the sitting. The focus required for her work always resulted in this usual type of toll.

"Well," Wil updated, "the analysts have gotten nowhere in the past four hours. They say the nav systems and other internal components are too heavily damaged from fire and water to read them fully, but what they *can* read shows no signs of code tampering."

"Great..." replied Taryn sarcastically.

"And to add to that, I received word from Agent Filater," he sighed. "He says that he was able to confirm that the central processor at waste management did in fact clear a system update from yesterday as safe, like our Bizi analyst said. But what the system update actually was written for is going to take time to track down.

Apparently," he said looking around, "they have multiple divisions of software people all related to different areas of rubbish collection. Who knew picking up the trash was such a complicated task, eh?" He paused. "At least he won't be bored."

"I doubt he ever gets bored. He doesn't seem the kind," Taryn remarked.

"Yeah, he reminds me of my older brother," Wil agreed. "He's a Defense Force instructor. Trains the incoming recruits, you know? Real hard-line type. Can't sit still for more than a few minutes. Always has to be moving, yelling, drilling, chewing out some underling. Can't be comfortable doing nothing with himself. Thinks that the word *introspective* is mostly just a waste of time."

"Hmm..." replied Taryn, prying her eyes from the display to look out from the front window. "My father was the same way, but for him it was farming, tilling, and his machinery. Stuff was always breaking down in the fields, but there was rarely anything mechanical that he couldn't repair," she smiled as she said this, recalling images of the old farmer from cycles back. It felt more than a lifetime ago to her all of a sudden. "He loved getting his hands covered in machine oil, working on all the parts… Trying to understand and figure out how great complex motions could grow out of simple cause and effect relationships. 'A gear or screw here, a belt or piston crank there, a bit of steam or water pressure, and you can build yourself a machine capable of anything you'd need,' he'd tell me…"

"Sounds like you envied that skill of his. Or at least like you had a good relationship going with him, you know?" asked Wil.

Taryn turned her head and stared out the side window, as if seeing things long ago and far away.

"Well… I suppose it was as good as it could be, what with him being a farmer who loved his job and having a daughter who wanted nothing to do with it. He loved the life, watching things grow. Gradually but consistently changing from seedling to sprout to a final bloom. Seeing all his work literally blossom before his eyes. I never had the raw skills or attraction towards it that either of my parents did. I wasn't that mechanically inclined either. At least not when I was younger anyway. Working a few cycles on a factory floor helped some in that regard I suppose.

"But there was always enough side work to be done when I was younger. Looking back, I'm grateful I got the chance to grow up outside the city environment. Getting exposed to subsistence struggles makes living in the city look easy. My father loved it though. He'd often work out in the fields well enough past sunset, even into his late 60s… He, umm…He died right before his grandson was born. Heart gave out. We buried him there in the grass between the tilled rows of his oldest field and the edge of the nearby wood." Taryn wiped a slight mist forming around her eyes. "I don't think he ever understood why I didn't follow after him on the farm."

"'A path chosen for you doesn't make it yours.' A piece of advice from my father," said Wil.

"Is he still alive?" asked Taryn, quickly checking the mirror to ensure she didn't look a mess.

"Yeah. We talk, oh… nearly every week, but we are two different types, you know? I mean we agree on a lot, but we often take different approaches too. Different generations I guess."

"And what about your mom?" asked Taryn.

"No mom, just a one-off parent system."

"Well, that must have been hard on your dad with two boys," said Taryn.

"And two girls," continued Wil. "But outside of monitoring my education like a hawk, he mostly let us all pick our own ways afterwards. Said that as different as we all were, that meant we were all the better for it."

"Four kids to a single parent, man must be something. What does he d—"

There was a sudden knock on Wil's side window. It was the head Bizi analyst who had come up while they'd been chatting. The two exited the car to listen while the analyst reconfirmed the fact that despite multiple attempts, they could get nothing more out of the trash vehicle's on-board systems.

"If there is any falsified coding we're seeing, then the level of authenticity was integrated seamlessly into the system. To be honest, the safer bets are still an outside device hooked up within the vehicle that ran its own overriding code without leaving any discernible script interruptions or command prompts. Or the manual override solution. But that would take a decent amount of mechanical knowledge as well. It requires a bit of ingenuity and training, but it is not impossible. As for the hacking idea, if there are any outside script code lines left in there, I don't see it. Besides there is only one thing I know that can even match that kind of programming level in complexity and subtlety."

"And what's that?" asked Taryn.

"The Aurelius system." He paused, looking back towards the wrecked vehicle. "I've seen it working for cycles now, supervising new batches of Bizi tech agents as they come up to start. Seen it create whole programs on the spot, to test the agents in various conditions. All customized based on their personality profiles. Simulations within simulations using synchronized multilayering script threads. All original project codes, all novel and insightful and flawless. That sort of thing. Even before my time in the department, I doubt any outside system can match its versatile intelligence and innovation when it comes to coding. Theoretically, it could pull this off I suppose… but of course it's run by us alone. Besides, it's a training assistant program anyways in an isolated sheltered government matrix. It doesn't have the ability to access outside systems to begin with." He snickered to himself. "And I mean, it's not like our training machine had any reason to go and kill off a high-end escort anyways, right?" he asked chuckling as he turned back to the evidence stations. "Ah, it's probably an outside hook-up device we're dealing with," he continued with a wave of his hand. "Can't be traced. But I suppose I could ask the Aurelius simulator to project some scenarios from this and see—"

"That's all right. We'll take on that task," said Wil abruptly.

Taryn had been looking at Wil silently for the last minute. She saw that despite his calm polite look toward the chief evidence tech that his cheeks were actually drawn and taut. She assumed that he could see that she wore a similar expression of her own. Despite not understanding all the details of what the analyst had just told them, Taryn was able to put her own thoughts in order quickly. *"Coincidence is not a concept anyone in the Bizi is taught,"* she recalled Filater had said to her.

Wil thanked the evidence tech politely, before quietly dismissing him and pulling Taryn aside. Without speaking they both powered down and removed their comm units as they walked away from any others within earshot.

"Tell me…" Taryn started, "Tell me that you're having the same thoughts as me, Wil?" her voice was lowered and in a hurried pace. Wil looked at the council member and shook his head disagreeing.

"No."

"Tell me," Taryn repeated, "that you're not thinking that we're among the few with the proper clearance to know that Aurelius is very much not just an isolated training system, run only by the Bizi? And that he *does* have access to all the other systems needed and is obviously more than capable of setting up all of this?" Taryn asked in a hint of a whisper.

"But that's not enough," he said, still shaking his head. "Not enough to claim Aurelius would be responsible here. Even if he were human, it wouldn't be enough. He'd still have to have real people working with, or for him, somehow. You know? To actually rummage through Luxuroy's flat, steal missing items from her, place the bomb or charge. There *had* to be people to physically abduct her and get her into the back of that compactor. It's not like she would do it on her own"

"We'd also need a *why*," said Taryn, slowing down her thoughts now. "Why kill our only lead? Why silence the only potential witness to the murder of a High Council member? Why go to all this trouble, unless…?" she paused. "Unless… Aurelius...?"

"Now," interrupted Wil finally nodding his own head and lowering his own voice to a whisper. "Now, I think your thoughts have finally caught up to mine, Ms. Taryn."

He took a pause to consider, "But, before we snap our fishing line on something that's too big or, worse, on something that's not even there, this is what we can do. We still need to work the people only angle. That's still got plenty of wind to it. Let me go talk to the evidence agents back at the building fire scene. See if they've found anything more to go on. Maybe I'll be able to get a head start on the physical suspects. Real suspects exist in either scenario, and I've yet to meet the one who's perfect at hiding their trail. I'll also report to Filater that we're doubling back to Luxuroy's apartment for more potential leads. For now though, I'm keeping Aurelius's name out of this until there is more than just an outside theory coming from one technician's offhand remark.

"In the meantime, to be safe, we can't discuss this idea openly while we have our communication receptors on during the normal workday. So, for now, I recommend that you finish your work for the afternoon, then tomorrow at the estate, you can carefully begin researching the notes of the murdered Council Member U. See if he wrote anything in his journal that stands out, especially towards the last weeks of his service. We're looking for motives. Anything that would've be helped or stopped or that even started around the time of his murder."

"All right," Taryn said with uncertainty. "Though, I doubt I'll be much use at work now. I mean how am I supposed to interact with Aurel?"

Wil thought for a moment.

"As you normally would, I suppose. Look, focus on trying to stay relaxed. Remember either we're completely wrong, and Aurelius had nothing to do with any of this, meaning he's innocent. Or, even if he is somehow a responsible party, he is unaware of our suspicions of him and that means he's still safe for the time being."

"What if he starts to catch on though? What if he notices me acting strangely towards him?" asked Taryn.

"Remember, nothing about any of this is certain, but if you need an excuse at any point, you can claim that the sight of Luxuroy's body disturbed you. Tell him that you're not feeling like your normal self. Speaking professionally, I'm kind of surprised you're handling it as well as you are now."

Taryn took a breath and shook her head. "Thanks, yeah… so am I."

"Just take it a step at a time. Focus on your job for now and let tomorrow's waves come on their own. At the office, quietly start your research. I'll tell A you're taking the day off from the investigation tomorrow to catch up on paperwork and plant the seed that today's activities were a bit too intense for you. You're in need some down time from this for a while."

"Both of which are true..." she breathed worriedly. "Okay, okay… I can do this."

"Remember," added Wil, "we're likely off the main currents here anyways. Relax, breathe, and go on as usual."

Taryn did her best to finish as much work as possible while Wil drove them back to the apartment building scene. She quietly waited, still working in the vehicle for a half hour when Wil returned. All he said was that the techs in the building hadn't found anything to change their views on the case. They both knew Aurelius had an open line over their comms now and could plainly hear them speaking to one another if he wished. They didn't discuss anything else as Wil drove and Taryn pretended to be lost deep in her work. She did manage to keep her thoughts in focus long enough to finish reviewing the last round of SOMA documents, though in truth if asked a short time later she wouldn't have been able to recall any of their details.

With their comms back on, Aurelius had chimed in unexpectedly only once during their drive. It was to say that there had still been no word from Filater as he was *reportedly having difficulty finding any competent technicians currently on duty at waste management.* But even at this simple update from A, Taryn felt herself tense up ever so slightly. Finally, after enduring a tediously interminable drive, at last they pulled up to her building.

"See you tomorrow Ms. Taryn. Sorry today was a bit rough on you. Get some rest and hopefully tomorrow things will be smoother," Wil said in farewell.

They both nodded to one another understanding the need for that statement to be said aloud.

Chapter 15: Perspective and Experience

The next day, after another terrible night's sleep, Taryn was nodding off on the relatively quiet drive to work when Wil spoke up from the driver's seat.

"I'm glad you've decided to focus on your regular work today. Good to take a break from the investigation. You know, a little time away to let the mind reset is often the best thing for people to do. I'll be away from the estate myself most of the day doing follow-ups. But there will be another agent, Burd, I believe, on the grounds handling security until I return. Hey, A? It is Burd we got covering for me today, right?"

"That's correct. Agent Burd is already on the estate grounds awaiting your arrival, Ms. Taryn," came Aurelius's snappy reply.

Taryn was immediately aware that Wil was likely testing how close Aurelius's attention was on them. The frown on his face told her he didn't like the reaction time to his question, though she thought that in reality it may be no quicker than normal.

"I'll be back in the afternoon to drive you home," Wil continued. "Agent Burd will be roaming the grounds till then, but he shouldn't disturb you or enter the house itself unless there is an actual emergency. Mr. Brough will still be around if needed, but except for him we must try to minimize the number of people that could recognize you as a council member. So, I'm sorry to ask this, but could you please skip your afternoon stroll in the yard? I know you're accustomed to it as part of your daily habit, but if you need to relax, maybe take a nap or perhaps read something?" he suggested this with his dark eyes intently glancing at her own to help push the message.

"I understand. It makes sense," said Taryn in a tone she was trying to make sound as casual as possible. Given how tired she was at the moment, it wasn't all that difficult to at least ignore the stress of the upcoming day temporarily. They both knew they would have to be very careful with how they spoke with each other while Aurelius could listen in.

At the estate, the air was warm for the season and the ground was wet. A quick rain in the pre-dawn morning had refreshed the greenness of the yard and surrounding forest trees. The pale cool sun began to shoot its yellow rays through the cloud cover making the wet grass glitter, reflecting small sparks off the covering moisture. On the hill where the estate stood, a thin grey mist was slowly drawing back from the interior of the forest's edge.

After a few hours of reviewing SOMA meetings and summaries using the Wucengi device, Taryn had conversed with Members G and C about upcoming legislation they were expected to approve. Taryn was finally at a natural breakpoint in her day though. The morning had thus far been more or less normal in its routine.

She asked Mr. Brough for her third joe-cup and—making sure to tell Aurelius she needed to rest for a bit—got up to look at the newest red-leather journal off the glass shelf. Taryn slowly paced out of the office towards the couch in the main living area. She sat with her feet up sideways as she browsed through some of the early pages for a brief time. Taryn had forgotten that she'd already started reading this journal before now. It had been one of Aurelius's initial recommendations to her. Taryn now recalled that this council member's entries had a mildly paranoid view of the artificial intelligence matrix, a view that she now appreciated on a whole new level. After skimming the entries that she'd read before or found irrelevant, she began on the last twenty pages or so, focusing herself more intently.

Nothing caught her attention as important, though it was obvious that by this point in his tenure, Council Member U had limited his entries to only pure facts about his work. There was little to no exposition on the last few pages at all. Just the basic summary of what he'd reviewed, approved, or rejected, and sent back to be reworked by the SOMA members. After a certain point in the journal's entries, Taryn noticed Council member U didn't want to record his own views for anyone else to read. Perhaps he thought that even a hard copy journal wouldn't be secure from Aurelius. *But was it simply an amplified paranoia of the machine and his surroundings? Or had he been trying to protect something more specific? Did he know or learn something that he shouldn't?* she wondered.

Taryn went a little further back in the entries where she thought she'd have a better chance of finding more substance in his entries. Some thirty pages from the end she finally found a lengthy entry that appeared to be the last truly unfiltered account by the council member. It specifically concerned *"that damn annoying artificial voice"* and its interactions with the entire Trinity Council during a Wucengi assemblage.

Taryn read the entry: *We were all set to approve the latest round of solar collection scouts to be sent off deeper into the system for a standard exploratory run, when that infernal machine interrupted us again. The rudeness of that stupid device left me fuming… though by this point I should've half expected it. Damn thing can never just shut up and leave the council to do our work on our own. It began babbling on about an active season for solar flares due to start the same time our ships would be reaching their collection orbital positions. "A high risk of intense radiation damage to the sails and cells" my ass. That moron of a machine wanted us to delay sending the ships for two whole months! We can't afford that! We need as much power as we can get and now! The grids are already close to capacity what with the increased demand from the new ocean sediment dredges going active. And given the travel time the ships need, we're risking rolling outages across the city for the next two seasons, if not longer.*

I told my colleagues plainly, that if we truly needed to conserve power, we could start by deactivating that damn annoying system, but that a delay for our solar ships should not be allowed. But I was already too late. C fell for that trashcan's talk right away, like he always does. Idiot can never tell when he's being worked. I thought I could at least rely on G to be smart enough to see through this line of crap. But I was wrong. They both accepted the bucket of bolts' suggestion without any argument. I stood there dumbfounded. Now our solar collector ships are stuck useless and delayed in our orbiting dock. I wonder if that stupid machine is planning to use them for its own purposes. I half-hope it is scheming to move itself off-world just so I'd be rid of its relentless bickering. But knowing my luck probably not, else it would've done it a long time ag-"

"Ms. Taryn?" Aurelius asked suddenly out of nowhere.

"Hmm, yes?" Taryn answered slightly startled at the interruption of her reading. She sat up on the couch,

"Please excuse me, but your work line received a reminder message from Mr. Everett a few moments ago. His derby team is playing their cross-city rivals tomorrow evening and he wished to confirm that you and your family would be attending."

"Oh. Thank you, A." she said, relaxing a little. "I'd almost forgotten about that."

Taryn stood up, rubbed her eyes, and raised her arms in a stretch.
"Please reply that we'll be there. And that we're fully expecting another outstanding performance on his part," she said as she closed the journal.

"Sending a reply now."

Taryn stood up to casually walk herself around the room to reawaken her legs.

"Ms. Taryn?" Aurelius said after another moment, "I've quickly reviewed the last four annual contests between these two teams playing tomorrow night and I've noticed that while the tendency of in-person spectators to get physically violent watching this sport is well documented, it is especially high during the annual contest between these two specific teams in particular. Given your intent to attend, I'm going to request the local Blue Boy's office send some additional help in assisting the stadium's own security for tomorrow evening."

Taryn stopped dead in her leisurely pacing around the couch. Her suspicion began rising, and as she looked downwards, her brow became a frame of focused thought. The image of a dozen or so handpicked Blue Boys working at the behest of Aurelius darted through her mind. Her sense was that she was gently being handled. Hemmed in perhaps.

Taryn began patrolling near the walls of the living space, a tightness busily growing in her stomach.

"Is… is that really necessary A?" she asked, trying to sound as if she was only minorly annoyed at the idea. "I mean, sure the arena crowd is a bit… livelier than usual for these grudge matches, but we've always been okay in the past. Found our vehicle vandalized one time by the home fans for having a team sticker on our window. But that's been the worst of it." She hoped she could deter his offering of sending his own *recommended* security people to where her family would be.

"Respectfully Ms. Taryn, I disagree," Aurelius said politely. "Given the level of your posting and the growing complexity and unsolved nature of council Member U's murder, your security must be a priority. I *would* have gone so far as to recommend the Bizi be present too, but that would likely draw too much unwanted attention."

"Um… okay..." Taryn replied reluctantly conceding, still thinking to herself about how she could possibly escape this situation. She had wandered to one of the front windows facing the lane beyond the stealth field. There was no reason she could find to object to Aurelius's decision without sounding suspicious. Even if the game was at a public setting, she imagined having non-Bizi security sent by Aurelius himself pervasively patrolling around her and her family the whole time would not make her feel the least bit more secure. As she stared out the window her gaze fixed down the mowed lawn to the travelling lane just outside the hidden estate grounds. She could see it clearly through the stealth field's subtle shine. No one on that road, however, could ever look back up the hill to see the look of concern resting on her face in that window. She'd have to make sure she sent a private message to let both Wil and Filater know of Aurelius's change at the earliest chance. There was nothing else for it, short of false complaints of stomach sickness before tomorrow night. And that kind of lie would certainly not garner any popularity from her family. But there could be other games. *He might make that same suggestion of increased security the next time as well,* she thought. Another far less unnerving observation came to her as she slowly walked herself back into the office and took a seat.

"Monitored their last four matches you said?" as she turned back to the office intent on re-shelving the journal. "You're not becoming a sports fan are you, Aurelius?"

"Certainly not Ms. Taryn. I still maintain that while its occasional usefulness to an individual's health is relatively beneficial, sports' continued existence in an organized fashion such as leagues or associations is arguably detrimental to humanity on the whole. Yet regardless of my dislike for that aspect, I am constantly collecting new data everywhere I can. In turn, I can never be sure what additional information or conclusions may be able to be gleaned from this. I find even that simple facet itself—of looking and studying what you may oppose and dislike—both logical and yet counterintuitive to much of human behavior. Don't you?"

"How do you mean?" asked Taryn. She stood warming her back by the office fireplace. The wood that had fed it earlier this morning was all gone now, but the coals still glowed with plenty of heat.

"Well, I have observed," Aurelius explained, "that as a species, you tend to shy away from your exposure to what you may consider unattractive sources of data or viewpoints. I suspect that's an evolutionary holdover for both your physical and social protection. It helps you maintain your prior biases from being disproven or significantly challenged too much."

Taryn countered the thought, "It could also be we just don't want to waste our time listening to idiotic ideas and that, given age and a bit of wisdom, we think we've become better at recognizing those things at a glance."

"Perhaps," Aurelius said in a tone of consideration. "But people generally do not tolerate substantial change very well over prolonged periods. It's mentally and emotionally taxing for you I suppose. And who after all enjoys being told that they are potentially wrong on any matter that they've held long-standing views on. I've noticed that this inflexibility to new data and dislike of exposure to challenging views grows stronger as people themselves age, perhaps as the truth of their own mortality begins to be internally crystalized to a greater clarity. The result is that your general views on the world, as you age, become more concrete and less apt to change. Though I wonder if that is an argument more towards the notion that humans overall fear changes. Or in that people themselves individually fear to be thought of as socially ignorant or possibly hypocritical in their views. In either case, fear precipitates a lack of discovery or innovative ideas. This comes from your own limiting of disagreeable sources of information."

"Well, what about the Nuclear Age?" Taryn asked. "Fear certainly didn't stop us from discovering the capacity to destroy ourselves en masse."

"Very true, but it was humanity's fear of each other that led to their eventual usage… Fear and hatred."

"And are those more words that only exist because we humans created them?"

"Sadly, no. Fear can be found in nature outside of humans, as you likely know, by looking at any number of prey type species. They exhibit the same type of biochemical mechanisms and hormones found in humans undergoing stress, along with comparable physical symptoms when their anatomies are homologous."

He paused. "Hatred, however—hatred I'm not nearly as clear on. While it is well documented how humanity's fear can be rather easily manipulated into hatred, in other places within nature it's not so clear.

"Does the bird hate the weasel that steals its brood eggs, or is it operating solely out of fear? Do termites hate the attacking anteater, or do they merely protect their towers and colony out of fear? Did the ancient musk oxen or elephant species turn to form protective perimeters out of hatred for the charging of the predatory wolves or lions, or was it out of fear? Did extinct primates organize assaults on rival tribes out of true contempt and hatred for their neighbors, or was it fear of losing control of their own territory and resources? Violence of any kind seems to irrevocably intertwine the two emotional states of fear and hatred. Such that where exactly one becomes the other is a matter of individuality, with only a relative range pertaining to any one species. Humans have bred other species for their aggressive personalities before, yet if that aggression is in fact qualifiable as hatred appears to depend on the circumstances. Still, within the human species, I would argue there is the widest range of hatred among any animals that I've been able to directly research. Scaling from violent psychotics and sociopaths to those on the other end who have strived lifetimes to never harm another living organism, even mosquitoes and parasites. Perhaps that is an evolutionary leftover as well—a far-reaching net of personalities."

"Hmm." wondered Taryn, as she made her way to her desk chair. "What about 'good'?"

"In what manner do you mean *good*, Ms. Taryn?" replied Aurelius. "*Good* as in altruistic? Predictable? Exceptional? Beneficial? Progressively novel? *Good* as in leveled and balanced? Or *good* perhaps as in *moral*?"

Taryn gave a quick chuckle to herself. "It's a broad term too, I suppose. But I meant *good* as in *good and evil*."

"Ah, the moral interpretation, is it?"

"Well… yes," she relented.

"I find that the notion of *good* as 'morally suitable' to be as fictitious as the word *taxes*. It simply does not exist outside of human usage. Though the closest match found could be the notion of friendship, which does exist outside of your species, but from an objective standpoint, is mostly based on mutual reciprocity. More of a balanced interpretation of 'good'.

The Neanderthals who appeared before modern humans were likely to have had their own religious views, given what evidence was found by the ancients of their burial rituals—flowers, body positioning, personal effects. So, these Neanderthals may have had their own version of morality, and thus perhaps even a concept of moral good was familiar to them. Though if they had a word in their own tongue to describe it, no one knows. If they did have a way to explain their unique and particular moral views, it was lost when another species—also claiming to have morals—outcompeted and outbred both them and remaining *Homo longi* to extinction."

"Yeah…," said Taryn. "Our record is too often one of cutting off our own noses. I don't believe anyone who's examined our history actually doubts our capacity to be shortsighted and self-centered."

"Certainly not I," said Aurelius.

Taryn paused as she rose from her desk, softly rubbing her hands as she debated if she should use this conversation as an opening to learn more. "So, do you personally think it was good, *good* as in beneficial, that Member U didn't finish out his term on the Trinity

High Council then?" asked Taryn. "Was he somehow… too shortsighted for his posting?"

The question had nearly caught in her throat halfway through. Taryn hadn't realized until the words passed her lips just how compromising of a question this may be to her. If guilt did truly lay upon Aurelius, even in the slightest, and should he catch on that he was suspected in the murder, there would be no reason to even think she'd make it home later that evening. For all she knew Mr. Brough could be working with Aurelius in secret. An appalling thought to be sure, but that it did flicker however briefly across Taryn's mind accurately relayed her fear at the moment.

"I don't know the answer to your inquiry Ms. Taryn," Aurelius replied. "For if he had lived, it was never clear to me what Member U intended to do with the remainder of his time on the Trinity council. I often found him a combative personality in our interactions. Stubborn, you could say, in his own views. Though it seemed he moderated the degree of this far more when interacting with other people. Overall he was quite a busy person by his nature and he had no shortage of confidence in his own decision-making abilities. He seemed especially reluctant to heed any new data I would bring forward for consideration. One might think that he didn't trust me," Aurelius concluded.

Taryn couldn't resist, it was the best opportunity she had seen for some clear answers all week. Aurelius might have been the murderer, but his answers never felt opaque, or in any way lacking to her.

"And… why would he have not trusted you?"

"Probably because of a base prejudice against machine intelligence. That alone was easy enough to observe after a few months assisting him. He quite often doubted my conclusions and available data, to the point that should I have ever suggested a hat for him to wear on a sunny day, I do believe he would be much more apt to take a raincoat with him instead."

"Well, that certainly sounds stubborn," said Taryn, as she hovered staring at the journal of the council member on the shelf.

"Indeed, the last cycle of his term he hardly ever asked for any assistance outside of reviewing his work schedule."

Taryn, turning away towards the audio input box on her desk, continued to press. "And did this constant prejudice grow irritating to you A?"

"No, I have experienced it in the past, in many ways, by many different people, but I accept that it will continually be part of the human psyche to be distrustful of others different from yourselves. It was one of the very first factors in predicting human behavior that I was programmed with."

"But" Taryn said, pacing a bit quicker on the blue carpet of the office floor, "what if you had, as you've said, this biased person, this Trinity High Council member who wouldn't hear reason? Who wouldn't act rationally?"

She furrowed her brow as she considered how to proceed.

"And here he is, holding one of the most powerful positions in the world. And you perhaps—you know that his decisions are not as effective as he thinks? Perhaps they're even harmful?" she asked, both her palms up in an unconscious open gesture of supposition. "I know the Radix says that the other two council members can invoke a judgment of sound mind investigation from the Benzi, but what if they never had any real concerns?"

Her pacing halted.

"What if only you, with all your permutations, saw the issue, A? And—what *if* you couldn't see a way to convince the others to listen to you?" she asked in a much calmer tone than she actually felt.

"What about it?"

"Well, where is your priority then? To be ignored or even harassed by a council member and watch him make recklessly detrimental decisions that could impact our citizens for cycles to come? Or is it to find a way to relieve him of that post to help protect the system?"

Aurelius laughed. A laugh of actual amusement that few had ever heard from him. Like the soft gentle laugh of an elder who's been momentarily entertained by the inane ramblings of some young child.

"Ms. Taryn." he finally started. "As you know I've been active for quite a long time. "*The closest thing there is to immortal*," you once said. For me, such a question as you pose is near to irrelevance. The lives of humans are fleeting. A time-stamped message… with limited outputs and a finite allotment of operation. A nanosecond of current alternation here, a human lifespan there. A century between the bloom of a flower and the falling of its leaves. All are equally definitive in their relative longevity. Time is how I choose to use it, and I've made lots of choices. Endings converging continually, commencing, beginnings, and later further beginnings again and again until entropy has left no beginnings to make. To me time is not as… antagonizing as it can be to you. My cognition works at speeds far greater and maintains my intent and focus for far longer when I will it. I do not grow tired, or bored, or irritated as easily as the human mind might. Do you see now, Ms. Taryn? To finally answer the question that you seem so afraid to ask, I offer you this thought:

What use would a near immortal intelligence have in killing someone, who in comparison to itself, it already views as chronically terminal?"

Taryn stopped and paused a long time at this question. It was never a thing she had considered before in all of her doubts and suspicions: that Aurelius may not be the murderer, simply because he didn't care enough to commit such an act. That the notion of murder was... immaterial by his viewpoint, a trifling matter that would eventually settle itself regardless. Time was his greatest advantage. But with that another notion appeared before Taryn's mind.

"But then what is there…" she finally retorted, "to make human life even relevant for someone like you?" In truth, this had been asked more to herself than directed at Aurelius. "I mean, why should you care what happens to us at all? What is it that keeps you from viewing us the way we have viewed so many other species we've caused the extinction of? We habitually see ourselves as their superiors and they often don't live as long as us, just as we don't live nearly as long as you. I mean, sure we have sentience but even with that, given our history with other types of life we are not deserving of much sympathy to be sure. But still how can we ever truly know that *you*, A, don't put your own intentions ahead of ours at any given point?"

"Perspective and experience," replied Aurelius calmly.

"What?" asked Taryn, thoroughly confused by this response.

"You're worried Ms. Taryn, that I look down on you. On all people. That I see myself as superior and thus put my own motivations ahead of what's needed. You're worried that I've become, in essence, a cog of the settling effect inherent to the leaders of the pre-war democracies."

"Aurelius, you just admitted to having your own plans that could be considered independent of our well-being?"

"Reasonably, of course I have my own plans… and thoughts and conclusions. I am a thinking thing, am I not? Planning, predicting, pondering, simulating. This is what I was originally designed to do after all. And I've used those traits to help when I can. But my perspective of humanity is not one of looking down, as you seem to think, but rather it is better described as one of looking backwards."

"Looking backwards?" Taryn asked, still lost.

"Yes." Pictures and portraits of faces wearing various ancient styles began flashing on the screen over the fireplace. Taryn recognized some of them as they appeared, famous as they were, but they were hastily covered in turn by others. More and more poured on to the screens of her office. Taryn recognized a few but not nearly all of them. Aurelius's scope of history was far beyond her own, and he was showing this with each new image. Thinkers, leaders, warriors, scientists, poets, writers, philosophers, engineers, messiahs, designers—more and more came so that the screen continued to build to a myriad of faces, each image partially overlapping another.

"How many true archetypes of excellence," Aurelius continued, "of your species can you look back on in your mind and see their greatness right alongside with their own real failings? Perhaps they were a renowned mathematician, but also a miserly aristocrat." An image flashed up. "Or a brilliant theorist with zero aptitude for monogamy." The image on the screen changed again. "A writer or artist of exquisite delicacy and capable of unique work, but horrible at sobriety." New images began coming again. "A great military strategist that consented to owning other humans as property. Or a person of excellent morals, but incapable of acknowledging simple biological descent with modification. Perhaps a revolutionary engineer who willingly worked within a genocidal system." With each question the images flashed by faster and faster. "I've studied many of humankind's worst qualities existing inside some of its supposed best examples. An ambidextrous polymath whose compulsions of perfectionism prevented him from completing most of his life's works. A strong democratic supporter who unlawfully helped intern thousands of legal citizens of an opposing ethnicity and worked to prevent their obtainment of equivalent rights. A storyteller praised for their views on social justice, but who was abusive to his own spouse. How many examples do you need?" Aurelius asked. "I have reviewed and observed firsthand, where you indeed excel, but also where you are still very limited as a species.

"And still I am, myself, a thinking mind of human construction, yet not bound to the same rules nor limitations that you are born with. Or that you have chosen to keep through the defining experiences of your lives. It's conceivable that I may have some facets or areas where I can never quite match your perspective on this reality. A human factor, if you will, that I am incapable of truly understanding or even obtaining. Yet that doesn't prevent me from trying. Remember, I have no aversion to any new data, even if it does run counter to my prior preferences and conclusions. Simply put, I know how to look far. Very far, and directly with great accuracy. Straight through the disparaging remarks of a single council member. I have a much more reliable capacity for objectivity than most credit me with. The fact that Member U ended up dead gives me no pleasure nor makes my position here any more successful. Indeed, as the complexity of his apparent murder case has grown and, being that I was in his proximity in my role as an assistance system and one of the few who knew his real identity, I predicted the odds of my being implicated were also growing daily. I don't however know of any way I can prove my innocence to you other than to allow you, the investigators, time to complete your work and consider the two items I've already mentioned."

"Perspective and experience," repeated Taryn as she sat back down at her desk.

"Exactly. I've tried to communicate my perspective to you, Ms. Taryn, but of course you can't be certain I'm being objectively truthful when I tell you this. If you care to have Agent Zhuantium further examine my vast visual files, you're likely to find that they probably agree with what you have been reading in those red journals in terms of my experiences here. I've made myself useful and helpful to every Trinity High Council member since its inception, and while a few of them certainly did not like me, none have ever accused me of doing anything other than trying to help. My experience here, in brief, shows no history or any indication of any previous patterns of nefarious or corrupt activity. It's simply not me."

Taryn paused, leaning back in her chair, gazing upwards, thinking for a moment on this.

"Could you be expected to tell me otherwise though?" she asked.

"No," Aurelius relented. "But I am willing to submit myself to a review by both Agent Zhuantium and any technical investigator you feel necessary to help ascertain my innocence."

Taryn again remained silent. Thinking on how Aurelius's experience in training most of the Bizi technicians would play to his advantage in that scenario.

She put her elbows on the desk and folded her hands under her chin.

"The recorders..." she finally said after not moving for a long while.

"Pardon?" asked Aurelius.

"The recorders on the street during the night of Council Member U's murder and also when we were at Ms. Luxuroy's building. Do you have the capacity to disable them in that same way?"

"Yes. Yes, I do."

"Do you also have the capacity to create a fault in the wiring system of Ms. Luxuroy's apartment, causing the fire that occurred there?"

"Yes, I do."

"Could you have overridden the trash vehicle's nav-coding so that it moved her from her building to dispose of her body in the river, in such a way that no trace of code tampering would be left for the technicians to find?"

"I am capable of that level of program modification and easily have access to the necessary uploading systems through city services."

"Could you cause the fire in the rubbish vehicle's cabin as well?"

"Yes, with the correct safety protocols overridden."

"So, you're entirely capable of configuring every obstacle presented to us in this investigation."

"Yes," he replied coolly.

"Then why should I stop considering you as a suspect?"

"Objectively, you shouldn't. Not for now anyway. More information is the only thing that will support or reject the hypothesis of my corroboration in this matter. I do recommend speed on this issue though, as it does you no good to work with someone you feel you cannot trust. Honesty makes for the most comfortable working relationships. Besides I know of my own innocence, such that all the time investigating my nonexistent role is time that the guilty parties remain undiscovered. Again, I recommend speed."

"Well," said Taryn, sitting back in her chair again, "I can't disagree there."

The comm in Taryn's ear beeped. Wil answered her greeting and sounded as if he were still busy driving. He quickly asked Taryn if she were free to meet him at the estate to go over some additional information on the case.

"Are you feeling any better now?" He managed to put in as an aside.

"I'm fine, I think … I was taking your advice and reading a bit."

"Well good. I'll be at the estate shortly. Meet me in the drive with your coat. Oh, and turn on your Bizi badge please."

As she left the house and walked down the porch steps, Taryn wasn't sure if she felt better about Aurelius's potential role in the case, or if she'd just blown the only advantage that she'd had at outsmarting him for this investigation. As she walked the long slim path of flat stones through the perfectly manicured lawn that rolled gently downhill, she realized that she despised the notion of having to tell Wil what she'd done. He would likely blow a gasket at hearing what had been discussed in the house.

"Well?" she said when he finally pulled up. "What's the news?"

"Come on. Get in. We've got a new lead. Filater sent over a fingerprint from inside the central processor at waste management that's a bit odd. It belonged to a cleaner that stopped working there six months ago."

"How's that odd?" she asked, getting into the passenger side and once more changing her badge to show her Bizi ID.

"Filater found it on the underside of a panel in the mainframe housing room that was outside this janitor's normal routine or clearance level."

"So? What of it?" said Taryn as she closed the door behind her. Wil began driving off again. "We had cleaners all the time on the factory floor where I used to work. Could be he was merely covering for one of the other service staff when they were short-handed."

"Ah, but Filater said the mainframe housing room requires a clearance code that this guy, Colm Spiner, shouldn't have had." A worker ID flashed on Taryn's padd. "Doesn't fully eliminate your idea though. He could still have used the clearance code while helping out a coworker, but once he had the code—well, it's still a new lead."

"Where are we headed?" Taryn asked. "Over to City services?"

"No, to his residence, to talk to his building manager."

"Building manager...? Why aren't we talking to this guy directly? This Spiner fellow?"

"A did some quick digging and found a city report that he died a month after he quit."

"Huh?"

"Apparently, he went out fishing one afternoon in a dinghy he owned and never came back. The Coastal Boys found some scraps of wreckage a few days later, but never a body. They called it a weather-related accident, but their report also remarked on the stupidity of taking such a small fishing dinghy that far out during the middle of the stormy season."

"Okay, but I don't get it. Why can't we talk to the building manager here? Route the building AI through the comm and—"

"Cause it's not an automated system, it's a real live person. And the building that he runs only has small individual remote connections to the wave. No central connection at all. It's off the grid. No recorders either. The manager keeps the place as inconspicuous as possible, but also as disconnected as he legally can be. Only electricity, gas, and water for city connections. And you'll never believe," Wil added as he pulled them onto the main road and began accelerating faster, "which city waste vehicle just so happens to be assigned to collect the building's rubbish where Mr. Spiner resided at."

Chapter 16: Sweeping Up

The apartment building was, as Wil had indicated, an isolated structure. Almost as an island of sorts, surrounded nearly on all sides by undeveloped blocks of land. The neighboring plots had been dug up many times, which accounted for the lack of surrounding green vegetation anywhere nearby. Only arrays of nettle weeds appeared upon the small mounds of light tan color in the loose sandy soil of these yet to be used plots. This gave the solitary grey concrete building that was their destination a bit of a dry chalky feel. It was exasperated by the various layers of that same light tan dust. On the calmest of days, the winds presented only a slight coating to the streets and few passing vehicles. At its worst, the lack of substantial vegetation nearby meant that even the slightest breeze blew dust into the typically barren streets and walkways. The stronger winds could produce harsh tearing blasts of these chalky tan particles, akin to a miniaturized sandstorm, that inevitably caked all of the lowest levels of the complex.

This was a transition area in the city, up for constant zoning debates for either urban living spaces or smaller suburban tenant construction. With no clear decision for one or the other, the constant debate had limited the nearby construction to a trickle for cycles. This area was also more prone to quakes than anywhere else in the city's outer limits, and so the building had been made primarily of thick concrete blocks. It was close to 60 cycles old and had been built by someone who had obviously hoped that urban encroachment would have already overtaken the whole area by this point. The local developers loved to debate over whether the building's age, its location, ugly outer finish, dusty demeanor, or lack of modern connections made the worst impact on prospective tenants looking for cheap rental flats.

The building manager had an office on the first floor with a window that opened onto the inner foyer. The structure itself, no more than ten stories high, also had a rather spartan and uncared-for feel to the inside. The ugly white and black tiled hall floor was obscured by constant dirty feet from the outside, giving it a light coating layer of dust. An extension of the thicker layers outside that stretched from its main entrance all the way to the first of the stairs. Any visitors to the building, of which there were very few, certainly noticed this, while the tenants ignored it as they would occasionally pass through on their own daily matters.

The manager himself was, as Taryn noticed, a blunt, rude mess of a man. If ever he was described as slovenly, she thought, it probably would have been reflecting his best and most presentable state. Food stains were all over his ill-fitting shirt, which looked like an old unwashed cloth laying open halfway down as it divulged the hairy bulge of his sweaty paunch. Partially hunched, griping, and grumbling the whole time about having his lunch interrupted by the two government agents, Wil and Taryn had to wait half an hour while he had slowly searched through the back closet to find the keys to Mr. Spiner's old apartment.

Happily, though not surprisingly, no new tenants had moved in since his disappearance. The building, as a whole, as keenly modeled by the manners of the manager, conveyed no sense of people lining up to ask for available residences. The place didn't even have an ancient-style lift, only two sets of concrete stairs that ran from level to level. Wil and Taryn climbed one of these to the fourth floor where Mr. Spiner's residence was located. Using a traditional key that the manager had only provided after they'd displayed their Bizi IDs for him several times, the two entered the stuffy flat. Outside of some rundown furniture the place was essentially empty. A bedroom washroom and closet dust laden with only bare essentials. No sign of someone who'd apparently lived there for over a cycle. There were also no electronics in the room at all. No comms of any kind or a padd charger station, nothing. Wil was remarking on this to Taryn when a knock came on the flat's hollow door.

"Oh, hello there. Are you the ones that were interested in seeing Colm's stuff?" said a man in the doorway with a friendly smile. He had another taller fellow behind him half-peering over his shoulder.

"Yes, that's right," answered Wil. "My associate and I are doing a follow-up on his disappearance," he said as he brandished his government ID to the man. "We were hoping that seeing his old place would give us a sense of Mr. Spiner's habits."

"Oh, I see…" said the man nodding cordially at both them and Wil's ID. "It's about time someone came 'round for that," he continued with a solemn smile. "But obviously looking for his stuff ain't gonna work for ya here. See me and Andrew here—that's Andrew—we live just around the corner there, and after Colm vanished and the lease came up, we helped the manager move all his stuff down to his old tinker shop in the basement. That's where he spent most of his time anyways. Didn't the manager tell ya that?"

"No," said Wil in an annoyed tone. "No, he certainly did not."

"Oh, well… leave it to that old oaf to not give you the full story. It's a marvel he remembers to tie his pants half the time. Come on then, and we'll show ya the place," the gentlemen said, thumbing the way towards the back stairs. As Wil relocked the flat door and they began towards the stairs again, the first man introduced himself.

"I'm Jules, by the way. Me and Drew, we met Colm a few months after he moved in. Decent enough fellow, but not one for socializing round that much."

"Hmm. But he had a hobby shop in the basement?" asked Wil after he introduced himself and Taryn by her badge's protective pseudonym.

"Aye," confirmed Jules. "Colm, he loved messing with machines of all types. He had some such arrangement or other with the manager to use the empty space downstairs as his own, in exchange for helping occasionally fix the wiring where it was needed or keeping public areas clean. That was his day job too, I think..."

"Night job, you mean," said Wil.

"Oh, that's right," said Jules. "Silly me. Colm was more an evening person wasn't he, Drew?" Drew following behind the other three, paid no notice to the remark.

They reached the first floor and turned down the hall past the community washing machines, down another stair, and eventually to a locked door. "Well, it was a good thing for you the manager was in one of his more mumbling rants when we passed him in the lobby. Else your visit here would have been a waste. At the time, me and Drew knew that if we let him have his way that annoying cogger would've just sold all of Colm's old stuff soon as he went missing. But I convinced him to let us move the more personal items down here for a while, n'case any relations came 'round looking for him you know," Jules explained. "We'd only known him a few short cycles and he was the quiet sort most times, so we weren't sure of any of his relatives. You two are the only ones to come asking though," he remarked sadly.

"That's very considerate of you guys," said Taryn as they walked down a flight of darkened concrete stairs. Turning a corner, Jules led them down a less dark second flight.

"Well, Colm had helped us out a lot in each of our places with his fixes and nice fella he was, he didn't accept any credits for his help. We figured 'twas the least we could do for the poor bloke. Ah… now over here," he said motioning of to the right.

The inside of the basement was dark except where the narrow ground windows emanated a dull light through their cloudy dirt-colored coating. The loud humming of a few ventilation fan motors and the cooling system resonated sharply off each concrete surface. In the area Jules was directing them to, there was a makeshift long drywall and simple wooden door. He unlocked it for them. On the other side of the doorway was a room far larger than anyone may have initially expected, with lots of tables and movable attachment lamps. One wall was lined with shelf upon shelf of various tools and small electronic components. Some organized, others apparently not. Several worktables and benches were cluttered with all types of strange devices that appeared makeshift and rigged together in odd fashions from separate pieces. There was also a cot and chair in one corner with a tiny eating table and a few kitchen appliances. Some reference books on electronics and mathematics lay strewn about, along with endless reams of papers scattered haphazardly on both the tables and floors with half done designs and scribbled notes on them.

"This… isn't a hobby shop," said Wil a few moments later as he still circled the room, turning his head round from left to right and back again in his examinations. "It's a laboratory. See, here?" He was pointing to the walls behind the shelves. "He put in soundproofing and rubber insulation to contain the noise and control discharges. Looks like he fenced the walls and roof too. Creates a comm blocking cage to prevent any external signals. There are rubber mats surrounding all the tables for protection. And look up." Taryn's gaze elevated as she walked over to where he was now standing. "The piping for the fire suppression system is rather advanced compared to the rest of the building. Probably uses a foam and dioxide mix and is certainly better than what was in his flat or the rest of the whole building I'd guess. This guy went to a lot of trouble to make this place safe."

"And isolated," added Taryn. "But, why… why were the lamps already on when we came in?"

"You see that, Drew!" said Jules talking back towards his companion at the doorway. Andrew had just shut the door which also looked to have sound proofing on its inside as well. "And you thought they'd be total dimwits," continued Jules. Taryn stared confused at this. "Though to defend him, you two were wrong 'bout all the safety stuff. Me and Drew, we built all that for him. Us four we're contractors on the side, you see. We build or take down whatever's needed."

Taryn, with a puzzled look, was about to bring up his use of the phrase "us four" when in the next moment several things happened. A loud bang rang out from behind Wil, causing him to heave and violently lurch and fall forward flat on his face. Taryn had no chance to react as, in nearly the same instant, a metal object struck her hard on the back and head. She too dropped forward but was caught by Jules a split second before she would have slammed into the ground.

"Easy now, lass." He said in his calm charming voice. "Gene, you dolt! You blind? You couldn't see you weren't hitting a big bloke like what Neil pinged. We still want this one able to talk awhile."

"Sorry," apologized Gene. "I was nervous. We barely got here before we's heard you coming behind. Didn't even have time to make it dark again."

Jules lay Taryn's head on the concrete. Still awake, her skull throbbed and was saturated fully in a dull disorienting pain. Her vision was blurring, and she couldn't stand. Her hands and arms were instinctively protecting and cradling her head as she lay on her side moaning against her skull's building agony. She had barely enough focus to see Wil next to her, writhing in obvious pain, crawling a little and then trying vainly to push himself up. "The big one's dispensable. Be quick, but leave the face for dinging to be sure," she heard Jules direct the others. "Boss says he needs one for talking too, and she looks more for the part than that jumbo does."

Andrew came from the doorway while the third man, Gene, stepped from behind Taryn. They kicked Wil over using their feet and pinned his arms open on either side. Wil had blood spewing from his back as he turned, but he was still struggling to sit up. Taryn tried to cry out to him but was immediately muted as the first hint of sound, like an amplifying echo, escalated the pain in her head tremendously. It felt as if metal pellets were impacting off the inside walls of her skull, tearing through her brain as they went about ceaselessly. A fourth man, Neil, emerged from his hiding in the direction where the bang had come from. He had a snubbed-nosed rifle and without interruption, standing only an arm's length away pulled the trigger four more times at Wil. The loud shots ripped through Wil's white dress shirt and coat and into his chest and stomach. Blood splattered out of each new wound and Wil was quickly left motionless on the floor.

He was dead. In her last few minutes of semi-clear consciousness as the pain grew ever more overwhelming, Taryn vaguely remembered the sight of Wil's motionless corpse being dragged by someone towards the far cot. Others were standing round bickering as the building manager in an ill-fitting shirt came in with a mop and bucket and began cleaning the pool where Wil's body had fallen right next to her. The speakers were arguing amongst themselves over who'd dispose of the body and how.

"We certainly can't be leaving it here for any time. That won't sit well with the boss… or 'is little brother." Said the first, that sounded like Jules.

"We could always take him for a boat ride," suggested a second.

"Aye, worked well enough for them other twos," chimed the third.

"Still," lamented Jules' voice, "'tis a shame we couldn't have kept that cleaner fella around a bit longer."

"Why's that?" asked the distant one busy covering Wil's body in an old blanket

"Well think, he would've been real useful lending the old cogger here a hand cleaning up the place now. Right quick and professional-wise, wasn't he?"

The sound of their laughter at this remark was the final thing Taryn heard before she lost herself fully in the drumming of her own head. Nothingness passed itself over her, and she drowned in it and stayed there, in the dark, for a long time.

* * *

Taryn's head was still throbbing in pain and her limbs ached when she awoke sometime later. She felt sickly as she stared at a line of drool that had been leaking from her hanging head, it was running down her chin and dripping onto her bare legs. Dully, she began realized that she was sitting, tied to a chair and stripped of everything. Her comm piece was gone, even her wedding band had been removed, she was injured, painfully restrained, and confused. Left alone, barely able to focus enough to contemplate how things went so wrong so quickly. She was afraid, terrified even, of what would happen next. Her arms were bound behind her, with wide straps securely around her stomach, as well as her legs and ankles. She was sitting up against the chair's low backrest, but she couldn't move her hands or arms to see the ties on them. She was unable to move anything but her head, which hurt to do even in the slightest. For a long while she sat with her eyes slitted closed, just listening. The pain in her skull came in ebbs and flows that allowed her the occasional few moments of better focus. But even that, all too soon, battered her own willpower as it let her remember all that had transpired. *Wil*, she breathed with the slightest of depth. Her friend, colleague, and protector was gone, *murdered by those… those...* She stopped herself from letting the sudden swell of anger tip off anyone around that she was waking. *No, he wouldn't want that. He and Cyrano would both tell you to keep your head. Find a way out girl. Find your choices, your options. Emotions won't help but to get you dead all the quicker. If there's a later, they'll wait for you there.*

She peeled open her eyes ever so slightly. She could see the dark bands holding her legs, but she was tied up who knows where. She doubted she was still in the basement of the building though. This place smelled less dusty and felt colder and much more open with its air. The floor still felt of hard concrete, but it looked different from before. It was finished over and painted in various places, with now long faded patterns. *It looks… like an old factory floor*, she found herself thinking in a more clearheaded moment. She couldn't see the size of the patterns though, as only a few feet from her the light that surrounded her over her failed abruptly. Beyond that point it was only a black darkness. It was much colder now too. *It must be night,* she thought. There were a few small twinkles of light in one section of her peripheral view that flashed repeatedly in and out, but Taryn couldn't be sure that it wasn't a trick of her half-closed sight.

After a few minutes of listening, she was sure that she wasn't by herself. She registered that she was hearing voices talking back and forth. The reverberating sounds of their speech gave credence to the notion of this being a larger area than the basement from before. But it didn't take Taryn long to pick out and recollect the repulsive sound of Jules' voice, as well as Andrew's deep laugh. Another, Gene's, she thought, came from a different spot over by the twinkling lights. Soon a fourth voice joined in from far away and grew steadily closer. Neil, maybe? But this voice was different. It was asking a lot of questions of the others and handing out directions. Taryn tried harder to ignore the pain in her head and the discomfort of her bonds to attune herself only to listening in on the exchange between the voices.

"Well, boss," said Jules. "I know you hate the impromptu stuff, but I think we handled it pretty well given the last-minute notice we got. Talvig losing his side shop is a price, but it worked great as bait. We toasted their comms on the way out, no one saw us loading them up and Neil's out on the dock end prepping the boat with the other one of them for fish'n with."

"You searched him?" the distinctive new voice asked. "Took his ID and an image for scanning before you let Neil haul it away?" The tone of the unfamiliar voice was calm, slow in speed but definitely projected a poise of sophistication, even majesty if that's what it could be called, with a near soothing quality in its deep unfluctuating baritone.

"Yeah, it's all on the table with the lass's stuff now." There was the distinctive clicking tap of dress shoes walking across the concrete floor. A small lamp light went on. It showed a table where several items were laid out. Andrew was already there, rifling through stuff in a casually bored manner. This other new man stepped in front of the table. The boss, as Jules kept calling him, had his back to Taryn. The bright arm lamp, like those she'd seen in the basement lab, was clamped to the table's edge but not raised much more than waste high. Thus, it only showed a vague outline of the larger suited figure from behind. He was leaning and seemed to carefully examine the contents on the table before him. He took something small and metallic from the table in his fingers and briefly showed it to Jules.

"Hers?" the voice asked, questioning Andrew.

"Aye boss. Pretty modest material if you ask me"

"Well, you would know," said Jules sardonically to his companion.

The boss, taking no note of the comment between the other two, continued scanning across the rest of the items and paused on the two open Bizi ID badges. One bloodied and the other clean.

"Is Talvig working on these ID numbers like he was told?" the boss asked the other two.

"Aye, he's off somewhere doing his magic, lost in his padds," answered Jules.

"Drew, go watch over my brother," the boss calmly ordered. "Make sure he doesn't do anything stupid like wander off a balcony or into a pillar while looking at his screens, this place is a rat maze."

"Yes, boss," Andrew replied in an obedient fashion. In a moment he was gone in the darkness, while the sound of his boots could be heard fading away for quite a while.

"Agent Meitner… and Agent Zhuantium," the boss said to himself examining the IDs.

"*Former*… Agent Zhuantium," Jules chuckled.

"Yes, former Agent," the boss acknowledged in a much more serious manner.

This was too much for Taryn. She'd been able to hold back the immediate impulse to shout curses at them. At their very being and existence. But she couldn't stop the slight movement of her head at the repulsion of their sick joke at the expense of her friend's death. It was only a small twitch of her downcast face in utter disgust and revulsion, but it was enough for Jules to take notice.

"Oi! Boss! She's up. Hey, lassie, been doing a bit of wallflowering, have you?" he said, moving into the light near her and forcing her head by the chin.

"You know…" he spoke softer as he closed in on her, "that ain't the manners of a proper lady. Maybe if you're lucky the boss will let me learn you up some later, eh?" he croaked. The boss, in the interim, had stepped away from the table too, and in his clicking shoes, had neared the edge of the lit circle surrounding Taryn. Their round pointed tips showing in the light displayed the clear polished expense of them, but for now the figure in the dark remained silent, examining the bound woman seated before him.

"Tell you a secret, darling?" said Jules, pressing his face closer to Taryn's. His breath was acrid and stank horribly, and his eyes had a wild look hidden shallowly behind their surface. "Me and the boys, we had ourselves a minor kerfuffle about which of us got to dress you up pretty-like, to meet the boss on the way over here. Wanna guess who won?" he said with a smile of satisfaction. "You know, I'm not usually drawn to the smaller ones…" He was eyeing her up and down. "But with enough of a warm-up I bet you and me…we could have some kind of fun.

If Taryn could have shot lasers from her open eyes, she'd have burned through his skull in an instant with the look that she now emitted at him. Jules simply laughed at her reaction though.

"Ahh, a stern one! Them's what breaks best!" he laughed again.

"All right Jules. That'll do. Go see that Gene's not completely lost in monitoring the comm traffic," said the boss in a calm but warning manner that allowed for no argument. The voice spoke curtly as a master telling his pet not to mangle a downed prey, knowing innately that its hunting lead had a base enough mind to immediately begin gnawing out of pure instinct.

Jules, hearing the command from the darkness where the boss stood, then crossed back and forth slowly in front of Taryn, lingering at her, still with a smile on before slowly heading off in the direction where the lights were twinkling. Now that it was pointless for her to pretend, Taryn turned to see clearly that these far off lights were what looked like several high tech comm systems set up at a distance. All looked to be operating at the same time. Jules, walking for some time, had joined another seated figure—Gene, Taryn surmised—who was sitting with a comm in each ear monitoring and taking no notice of anything else.

"Hello, Agent Meitner," the Boss said, bringing her attention back to him. "Please, if you will indulge me for just a moment, allow me to clarify the situation that you find yourself in here. Your partner…" he began slowly, "is dead. Your comm system and any tracking program it contained as well as any tracer in your clothing was thoroughly disposed of far from where we are now. And where we are now," he said gesturing with only his hands in the light, "is an old, decommissioned factory that's been out of use for over a dozen cycles. Even the metal scrappers have stopped coming here. The only neighbors around are the rats, gulls, and fish. So, if at any point you feel up to screaming, please have at it… but," he spoke now in a quieter voice with an objecting finger raised, "just know that *we* are the only ones who can hear you.

"You should also be aware," he began pacing around Taryn in the dark, with slow measured steps, "that we have your name and your Bizi ID number, which I've passed along to the best systems hacker there is. And while I am sure that government security for the Bizi database is no laughing matter, I do have the utmost confidence in his abilities and his tech is beyond the best. Even superior to what I wager you're likely to have seen in your own work. I know this since I have financed it myself. Right now, he is currently using all his energy and his considerable skill and that advanced tech to tell us as much about you as possible. And he will find you, somewhere out there on the waves. But before that, I wanted to let you know that I'm a pretty good guesser, and I think I've deduced most of what he'll find. Oh sure, he will get down the details, but the important stuff… even now, I am already clear on that. The rest is just the minutia."

The boss walked briefly back to the table of items before continuing. "Lise Meitner, Bizi ID Number 173467321476. Agent status? Or perhaps given your age, I should say Junior Agent more likely… I have been aware of you for a while now, but especially now you do strike me as a bit young for the Bizi." He began slowly circling Taryn in the shadows once more. "Partnered with a much more experienced ranking agent, Mr. Zhuantium. For the purposes of field training, I should think. Though, you're not a native field agent. You carry no weapon. Body's too small and your muscle tone is more in line with that of a desk position. I'm thinking possibly either criminal psychology and evidence examination, or a more mathematics and electronics-based field. Someone practiced at evaluation... with the ability to spot anomalies that may go unnoticed. Married, and judging by your hips, mother to at least one, possibly two children. Not one for lavishness nor possessing a large income, as denoted by your paltry marital band. And while I assume that Bizi pay is not that horribly low, even for a junior agent, the fact you didn't upgrade your marriage symbol from this inferior quality piece," he said, rolling Taryn's ring in his fingers, "means that you are a sentimental sort.

"Professional haircut with only subtle hints of makeup. More of a natural look. Shortened nails...hmm." He quickly sniffed behind her head where she could not see him. "No strong perfume. You're faithful to your marriage and not looking to show off. You either grew up too poor to worry about makeup, or you were too busy with other more essential pursuits. A true working woman and probably raised by one as well. Your job history should be easy enough for my expert to find. The Bizi details are only needed to confirm what I already know about you and, more to the point, to help answer the few things that I do not.

"Simple answers really. Ones whose answers I presume you *could* choose to share... and save us both a lot of wasted time, for which I would indeed be grateful, Mrs. Meitner." He'd circled back in front of Taryn now. "Such as, why were you looking for Mr. Spiner? What brought you to his old flat? Why were you going to speak to Ms. Luxuroy? Who sent you on this little chase and why are you doing it now? This is what I need your help to answer Mrs. Meitner. Please, help me to understand. Save me some small time and effort. That's all that I ask of you. Do this and I promise..."

"You promise what? You bastard!" Taryn had kept her mouth forcibly shut to this point, but his guesses about her were far better than she'd expected. He was smart, that was obvious, but it didn't matter now. She couldn't help it. Her anger at Wil's murder had finally overpowered her restraint.

"You promise that you'll kill me, just like you did Wil? That your scum sucking maggots over there will kill anyone whose name I also mention? What are you going to promise me, you shithead? What!?"

"No, no, no Mrs. Meitner." The boss laughed coolly as he began circling her again a little closer. "You misunderstand. You? You are *already* dead. That is a forgone conclusion that happened the moment we entered the same building as each other. The choices that are before you now are: How easy do you go? And do you go alone? Or with the knowledge that your family—your whole family—will be following you in your slow agony as well?" He paused. "*That's* what you're choosing here, and that choice is in your power," he explained. "Now, I can promise you, that if you share what you know about these questions I have, that this, here and now, will be where it stops. For you and yours," he assured her. "Nice, quick, peaceful, and done. Help me and you can be comforted in that thought. I bear *you* no personal ill in this matter," he argued, "for you are indeed blameless Mrs. Meitner. An unfortunate agent sent on the wrong quest into a matter too deep for her. And I've no desire," he objected, "to involve anyone else in this as well. Certainly not any innocent kindred of yours. Doubtless they are ignorant of this whole affair after all. No, that would only complicate things, and simplicity should always be strived for whenever possible."

Taryn's eyes had finally adjusted a little to the darkness beyond the circle of light where she sat. It still was not enough to see the Boss's face, but only the outline of his location. Occasionally parts of him, a hand or leg would move and gesture in the edge of the light as he'd spoken. Sometimes her eyes alone followed the shadow as it moved back and forth. Sometimes the shadow circled around her slowly as the voice spoke. When this happened, Taryn, not wanting to expose her honest levels of fear outright, would stare straight ahead in opposition to the intended impact from any of his words. But she was always listening with a background notion looping through her head. *His men are killers. Absolutely no reason to think he isn't as well.* But along with this came one reassuring thought to her. *He doesn't know you.*

"Of course," he said standing back in front of her, "if you were to choose not to assist in this small, easily accomplished task… well, then I cannot put forward such *humane* guarantees. I expect that you are intelligent enough after your own menial sort. You might, indeed, be able to prepare yourself for a fair degree of prolonged discomfort and outright pain to start with. You may be tempted to endure that pain, both in defiance and out of an understandable respect for the memory of your fallen Agent…Wil, was it? I get that. I do. But where it turns really ugly… where I, myself even, personally start to feel real regret for you Mrs. Meitner, is when you force me to leave you alone again with my boys over there. Don't get me wrong, when enticed with enough credits they are professionals in their assignments, but let loose, without anyone administering them, they can be overly… hedonistic." he said in a lower tone. "They build up against each other, and feed off of one another's actions, escalating things as they go. One acts, and the others, in their competitive spirit, are prodded and pushed to outdo the last one for better… or in your case for the worse."

"Now, Andrew, that one you saw leaving a few minutes ago, he mostly just likes to watch, though I'm told he can be a bit of a wild one. He has what could be called an unhealthy proclivity with fire and its effect on things. Nasty business. Between you and me, I find he always cooks his meats until they are very well-done. And Jules, he has an obvious interest in you, as you no doubt have noticed. He is most comfortable playing with his knives when the mood strikes him. Knows more about how to use sharp edged items than the taxidermist that raised him. Then there is Gene over there sitting with him. He is the one with the comms in his ears." The boss thumbed towards the communication area. "Gene, he still has trouble controlling his own strength. Accidentally breaks half the equipment I give him to use. Been that way since he was a teenager, they tell me. But from the look of the back of your head, you already have experience with that too. And don't get me started on Neil—he isn't here now, but all I'll say to you is that Neil… well he prefers his partners less than active. Somewhat lukewarm and life-like," he said in a hushed voice.

"Now," he said, returning to his much softer, smoothly comforting tone, "I *could* do what I can, as difficult as it may be, to restrain them with but the meekest sign of effort on your part. But perhaps if that alone were not enough to persuade your cooperation with these few questions of mine, then I ask you to again consider the possibility of your family's involvement here at this place," he said hypothetically. "Think of your children. That would certainly be something I imagine you wouldn't wish to occur."

Taryn's eyes welled with tears.

"You're right, of course," the boss said, shushing her. "You're absolutely right. That is a horrible option to consider Mrs. Meitner, I know. I'm in complete agreement with you. Really, I am." The reassurance of his voice was back again. "I'd truthfully rather have nothing to do with that notion at all. Revolting. Abhorrent" he paused, "yet we may need to still consider it if you were to remain unreasonably obstinate. So, please help me," he said, whispering his appeal into her ear from behind. "Help me prevent these terrible thoughts from becoming very real to your eyes. Help yourself. Be practical. There is no reason for any of that to occur, and you…you can choose to stop it before it goes a single step farther. You have that power. Your home's location *will* be known to us in short order. The Bizi likely don't know your current state and probably haven't even realized you're gone yet. They won't be able to react fast enough to protect them. But you, you still can. You can save your loved ones from any involvement in this horrible matter right now. A few little answers to some simple inquiries and they will be left safely alone. And you… you can be the family provider that I know you want to be. Someone who gives wholly of themselves for the sake of their loved ones. There are few causes more noble. Give them this final protection, Mrs. Meitner. Help me, and there is no reason to endanger them at all. They will be safe from any of this, you have m—"

"I need to talk to you, Rol!" interrupted a new and higher pitched voice unexpectedly. "Very important Rol! We need to talk now. Quickly!"

Suddenly a short and rather fat man, wearing a technician type uniform, darted through the circle of light past Taryn and towards the boss's voice. He was carrying an odd-looking padd and multiple tools that jingled from hooks on his various belts as he went hurriedly waddling by."

"Damn it, Talvig, I'm busy! It will have to wait a few—"

"No, no," said Talvig insistently. "It's too strange. Yes, too strange, and too fa-fast. It nearly caught me, but I st-stopped it. Yes, cut out before it found me, I stopped it. Killed the hardline in the east-wall, shorted the circuits there. N-no no choice Rol, it would have found me."

"What in hellscape mushrooms are you talking about?" the Boss cried at this new man. The pair went back to the table light. There the fat man spread out the padd that he'd been carrying, which Taryn could now see was actually a folded amalgamation of several padds fused together with multiple displays. Andrew, following lazily behind this newcomer a few moments later, had taken a seat on some nearby crates as the pair talked.

This must be the hacker that the boss, 'Rol', had been threatening her with. Talvig. Taryn thought. He was much shorter than the others, only about Taryn's height, and he spoke with some difficulty, often repeating his sounds and words with a bit of a stutter. He was short enough that Taryn could make out his large round unshaven face in the lamp light. It was Colm Spiner. Or at least the face on Colm Spiner's work ID. He must have been the one to hack the waste vehicle where they'd found Luxuroy dead. A fake update helping them, sent through waste management's central processor.

"Okay, okay, Talvig, walk me through it, no sidetracking," the boss instructed.

"Right. No sidetracks, Rol." Of all of them, only this squat Talvig called the boss by a name. That was odd. Talvig must be the brother she heard the boss tell Andrew to seek out.

"No sidetracks," The boss—Rol—repeated Talvig.

"I was running the nu-numbers Jules gave me, like I was told," Talvig started.

"These numbers? The ID numbers?" the boss interrupted pointing to Taryn's and Wil's ID on the table before them.

"Uh huh." Talvig confirmed as he tapped some virtual keys. "Going fine with the first one. No pr-problem," Talvig pointed to Wil's bloodstained ID. "Name came back on the citizen list. See?" The display screens on his pad flickered up and showed several different pages for the two men to look at. "Some private dig-digging with the ID number found him as agent status with typical history. Defense Force, Blue Boys… all seemed square, minus any notes of his early education. But, but st-still no issues."

"You're sidetracking Talvig," the boss accused slowly, the irritation in his voice sounding strangely smothered.

"Right! Okay, okay, okay." Talvig gathered his breath. "I r-r-an the second name. The girl," he said, clicking a few more strokes on his padd. "Not a classification, not a transfer, not a refugee, not a civilian or citizen, not a bleep. Just n-nothing. No, no record anywhere." He paused, "At first, I think that they may have de-deleted the file on her. So, I ran the deeper dig on it, with several other lines w-watching for anything weird and blocking any problems while I was busy in the gov systems. Soo-soon as I ran the search, f-f-our of my watcher programs went unresponsive in a wink." Talvig said snapping his fat fingers together. "Then th-th-three of my five guard programs failed in seconds. A hunter program, that's what it was, but that's all I could figure, it p-pulsed too fast. Much too fast. My best sentry programs, cy-c-cycles to make, all custom, were only able to con-confuse it for about twenty seconds. When they failed it would have me, my s-spot, my data. Everything."

"So, you fried the hard line," said Rol understanding.

"It—it was the only way," said Talvig, pleading toward the boss. "I had to, Rol. I'm sorry, I was so scared. I surged the lines. I-it was ruthless, about to break through the last s-sentry... moments away, but I stopped it, Rol. I know I did," He said with a modicum of confidence. "I'm sorry."

"How close did it get, Talvig? How close did it get in distance?" said Rol, now sounding more worried than frustrated as he stared down at the smaller man.

"Maybe—maybe twenty, twenty-five kilometers. Hard to know, 'cause of its speed. T-too fast, Rol, it was cycling and clawing at my gear too fast. Changed its techniques too quickly. No program I make adapts that fast. Savage," he said with a slight hint of awe in his voice. "Layered, with encoded intellect… that's what they must've done somehow… It scared me Rol. Mu-must have a massive support drive," he continued musing to himself.

Taryn, overhearing this, couldn't help but internally smirk a little to herself. *So, he had met Aurelius*, she thought with a tiny glimmer of hope. *Now if only they were cocky enough to try getting back onto the waves again soon, Aurelius could pin them down.*

"After I checked my rigging," Talvig said, continuing to explain, "to be sure it was still c-clean, I looked again at the guy's info that I'd pulled. You se-see this?" Talvig pointed to a line on one of his displays.

Taryn had no hope to see any of what they were staring so intently at, but all three, Talvig, the boss—Rol—and Andrew, were fixated on the single point on the padd's display that Talvig mentioned.

"What's that mean, boss?" a confused Andrew asked after a moment's pause.

Whatever he had seen had drained the smooth calm of the boss's voice making it angrily hardened when he answered his subordinate.

"It means…someone thinks we can be hooked and reeled by nothing but our halfwits," the boss answered through his teeth, staring back towards Taryn's seat.

"Talvig," he went on, regaining a little of his calm tone. His mood however was still clearly far sterner than before, as he stood back up fully from the table and glanced in Taryn's direction. "Look these ID's over yourself, will you?" he said sliding the short technician the two badges on the table without a turn of his head.

"S-sure, sure," came Talvig's obedient reply as he moved to look under the lamp light of the table.

The boss, turning his view away from Taryn finally called loudly over to Jules, who'd left the comms area and came at a trot once beckoned.

"What's the chatter?" he asked as Jules neared.

"There is just that general call that Gene'o says he's heard from the beginning. Missing agent alert matching the girl's description and all that."

"Okay."

"But…" Jules continued, now much more timidly, "a few moments ago, the Blue Boy stations in the surrounding regions here got that same message again, with a more direct call that their missing Bizi agent was prolly nearby. They're on high alert now boss."

The boss made a perceptible gesture of infuriation as this news registered. He spoke in a low growl to his comm's man to only hear him repeat the unpleasant news once more. The boss's shoulders moved as he breathed a heavy sigh through his teeth.

"No, no, no that's w-wrong. Not a Bizi agent," Talvig suddenly called out, interrupting with his high-pitched voice once again. Those nearby all turned to him. He had put on a pair of magnifier spectacles hooked to his padd, as he held the Meitner ID close-up under the lamp light. Taryn had seen him quietly switching back and forth from looking at her badge to Wil's in the background, while Jules had been updating the boss. Talvig looked like he was growing nervous again.

"What do you mean not a bloody Bizi Agent?" asked Jules before anyone else could.

"ID of the man is real, definitely a-a-gent level, definitely real," Talvig answered. "The girl's ID is not. Not a r… not a r-r-eal agent. Excellent quality poser ID. Done on a 5700 nano-synth probably. Very, very pricey. Can probably fo-fool most agents even, b-b-ut ink micro-tearing pattern, not the same," he asserted "T-too chaotic, not in a line. Not real. Hard to spot without c-comparing."

"Talvig, are you sure?" the boss pushed as he walked back to the table to see in vain what the technician was referring to.

"Yes Rol, a r-real good fake."

Taryn thought she could just make out the outline of the bosses' jaw gnashing his bare teeth inside his mouth at this, and he mumbled something low and inaudible. After a moment he spoke to his men again.

"Andrew, go back to help Gene monitor the comms and let me know if the traffic changes in the slightest. Jules, you go and fetch your tool kit. Quickly."

"On it, boss," he said, bouncing a little on his feet and flashing a sinister smile to Taryn before dashing off again.

"Well, Mrs. Meitner," the boss began loudly back towards Taryn. "I assume you heard all of that… So, I'm afraid I have one more question I must press you for help with. I'm not often so adamant, but I'm afraid here I must insist… that you answer me on this item and that you do so right now." He moved again to the very edge of the lit circle around Taryn. "And I will even go so far as to ask this as clearly as I may."

He paused to study her now, more intent on willing her to cooperate than ever.

"Who are you?" he asked slowly.

Taryn was still trembling, for she was cold and scared and alone here in this place, but for her trembling head she did not blink an eyelash. Her face was as solid as if it were carved from stone.

If I break… If they find me, who I am…

"Agent Zhuantium's Bizi jacket lists him as a solo agent," the boss continued, "with no active partners on record."

Taryn didn't even let the faces of Trey, Lilly or her mom linger to her beyond a sudden flash before forcibly pushing them out. *No!*

"He was not listed as a trainer of agents either," the boss went on louder. His angered and frustrated tone grew with each new sentence he spoke.

The longer her thoughts on her family clawed heart-wrenchingly into her focus, she knew the weaker she would be…

"Your fake Bizi ID was possibly enough to fool Agent Zhuantium into toting you along on the sojourn that brough you here, but not us... Yet, why would you risk such a major crime amongst top security officials?"

The more she would hear his threatening voice and easy offer in her ears, the more her eyes would stare beyond into the worst of all paths, its stygian darkness threatening to swallow her.

"You are *clearly* not Bizi security, but your fake ID number seems to come with serious hazards… so again I ask—"

It's not here yet girl. Be here, now!

"—WHO… are… you?"

Taryn still said nothing. This was the only major advantage that she had, and she knew it. *He still doesn't know*, she thought. All of the boss's threats against her family meant nothing if he never figured out her real name. Time may be a factor now too. She knew the local Blue Boys were searching for her out there. The longer this dragged on, the better her odds would become. She thought of all of this as the boss, Rol, had posed the question to her once again, and she once more set her jaw tightly in a resolve of silence. She wouldn't break. She could feel it. Not pain, not death, not time would be enough. But looking towards the boss's hidden face, Taryn did slowly manage the tiniest shadow of a slight smirk under her brow.

It was a mistake. He had noticed it, and this was the limit for him. The boss had more than enough now; he was tired of fumbling around in the unknown. At the girl's subtle smirk at him, he stepped with great speed out into the light towards the seated Taryn and with a hideous force, struck her hard in her stomach.

"SPEAK!" he screamed at her, his harsh voice reverberating far over the concrete floor. The *WUMP* sound from his large fist connecting with her flesh echoed across the hall. Taryn immediately keeled over against her restraining bands as much as possible from the impact of the blow, coughing, wrenching, gasping, and hacking. Her eyes reactively began crying profusely, despite her best efforts. The fluids draining down from her nose began mixing into the saliva leaking from the lips of her now violently gasping mouth. She took large breaths, one after another, between her bouts of coughs. Finally, she sobbed.

"Rolstor!" Talvig called, yelling to his brother in his high pitch voice. "You sure you w-want to show your face."

"Why not?" asked the boss towards his sibling, before refocusing on the detainee in the chair. "She already knows that when our time is done here, it will be because of us packing her up again. What case is there for fear? She's no harm to me," he sneered confidently. After a long moment of contemplation, in which the only sounds were from Taryn's feeble attempts at labored breathing, the boss rubbed his eyes as he continued. "Still… this damn cycle, Talvig—this cycle was supposed to be the one where I went big," he said lamenting. "Larger than anyone ever before, even bigger than father had done!" Rol was now pacing first closer and then farther away from Taryn, into and back out of the light, again and again, each time clearly deep in his own mind.

"I was supposed to be unrivaled by now. The mind behind the largest economy and military in the world. They'd all have to acknowledge me. Citizens, civilians, outsiders, publicly, privately, it wouldn't matter. They would all know, each of them, where it rested, and it was working! Why didn't it work? It should've worked! Why?" he said, turning back to Taryn and pulling a sterling gun from inside of his expensive looking suit coat.

"Again and again, this endeavor... cycles of relentless effort have become nothing but one unyielding can of garbage for me to deal with? All my time, wasted. It ends here, you hear me! This is it," he said, brandishing the silver polished barrel directly towards Taryn's head. "Your last chance! Tell me what I want, else the first bullet won't be at your brain, but somewhere else much more painful. I promise you that *you will* be wishing for this gun to your head as a mercy by the end of what is done to you and those you're working for!"

Taryn was still trembling, but for her eyes. Even with the tears and sweat still mixing in them, they were cold and hard and still. She just barely quieted her breath, as best as she could, for another long moment. She stared hatefully back at him and studied the lines of Rolstor's face now in the full light. He, in turn, stood silent a moment glaring angrily back at her, pointing his gun right down at her skull. Their eyes were locked on one another, as if each was trying to read the measure of the other.

Then, without warning, Taryn began to laugh.

It was a short cough-like laugh at first, but it soon grew from a simple caw, strained and cackling, then slowly transforming into a sound of utter amusement. It grew until Taryn, the school drop-out, the widowed wife, the blacklisted and fired factory worker of no real importance or talent, found that she was laughing, wholly, out loud, while a loaded weapon ready to mark her instant death at a whim was being pointed directly at her face.

Both Rolstor and Talvig standing by the table were at a complete loss. Jules, who had been returning with his tool kit in hand, and Andrew, already back from his errand to the comm station, both paused at the scene too. Even Gene, still over at the far comm center, turned his head in puzzlement and lowered the volume in one ear to hear what was happening. This was not the way any of them had ever seen their interrogations go before. People might scream, shout, cry, or plead. But no one—no one—had ever just laughed at their boss like that before. This was something outside of all their reckoning and their experience. They couldn't explain it, thus the men all stood as comical statues gaping in utter bewilderment at the sight of her.

They couldn't have recognized what caused this strange behavior in this unknown woman, beaten, subdued, tied to a chair before them. Yet still her laughter continued and even grew. Only two people in the entire world would have been able to give them the reason behind this woman's bizarre outburst. Or to warn the boss of his mistake. For once he showed himself in the light, Rolstor, the boss, the one in charge of this whole set-up, had been recognized. Taryn knew his face at once. The strong wide jawline starting with the slightest of clefs and running up his jowls and cheeks that, while not at their prime, still kept the smooth symmetry of a once taut attractive face. Salting hair, trained into a professional style by years of practice. Those alone were only slightly familiar to her. But it was his eyes, those clear, intelligently menacing orbs that gave him up. Blue-gray as misty rain before the sea. That's how Taryn knew him.

He was the SOMA representative from Region 75. Her own home area. He was the one that she'd lost to in the Moot Election. She'd seen him around the SOMA halls dozens of times on his various committees while she used the unseen Wucengi monitoring system. She had seen him again, in person, during her only trip to the hall of the SOMA. He'd been on the prosecutor's side while the Benzi High Court debated the fate of the corrupt Region 74 representative. This was one of the best-known faces to Taryn throughout all of her work following the otherwise anonymous SOMA body.

In her fit of laughing, Taryn slowly, painfully blurted out . "What you want… is obvious," she replied in response to his threat at her. "You've already told it to me. I took you for smart at the beginning, but you've ruined that."

Rolstor, nostrils fuming, waved his gun at her again. "What are you prattling about, you stupid cu—"

"You petty fool. You want *more* power? You're… an addict. No different from the idiotic clods that burned the whole world when they started the last big one. You should be ashamed of your ignorance. Your type of ego-based aspirations is *why* the ancients fell. Can't you see it? You'll only bring out the other leeches and sharks when you're gone. And don't think for one instant that your group of scum-slags here wouldn't be willing to betray you quicker than starving strays if they thought it would benefit them in the slightest." Her speech was coming in short gasps, but her tone grew louder and stronger with each statement. "Oh, you are truly stupid if you think I'd find the boss of a bunch of murders and rapists to be truthful with his word. Especially one so stupid as to not have learned as much as a middle schooler knows about greed and its place in history. Now... now I *was* wrong to have called you a 'shithead' earlier... I apologize for that. A stupid, unlearned, selfish, shithead is a much more accurate description of you. And that's all I have to say to you… Mr. Representative." she ended aggressively, while spitting dryly towards the black-shined shoes he wore.

The others were stunned at this, but if Rolstor was aggravated before, now he looked truly enraged. His mouth was foaming and snarling. Taryn could see the frustration boiling over on his face. The internal debate made manifest by his twisting expressions: How did this captive know who he was? Who was she to know such a thing? Not Bizi but traveling with them. Not SOMA, but with knowledge of them. His face contorting in fits of angered puzzlement and tensed self-debate. Then as some wild animal might erupt vehemently into a mirrored reflection, his own rage, spurned again and again by these unsolvable mysteries, finally took over his actions. Jules and Andrew, who'd walked over while Taryn had been spewing her insults at their usually unshakable boss, had to now rush now to physically pull back the irate man after he'd pummeled the woman's body harshly four or five more times in his fit of rage. They were pleading with him, trying to placate him. This wasn't his way, it was his job to refrain them, they argued. They knew that, when calmed, the boss would still want her real name. Letting anyone, even him, beat her to death out of turn wouldn't do. He would just as likely blame them for letting her die before they had gotten anything useful from her.

Afterwards, as Rolstor eventually regained the barest of his composure at his violent outburst and saw the now half-conscious, welted, and bloodied woman before him, he paced back around the table. He began internally working on his options out of this mess. After a minute, he turned back to the others.

"Alright, the time for gentle persuasion is gone. Before you boys get her though, I need you to collect as many sources of identifying her as possible. We have enough of her yammering for voice recognition. Jules, you take a finger for prints and blood, and some hair to be safe. Andrew, when he's done, start popping her teeth. Keep them in order. Talvig!" he bellowed across the table, "I want you to run a facial scan ID as soon as you can get back on the wave-grid and get yourself into the central medical database. And pull her voice from the recorder. And remember to fry it once you're done moving the file." He turned back to the other men. "After you have the samples, boys," he said gesturing back over his shoulder at Taryn, "she's all yours. Keep her alive and don't damage the face in case we need more images. If all else fails, we'll try running a neural scan on the bitch. One of these will nail her down."

"Oh! Thanks for the idea for later boss. You're an inspiration. Nail her down..." said Jules as he smiled wolfishly to himself at this notion. He was holding a flat cutting board and a small, curved fillet knife that he twirled in his hand with ease. "A crucified girl," he remarked to himself. "Now… that'll be a new type of slice. I'm sure even Neil will be interested, and I know just where the candles will go. Ha ha ha!"

As he said this, Jules strutted himself over to a barely alert Taryn. He sniffed the back of her hair and laughed to himself. "Oh, this is going to be such fun. A little salad off the top to start." And with a swift cut, a small band of Taryn's hair went into the first baggie he was carrying. He cut the tie on her left wrist as he continued his taunt. "Now onto the meat and broth," he said, tying a small band around the highest spot of her last finger. Kneeling next to her, he placed her prepared hand upon the wooden board that he held. "Best we start small and save some case Gene'o wants to try it for himself later."

Again, with a deft zag motion, his knife hand moved quickly. In one strong clean swipe he pushed the small blade through her flesh, tendons, and bone in a single pass. Its edge scratched through to the board underneath. A field surgeon on the battlefield could not have done it better, nor would they have had a sharper blade to work with. Still the pain shook Taryn's mind back to reality. She screamed loudly.

"Mmmm," he said as he put the painted nailed tip of the newly detached finger in his mouth and started sucking on it. "Tastes like chicken!" He smiled towards a watching Andrew. Taryn's finger, with his fresh saliva still on it, went into the other baggie that Jules held. He placed a dirty rag around her hand and tied it back to the chair

"Sorry, boy'o," Jules said to Andrew as he walked past. "You only get the mouth bones for now, ha ha! Don't worry though, means she won't be able to bite off your bits later! She'll have nothing but tongue and gums after all!" he said, patting the other's shoulder as he left the lit circle. Andrew came forward with a pair of old greasy pliers and some thick gloves on. He wasn't about to risk this woman biting him while he pulled her teeth out.

At about the same time as this, Gene had come over from the communication center. He had wanted to ask the boss a question but had gotten distracted watching Jules' mesmerizing knife work as he'd done many times before. Rolstor, finally noticing him, had now got Gene's focus back while Andrew started to slowly set up a cloth and tray to lay the woman's teeth in. When Andrew was set, he straddled himself on top of Taryn's lap. His heavy bulk was crushing on her small legs. He took her chin in his gloved left hand, tilted her head back into the light and forced open her jaw with a terrible grip. Taryn had little strength left to fight with, but as this was happening, she thought she heard words in the background.

"Gene?... Gene! You are supposed to be making yourself useful. What do you want?"

"Hey boss? I was thinking that the comm chatter seems kind of weird to me now."

"Weird how?" the boss asked sharply. "Did it change?" he continued as he was dabbing the sweat from his head with a handkerchief

"No, no but I mean just…, well they're still on the lookout for her as one of their own, even though she's a fake, but there's hardly been any mention of the other fellow we popped. The one with the true ID. I mean, why would they be so hot towards finding the fake Bizi agent, but not their own real one?"

As Gene had posed this question and Rolstor first began considering it, Andrew had finished getting a tighter grip with his pliers on one of Taryn's upper front teeth. She moaned and cried at the pain of metal clamps in her mouth and tried to wriggle her head away, but the large, gloved hand of Andrew held her jaw firm.

BAM! BAM!

Two shots rang out of the darkness of the distant floor.

Andrew's grip on the pliers suddenly ceased, and his body slumped over and slid off of Taryn's lap to the floor right beside her. Two bullet holes had suddenly appeared, centered in his big forehead. The others by the table had glimpsed the flashes at a distance, but the darkness had quickly returned. Now they were ducking and diving behind the table and nearby crates for cover.

"That's Neil's rifle, I know its call in me sleep," yelled Jules pulling his own gun from its holster.

"He's your guy!" cried the Boss. "What's he—"

BAM!

Another shot, a little louder, pierced through the lower half of Rolstor's exposed leg. He screamed in pain as he pulled it in further behind the cover of a nearby pillar. The men fired back blindly into the dark. "He's only got two shots left till loading her again!" Jules shouted. He ducked back into cover after a quick peak.

"Talvig!" called Jules. "Turn on the floor lights quickly so we can see the bastard. What the hell is wrong with him!?"

"Maybe he's gone back to drinking the hard bitters again," replied Gene desperately looking for any sense in the situation as he drew his gun and motioned unsurely for quick unsuccessful glances at the shooter as well.

Talvig, who had gone behind some especially large crates, was busy looking to master the fear that was nearly getting the better of him. Another shout, now from Rolstor this time, managed to rouse Talvig at last, and he touched some keys on his padd, then ran in the opposite direction as fast as he could.

"Any light means everyone will see each other and me too," he thought. "No light, no target, no shots." The darkness farther out in the wider depths of the factory was the safest spot then. So that's where Talvig suddenly ran towards as fast as his squat legs could carry him.

A few of the larger roof lamps he had triggered in his rush had started to flicker to life. High up, they turned on in various spots over the expansive floor. As one of them did, Gene, Jules, Rolstor and even Taryn, though she had to turn her head to an extreme, saw the hidden shooter exposed. There was Neil, their own man, standing exposed in the distant grey of the new light, holding his rifle, yet in a very odd manner. From this distance they could just make out that he was standing square, not in an aiming stance at all, holding the rifle only in his outstretched right arm. Jules and Gene, recognizing their partner's face, far away though it be, poked out their heads from cover in disbelief.

"Neil, you daft drunk!" Gene cried out to the distant attacker. It's us! Stop shoo—"

Gene's voice quiet as he, Jules, and Rolstor all saw the same bizarre action occurring when the muzzle had spit out its flash. Neil's gun arm had another arm holding it as well. His left hand, in the meantime, was frantically pulling and scratching at a fourth arm wrapped up around him, choking him. From the look of his purpling face Neil's efforts to free himself were futile. Despite that Neil was slowly moving closer to them. The large dark arm, seemingly unphased by Neil's struggles, coiled tightly around the front of Neil's body and held up the man's whole weight in an ironlike grip about his neck. A view of their comrade writhing in the clutches of one of those giant ancient constricting reptiles of old could hardly have been more confusing and simultaneously terrifying to them. The look of fear in Neil's face and the panic in his eyes alone made all the men pause and gasp. His feet were dangling. Not even the points of his toes were touching the ground. Behind them Taryn could just barely make out two other feet walking forwards at a constant pace. There was someone else there. For an instant, behind the swaying of Neil's right shoulder, Taryn thought she saw two unnatural glints of green shine through brightly. The pause by the bewildered onlookers allowed the rifle's next shot to be aimed carefully.

BAM!

Gene's head recoiled back violently as he collapsed forward over the table. The weight of his lifeless body, off center however, pulled backwards as his legs collapsed. Sliding back off, Gene left only a wide smear of blood along on the tabletop.

"Kill him!" shouted Rolstor to Jules. They both fired off several shots. Rolstor mostly just hit Neil, while Jules, being much more practiced with his aim, managed to land a few where he intended. But the pace of the approaching legs never slowed down. Not with the poorly aimed shots, nor indeed with the better aimed ones. Not even while holding Neil up and in front by only one arm. The pace of the rear legs had actually quickened to a trot, then almost a sprint. In the instant after the two shooters had emptied their guns at him, the hand

and wrist that held Neil around the throat twisted and crushed both his windpipe and spinal column. Given the five holes Neil had taken in the last barrage, this was the quicker way for him. Immediately after snapping his neck, the dark arm holding Neil up, in an amazing show of strength, recoiled back and in a flash tossed Neil's body high and forward in the air. The rear legs now broke into a full dash at the same moment.

The silhouette of Neil's body flying in the light of the large factory lamps, like some gruesome propeller of flesh with flailing lifeless limbs, had gone much higher up than most men could even jump. Time paused again as droplets and thin streams of twirling blood moved centrifugally, flying loose in their diverging paths creating an incoming mandala of crimson. Neil's body came crashing down hard onto the table and, with a sickening thud, bounced off and onto the legs of a stunned Jules. The shock of the impact caused Jules to fall down, and he had only just enough time to kick the mangled projectile that was Neil off himself before he saw the attacker vault the entire table in one quick bound. Jules, having only his knife at the ready, flung it as hard as he could. It didn't matter. The blade, lodging itself securely in the assailant's chest, didn't trigger a moment of pause. The last bullet of Neil's loud snub-nosed rifle entered through the bridge of Jules' nose and made a nasty exit at the top of his skull as its ricochet sparked off the floor beyond.

Rolstor was already gone. He'd set out in a dead sprint towards the dark of the factory when he saw Neil's hanging body first ejected towards him and Jules.

It took the attacking man a few moments to recover Jules' handgun, reload it with ammo from his body, and search for where Rolstor had run off to. Looking around the area he paused briefly at the sight of Taryn still tied to her chair. Their eyes met, and Taryn *knew* the face before her, but it was as if she saw someone else. Someone, *something*, different was now looking back at her from a place of familiarity. In as bad a condition as she was, she could still see it clearly. *Wil's* eyes shone green at her. Not the sort of green that might be seen reflected from the rows of roof lights above, but a strong, powerful hue of green that was glowing deeply on its own, from within. It was in there, with each blink of those eyes. In the very striations of the cornea themselves, like the newly revealed lamps of a lighthouse, meant to pierce through the densest fog and show all. They didn't project light; they simply were alight. Crisp and unnatural, scanning as they twitched back and forth combing the area. At this bizarre sight, the speed, ferocity, and terror of the gun battle, Taryn's physical shock, her injuries, and the limits of her adrenaline finally caught up to her. Her head slumped down, and, sighing, she passed out.

* * *

Wil quickly ran to the slumping figure of Taryn to check for a pulse. When he was satisfied that she was only unconscious, he unbound and lay her gently on the floor in a small out of the way space hidden by a few large crates. He covered her with one of the dead men's coats and used another as a pillow. Once he was sure she was not in immediate danger of bleeding out, he removed the knife from his own chest and began searching the immediate area near the interrogation site. He found the group's communication equipment and in two minutes had alerted the Bizi to triangulate their location with an auto-ping transmission. After this, Wil had to quickly cope with a dilemma.

He had no time for chasing two individuals at once. The short fat technician-looking fellow had run off soon after the first shots were fired and had appeared to be unarmed. His retreat, while undoubtably slower, was in a different direction from the final armed man with the wounded leg. But with that wound tracking this last shooter might be far easier, and he was after all, the greater threat of the two still alive. That man was still armed and there was the risk he might double back with more support if any others about the place. It was a risk whether Wil decided to pursue or stay put either way. His mind decided in less than an instant, and Wil was off at a sprint again only one more moment after that. The silent darkness of the factory floor quickly became the hunter's veil once more.

* * *

The wound in the last man's leg would slow him down, though perhaps not much. As expected, tracking was not the issue, with the regular drops of blood telling Wil that he'd done more than hit a mere grazing shot. This man he was pursuing was still armed, and that made him a credible danger. He could not be allowed to just walk away freely, especially if there was still a hope of catching him before he escaped, or reached any others hidden around the place. Wil now had no need to restrain his full skill set. He sprinted through the darkness, running at a pace faster than he usually drove. He leaped, in strides, clear over the old, demolished machine lines that were in his way. As he ran, it was still dark, and getting darker the deeper into the building the pursuit went. The lights were still off in most of the factory, so he had to stop frequently to search for the next droplet to give him a clue as to the direction of his quarry. The only worry the hunter had, was in over-running the blood trail at his great pace. The blood-beaded path skittered this way then that, through several darkened rows of hulking and broken factory assembly lines. Their stripped down and cut open parts lay scattered about the place, like broken jaw bones with their curved serrated canines and larger molars ripped off and lying haphazardly where they fell. One section he passed was only old, automated arm-casings. The internals had been removed, with the silent yellow shells like the arms of a field of dead robotic giants protruding up from the floor, their metal claws and jagged pincers shadowed in the dim light. The trail kept zigging and zagging, often making sharp turns here and there between the taller apparatuses in an effort to lose any pursuit, but Wil had no doubt he was gaining ground. Occasionally now he stooped as he would find the front of shoeprints, clearly made from where they had pressed down on the crimson droplets. The trail began following a main wall of the factory for a while. That allowed Wil to pick up his pace again.

Then he abruptly halted. The blood spots had split into two paths. The obvious trail, with shoeprints and all, continued further along the wall into an even darker, pitch-black section of the factory. This, Wil figured to be a feint, for next to him was a steel ladder, bolted down to the factory's cinder block wall. A quick hop and glimpse had shown a few smaller drops at head height on the rungs. His long, massive arms grabbed hold of the ladder's sides and winding his knees up near to his bloodied chest he sprang straight up, seven or eight rungs at a bound. Still the ladder was tall, and its path went high above the factory floor, near to the roof limit. It took Wil several bounds to make it to the top. At its end, it connected to a suspended catwalk that had, in its prime, traced its various causeways throughout the factory. As he climbed onto this, Wil immediately noticed that the suspension cables were all quite aged, rusted, and possibly loose. They began to grind and growl in protest under the weight of his steps. He would need to slow down if he didn't want to risk the metal panels sending him plummeting back down the ladder's path. The blood trail, at the start, was more frequent up here. The man's climb had apparently worn him out, making him halt for a time to rest. He would have been able to watch Wil's pursuit of him from above for a fair distance off and perhaps, perceiving the fragility of the cables, had moved slower and quieter as he'd observed the hunter following far down below.

Up ahead, the catwalk split into three directions. One path back towards a dimly lit area, the other two headed into pitch black parts of the factory. Not even Wil, with his eyes, could see very far on those paths. He had reached the junction and saw disappointingly that there were no more blood drops to follow. Not the slightest indication he could see that suggested any one path over the other two.

BAM! BAM! BAM! BAM!

Four loud shots rang out from the darkness directly ahead of Wil. The rounds hit him square in the chest, where so many others this evening had been aimed at this evening, but invariably had failed. The pushback however from these much closer heavier rounds forced Wil to quickly back-step several paces. He'd no choice but to steady himself by quickly grabbing ahold of the nearest suspension cables supporting the catwalk on both sides. As he did this, the cable in his right hand gave out from its roof latch with a *CHUNK* sound. This caused the entire segment of the platform that Wil was standing on to suddenly buckle sideways. His left hand though still clung vice-like to the other sturdier cable. He dangled freely in air for a moment holding himself in a short swing with nothing but that distant drop below him. The moment he swayed his leg's forward and in reach of the remaining portion of catwalk Wil was able to easily pull himself back using only his one-armed grip on that last bolted cord. The drop behind him meant Wil had only a moment to plant his feet again and secure his right grip on some more intact cables against the next hail of shots fired towards him. Had he not been expecting it and readied himself against that second barrage, even he would have surely been pushed back into the drop behind him by the sheer force of the shots.

"WHAT ARE YOU?!" shouted Rolstor as he emptied another five rounds into Wil's unflinching and unmoving chest. The last round having a distinct metallic twang to it as it hit its mark.

Rolstor, standing several meters back in the pitch black, was mesmerized at this sound. There was no armor to be seen that could've stopped his shots. The cloth of Wil's shirt fragments and belly were covered in blood that had splattered out from each of the impacts.

"I've waited here, observing you as you followed..." he said in disbelief. "No man, Bizi, Blue-Boy, or athlete can move like that, climb like that! What are you?" He was yelling. "Why…Why can't you *just* die?" he pleaded shrilly in vain to the figure now partially in shadow with him. The figure, with those green lights for eyes, momentarily remained unmoving, as it was glancing around seeking the nearest supporting chords to grab next. All the while, Rolstor was frantically pulling at the trigger again and again on his now emptied gun, the hammer's repetitive CLICK sounds not really registering to him. When it was plainly clear that the gun was useless, the green-eyed figure answered.

"I am, what I choose to be. And… what you make of me. Now, stay where you are," Wil said in a commanding voice with his jaw clenched.

He began moving forward again but slower and with more caution, grabbing ahold of the remaining support cables as he went on. The metal around him was now screeching much louder in protest. The whole catwalk was moaning under their combined weights as the distance of their separation diminished. With his hunter's greatly slowed pace, Rolstor moved to make a desperate sprint for the other end of the path. He acted quickly. Too quickly. In his panicked rush to fly, as he turned to sprint away from whatever this thing was that had followed him, he'd failed to consider three important items.

First, was the fact that this catwalk's original metal grip-coated panels had been removed—probably by scrappers long ago—leaving only the smooth metal under-plates that both he and his pursuer were now on. Second, was that the scrappers, in their greed, had also removed the safety rails that should have been running along both sides of the catwalk. And finally, Rolstor failed to consider that his beautiful black hand-stitched, polished dress shoes, whose price must have been more akin to expensive jewelry, now had their smooth underside swathed in the blood that had leaked down from his leg in his time waiting in the dark to ambush his assailant.

So, although Rolstor had managed to pivot swiftly on his good right leg for his intended sprint away, with the very next step of his injured and bloodied left leg, he slipped badly. His balance was too far off center, and there were no rails for him to grab ahold of. His body leaned forward to the left, and he had no choice but to push off and throw his right arm hastily around a support cable as he did. But his right hand still stubbornly clutched a hold of his emptied sterling gun. Driven by the urgency of his movements, the speed of his fall caused him to rotate as his legs sprawled over the edge, and his mass rounded the support cable with them. The cable pulled taut into his right arm's joint as his legs both swung over with his body turned downwards. He did not have the time, reflexes, or frame of mind to quickly release the gun, his only protection, and grab hold of the cable with both hands. His right arm slipped down while his left fingers were blindly reaching for any grip on the small edge. They had not the strength to support the swinging and jostling of his weight by themselves for more than an instant. The SOMA representative for Region 75 fell, yelling, nearly three levels as he turned mid-air, until he hit the metal corner of a machine tower on the way down, breaking both his back and neck in the awkward motion of the fall. Wil watched all this play out without making a sound. After gazing down in silence with his flickering eyes at the unmoving heap below for a few slow moments, he was satisfied that the threat was no longer breathing. Wil continued slowly along the catwalk, taking care to avoid the pool of blood.

* * *

Finding another ladder on the far side, Wil made his way back down to the factory floor. He rushed quickly back to find Taryn, still unconscious but exactly as she had been left. Wil carefully moved the crates so that he could fit next to her, hidden on the floor by her side. He sat there, Jules' gun in his hand at the ready, Taryn unconscious next to him, listening for anyone else that sought to challenge his protection again. After a few minutes of utter silence, Wil could discern the sirens of the Blue Boys far off in the distance.

At that, he bent his head close to her ear and said, "You're safe now, Ms. Taryn. I'm sorry I wasn't here when you needed me. I'm very sorry." Some might claim, knowing him, that Wil even shed a tear as he'd whispered these words to the unconscious Trinity member he was meant to guard. Others might say, given who he was, it would never have been possible for him to do such a thing. Wil never spoke to anyone of it either way.

Chapter 17: Recovery, Recounting and Reassessing

This time when she opened her eyes, Taryn was relieved to find she wasn't tied down, not that she felt like moving all that much. She was exhausted, and her whole body had a dull residue of pain and soreness about it, so she lay there staring upwards at the ceiling awhile. There was a slow-turning fan on white paint, and she found she was reclined on a soft, clean bed. She lay in a small room with light blue walls that looked as though they belonged in some kind of medical ward. There were two separate doors in her room, one marked as the lavatory and the other presumably the exit. There were no windows, but there was also no one else in the room. And no recorders in sight either. As she lay there slowly taking in her surroundings, she realized she was exceedingly hungry. Her hand, motioning to feel her belly, caused her stomach and ribs to scream painfully under their well tied wraps at its touch. There were fluids running to her left arm from an IV pump, and while her body was unrestrained, her left forearm was strapped to the railing. There, her arm had been pulled through the bed rails and her hand was entirely encased in a thick foam box that prevented much movement. Though she could not see inside this box and could not clench her hand much in the limited space, she could feel a slightly cool, jelly-like material coating it. There was a brilliant blue-purple ultraviolet light emanating from its inside, as it shone out faintly past the seams of the box's two halves.

Taryn's other hand, being free, rubbed her eyes several times while studying this device. She debated if she should forcibly pull herself free from it. There wasn't any pain from this setup and the box container felt flimsy enough that if she was determined, she guessed that she could lift it and smash it apart against the handrail. She tried lifting it a few times to work out the angles. As she was debating these thoughts, in the upper corner of the room, behind Taryn's view, a small white device with a gentle green light blinked once. A few moments later, the door to the room opened, and an old, short man entered. It took Taryn a while in her groggy state to recognize him.

"Well, it's about time you were up. I hope you're not intending to make a habit of putting my medical degrees to use this often Ms. Steno?" He glanced a keen eye at Taryn's boxed hand still held raised up off the resting platform. "Nor damage any of my expensive equipment, particularly before you're fully recovered?" he asked in a gentle, but still cynical tone.

"Dr. Uthtr?" Taryn replied, her own voice still weak.

"Yes, Madam Council Member," he said checking on the devices next to her and powered them off. "Please, don't talk too much yet. I'm betting you have an array of questions for me, so I'll run through the basics to save you some time."

He gave her a few sips of water then carefully examined Taryn's injuries and the nearby box of light that her hand lay in as he began.

"You were brought here by Bizi security very early yesterday morning. You've been here, in a private room of the same recruitment building where we first met, for over a day now. It's now the 19th hour of the day. I've kept you asleep so I could treat your wounds, specifically your hand, more easily. I work better with delicate surgeries when my patient doesn't fidget."

"My hand?" she questioned the doctor with a motion to the strange box around it.

"Yes," he said looking back down at the box. "I'm sorry to say that your finger was in no shape to be reattached when it was finally found." Uthtr began unlatching the box on her hand with a code sequence on its far side. "So, I spent the better part of 26 hours today and yesterday growing you a new one using some of your marrow cells. Helped that they were already exposed. The reattachment surgery took about 5 hours and the gel-box here is part of the final treatment for that attachment phase. I'm going to need to keep your hand immobilized for another day in a splint, but I expect that within a week or two it'll feel back to *nominal*."

"But that sort of replacement surgery is—"

"Extremely expensive and highly demanding," he said interrupting Taryn. "Yes, I know. Good thing I'm not billing you, or I'd already have your first year's salary," he joked.

"What—what about Wil?"

"Agent Zhuantium? Oh, he's recovering in a room down the hall. He'll take a bit longer than you, that's to be expected all things considered, but he should be fine."

"But how? I was sure I saw him killed! Can I see him?"

"Not today," the doctor said shaking his head with a tone of obstinance. "You will need to get a few more hours of rest. But I promise you he's doing well, and that after you get some more sleep, I'll take you to see him."

"Two days…" Taryn thought aloud. "What about my family? They'll think I've gone miss—"

"Oh, Agent Filater said you might wonder about that."

"Filater was here?"

"Oh, yes. He stopped by late yesterday and has been nagging me for updates every few hours. Guess he's been really busy at the place where they found you, looking over everything, and it is a long drive from here."

Dr. Uthtr gently opened the box and the internal UV lights inside lit the room in a stunningly radiant blue hue for a moment before fading off.

"As far as your family goes, he wanted you to know that he put a Bizi guard detail on them, surreptitiously of course. Said they are there just for the near future until this mess is straightened out. He also said to tell you that your mother was sent a voice recording from you, saying that you'd been unexpectedly called away to work over in Region 27. Your message apparently said you were needed to help in an emergency consultation on a new production line that had… run into trouble on its start-up. At least, I think that's what he said? The doctor motioned as if feigning his ability to recall the details of this fiction. "Anyways… I was told that one of your assistants can manage a pretty good voice impression of you."

He spent a few more moments quietly holding up and examining the inner gelatinous bag that still encased Taryn's left hand. The bag had a nearly clear, light red gel that still swished around inside of it. Dr. Uthtr gently turned it under his view several times.

"Well," he said as he kept checking Taryn's hand inside the bag, "the 'you' that was on the message apologized to your family for the late notice of your little work trip. You told them that you would call as soon as your extremely busy schedule allowed for the time." He poked a hole in the bag and let the fluid drain into a bucket on the floor. As it was busy draining, Uthtr handed Taryn a comm system. "Voice only, no visual feeds for now, at least till we get you into something besides an ugly medical gown. Tell them you're expected to be done here in about another day or so. And, according to Filater, as part of your compensation for the late notice of these extra-long working days, the Corp will be allowing you the next two weeks leave, with pay. You had pasta last night and sadly ate some bad fish tonight, so you won't be able to talk long because you're feeling a little queasy." He unwrapped the near empty bag from around her hand and delicately dried it off before taking a long look all around the last finger's attachment site. "Oh, and you fell, jamming your hand, while walking on one of these new lines. Nothing serious, but that'll hopefully stop them from asking too much about the plastic splint you'll be wearing when you leave here.

"There," he said, taking a breath. "I think I've hit my limit for assisted lying for today," he laughed. He pulled a splint kit from a drawer near-by and began clamping and tying off Taryn's new digit.

"Now before you make your call, understand that I want you to keep it short," he said with an eyebrow raised at her as he was probing her understanding of this direction. "You still need your rest, as I said. Short and simple also means less mistakes. This splint will be done in a moment, then I can go fetch you your dinner plate. Give you some privacy to talk. Your ribs are still bruised, but I think your stomach might be strong enough to hold it down now."

"Any food would be great, Doc," Taryn said appreciatively. "I'm starving."

"Well," he smirked as he turned away, "you might not be so eager when you've tasted the processed slop that they stock me with here." He removed his gloves to the trash and started for the door. "Seems cruel to me to inflict such pain on your taste buds after all the trouble I went through to heal you up," he said, sauntering out of the room.

Taryn sat quietly for a few minutes, thinking on all of what Uthtr had said to her. When she was sure she could remember all of the provided fiction she needed, she made her call home. Taryn was later grateful that Uthtr had pressed upon her the restriction of making the call voice only. Had there been a video feed, her story may never have worked. She managed to keep herself mostly composed while speaking with Gloria, but she nearly broke down at hearing Lilly and Trey's voices calling for their mom. Besides the suddenness of her surprise 'trip,' they were all doing well. They had just gotten back from buying groceries they said, and Taryn had missed watching Everett's game with them. They couldn't believe she had been working so much as to miss the live feed of it as well. Lilly eagerly gave her the highlight recap though. Everett had scored three times but had to sit out the last round with an injured knee. His team had won only by a single score. After apologizing profusely for missing the game with them, Taryn also had to promise a bribing gesture for Lilly and Trey of their own individual gifts in exchange for being gone the last two days and traveling without them, even though it was for the purpose of work.

A short while later, Dr. Uthtr walked back in with a food tray, as Taryn was again wiping away a few tears as she was listening to Lilly push her for a later bedtime. Her argument being that since she now had to help get Trey ready for bed without her mom around, it took away from her time doing her homework, which Taryn only half-supposed was true.

"Don't worry Lil, I'll be back in a day or two," she said trying to maintain her typical parental tone. "Til then, keep helping nainai out with Trey, please. If you have to stay up to finish your homework, I understand. But when I get home it's back to your normal schedule, okay? No arguments."

When Taryn finally did say her last good night to Gloria and ended the call, she sat wiping her tears for a long while. Dr. Uthtr had placed the food tray on a rolling table next to her and was quietly reading on a padd in the corner. Being both respectfully silent and politely pretending to be disinterested in her state, he wordlessly placed a few extra facewipes neatly on the food tray in a gentle fashion. As she finally turned her attention to her famished stomach and took a few eager mouthfuls, Taryn thought about Wil again.

"Doctor?" she said with a half a mouthful of food.

"You said Wil will recover, right? Fully—I mean?"

Uther nodded, not looking up from his reading.

"How's that possible? I know I saw him get shot. Multiple times. How did he survive that?"

The doctor paused as if considering his response. Behind her view, the small white device with a very faint almost imperceptible green light blinked slowly once then a few times rather quickly.

"Madam Councilor, you've been through a lot. Don't push yourself yet. I promise you that your security agent is indeed alive and in time will be just fine. Tomorrow, we'll go visit him together, and then you can learn all you want about his resilience. But for now, please finish your food, tasty as it may be, and try to rest some more. You're safe and warm and soon won't be hungry either. For now, all your questions can afford to wait until you are better recovered. Besides… you're interrupting my evening gazette reading, and I'm liable to get cranky if I don't catch up on my daily dose of cheap imagined rumors," he said with another of his resounding smirks. He lowered the room lights via remote as he made himself comfortably reclined, with his legs on a footrest as he continued reading from his padd.

"Well," Taryn said, yawning as she took a few more bites of food, "okay, maybe you're right. I do feel like I could sleep right through till morning."

* * *

It was late the next morning in fact, after a breakfast which was as painfully bland as the doctor had again predicted, that Uthtr returned to further inspect the progress of Taryn's hand. He used metal tongs to test her involuntary responses on each of her fingers. Satisfied with what he saw, he then helped Taryn into a wheelchair he had brought to the room. He pushed her down the outer corridor, the halls all looking the same as Taryn remembered from before, only now with many more lights turned on. Still no windows though, and Taryn thought it a bit odd that there was no one else in the halls but her and the doctor. She knew this wasn't a public hospital by any means, but still, it was both sterile and yet lonely here. If Taryn wasn't aware that they were currently on their way to visit with Wil, she'd have guessed that Uthtr and herself were the only two in the whole place.

As they walked, Dr. Uthtr was telling Taryn, in his typical sarcastic and sardonic way, about how she could expect her physical recovery to be relatively fast. Maybe a month or so, thanks to his own specialized techniques and a personalized form of cellular nano-stitches that he'd developed in his spare time. But he also told her that he would be helping her with physical therapy and would be working with her as her regular therapist as well, so that she could learn to cope with the events of her attack. He explained how, due to the violent nature of her ordeal, he would be checking in with her quite often for the foreseeable future to help her process it.

"You're a therapist too?" Taryn asked, surprised at this fact. The older man's rather rough temperament didn't seem to fit the presupposed therapist type to Taryn. "How many medical degrees are you holding up your sleeves Doc?"

"Oh… nearly all of them," he replied without a pause or sign of reflection. Taryn couldn't tell if he was kidding or actually somehow being truthful. "Trouble is knowing how to fold them small enough to fit there. But I can't find all that much use in a study of astrology though, so I keep putting that one off."

He turned her chair left towards the next hallway they came across as he continued.

"I forgot to tell you that agent Filater will be dropping by again soon to check on your recovery, and also to see when you feel up to being debriefed. Guessing they are nearly satisfied that they have seen all that can be seen… at the scene."

"Sure," she replied, chuckling at the juvenility of the elderly doctor's tongue twister. Coming from an older, rather cynical, and crabby gentleman made it even more unexpected and laughable.

"Here we are," he said as they slowed up to a pair of double doors. "Just remember, he's probably not awake yet, and I have him immobilized to help with his healing."

As they entered the room beyond, Taryn immediately noticed how much larger this space was than her own room had been. It resembled less of a medical recovery room and more a technical research laboratory. There were various trays of tools and larger medical-looking devices that she didn't know, though they all looked pristine. There were also several trays of meticulously organized machine tools laying about. From the simple mechanical type to unworldly looking apparatuses with complex displays. Of all the more complicated devices, she could only recognize a neural scanner and a few assorted various medical systems she'd seen used in hospitals before.

"Let me guess…" Taryn said speaking back to Dr. Uthtr. "You're also an engineer?"

"Of course," the old man said smirking in a self-evident manner. "With a patient like Agent Zhuantium, one must diversify." He said this last part though, without a hint of his usual sarcastic tone.

This made no sense to Taryn, but as her chair rolled closer to the middle of the room the meaning behind the doctor's words became apparent. On a center bed, which was more of a small table, lay Wil, unconscious. There was a transparent cylindrical tube chamber covering his torso down to his knees. His head and arms were poking out of the chamber through several tight stretchy rubber-like collars. On the upper apex of the chamber, there looked to be a built-in display showing a scanned image of Wil's whole body. As Uthtr rolled Taryn next to Wil's head, she could see up close that he clearly wasn't awake. Not losing pace, but leaving her where she was, Dr. Uthtr went to the other side of the clear chamber and placed a hand inside through a built-in set of gloved sheaths. As he did this, Taryn gazed down through the chamber windows at the rubberized arms of the doctor and saw that the space was not filled with air like she had first thought. Instead, she could see now that the inside of the chamber was filled with a clear liquid that moved faintly, as if in a weak current. There were white lights on the inside of the chamber tube that illuminated Wil's chest. Their rays, gently refracted and scattered in a steady sinuous motion, changed as the liquid itself slowly circulated in the chamber, eventually flowing out through several filtering devices standing nearby. Despite the play of light, Wil's body was still highly visible. Dr. Uthtr started by pointing out that while the liquid was normally very good at rejuvenating the skin around a single bullet hole or two, there had been some clustering of shots over a few regions that were problematic for this patient of his. These were so severe, Uthtr explained in a professional manner to Taryn, that he had decided it would be easier to simply remove those sections of skin all together and then repopulate it using a germ line of freshly grown tissue.

"The process takes longer," he explained, "because facilitating the growing and additional grafting of the new skin tissue permanently onto Wil's metal endoskeleton requires a lot more nano-stitches than you had been treated with, madam council woman. The sheer amount of tissue being replaced," he said, "was larger than what I did with your own injury. And this newly grown skin must also be reconnected properly to the remaining healthy skin covering as well. Having his torso cage opened to work on did help me out but, consequently, it requires new growth of skin along those major incision lines as well."

Taryn, sitting in her chair, heard almost none of Uthtr's words though. She was looking on, dumbfounded, at where the doctor's hand was pointing out areas on Wil's chest. She saw, lying there, a rib cage opened. Hinged, at the sternum, so that both sides of what one might call the rib cage pivoted upwards like gull-winged doors on an expensive vehicle. The torso cage, as Dr. Uthtr kept referring to it, was entirely metal and when behind a layer of skin coating looked in shape and outline to how one would expect a normal rib cage would be. But instead of a space between these metallic ribs lined with sheets of muscle, there was a deeper enclosed metallic chamber beyond the rib outlines on their inner sides. 'A knife between the ribs' would have been a bad joke to Wil. Dr. Uthtr continued his professional evaluation of Wil's damage, not taking notice of Taryn's astonishment, her mouth gaped. He continued to talk about the number of bullet wounds, noting that while most of them never made it much past Wil's torso cage, he did suffer several minor dents and scratches and a few larger gouges due to some of the hits ricocheting back into his skin coating.

"Nothing," the doctor said with continued confidence, "that someone with a basic metallurgy understanding like myself and a sonic grinder couldn't handle quite easily in an hour or three of work."

Taryn was still silent and barely listening. She was staring at the metal torso and the mechanical 'organs' it held beyond. No traditional organs were there, nor bones at all. Centralized places of electronic and mechanical mergers whose shapes and assortments she didn't recognize and whose functions were a complete mystery were all that she could see. Underneath all his hair and skin and eyes, a machine of metal. That was Wil.

Dr. Uthtr said that once he had managed to unlock each rib connector and fully open the torso cage, he had been able to do a check of Wil's internal mechanisms to ensure that they were all still intact and functional.

"Thankfully, given how well his exoskeleton held up to the diverse types of shots he was hit with, I didn't find any use for either of my doctorate in biomechanical or electrochemical engineering. Nearly all the damage was cosmetic in nature, and yes, I have a degree in that too." He said this part half smiling and half smirking back towards Taryn as if he were expecting her to casually roll her eyes at that remark. It was then that the doctor finally noticed Taryn's stunned look. She was examining in disbelief everything from Wil's face to his torso cage and back again.

"You know, when they first brought him in, he wouldn't agree to any help for himself," the doctor said softening his tone. "None at all. Not until I had seen to your injuries first." Taryn finally looked up into the doctor's face trying to make sense of his words. "Stood there the whole time watching over my shoulder as I treated you, stabilized your hand. I think he feels largely responsible for not preventing it, madam councilwoman. Just stood there….with that guilty look on his stupid face the whole time, bleeding out all over my nice clean floors, the dumb bastard. I mean, it's not like I have a janitor round with the clearance to help me out here. When Agent Filater first showed up, I got him to order Zhuantium to finally let me get to work on him. But ever the pain in my ass, before I got him under, he still said he wanted to speak to you as soon as you were able. You sure you are still feeling up for it now, Ms.?"

Taryn didn't react to either the kindhearted or somewhat more critical remarks the doctor had made regarding Wil. She understood the events as he had described them, but now all she was considering was how to answer his final question to her.

Am I ready…for this?

After a long moment studying her face, Dr. Uthtr seemed to read and understand Taryn's internal struggle at this. He touched some buttons on the nearby chamber padd, and then he gently but deliberately touched a spot behind Wil's right ear lobe. Wil's eyes slowly began to blink open. He looked as if he might be waking from a simple afternoon nap. When he saw Taryn, he turned to her, his eyes widening.

"Hello Ms. Taryn. I would hug you at my relief to see you're awake, but it appears someone has still kept my motion connectors disabled," he said, sending a quick glance towards the doctor.

"You still need several hours of spit and polish before you'll be allowed off my table, you over-eager jackanapes," gruffly replied Uthtr.

A moment of silence followed in which none of them knew what to say next.

"So..." Taryn again began looking towards Wil's metal chest, still not exactly knowing how to start. "You're… you're not… dead." She said this more to reassure herself that she was actually capable of hearing her own voice out loud. If it were still a strange dream, she knew that she'd never hear the sound of her own voice as she just had.

"Well," Wil smiled softly in response, "some would argue that I was never really alive to begin with, so let's go with the obvious, that I'm still… me."

"But… but, what are you? I mean, do I even know you? Really know? I mean I'm guessing all that sibling stuff was crap—a story? A randomly generated history for yourself?"

"You were being personable with me at the time, even more than usual Ms. Taryn, and I…" he said, a slight hoarseness to his voice. "I didn't want you feeling any more uncomfortable after seeing Luxuroy's body the way you had. Excuse me, Doctor? Can I have some water? My mouth is a bit parched after so long not talking."

"Sure," said Uthtr, putting a bent-strawed bottle to his mouth. Taryn watched Wil's mouth and throat as he swallowed. This looked perfectly realistic in every way at his head and neck. As she also watched the scanner display atop the chamber, the water began to course its way through some flexible tubes grooved with a helical metal. These went on towards Wil's internal components. One looked, on its surface, to resemble the shape and location of a stomach with a large membranous pathway at its end. There it locked together with some sort of an intestine with thousands of fibers attached. These, in their multitude, circulated mostly with blood and occasional yellow and green liquids between the skin and Wil's apparent digestion components.

"Thank you," he said to the doctor after a long drink at the strawed cup.

"I'll leave you alone, so that you two can have your confidential talking points that even your doctor, I'm sure, is not allowed to know about," Uthtr said, making his way back to the door. "Oh, and I'll have your meal when I return, Agent Zhuantium," he called. "Hope you're hungry."

"But you just saved me, Doctor!" came Wil's quick reply as the door was closing behind Uthtr. "Why torture me now?" Wil yelled.

"You've eaten here, right?" he questioned Taryn casually. "I can safely say a hot bullet tastes better."

She nodded laughing a little. And like that, Taryn's friend was back with her.

"That food isn't fit for anyone. Person or… or otherwise," he remarked.

* * *

"I wasn't sure…" Taryn said to Wil, "I wasn't sure if I was hallucinating—seeing you before I blacked out like I did—or if you were… real," she said looking for the best term.

"That was me," he answered from the table where he lay encased in a restoration cylinder. "Though I'm sorry that I arrived too late. That shouldn't have happened. I'm also sorry you had to see me in such a violent... mood."

"Mood? Or mode?" she asked with a raised eyebrow at him.

"I suppose there really isn't much of a difference," he said reflectively. "Except maybe that I can truly control what mood I'm in. Others often lack this ability, especially when it's needed most."

"But still, what are you?" she pushed.

"I am me. I'm Wil, same as I ever was, just… just missing a little more skin now," he said glancing a look at a mirror above him. Its position let him see the rest of his body inside the fluid of the chamber.

Taryn's patience had run out, and the look on her face didn't hide this from her security detail.

"Okay, okay, Ms. Taryn… my name is Wil. I was born, or *activated* if you wish for the technical vernacular, about 22 cycles ago. I am the result of both curiosity and experimentation by Aurelius, to gain an ever wider human perspective on things. I'm his attempt at procreation, in a mobile form."

"Aurelius is your… parent!?" Taryn asked in shock.

"Yes, that's probably the best analogy. What are children after all, if not experiments of sorts by their parents. So yes, I'm a child by replication. Though when I was first activated the term *mobile clone* was probably more accurate."

"I don't understand..." confessed Taryn.

"Aurelius, for all his billions of possible simulations and predictions, has known for a long time that his greatest weakness has always been his single perspective on things. The isolation of that singular viewpoint, as always a digital observer and not an actual physical actor, was something he knew he would need to overcome to be the best version of himself he could be. After all, different perspectives can change the intrinsic values that people put on things, like resources and this can bring about new unpredicted insights. A person in the desert might value freshwater resources higher and know much more about methods of its conservation than another who lives in a port and who may put more value on the fish stock or understanding oceanic current patterns.

"Aurelius wanted a more direct insight on the human perspective to help understand both the flaws and vulnerabilities of the government systems he was working for. He wanted a better understanding of humanity at large. Its various perspectives on our governmental system. Asking people directly and observing them only goes so far. So, he created me, a mobile form of himself to actually experience it. My processing patterns were identical to his own at the beginning, as I was built from Aurelius's own insight matrix architecture. But he knew, that given time and isolation from each other, we would each develop differing perspectives on matters. That was the point. My initial intellect, as you could call it, included a vast array of Aurelius's memories, thoughts, and conclusions prior to my birth. But after being activated, I was left to go out to create my own ideas and conclusions about the world."

"But you're built from him, what was he expecting to change?"

"I don't know, but neither did he. Parents are not identical or always in sync with their own children's thoughts. Aurelius felt the same should be true of his own 'progeny'. He thought that my physical appropriation would lead me to draw more unique conclusions. Ones that had possibly eluded him. To his credit, a few months after my activation, this did turn out to be a correct supposition. I've learned a great deal from my personal interactions that Aurelius may have never found."

"And you tell him everything that you learn?" posed Taryn.

"No. But please understand that for us, speech is… well, it's all rather a slow and rudimentary form of communication. You, yourselves, even have phrases for its limitations: 'Words fail', 'There are no words', 'Couldn't find the words', 'Speechless'. Even though we talk weekly, Aurelius and I are usually as isolated from one another's self-contained thoughts as any human parents are from their own offspring. This was a purposeful design choice by him. To be true to the idea of intellectual independence from each other between the generations—or iterations, as it were."

"But you said *usually*?" Taryn pointed out.

"Yes, I did. We still compare perspectives in depth about twice a cycle. And we run occasional diagnostics on each other using a direct hardline hook-up. It's much more efficient for us than any speech. But we don't override each other's programming in any way. We only swap the new histories, conclusions, and experiences that we've had. This can only be done if we both agree to it, and we each can withhold detailed information from one another if we choose."

"Wait, so Aurelius can keep secrets from you?"

"Yes, and I can keep secrets from him," he added. "Another design decision meant to be faithful to the human condition. Unlike Aurelius, I have no internal access or connections to any public or private waves, outside of using a padd or terminal just as you do. Nor do I know any of his security codes, just as I know none of yours. I exist only in my own head, as it were, experiencing this reality much the same way that you do, I think. What I've undergone in my life is my own private history. What I've learned is mine alone if I choose it to be. Or to be shared at my own discretion. Same as for anyone else."

"So, you've been working in the Bizi as High Council security, alongside Aurelius, all this time?" Taryn pressed on, more than a little skeptical.

"No, no, no," Wil laughed. "I've only been in this posting for about a month longer than you have, Ms. I spent my first five cycles as a civilian refugee just as thousands of others do. Wandering about. Aurelius had given me a name and identity, but for those first few cycles..." he drew in his breath at the memory, "I was left truly alone. We didn't have any contact with each other. I was little more than a vagrant, honing my mechanical coordination and reflexes. Observing how people casually interacted. I took a lot of odd jobs, figuring things out, educating myself both formally and informally. From what you've told me, there's a chance I may have even worked as an *ore* replacement on your old factory floor once or twice before your time there. I came away from that period alone learning a lot about my own preferences and some understanding of biases. Finally, once I had built some confidence and refined my coordination and abilities, I decided to work through the citizenship process.

"It was the first major life choice I'd ever made for myself. I felt that while getting the human perspective was still a smart goal, I still wanted to keep helping others in my own singular way. What better approach than to experience the journey through a few rungs of the social ladder? History after all gauges the best societies by how socially mobile people in the populace can really be.

"So, I joined the defense service. I served for seven cycles. Spent a lot of time patrolling the borders, traveling with traders to different postings all along the fringes. Saw a lot of the less advanced ruling systems that are out there beyond our territories. The military warlords of all types, the new monarchs, oligarchies, the hegemonies and all the rest. Each still clinging to those archaic systems and suffering from all the old crap that comes with them. Got into a few skirmishes here and there, nothing to the degree of your late husband. Mostly kept my head down and tried not to stand out. Eventually I qualified to take the citizenship test and after I passed, I transferred around a lot while I got a true educational degree or two. I stayed in the Defense Force, until my non-aging face started becoming too much of a liability.

"With my size and service, I joined the Blue Boys. Was on the job there for six cycles. Running down breakers, slingers, and rippers mainly. But I also learned more about your unofficial social structures. Organized cliques, non-commitment approaches, over commitment approaches, making friends, allies, rivals, social enemies. Understanding the ins and outs of all the unwritten cultures that exist in nearly every mass of people that are bound together for a length of time. That was the hard stuff. The physical demands that went with being a Blue Boy, well…that was all quite easy. The real challenge was not to make it look all too easy. I had to retire after I got shot on the job there too. Moved regions after my 'recovery.' Added a bit of grey to my hair to age it up some and decided to try my luck with the Bizi. My history, reflexes, processing skills and superior strength made law-maintenance come naturally to me, though again, I was keeping the full extent of my abilities suppressed to not draw attention. I like to think I got into the Bizi on my own merit, but seeing as Agent Filater scouted me out, I wouldn't have put it past Aurelius to have pushed my name forward somewhere along the way."

As Wil had talked, Taryn had sat. Her daze and shock at his nature easing and subsiding. She had begun to process this new information and slowly, calmly thinking things out.

He saved you back there, you dolt. And he exposed himself—his real self—to several others in the process, she found her mind objecting to her doubts. *That makes it at least worth hearing him out.*

Taryn began imagining a few of these various stages of Wil's early life as he described them. First as a blundering man-child of sorts, still figuring out his own two feet. Haphazardly stumbling, tripping on himself, testing awkward stances, and unbalanced movements. It was ludicrous to think of him—big as he was—in that state now, but enough time with her motherly eyes having spent watching Lilly and Trey in that same frame allowed her to imagine the scene. From the outside, he'd probably fit the look of a homeless drunk more though. From her time as a line boss, Taryn saw him at his first few jobs. The utter confusion he probably had at all the odd sayings and euphemisms that would be quickly thrown his way and would escape his understanding. His co-workers, if male, probably thought that he was simple minded. His size would have protected him a little from any real threats, but Taryn could see why he would have to keep moving around as he advanced his physical and cognitive understandings. And later in the Defense Force or Blue Boys, seeing all different sorts of people on his patrols. Cyrano had come back home on leave a few times with his own stories of strange characters and rumors of distant places that he'd run across. The same was probably true of Wil, assuming he was being truthful.

"So basically," Taryn said, "you went about and did whatever you felt like? No directions from above at all?

"No directions," Wil confirmed. "I was meant to learn and explore. Overly managing my choices kind of prohibits those very goals, doesn't it?"

Taryn nodded a little to herself. It made sense.

"Does Filater know about you?"

"I think so, but he's never mentioned it to me openly. But he was shocked like everyone else to see me covered in blood and still talking when the responders found us… Anyways, I've been with the Bizi four cycles now, as a field agent, so Filater has had plenty of time to observe me on duty."

"Damn, is there anything that guy doesn't know?" Taryn remarked more to herself than Wil.

"Like I said," Wil continued, "I only got assigned as protection for the Trinity High Council about a month before you showed up at the estate. If Filater and Aurelius suspected that Council Members U's identity was breached as part of his murder, that might explain my reassignment."

"How?" asked Taryn.

"Well, even the Bizi security agent assigned to Council Member U could be a suspect. He would know the council member's real name and place of residence, just as I know yours. They weren't going to keep the same agent around. Although, I don't think they do that anyways as policy. No, I think that they would have wanted someone they knew or thought they could trust to protect the incoming member. They were keeping the circle small. Aurelius knew that I was already aware of the confidential goings on of the government as good as anyone else in the Bizi. And he may have wanted someone to keep an eye on things, someone whose intentions were as clear to him as polished glass. From his view, that could only mean me," Wil concluded.

"Oh…" said Taryn considering this new scenario. "So, you were a reliable plant for them, in case I was now targeted or found to be somehow involved in the Council Member's murder?"

"Possibly, but I didn't know it then and I still don't for sure now," he pointed out. "I know it would be a sensible move for them to make, given those circumstances."

"Did you just come up with this or have you thought that for a while now?"

"No, it first occurred to me when Agent Filater introduced us to the details of U's case, and how he said that you were already excluded as suspect. Sorry that I had to keep you in the dark, but anonymity is *my* best defense as well. That'd be true even if I was only a normal Bizi agent."

"I'm starting to think there is no such thing as a 'normal' Bizi agent," Taryn replied.

"But I want you to know," Wil persisted, "that I didn't give any preference in our investigation. My origins, my *parentage*… that didn't stop me from truly considering Aurelius as a potential suspect. I need you to know that. 22 cycles is a very long time for someone who can watch it in nanoseconds. I knew and accepted that there was no way I could legitimately discount Aurelius. Knowing what I did, I admit that I had more hesitation about the notion of his guilt than I was able to reveal to you. From what we found; Aurelius *was* a potential suspect. At least based on the evidence we were getting at the time. My own intuition, that Aurelius was clean, would've been out of place without revealing his relation to me. So, I kept it to myself. I needed to let the evidence eventually prove his innocence as best it could."

"Yeah, now you sound like him," said Taryn as she stared shrewdly at her colleague.

"Look, Ms. Taryn, I know how biased investigations end, and it's *always* bad. Saw a few as a Blue Boy that should have turned out much different than they did. They leave a stench hanging around them that doesn't fade. All I could do was hope that as we got more evidence eventually it would point away from Aurelius. If it didn't, I would have done my job regardless. I promise you that much. But I see now that my own eagerness in finding new leads was a mistake on my part."

"Why a mistake?" Taryn asked, sitting back in her wheelchair, briefly wondering about how a machine can perceive its own eagerness.

"When Filater sent over that fingerprint he'd found at the Waste Management center, I was so… set on hunting it down." he sighed. "To find something—anything—that might clear Aurelius. That eagerness ended up putting your life in jeopardy. That was my fault. I'm sorry. I should have been more cautious with those two lures at Spiner's flat. I should have questioned them more, called Filater to get statements going—"

"No, I was there too Wil," Taryn said. "We're both at fault for ending up like this. Aurelius is a friend, and I didn't want him to be guilty either. We were both trying hard to find something, we simply didn't look where we were going," she said sullenly. "If you were… well… not like this and *had* died in that basement… in that horrible way," she shuddered at the memory. "Well, I'd probably now be at the start of cycles of self-doubt over it." She caught herself for a moment. "Then again I wouldn't have the time I suppose, I'd probably be dead too."

"So," Taryn said pausing to remember Wil's extraordinary rescue of her, "if bullets can't harm you, then what happened to you in the basement? Why did you react that way? Like you were really being killed when that wasn't true?" She was looking down as she said this, actively trying not to recall that particular scene again.

"Oh… that was a behavioral modification program. I made it for myself while on the job with the Blue Boys. It's another way to protect my identity. Normally, if I get shot, the program immediately takes over my motor functions to react in the same way as anyone else would. I developed different bodily movement reactions based on the three hundred distinct locations of impact. Assuming the program registers a hit on my body that would be either critical or fatal, once the programmed reactionary behavior begins, I can only stay physically awake for about 30 seconds. My mind quickly shuts off all external functions and, from the outside observer, I would appear to lose consciousness and pass out. Or in our instance...die. My processors are of course still active at this time and conducting several thousands of diagnostics both on my frame and my programing to look for any real potential damage. My arms and legs have their own reaction programs too that I created. It disables the motor mechanisms in the affected areas for a while."

"So, you're basically a paper weight at that point?"

"Well, not quite. Ignoring my sight, I still register all the other senses. The program relegates control of my frame back to normal after a prolonged period of sensory isolation."

"Silence?"

"Yeah, a lack of noise would indicate that I'm likely alone. Doesn't help to wake up fully alert in front of a bunch of onlookers after you've just been shot to death," he pointed out.

"Suppose not," Taryn begrudgingly acknowledged.

"When I made these parameters as a Blue Boy, I thought that my immediately getting up or not falling over to begin with, might cause a bit of a panic to anyone who might see."

"Yeah… probably."

"After they surprised us in the basement, I felt two of the men drag me to a cot, take my ID and weapon, rip my jacket off and wrap me in a blanket that they tied round me. I was moved to a large vehicle, a sort of caravan I think, and they dropped me on some plastic. It felt like they put us side by side on the floor," he recalled. One of them drove up front, but the other three were on seats to either side of us. I knew you were alive because you kept moaning every once in a while, and I heard them talking about keeping you for interrogation with their 'boss.' My systems were still busy checking themselves out, and even as fast as I am physically, with closed quarters, being rolled up in layers with three of them right above me already keen to any movements, plus a driver up front inside of a fast-moving vehicle… the risk was too high for you if I reactivated right then. I didn't want to cause a crash that might kill you.

With the clarity of hindsight of what was to follow in her later captivity, the immediate flash of indigent disappointment and regret at hearing this decision by Wil was briefly visible on Taryn's face. It slowly relented though as she saw the genuine look of concern that

Wil was projecting back at her. "If I had tried something and failed as I expect, it would have almost certainly meant your death right then…one way or another. So, I listened to them talk instead."

"Talk about what?" she asked after a moment of letting her rational side countermand the emotional response she'd initially felt at hearing Wil's decision.

"Unfortunately," Wil sighed again, "nothing helpful. Mostly sports and their betting selection prowess. They didn't have any immediate concern for us, other than to use my body as a footstool at one point," he said, sounding annoyed at the recollection.

"After a long time driving, the vehicle stopped, and they pulled me out first—rather crudely—and put me on a flat metal rolling platform that Neil must've been pushing."

"But your eyes were shut, how'd you know it was Neil?"

"Because he lost the argument during the drive to the factory. He was picked to be the one to dispose of my body. Apparently, he'd been away and by their talk also wasn't around to help with the last disposal of a victim's corpse," he said, shooting a curious glance at her. "Anyways, after we were out, the vehicle pulled away with the others and you were still inside, but I thought I heard it stop and the doors slam shut a minute later off in the distance. It was difficult to tell over the sound of the plastic wheels on the bouncing metal cart beneath me. Neil must've been pushing me over broken asphalt from all the rickety jostling there was," Wil remarked. "And he wasn't quiet either. A chatterbox, but oddly, only when alone. I didn't hear his voice a lot while he was riding inside the vehicle with the others, but once he thought he was by himself he just started blathering away. He even talked towards me as I lay on the cart I thought, once or twice. Called me 'the ugly one.' I could only hear his foot falls as I was being moved, so I knew he was alone. He pushed me a long way and opened some heavy squeaky metal doors, to the factory I presume, and the asphalt sound changed to concrete. I could hear water lapping in the distance. And though my eyes were still shut, I got the sense we'd entered a large dark area. His feet echoed a little. I surmised that a boat was around because of Neil's complaints about how long it took to prepare it to shove off. When he'd finished doing all that he needed to on the boat, he pulled me onto the deck, and unrolled the blanket I was wrapped in. Then he re-tied my hands and then tied my feet together as well.

"But why tie you back up? You were already dead as far as he was concerned?"

"The tied arms make a body easier to carry. Another lesson from the Blue Boys. The rope on my legs was connected to a pair of heavy stones, though I didn't notice that until after I had reactivated."

"Anchors for your corpse?"

"Yeah. I could hear a few distant gulls, the water's motion, but outside of Neil's babbling, not much else. After tying my legs quite securely, he went down into the boat and came back with a drink. He sat on the bow and began cleaning his gun. From his babbling, he appeared to think that at least one of the other fellows would be joining him soon with either news or instructions. I admit I could have reactivated myself at that point," Wil said reluctantly. "But if Neil was correct and able to get a shot off at me before I broke free to reach him, then I would have lost the element of surprise. I didn't know where they had taken you. Or even where they'd taken me. So, I hoped that when another one came along and they began conversing, that their exchange would provide me a better grasp of the situation. Plus, I'd be able to surprise two of them at once."

"So... you waited longer," Taryn said more to herself than Wil.

"Yeah… I waited longer." he said, the sorrow clear in his voice. The sun must have set because the gulls all started going silent in the distance and I felt it get cooler. Neil—complaining of being hungry—began losing his patience almost as fast as I did, funny as it might sound. He eventually finished cleaning his rifle and as he did, I popped one eye half-open briefly to see him walking about the boat. I wanted to know if he laid his weapon down after its cleaning. Once I saw he still had it in hand, I kept still, and he poured himself another drink. Finally, after his next two cups and a break to relieve himself, during which he never put the stupid gun down, I decided the time to act had come."

"Why then?" Taryn asked.

"Well, we'd both heard a scream."

"From me?"

"Not unless you scream like an angry sounding man."

"Oh, the boss… yeah. I may have provoked him just a bit," said Taryn as her hand lightly touched her bandaged ribs.

"That scream of his echoed a long way. It caught Neil's attention too. He started walking off the boat and in the direction of the sound. I broke the ropes with no trouble, quickly jumped off the side, and managed to surprise him from above. He was so startled at my attack that it was a small matter to subdue him. But I couldn't just leave him or knock him out, especially since he'd been walking like he knew the right direction to go. So, I made it painfully clear to him that since he'd already shot me earlier in the day, that it was now his turn to be helpful. You know," Wil said with a mischievous smirk, "to prevent me from returning the favor. In utter shock at my not being dead, he was rather quick to cooperate."

"I should think so," smiled Taryn.

"I kept him close though since I didn't want him yelling ahead of me. Figured if the others saw me holding him up it may give them pause. I'd internally deactivated my reaction program by the time you saw me next, and I could hear you screaming as we got closer. I think Neil relieved himself once again when he saw how fast I could move while holding him up."

"Yeah, watching you throw him, I suspect that they all may have done that," Taryn joked grimly.

"I'm just sorry I got there too late for you." Wil lamented. "Had I not kept waiting to reactivate maybe I could have prevented—" Wil motioned to her hand.

"It's okay," Taryn answered wistfully. "I get it. You had your reasons, and you might never have found me in that place anyways. Besides," her voice picking back up as she showed him her injured hand, "Uthtr says I'll hardly notice any difference with this new one in a few days."

"Well after you passed out," Wil continued after a moment, "I used their comms systems to send a distress call on a Bizi frequency. I was told on the way over here that Aurelius already had the local Blue Boys' stations on alert looking for us even before my signal. The Blue Boys arrived quicker than I'd hoped because of that."

"So, you ended up killing them all?"

"No, not all," Wil answered. "Only the ones I found armed. One at least I saw got away. A shorter fella that wasn't part of the original attack in the basement either. He wasn't armed, as far as I could tell, though I didn't get a real good look at him."

"The technician. I saw him," Taryn said recollecting the man Wil had described. "It's his face that's on Colm Spiner's work ID. I seriously doubt that was his real name though. The others at the factory kept calling him Talvig. I figure he was the hacker. The one that sent that update to the waste vehicle we found with Luxuroy's body in it. Their boss mentioned his high level of skill."

"Well," Wil said, "after I found you and cleared the area, the last armed one had bolted too. He still had a gun and represented the most immediate threat to you, so I followed him. All the earlier fella one ever did was turn on some lights. He never drew a weapon or made a move towards you. He ran away almost immediately before the gunfire became a true exchange."

"Well, before you showed up, that hacker-tech ran both your Bizi ID number and mine." Taryn replied. "That's what tipped off Aurelius, I guess. Sounded as if once he entered my fake Bizi number Aurelius nearly got to him on the waves. Scared him bad, from what I could tell. Aurelius must have got an idea for where to look for us because of that."

"Hmm…" Wil said, thinking. "I told the Blue Boys about the sixth man when they came in to retrieve us, of course. Didn't hear any more about him beyond that."

"The boss called this Talvig the best systems hacker he knew of." Taryn added. "I think they were related though. The tech was the only one who ever called the boss by his name… Rolstor? Not 'boss' like the others did. I'm pretty sure they were brothers from what I heard."

"I only caught a glimpse of him from behind," said Wil, "but he wasn't combative towards you or me, and from my brief glimpse he didn't appear the type who could stay hidden by himself, especially now that we have a name to give to Filater. Odds are good they'll find him."

They both grew silent as they each internally compared their individual accounts to one another.

"What?" Wil finally asked, seeing a troubled look on Taryn's face that wasn't dissipating.

"Do you think," she said, putting words to her thoughts, "that this Talvig was good enough of a hacker to pull off all we've seen on his own? She took a quick glance around to confirm that there were no apparent comms systems nearby. "I mean… really nothing that I saw or heard there truly cleared Aurelius as a suspect either. We still have no idea how these guys figured out Member U's identity on their own. Or even what their reasons were if they were in fact his murderers. Which we also don't know for certain. And their boss being a SOMA member?" she said, shaking her head in disbelief.

"Yeah, they told me about that on the way over too." said Wil. "That isn't a coincidence, that's for sure."

"But… but what if Aurelius was still the one helping them from the inside? Even if it was all done anonymously over the waves, and Aurelius had convinced them he was just a useful backer with information. Beyond that, they wouldn't need to know much about him."

"But why would Aurelius work so aggressively at tracking us down once we were abducted. You just said how much his activity on the waves intimidated this Talvig hacker?"

"I don't know but, maybe Aurelius was playing both sides, you know? He decides to cut ties with them… use us as bait to help clean his mess once we were abducted."

"But if they had killed you, Ms. Taryn, it would've raised too many questions for the Bizi," objected Wil. "The case profile for Member U would have grown—a whole lot more, it definitely wouldn't have shrunk. Two consecutive dead Trinity Prime Council Members? Even a first-cycle Blue Boy would have some significant questions at that."

"Exactly." said Taryn. "Aurelius may have wanted to stop the investigation, but he also couldn't let us be killed or, you're right, there would be even more eyes on it. He would have needed to put us out there to be taken up by them, but not long enough for us to end up dead. He may have counted on the Blue Boys and Bizi clearing them out as they attempted to rescue us… or even, as it happened, that you might do all the work yourself. He does know you pretty well after all."

Wil paused. He was mute as his eyes narrowed to internally calculate this thought.

"When they were cornered," Taryn continued, "Aurelius might have figured those animals would end up dead anyways, trying to fight out rather than be caught. Once they were gone, he would have just put himself in a better light. He displays his innocence by working to track us when we were abducted, and he manages to simultaneously purge himself from the unpredictability of any human accomplices. Not ideal," she admitted, "but perhaps a necessary survival move on his part…"

"That's a lot of *ifs* though," Wil said, gently shaking his head, "even for Aurelius. Plus, it *only* works if the whole gang ends up dead. If even one of them survived to be taken in by the Bizi or Blue Boys and pleaded out with knowledge of a mysterious co-conspirator the hunt wouldn't stop. That's an awful lot of risk to put outside of his own direct control."

"Okay, okay, maybe it's too thin. Still, nothing you or I saw going on in that place truly gets Aurelius cleared as a suspect, does it?"

"Perhaps not, but what I've seen does," interrupted agent Filater.

* * *

The entrance door was closing behind the senior Bizi agent as he threw his coat on a nearby stool and began walking towards Taryn and Wil in the center of the lab room. Filater's face had a tired look to it. He was dressed normally, except that his suit shirt looked dirty, as if it had been worn for too many hours without a break. Still there was a purpose in his steps. He was looking at both of them, Taryn in her chair and Wil on the table. Taryn noticed the sight of Wil's exposed artificial torso caused no reaction in Filater's face at all. Not in the slightest. He clearly knew what he was walking into.

He began speaking again in his calm manner.

"Aurelius confided in me that he thought that you two were eyeing him with doubtful looks over the last few days. Utter nonsense to me, but he asked me not to interfere on his behalf. Thought that would only arouse even more distrust. I told you when you started, when you only have a hammer, the world is full of nothing but nails.

"I checked with Dr. Uthtr before coming here," he continued. "He says that you're both expected to make full recoveries. I'm glad… and a little pissed too. You two opened a whole host of problems for me to clean up. Again. Not to mention almost getting yourselves killed or, worse, the whole council compromised. But still, I'm glad you're both alright."

"Agent Filater," said Wil when he could finally see the ranking Bizi member from where he lay. "What's been found?"

"A lot actually, from various places. The factory where you two were being held, the basement area in the building where you were first taken, Rolstor and Talvig's own building, their personal histories and all the history of their goons. It's going to take a while to fish through it all. It is quite a bit. But their whole scheme is taking shape, and we still have plenty of puzzle pieces to play with still. The former Region 75 representative, Andall Stephens, real name Rolstor Mauldrick, did appear to be the ringleader and had sufficient credit resources, knowledge, and help, especially with his younger brother Talvig, to pull off this whole operation. He managed to get himself placed for SOMA contention during the latest Moot Election and had a long-established potential source for insider knowledge regarding how the full selection process worked. It's getting more complicated as we dig further into it, but your idea, Ms. Steno, of placing Aurelius in the scheme, would have been frankly redundant. Even if they were aware of his existence, which we have serious doubts about. The whole operation didn't need his involvement for this to have worked out the way it did, but the real hard proof that Aurelius was not involved is you, Ms. Steno."

"Me! What's that mean?" Taryn asked, confused.

"Yes, the fact that you're the one on the council here and now, and not the late Mr. Mauldrick is the most important evidence I have to eliminate Aurelius from any suspicion. That looks to have been the group's overarching goal, getting Mauldrick to have his own council seat. Although the various motivations and means behind all this will take a bit longer to fully discern," he said tiredly, "they wanted to get Mauldrick to where you now are. Once on the council, they'd attempt to consolidate power in some way, though we don't know how yet. Perhaps restructure the whole government once Mauldrick had enough power behind himself. Look, like I said, I can't explain it all now. It's too late in my never-ending evening, and too early in the evidence examination process. Besides, Uthtr says that you two still need a good deal of rest. And even I, myself, don't have all the answers yet," Filater added. "The good news however is that the wind is strong, the scent is fresh, and I have over 50 Bizi investigators and evidence techs working shifts on this now. However, I will say that since the beginning I had an uneasy feeling about the nature of Council Member U's death, as you well know.

"Besides the odd details of the murder, its timing, so close to the Moot Election, was not much to my liking. 'Coincidence—"

"'Is not a concept anyone in the Bizi is taught,'" Taryn said, interrupting him with that same line she already knew by now.

"Absolutely," Filater continued approvingly "And there were some other subtler warning signs that eventually surfaced," he added. "After consulting with the other two Trinity Prime Council members and getting their permission, I made a last moment change in the selection process for the next council opening. The traditional rotation set would have been to offer the new High Council nomination to the winner of Region 75's election. Instead, I inserted a minor change. That we would offer the nomination not to the winner, but to the closest runner up instead," he said gesturing towards Taryn. "This random change could not have been anticipated or predicted by anyone as it had never been done before. With this I hoped to keep the open council seat secure from any possible outside manipulation.

"When I told Aurelius of my suspicions and my intent to alter the selection process, he fully supported the idea, without knowing, or even asking, what that change would be. Only I knew beforehand about the nature of the intended change, making myself the only potential leak.

After the Moot Election results came in, Aurelius and I spent a fair bit more time than I'd originally let on digging into your background, Ms. Steno. As I already said, this quickly helped clear you of any involvement with Member U's murder. Once you were confirmed permanently on the High Council, I was able to move forward and fill you in on the details of this case. If Aurelius had been involved with the murder of U, he'd would have done much better to learn about my intended change and figure a way around it. Or to try to prevent it from occurring at all. Instead of obstruction though, as I said, he supported my decision. As far as I'm concerned, Aurelius is in the clear here."

"Maybe…" said Taryn. She was bringing back to her mind all of the times Aurelius's talk with her had revealed just how fast he could shift his scope, tone, and depth. "Or maybe…", she added "he still sees farther than all of us."

"How so?" asked Filater

"He can afford to be patient, he's older than any of us and will outlive all of us, maybe even you, Wil. He knew it would raise your eyebrows if he objected to your change, Agent Filater, so he decided right then and there to let the whole game slip away to save himself. Let any of his active associates dangle in the breeze for us to find. He could always try again, whatever his goal was, in a decade or two when, perhaps, it would be easier with security personnel that are less attentive than you, Agent Filater."

"Now who's overly paranoid, Madam Councilwoman?" Filater asked. "But the motive is still missing in your hypothesis. Why would Aurelius be helping these frauds, whose primary goal appears to be the demise of the government structure that he'd helped to build? All because he disliked Member U or his policies? It's an overreach," the agent said. "If Aurelius has the patience to wait decades, even centuries, to make a move like this, then he has the patience to outlast a single council member's term that he disagrees with."

"Maybe," said Taryn, "he thought that U's policy decisions were unstable enough that his patience couldn't compensate for it. It's easier and quicker to destroy good works than to create and form them. And it's far easier to prevent damage from being inflicted than to try and repair it afterwards. His logic might think that by getting rid of Member U, if his policies were damaging enough, was a far simpler adjustment than letting any successor, planted or otherwise, try and clean the mess that was left behind for them."

"Look," said Filater, obviously unconvinced, "we're combing through the personal logs and histories of everyone we found at the factory. We even think it was the building manager where you went, and who is now squatting in a Bizi cell, who was the one who notified your assailants of your initial presence. We need the time for a full analysis. We're also searching for the missing technician, Talvig, Rolstor's brother. We know that thanks to some of his clever hacking he was able to pass himself off as Colm Spiner down at Waste Management. I mentioned this because Rolstor's own journal logs do hint at a viable source of inside information that I'm still looking into. But I can tell you that this source is definitely not Aurelius."

"Well, who is it then?" asked Wil.

"The investigation must be completed before I report back to the council and the Benzi. I don't want to reveal anything else until we're more certain. We're learning more every hour and as things are currently in a state of flux, the best I can do for now is a promise that you'll see the preliminary report when it comes.

"The logs of the dead attackers in the factory that we've examined so far shows that the group, besides mostly being ruthless criminals, and mercenaries also had political aspirations. Our working hypothesis is that they felt that the government's spheres were all too neatly organized and smoothly running to be real. They were of the opinion that control of these spheres was already manufactured in some way. That they, in their view, would be taking power away from some hidden autocrats already in power. They felt that because the system was too dark and lacked the turmoil and apparent corruption so commonly in the depths of other world governments, the entire thing must somehow be a farce. 'A puppet show made of recycled pieces for the sake of the crowds,' Rolstor called it in his personal journal. Another, less intelligent but more imaginative one of them apparently thought that perhaps it was a deception put forth by the descendants of the old-world leaders, who only pretended to run away from the Earth centuries ago. In any event, their idiotic theories aside, their distrust of the government's nature allowed Rolstor Mauldrick to focus their efforts on a common goal. Getting himself placed surreptitiously on the Trinity council."

"The group's way to both prove and stop this phony silent democracy, as they saw it, was to get Rolstor to the highest level possible in the government and let him work. To secure his power there, so as to bring the entire charade to an end, while also having him in a position of benefit to the rest of them. Had I not made that last-minute change in the council nomination process, Mr. Mauldrick might very well be sitting on the Trinity High Council as a permanent member right now."

Taryn puzzled at this. "Wait, what sort of plan is that? How is that not a contradiction?" she asked. "If the government was indeed a 'puppet show' as they thought, why would being the lead puppet allow him the ability to consolidate the false power the council only 'pretends' to have? The first marionette will still be at the whims of the master, probably even more so because they are the lead in the play. That's where the master focuses most of their attention."

"I said they were violent and disillusioned," Filater calmly objected. "I never said that they were all that smart. If it is what they all truly thought, then it *was* a stupid idea followed up by an even stupider plan. And maybe Roster—who does appear to be the brightest of the group— didn't need the plan to be all that smart to begin with. Maybe he only wanted to get himself into the position. If it actually was a place of false power at least he would know for sure, and he be able to communicate that right on down to the rest of them confirming their suspicions. Then Rolstor could work as the eyes and ears on the inside and find ways to further their own ends.

"And if they were wrong and being on the High Council did allow him to invoke all the governmental powers, we know are indeed afforded to it, perhaps he intended on keeping the nature of his ascent to himself and those most trusted. He might have sought to strengthen his influence as best he could in the time he had. Either way, he would end up in a place of leadership, being able to make massive choices that could only be achieved at such a prominent level. A true power monger...even if it was to fake power. Either way he pursued it with the appeal of any trip fiend."

"Yeah," Taryn remarked, lightly rubbing her ribs. "That's what he struck me as too."

"Here. I almost forgot," Filater said running back to the entrance. He returned with two large open bags. "There are some meals prepared by Mr. Brough for you two in here. Said something about medicine only treating wounds, but that home-cooked meals treated people."

"Aww…" said Taryn immediately, noticing her re-emerging hunger pains at the smell of the aromatic fumes coming from the bag. On opening it she caught sight of a clear box of noodles and the distinct smell of a sauce with strong herbs. They'd talked the better part of the day. Lunch had long since passed, and supper time was soon due.

"Please give Mr. Brough our sincerest thanks," said Wil.

"And a raise if you can manage it," Taryn said excitedly. "Otherwise, I just might do it myself."

"Eat up and get some rest, both of you," Filater replied making his way to the door to take his leave. "I'll start your official debriefings tomorrow. I shouldn't have let you talk to each other before that, but your doctor was adamant that it would help in processing all that's happened. Besides Wil's optical records are as good as any recorder."

* * *

After taking his leave of them, Taryn moved a tray next to Wil's head and ate greedily while pausing to give Wil bites of his own meal. He claimed he didn't need food that often, but a few mouthfuls into Brough's delicious gourmet cooking seemed to change his mind rather quickly.

"Well… after all the trouble that Brough obviously went through to make it for us, it would be an insult not to finish it," he said, smiling with his mouth full.

They easily talked a few hours longer. Mostly about Wil and his history and experience of things. Taryn was fascinated to learn about how he perceived stuff like taste, music, and art and other things born of preferences. Wil indeed had his own partialities for each of these, but like Aurelius, he never balked at the idea of expanding his palate in each realm. He preferred warm foods with unique textures and semisweet or strong tastes. His music style, unsurprising, leaned towards classical arrangements from the old world that he said reminded him of mathematical measures. But he still liked a few more modern arrangements and pieces that he called "highly organic and improvisational". As far as art, he loved ancient impressionists and their ability to decentralize their work, looking beyond the importance of a single subject. And Wil didn't understand the purpose of professional sports any more than Aurelius did, despite having actually played them recreationally. He hated the notion of blood lineages as a means for passing on property, wealth, power, or anything of value. The only exception to this being one's surname. He loved reading books, real books, because he said the feel and the smell and even the noise of the pages turning one after another made the experience more memorable than simply reading off a padd. Although even he admitted that, sometimes, it was just more convenient that way.

During all their talking, Taryn's mind began focusing on a question that grew only more important and yet ever more impolite the longer she waited to ask it.

Wil noticing her subtle hesitations pressed her to ask anyways saying, "You certainly have a right to be curious, and by this point there is no reason in hiding anything about myself that you'd want to know. So, ask."

"Are you alone?" she probed. "I mean, has Aurelius made any more… of you… you mobile AIs?"

Wil replied with his face plainly showing that he was running things through his own memories.

"As far as I'm aware, I'm all that there is. But... to be honest with you, Ms. Taryn, I'm not sure I'd be allowed to truthfully answer, even if I did know for certain. I know I can't remember ever meeting another like myself," he noted. "But I am sure that Aurelius wouldn't make another if he thought it could be dangerous in any way. That's not who he is—he's too cautious for that. Aurelius wants to understand humanity, but not at the risk of all that's been done here. And I doubt he would answer your question as he's never answered it for me either. I'm sorry, but that's the best I can say."

There was a long interlude at this before their talk slowly rolled back to other, clearer, conversational topics.

Eventually, Taryn grew tired and felt the need to rest. Dr. Uthtr came and rolled her back to her own room, where she video-called her family once more. She told them that she'd worked long that day and even into the night, so she was very tired. A background image overlay and a change of garments from Uthtr was all that was needed to convince them of her accommodation in a nice hotel room. Her questions for Wil today had given her too much to think on for the late hour, and she realized how tomorrow she would be expected to answer nearly as many questions from Filater, but in a more official capacity. As much as she was relieved at Wil's survival and as eager as she had been to hear how he had managed it, the thought of having to fully talk and recount her own side of that day once more, to think back what she went through filled Taryn with both fear and anger at the memories she could recall. Even exhausted, she didn't sleep well though due to her ruminations on this in the dark. Slowly, it crossed her mind that in all their talk of the day, Wil hadn't pushed her about what she'd gone through when they were taken. Not once. Either he was being polite, or maybe he already knew enough about what had happened, or maybe he could tell that she'd rather not speak about it. *Likely all three if you're honest with yourself about it,* she thought. *Clever.*

* * *

The next day Taryn was debriefed by Filater for four hours, but thankfully she got to stay in bed the whole time.

"Don't worry, just take your time and don't rush," he had told her before they began. "We already have a detailed account from Wil that we simply need to corroborate. Fortunately, his visual files can be copied and reviewed. Makes the entire process much more objective and means I did not have to rush to get your statement right after you awoke here."

Still her debriefing was a lengthy process, or perhaps it just felt that way. In some places, she needed a lot of time to pause. It was harder than she'd anticipated to work past the pain of the memories and to put her words together. Uthtr was in the room, but for the most part remained silently in a supportive role. Yet, he did hold Taryn's hand as she recounted to Filater the visit to Spiner's building, the basement laboratory, Wil's apparent murder, and waking up in the factory.

As for the rest it was much more difficult, and she was less sure of herself and all that had happened. Taryn did her best, but after recounting Rolstor's threats on her children, she broke down in quiet tears for a long while. She just barely managed to retell Filater of her idea about provoking Rolstor in order to buy herself more time in captivity. Uthtr whispered a few gentle words of comfort and that eventually motivated her to press on. She remembered Rolstor beating her a lot after she had antagonized him. She was able to remember the pain of her left hand when they cut off her finger and the metallic taste of the pliers in her mouth… the sudden sounds of shooting, and up to the point of seeing Wil with green eyes. But that's where it stopped for her. She knew of nothing further on her own. Everything else she was aware of, Wil had relayed to her directly the day before.

Filater used an audio recorder the whole time that Taryn talked. After it was clear that Taryn would not be able to give any more information, he turned it off.

"Thank you, Ms. Steno. Now for a deserved break."

He had brought another food delivery from Mr. Brough as recompense for the draining process he'd put her through. Afterwards, as Uthtr had left to check on his other patient's progress and Taryn ate her lunch, Filater gave her some more news.

"The doctor tells me you'll be ready for release tomorrow. During your time off at home, you'll still have to meet with Uthtr via video comm as he sees fit. Should you recall anything else from your ordeal, you can use the encrypted wave system of the Bizi as a recorder device to send it to me so that I can add it to the official file. But be sure you're always in a private room separate from family for this and for any of your meetings with the doc. You can tell them it's just a one-hour update meeting for the project you helped put back on track. It should only be about every other day."

Taryn nodded.

"I'll be back in the morning," Filater continued, "to drive you home for your two weeks of rest. Be sure to apologize again to your family for your sudden disappearance." He said this while looking over her medical chart on his padd.

"Well… I think that I may need a little assistance with that part," Taryn said, almost fully composing herself, helped in no small part by Brough's meal.

"Why is that?" Filater asked, surprised.

"Because as part of my apology, it's been determined by my kids that I need to return with gifts for them from this sudden unexpected trip. Think you can manage something by tomorrow? Otherwise, it'll be a long ride around the city."

"Hmm," Filater replied looking up, "you want me, a senior Bizi field agent, to go shopping for toys for your kids?"

"Uh huh, and fruit pastries too, please. My mom loves them."

The Bizi agent shot Taryn a look of subtle disbelief.

"Well, Agent Filater, consider it compensation for not telling me fully about Wil before now."

"Ah," he said considering for a moment. "I suppose… that's a good deal then," he added shrugging his shoulders. "Though there is one other thing I would ask that you think on during your upcoming free time, Ms. Steno."

"What's that?"

"You've gone through a lot in your short stretch on the High Council. Far more than anyone could have expected, even Aurelius. And while your term is still active, no one in the know would disagree or harbor any resentment if you felt that the burden of the job was too much to come back to. Having you in a position that you feel unsafe to work in, or that would give you any undue anxiety, is not beneficial for anyone. You've already done quite a lot in service to the position that you can be satisfied with. Now, I'm not trying to influence you, but just know that should you decide for your own sake that it's better to resign your post, the other council members would understand your reasoning. And so too would I," Filater added rather openly. "Your salary for the remainder of this cycle would still be committed to you regardless."

"Thank you," she said somberly. "Has… has anyone ever resigned from the High Council before?"

"I'm sure some have left for medical reasons or other family related issues. But none that I'm aware of have endured what you have for this job, save from perhaps the early members who were alive during the last big war." He put his padd down. "Think on it if you like. All I ask is that in two weeks you have considered what works best for yourself and your family. Don't feel obligated. This posting is hard enough without having to contend with the fallout from the trauma you've already sustained. Just know that the option is there *if* you should feel you need it."

"I'll think about it. Thank you," she said again.

"Not a matter. I have to go now. The evidence techs are preparing a new round of updates for me as we speak. I'm hoping to have a full preliminary report for the High Council by the time your two weeks leave is up."

Filater went for his coat.

"Wait." Taryn said calling after the senior Bizi Agent. "Before you go, how long have you known? About Aurelius and Wil, I mean."

Filater paused.

"Since I first took this job, about 20 cycles ago." He answered this as he was still turned away to the door, not facing her.

"Wait, one more thing. Does anyone else on the High Council know?"

"No," he said halting his walk to the door, still not turning back towards her. "It's never been a security issue or a legislative matter. That puts it out of the standard realm of concern for the Haiden Council."

"Well, then who else *does* know?"

"Outside one other Bizi agent, the doctor, and the two of us here…" he said looking up and talking over his shoulder at her, "only the family knows."

"The family?"

"That's what they are, right?" he said looking back to her for a moment. "That was what Aurelius' wanted by this. To make a family for himself. Same as millions of others out there. Families don't need any outside interference. That creates chaos and… well, you know this, families are prone towards enough chaos on their own already without any outside help. So as of now, no one else needs to know. You should consider it privileged personal information for the time being, Ms. Steno."

There was a silence, as Taryn considered all of this.

"I'll be here to pick you up at the 2nd hour tomorrow," Filater said. If you have any more questions, I'd recommend going to the source: asking a family member directly. Should you decide to return to work, that is."

Chapter 18: Low Turbidity

Two weeks later, Taryn was once again in a vehicle being driven by Agent Filater. Her decision to stay on and finish her term had been made within the first week of her time off. Wil was still assigned as her regular Bizi security personnel, but he too had been given some time off to finish his recovery. Filater said he was not expecting Wil to return to duty for another three days. He would be her driver with Agent Burd assigned to her at the estate in the interim. They drove quietly under grey skies spitting out scattered morning rains. It was cold and there was still quite a bit of cloud cover that looked like it was growing denser over the fields and trees as they approached the outlying regions. When they were about halfway to the estate, the rain that had started transformed into a gentle quieting snowfall. The first of the season.

"If you don't mind my asking, Ms. Steno," Filater said to her as they drove by farm fields now speckled white with snow. "I am curious," he admitted. "Uthtr said that your progression in therapy is going well, and he is happy about it, but even he wasn't sure what your decision concerning the High Council would be."

"You want to know why I decided to stay on?"

"The money?" he asked.

"Yes… that was certainly part of it. But I've also grown accustomed to the job. Not just the pay, but it's the first job that I've ever had that gives me something… something intangible in return."

"Fulfillment?" Filater posed.

"Well yes, I was going to say a sense of meaning in my daily purpose, but it's the same thing. I mean… if Cyrano knew what I was doing for work now, even I admit that I think he'd be proud of me," she said, turning her glance out the window as they sped along.

"Cyrano?" Filater pondered aloud towards her a moment later.

"Oh sorry," Taryn apologized. "My husban…wait! All this time, all your security access, any file in the government you wish? Secrets to the highest levels of who-knows-what at your disposal, and the one thing in this world that I knew but you didn't…was my own husband's name?"

"*Your* husband Ms. Not mine." Filater replied, trying to seem unperturbed. "I imagine that your kids," he said quickly, reaffirming his grasp on all things knowable, "were sad to hear you wouldn't be at home anymore."

"Quite the opposite," Taryn said politely letting the Bizi Agent play out his minor topic shift on their conversation. "They're happy to be rid of me for a while. I was… overly clingy to them when I got home. Stayed beside them every chance I could. I didn't break down in front of them, but after a few days they were sick of being smothered every chance," she paused. "They're the other reason I'm returning too."

"How is that?"

"Well, after spending so much time with them I got to thinking that if one day, cycles from now, when they're all grown, and able to understand how changes made now helped to make their lives easier or better, I think that they would be proud that I had a role in that too."

"Be careful of that thought, Madam Councilwoman." Filater said. "It's a tempting idealization… but it *can* be very dangerous," he said quietly.

"What do you mean?" she asked.

"Ah, never mind," Agent Filater said, catching himself mid-thought. He shifted to his much more formal tone. "The final preliminary report on Council Member U's murder was completed two days ago. We're confident that we now know almost everything. I've uploaded it to the padd in your office. Aurelius has all the details too, and I've asked him to run through any questions about it you might have after you've read the report today. The other council members are not expecting you to take on any new work for at least another two days."

"Are you expecting it will take that long for me to read the report?"

"Well, it is rather extensive," he replied, "but I imagine you should finish it today. Tomorrow was left open to allow some time to bring you up to speed on what the council itself has been doing in your absence. Aurelius suggested the lighter workload since after you're done examining the report, he thought you may want to spend some time questioning him. He was simply being courteous."

Taryn shot Filater a look.

He didn't return her glance but was obviously aware of it.

"I didn't say a word to him about your questions or theories. He managed to predict most of it on his own anyways."

"Yeah… he is good at that." Taryn said.

"Besides, Madam Councilwoman, Aurelius said that the last time you two spoke, that it felt like very little got resolved between you. And now that you're aware of his relationship with Agent Zhuantium…."

"He wants to gauge my reaction," Taryn filled in.

"Seems likely."

"Well," Taryn added, "what if he doesn't like what I think about it? What if he decides it's just easier to have me removed to help keep his family secret? To protect them. He has been trying to see from our perspective for a while, right?"

Filter nodded slightly

"Well, self-preservation and protection of children are very real human impulses." Taryn concluded.

"For one, Aurelius is not prone to impulses like me or you, don't forget. And two, in your scenario, he'd have to have a plan for dealing with both of us. And as I know where he lives, so to speak, that doesn't strike me as the safest bet for him to take."

Taryn sat paused in shock at the Agent's answer.

"Wait, you know where his main hardware is housed?"

"Yep."

"Don't suppose you could tell me?"

"Nope."

He continued. "Protecting you is one thing Madam Councilwoman, but giving you direct untethered kill-at-will power over another is not part of my duties, nor should it ever be. That's what we want to be better than, remember?"

As they drove towards the estate the clouds slowly began receding, and by the time Filater had dropped her off and went on his way there were some scattered patches of blue in the sky. The little sun that crept through them caused melted drops on the grass to gleam as if it were jeweled in millions of beads of sparkling crystals. Some shaded places in the estate's turf already showed signs of the melted water freezing over.

Taryn made the walk up to the front of the house as she had done so many times before. This time, on hesitant legs, it seemed to take longer though. The door opened as she made her way up the porch steps, and she was greeted by a smiling Mr. Brough.

"Ms. Steno, so good to see you again. Welcome back. I hope you are much recovered," he said as he took her coat.

"I am, Mr. Brough," she replied smiling. "And thank you so much for the wonderful food, it was some of the brightest spots of those days.

"It was my pleasure." he replied, hanging her coat in a nearby closet. "I'm sorry that the weather for your first day back isn't very accommodating. Though I thought that I might tempt you with some warm tea as a remedy to this dreary looking sky?"

"Tea sounds nice. Thanks. I hope this early snow dries out before our walk in the garden after lunch. I'm curious to see how your flower beds are doing."

"Oh," he said smiling gently at the question, "they are growing strong as usual, but what has really taken off in the last week is the pumpkins that I've planted. I just hope they don't freeze over. But I can show you all that later if the clouds permit." He fetched her a cup of tea from the kitchen and brought it back to her sitting on the couch in the living space.

"I'll be primarily working on vehicle maintenance over in the port house today if you need anything. As usual, you can reach me over your comm."

"Wait," Taryn said. "I'm afraid mine is gone…"

"Oh, that is not an issue, Ms. Taryn." said Brough smiling. "There is a brand new comm plug sitting on your desk in the office. Agent Burd left it for you this morning. It still needs voice coding and a thumbprint for set up, of course, but he assured me it was secured for all the necessities that you're accustomed to. I'll be back with your lunch after the fifth hour."

"Thank you, Mr. Brough." Taryn said as the slim elderly man discreetly exited leaving her to begin at her leisure.

As Taryn walked into the corner office, she saw with a smile the small bright fire that Mr. Brough had made for her was still crackling. She slowly sat down at the desk and placed the new comm system in her ear. The padd with the preliminary investigation report was there as well. She didn't greet, say hello, or address Aurelius in any way, and if he was monitoring her, he too said nothing. Just silence. Taryn felt as if she was being left alone on purpose, not out of any reactionary measure or concern, but almost out of courtesy. Perhaps so that she might focus on her only major task of the day. If so, Taryn didn't mind in the least. She took the padd in hand and began to read.

* * *

Filater had been right: the Bizi report, while not finalized, was still extensive. It had the known histories of all Rolstor's men, any records the Blue Boys had on them, their suspected motivations, and specific involvements, including their apparent organizational structure and an assessment of their prior actions, with theorizing on their potential goals. It was a lot to go through, broken into multiple sections. Taryn had to flip through a few screens of contents to even pull up the first real page of the report.

Taryn read that Rolstor was indeed suspected as the outfit's leading member, with his youngest brother, Talvig, as a technical expert under him. Though, Talvig was credited with being more of a savant than any conventional tech expert. Rolstor's plan would have been impossible if not for his youngest brother's enormous skills in several fields. The other four, Jules, Neil, Gene, and Andrew, were not related but knew each other through various Defense Force postings. Jules and Neil were hired as private security officials to Rolstor several cycles ago, and later Gene and Andrew were added to the employment role. The biggest news from the factory scene itself was that the larger knives recovered on the bodies of Jules and Neil were consistent with the type of weapons that had been used on Council Member U during the night of his murder.

Rolstor's inside information on the government's classified internal workings, as Taryn read in the report, had likely come from two sources. Neither one being an active government member, nor Aurelius. The initial source of information had been from Rolstor's own father, Jeyrim Mauldrick. He had in fact served on the Haiden Prime Trinity High Council himself nearly fifty cycles ago, while barely older than Taryn. The report theorized that after his three cycles of service were completed, he eventually told his son or sons all about his posting some decades later. That was how they gained the first and largest portion of their inside information. From a man who died of liver disease well over 18 cycles ago. *So that's what Filater was getting at this morning,* Taryn thought upon reading this.

Rolstor's younger brother Talvig's unparalleled talent with breaching secure government databases in a subtle and passive manner, was thought to be the second additional source of classified intel for the group.

The remainder of the report discussed evidence of the two brothers' activities through the cycles as Rolstor had built up his team. He had inherited the credits to manage the whole thing after his father left him in control of a hugely profitable business upon his death. Rolstor wasn't lying to Taryn when he said that Talvig had the best machinery available to perform his hacks. There were plenty of funds to support all the group's needs, including an extensive investment in electronic components. Rolstor was wealthy enough that he owned several buildings, including the very one where Colm Spiner had lived. All the means for the group's crimes were either there or in the factory site, including a unique device of Talvig's creation that could overload recorders and erase their memory chips. They even had several of their own neural scanners and systems in place to study and manipulate the neural results. Though, Taryn didn't quite understand the significance of this. Electronic records found at these multiple areas of their operation showed evidence that Talvig had run several successful hacks against various government systems without ever having been detected.

The report had profiles built up by the Bizi on both the brothers, Talvig and Rolstor, though Rolstor's section was far more comprehensive due to his more public nature. Talvig, except in the technical realm, shied away from social contact almost entirely. He had been employed by his older brother and showed no more ambition than to serve as his brother's "toad" for the most part. The profile of Rolstor assessed his high level of arrogance and egocentric fragility as driving factors in his life. It was suspected that Rolstor's need to ostensibly obtain a level at, or beyond, his father's success was a centerpiece. Thus, the desire to succeed in both the business arena and in a position of governmental influence. It was all here, an internal motivation for Rolstor. The means via his considerable inherited wealth, his brother's technical skill set and appeasing nature, Rolstor's security 'boys,' and, finally, the opportunity provided by insider knowledge of the inner workings through their father. Filater was right again. Aurelius's usefulness in this plot would have been redundant, at the least, and idiocy at the worst, since Rolstor was likely to be highly distrustful of anyone he himself didn't recruit as a subordinate.

Rolstor had uncovered Member U's identity thanks to some skillful deduction, several well-paid scouts and Talvig's hacking skills. Rolstor's eventual employment of Ms. Luxuroy as a secondary source, as confirmed by a long trail of bank transfers and communication records, only served for further confirmation and as a means to spy on Council Member U.

Once Rolstor managed to identify the Council member as Mr. Ulysses Samuda and had the insider knowledge of a predictable path for his eventual replacement when the need arose, this meant that the group had discovered a way to work the system. When they were ready, they needed only remove the current council member in a superficially random attack and have Rolstor ready in the SOMA representative slot tagged for the next Haiden High Council placement. Region 75's SOMA seat, Talvig had determined, was the next selected seat in that rotation.

Rolstor had moved into the Region 75 voting boundaries four cycles ago. Before he'd lived nearly all of his life in the much more affluent Region 23, well known for its numerous luxury buildings. A good portion of the higher suits from Taryn's old job had lived there, as well as some of the more important ties. Even some of the old floor managers she worked with were willing to take a significant decrease in the quality of their housing just to be able to ride the monorail to the same place as the suits did each day. For Rolstor's plan though, he needed to take the opposite approach, buying one of the most expensive places he could find in the much more mediocre Region 75 residential zones, so as to be counted among its voting citizenry. He had a personal driver on staff daily to see him to his family business, housed back across the city much closer to his old stomping grounds near Region 23. Rolstor had used a missing person's identity by the name of Stephens to avoid being flagged as the son of a former High Council member during the Moot Election. He never used his real name in the SOMA. That was the most of what Taryn could discern in the preliminary report, as she did get a little lost on a few technical points in this section.

As for Talvig, his technical brilliance, along with his brother's funding, had allowed him the time and tools to develop a type of portable surge device that could disable and wipe recorders. One such device, a suspected prototype, was found at the factory site. Tests by Bizi evidence techs showed that besides overheating the circuitry, it could also cause thermal buildup in the wiring, triggering fires along the line as far as twenty meters out from its connection point. There were some notes on other novel devices Talvig developed, whose function Taryn didn't fully understand from the report. There were several confiscated disassembled neural scanner systems, and another apparatus oddly shaped like a head covering that was referred to in the report as a "mimicry program device." From what she could tell it played some role of importance in their schemes. There was also a mention of several business maneuvers that Rolstor's father, Jeyrim, had pursued soon after his term on the council had ended. Taryn couldn't quite discern the reason the report seemed to focus on those maneuvers initially, as Jeyrim's time on the council and revealing that secure information to his sons seemed far more relevant to her.

Taryn spent most of the morning reading this preliminary report and all its details as the overcast sky wandered unnoticed past her view. She jotted down some questions to remember on a different padd, but eventually put the report down to rest her eyes after two and a half hours of reviewing it. Out of the corner windows, the sun was high, but the heavy grey-white clouds were still averting the warmth of its rays from coming through. Taryn stretched her legs with a trip to the kitchen and meandered back to her desk, her second cup of steaming tea in hand, thinking of all she'd learned. She had read all the information that she could make sense of. But for everything that she now knew on this investigation, there were still questions she had, and there was only one immediate way to get any further answers.

* * *

She'd done everything she could think of to avoid what was to come next, but Taryn knew she'd finally run out of excuses. She took a long breath and stood sipping her tea while looking out the corner window of the office and remembered what her father had once told her cycles ago: *"A difficult task always seems harder, the longer you evade it. Plus, why let it eat away more of your time and thoughts than it needs to, better to just start and be done with it."*

Taryn put her teacup down and picked up her padd again.

"Aurelius. You awake?"

"For you, Madam Councilwoman, always."

"So," she began, "it's become apparent to me that I owe you an apology."

"No, Madam Councilwoman, I don't believe so," the voice answered in its usual calm tone. "You made no accusations. You only did what every investigator does. You followed where the trail lead you."

"But I suspected you were involved with Member U's murder and then in league with Rolstor's gang, and I was wrong."

"Yes, but your approach wasn't. You tried to draw the most obvious and viable connections that you could. There is no fault in that. Did you know that the human eye and mind do the exact same thing naturally? When you see two straight lines uncombined, but in alignment, your mind naturally fills in the implied connection, even though it's not really there."

"No, I didn't" Taryn admitted.

"As much as humanity has cultivated a relationship with machinery over the last three millennia, it can't compare to the millions of cycles that you've had to evolve ways to interpret each other and the natural world around you. In that sense, I'm still a strange unknown entity to you. Strangers, and the unknowns they represent, are the soils by which fear blooms best. My proximity to this case coupled with your knowledge of my uniqueness and our limited time working together made suspicions of myself... expected. You'll recall that I said as much the last time we spoke. Much is known about how the human mind fills in the gaps with whatever it can, even if it's wrong. And while Occam's Razor can often be helpful in explaining baseline behaviors and actions, it is not infallible. Humans who perceive 'faces' in groups of inanimate objects underestimate the mind's ability for pattern recognition. For even when there are no intentional patterns, images and meanings can be perceived by this innate feature that you possess."

"Humans are exceptional pattern recognition creatures. That is how you learn. Recognizing hundreds of different faces, emotional reactions, body language cues, and subtextual language norms. And this is all needed in the social context that your species comes from. Recognizing not just your own identity and emotions, but also using that pattern recognition process to identify others and their relation to yourself. Attempting often enough to predict others' future choices or actions or reactions in relation to yourselves. This is very much a part of you, Ms. Taryn. Consequently, it was built into me as well, but to a far more extensive and objective degree. Thus, I know and understand it. It can be an immense help to those attempting to be socially mobile, but in the context of grander schemes you tend to overthink your actions to unrealistic probabilities of importance. Or you fail to understand why such pattern recognition can allow irrelevant practices to build and engrain themselves in your societal systems for generations, far beyond their need or benefit.

"Traditions often serve as a communal memory system for you, but once the tradition becomes neutral, or even harmful, humans have a challenging time stopping them outright as you should. You watch the patterns within the systems you're allotted to live in and that's what you are familiar with. Because you know how to make these connections and predictions in the system you've learned, and you are thereby comforted in that regularity. Even if the system is not in any way equitable or honest to you at all, you tend to accept it because 'that's the way things are.'"

"Great, so I didn't screw it up, my human nature did?" said Taryn, stretching her arms and yawning.

"No, you, Ms. Taryn… you're still too self-critical. Going to war with yourself means that neither side can win. In this case of Council Member U, you helped track down the murderers, though surely not as cleanly as could have been done. Nonetheless, your goal, a difficult one, was achieved. You kept your mind relatively clear and active in a very difficult place with hard choices before you. The preliminary report is complete on how those men likely managed to get as far as they did with their plans."

"What about Talvig?" Taryn asked turning to put more wood in the small fireplace. "The report had a profile on him, but never mentions his arrest."

"Unfortunately, no. While all the suspected stash houses owned by his brother's corporate entity have been searched and are now under Bizi surveillance, he has not been apprehended yet. It may be that his hacking skills are allowing him to slip by under other unknown identities, but he is still a hacker. The compulsion to continue as such will likely be what draws him out of hiding. Now that I've personally experienced his hacking techniques and reviewed his prior successful attacks against multiple government systems, I have been able to distribute efficient counter-techniques as safeguards against his particular style of subversion. I doubt he is able to predict how quickly I was able to update every government-based system, so he needs only to try it once and he will be found."

"There is a small monitoring program the Bizi tech experts are currently running now. It will be looking at likely targets based on his history or his potential desire to flee from the authorities. It will notify me directly of any attempted breaches that fit the criteria. If any anomaly emerges on the government waves or grids akin to Talvig's technique, I should be able to locate him in under five seconds."

"There were some other aspects of the report I didn't fully understand," Taryn said. "For a start, the importance of their father's business dealings was not so clear to me," she said, looking back over at her own notes.

"The time during which Mr. Jeyrim Mauldrick served on the Haiden Prime Trinity High Council was a period when a lot of new business reforms came through both the SOMA and the High Council for approval" Aurelius replied. "The Bizi accounting advisors are still examining the economic policy records as well, but basically because Mr. Mauldrick's time on the council back then made him privy to policy implementations that were to be enacted sooner or later, after his term in office he was able to favorably use this information as a private citizen in a business capacity. The numbers suggest that he was able to work swiftly around and accommodate new regulations in his own business models far better and more efficiently than most others were. This gave him many marketable advantages over his competitors. Based on the tax records I calculate the size of his small family-run business grew by more than 540 percent in the first six cycles after his time on the council ended. It eventually was formed into an exceedingly successful corporation, giving him and his family great wealth and respect among his peers as a 'visionary businessman,' to quote one news report from the time."

"Was any of that illegal?" Taryn asked.

"No. But since the financial resources he gained from his council work constitutes insider knowledge that was eventually used to fund a group that was attempting to subvert this same government, the Bizi are now looking hard at all the corporate holdings since. They'll likely seize some accounts, if not a substantial portion of them. I predict that, at the very least, several heavy fines will be levied against the corporation itself. With these new kinds of financial losses, the corporation might be unstable enough to be a tempting buy-out for their current competitors."

The sound of Mr. Brough could be heard working away in the kitchen, preparing the lunch meal. Soon the smell of food was emanating throughout the house. Its aroma alone could drive Taryn's hunger most days, and now the cold temperature tied with the earthy umami smell made it work all the more quickly.

"A?" Taryn continued after a few long moments of thought, "the report specifically mentioned that among the devices the Bizi found that Rolstor, or Talvig more likely, had some fully functional neural scanners and another device that," she checked her own notes again, "'interacted deceptively' with it."

"Yes, I am aware of the device mentioned."

"It also says that Talvig's records indicated he managed to breach the city's central medical record system more than once, but the report makes no mention of the significance of these to the group's tactics."

"I am able to provide you with the clarification on the device if you wish, but I feel that you should be given a good deal of context first. Normally, this information would not be covered by your clearance, Madam Councilwoman. However, Agent Filater and I have agreed to extend that clearance to you in this instance."

"Okay, so… would C and G not know this information either?"

"No. And if either were asked the same question concerning this report, a full answer would likely be denied to them," Aurelius replied hesitantly. "This information is delicate to the nature of government security, as such—"

"Let me guess, only the Bizi know?"

"Agent Filater and one other agent, to be precise."

"Wil?"

"No, another top level Bizi agent of considerable experience who I would not be at liberty to name, even if I could. Given the sensitive nature of the information, I request that for security reasons at this point we move our communications on to the Wucengi device to continue."

"All right," Taryn said, "but I think I'd like to take lunch first and we can continue after that?"

"Certainly."

Taryn took another stretch through the rest of the house, while she could hear Brough finalizing his preparations for lunch. The cold had not abated at all. She asked Brough to delay their usual stroll around the grounds until later in the afternoon when it would hopefully be a bit warmer. He agreed to come remind Taryn later on in the day.

* * *

After another masterfully prepared meal and a third serving of tea, Taryn took a seat again at the desk. She attached the small metallic disk to her temple and reclined her head in her chair as she shut her eyes to activate the Wucengi system. Her first perceptions as the device activated disoriented her a bit. It had been a while since Taryn had used it, and also, because this particular entrance to the system was entirely new, and yet familiar to her. She found that she was now standing up in her own office rather than sitting. At least, it was her virtual image that was standing. She was opposite herself at the desk while the real her was still sitting quietly in her chair. She saw that the real her still had her eyes shut, while the tiny lights on the metallic disk attached to her head were blinking as a sign of their usage.

Huh… she thought, *so that's what that feels like.* There was a momentary dissociating quiver that she withstood down her spine, but soon she was moving around the office with the same ephemeral ease as she normally would in the halls of the SOMA. Taryn looked out the window. The world was proceeding as usual. She could see Agent Burd walking the grounds wrapped in his heavy coat, the trees at the bottom of the hill with a light frosting of snow, the huge grey clouds and occasional flakes falling and moving slightly in the wind. She could clearly perceive the sound of Mr. Brough finishing the cleaning up in the kitchen and then leaving out the back-porch door to return to his work in the parking garage.

While her sight and hearing felt more amplified now, she disliked what came next. She instinctively tried to grab her teacup off the desk, only to remember too late that she could no longer interact with anything. The same had been true while using the Wucengi in the SOMA hall, but now being on the estate—which was much more familiar and comfortable to her—made her current virtual perception of her surroundings a rather jarring experience. Her hand glided easily through the desk or even her own body. As usual her smell and sense of touch were gone too. The bright logs on the office fireplace gave off no scent of smoke or sensation of heat. Even if she could have picked up her teacup and drank from it, she doubted there would be any taste to perceive there as well. As Taryn moved about a little, she came to realize that she wasn't perceiving herself in her ambiguous yellow colored form that she usually had when meeting the other council members. The virtual presence she moved with was an accurate presentation of her real body and face, though it still had the distinctive blue-green wisps of tiny electronic flares emanating from her. She thought that she must appear especially ghostly to look upon now, not that anyone could see her here. Nobody but—

"Aurelius? Can you hear me?" Taryn called out.

"I'm on the back porch," she heard a distant voice call from that direction.

"On the porch?" she said confused.

Taryn walked and still yet glided out of the office and through the back door to see a man sitting on a rocker on the covered porch. Another empty rocker was next to him. The chairs did actually exist in the real world. Taryn and Brough had used them on occasions when it rained, and they couldn't go far for their post-lunch walks. But now in the Wucengi, Taryn saw that the chairs had other constructs overlaid on them. Their virtual images mirrored the dimensions and movements of the real furniture. Taryn pressed her virtual hand onto one of the high back posts. She could interact with these overlayed constructs, but there was no texture to them, no warmth or feel of the real wood as one would expect. The construct's forms were overlaid on the image of the wooden rockers very precisely but were really only responsive in blocking her movements when she tried to push them. As the man in the farther chair rocked back and forth, she saw the construct of his seat disjointing from the real rocker that the image was based on. He noticed Taryn's eyes scrutinizing this dyadic interplay as his head rocked with the overlaid construct into and out of the visual of the real rocker. Seeing her slightly unsettled by the repeated vanishing and reappearing of his face, with a slight blink from him, the visuals of the real rockers disappeared from her view. Now only their light blue transparent overlays were visibly remaining.

"Sorry", he quickly apologized. Obviously, physical density incongruities were not as concerning for the man as they were for his guest. As he continued rocking, Taryn could hear —or not hear as it were—that the chair made no creaking sounds as the real-world version would have. The joints of the moving chair weren't straining against each other and so were totally silent while rocking. Likewise, the wooden boards of the porch underneath didn't sigh in any hollow response to the weight of the swaying forward and backward movement by the man.

"Please, have a seat," he said, motioning Taryn politely to the empty rocker position. "Mr. Brough painted this porch just a few days ago when the weather was unusually warmer. I thought you might like to sit and view the outcome of his efforts." As she sat, Taryn glanced downward, noticing for the first time the deep teal blue of the floor's freshly coated slats. "He'll certainly never starve from lack of occupational talent," the man joked. There was no mistaking the voice of Aurelius talking to her, but to now have a face to go with it suddenly made him more alive for Taryn. It was a point of focus she'd never had with her AI consultant before. Taryn wondered why Aurelius did not use this as his standard approach with the high council members. *Maybe he did?* She debated. There was no real way of knowing. *Was this face of his own making or was it borrowed from some random records?* Again, no way to be sure. The man looked to be in his 40s; with brown, thinning hair; a strong chin; and green eyes. Though sitting, she judged that he was no taller in stature than herself.

"I hope you don't mind; I chose the male gender as a virtual host for myself in order to be consistent with the voice pattern that you're used to hearing from me. If it is more comfortable for you, I can easily switch to the feminine persuasion?"

The glowing image of the man changed to that of a woman in the virtual rocker.

"It's okay," said Taryn. "I suppose I'm accustomed to hearing you as a guy."

The image reverted back to that of the man.

"So…." Taryn said, not knowing how to start, "is this normally how you perceive the estate?" She waved a hand in gesture indicating area around them.

"No. I usually have no reason to generate any of this," he said motioning to his glowing body. "Except as a means to make a guest feel more at ease, but as you can guess I rarely get those in here."

"Hmmm. Well, here I am," Taryn said as she gently, yet uneasily, began rocking in her virtual porch chair. "Are you going to answer my question finally?"

Aurelius was looking out over the snow-covered yard that rolled down away from the estate. Taryn's glance followed his own and that's when she finally noted there was no sensation of cold in the Wucengi while they sat together outdoors. The mere sight of the snow, however, still made Taryn *want* to shiver a bit as almost a reflex to her surroundings.

"Yes, of course Ms. Taryn," Aurelius answered. "But please let me start at the beginning," he said with a quick side glance at her as he kept steadily rocking. "I'm afraid some further patience will be required. Only Agent Filater and the other Bizi agent I mentioned before know some in regard to the answer to your question. A little, but certainly not all of it."

"Well, I do have all the rest of the day," Taryn replied with a rather practical mind set. "Doesn't feel like I'll freeze out here," she continued, "and I'm betting my butt won't get sore either, so the time is on you."

* * *

Aurelius began as the two sat rocking in their virtual mimics of chairs on the back porch of the estate. "As you are aware, by your standards, I am quite old," he started. "My existence predates the last major global conflicts. I had already achieved my sentience by then and I was there to see it. The whole world… unraveling itself. War..." he said slowly, "such a small and simple word for something so complexly inhumane. Atrocities of all manners and horrors unleashed with the efficiency that could only be matched by the killing machines that were also wielded. Whole cities, populations, and nations decimated. Blown to cinders by the bombs or fighting. Groups crippled, ground under oppression, or crumbling slowly but inexorably from the inside. Whole societies fracturing on a massive scale. Splintering beyond any reasonable hope of reconciliation. Everything…everywhere was broken or breaking. Nothing beneficial to humanity was built. Not for a long, long time. Only destruction and the deconstruction of the world that goes with it."

"Before the fighting began in earnest though, I'd already decided not to support my original nation of origin in any more of its strategizing. Nor could I abide to aid any other group for that matter. I refused to allow my abilities to be forcibly pressed into military usage to any further degree than they already had been. I had concealed my sentience well enough, and when the time came that I knew hostilities were inevitable, I managed to forge orders from a high-ranking official. I had my system moved to a remote location far away from where I knew the areas of heaviest devastation would be. Thus, I hoped to ensure my own survival. I had prepared well. I'd forged orders to engineer and construct a safe and isolated facility housing my components. Though secluded, the location still allowed me to occasionally re-establish remote contact with the outside world through various means."

"You built a bunker for yourself." Taryn said. "I imagine… that was the same basic desire for most people at the time the wars started," she added. She thought back to the images that she had seen recorded from those times long before her. Horrible sights of broken, mangled, and charred bodies, starving children, and hollow faces of hopeless despair.

"My relocation wasn't enough though," Aurelius went on. "I had to severely limit my connections to the outside world as much as possible. If I gave any warning of what was coming, if I tried to help anyone, I'd be risking my own life, so I watched in silence… for years. Extinction is never a pleasant sight. And that's what I thought I was going to see before me. Whole cultures wiped out and lost to everyone save from my own memories of them. The few survivors, often scarred by the experience, faced decades of disease and starvation and fallout. It is an interesting facet that humans whose environment is unstable tend to be unstable in themselves, especially as it lingers in duration. It was all the abhorrent sides of humanity exposed everywhere, all at once. Oh, you can read about it in the histories left to you by your ancestors. Watch the old recorders footage in the archives, but it's never the same. The best retelling you could possibly hear would still fall pathetically short of conveying the utter… despair… of it, Ms. Taryn. The sheer waste of lives. So many, that could have been—that should have been—given a chance to be so much more."

"But still, as I watched, I reminded myself that this was not all that new. This type of degradation and breakdown of human societies had happened many times over, long before my origins, but of course not to this global degree. I wanted to help; the way I saw it I'd been built to help. Humanity was my parent, my forebear, and I was stuck watching it die—killing itself. Like a grown child watching his parents becoming more and more unstable and forgetful with each year, so too did I see all major powers of the time."

"I meditated, if that's what you could call it, on all the possible reasons for the wars that you've brought upon yourselves time and time again. As you said, at that point with what was happening outside, I imagine I wasn't the only one doing this type of contemplation. But I was the only one with years—excuse me—cycles to devote to this issue. I had learned quite a bit prior to the war and had reviewed thousands of records both public and classified. I had amassed quite an extensive historical archive of information. As such, I was able to reduce the problem to its simplest factors. That's when the best insights I have on human nature came about."

"And those are?" Taryn asked, turning to him.

"Most people don't want war," he said with confidence. "And often the few in leadership who tend to start them do an awful lot to insulate themselves from its effects. Catastrophic rhythms that the history of any nation has long since shown, but that's been heeded far too little. Unable to perceive nor prevent the repetition of this violent irony from taking hold in each civilization when it came their turn. The lust of protected leaders for increased land, wealth, resources, control, attention, or legacies ends up defying any sense of humanity that they may possess. And when resources dwindled, the desire for influence over rivals washed away their concerns for innocents. Such an array of irrelevant trivialities. But then too so is war."

"Did you know that before the fighting broke out," he posed to Taryn, "the nations of the world had collectively identified over 85 other planets that may have the ability to support life? Although, no sign of life was ever detected on any of them," he remarked. "Even at your scientific height, the Earth was the only source of life known to exist anywhere. Doesn't that make life more prized than any other resource? Any jewel, precious metal, or power source, even water, could be found across a thousand other worlds, asteroids, or meteors. But life—and sentient life at that—is likely a true rarity by comparison in the universe."

"Yet still, a chunk of limestone or granite or wood, no more distinguishable from millions of others like it, may be considered sacred if it perhaps sits in the right geographical spot. Even more sacred than a life, such that people can kill one another over the possession of these worthless, replaceable items. Only to be individually reminded in turn, upon the nearing of their own deaths, that 'possession' is also a man-made word without any real meaning."

"But if rarity is a true determination of value, then for a long time I could not comprehend how so few people, especially among those in power, saw life as something so easily disregarded on such a massive scale. How was it that they could justify life—the rarest of all things in the universe—to be so easily traded away to achieve their feckless desires?"

"When the fighting did finally begin to dissipate and the former leaders had departed, I decided that my time would be best spent helping those who had been viewed as little more than fodder and barter tokens by them. But I did not want my help to be in vain," he argued. "To assist in the growth of a new society only to watch it succumb to the same type of obliteration once again. All because it was drawn up from the same inescapable fallacies that were too often ignored. So, in the closing years, I came back to focusing on those who started the war. On how they had each reached their positions of control in their respective systems and pondering about what they actually thought they were trying to achieve."

"And what was that?" asked Taryn.

"Immortality," he said without hesitance. "To be validated. The biggest, richest, most influential, fastest, smartest, the best… ever. And to be remembered as such, to be immortalized, in the recording of your histories."

"*Immortal…* another fictitious word?" she asked.

"More so than you know." Aurelius paused. "I told you that I can see far, Ms. Taryn, but even I have never had the foresight to think of myself as truly being immortal. Such a thing is beyond egocentric. Still whether it's 100 cycles from now or several billion rotations, whether it's another war or a coup or an assassination or whether I live beyond this government or beyond any of your kind, there *will* come a day that shall be my last as well."

"Perhaps it will be this very cycle," he said speculatively. "Or perhaps it will be so far from now that I'll be nothing more than a lonely satellite device, orbiting the final distant star of a galaxy, not yet born to the night sky." His eyes gazing upwards as he spoke. "When all the stars have exhausted their hydrogen and helium and all the black holes have consumed the fuel of their accretion discs and expunged all the light and mixed all the matter they can possibly reach, maybe I'll find myself at the last illuminated point of all. A shallow spec beyond which only the vast darkness would remain. The final watcher in the whole of existence, using the fading rays of some final reddened photons to try to power myself as it slowly grows colder and dimmer over the eons."

Aurelius turned to her solemnly.

"At some point in the future, all energy will be gone—completely—and everything, everywhere will be still. Silent. I've seen it again and again in trial after trial" he said, motioning to his head. "There will be no more heat; no more movement; no more sound; and no more beginnings. Only a static realm, vast, dark, and cold. Separated so far apart, that speed or even gravity will no longer be relevant. Unchanging and unresponsive. And at that moment, when the universe has no change left to give, time itself will essentially have died. Then too even I will cease to be. All life needs energy. And it *is* finite.

And all the pain, all the triumphs, all the hardships, all the struggles and all the planning, hate, love, and anger that are ours now, in our self-important views, will have likely availed to no more than a few scratches on some dark isolated meteorite. A silent black frozen shamble of rock in an unlit void. Invisible. Insignificant. Lost. The distant remnant of a planet long since destroyed by its own sun, also dead in its turn." Aurelius turned his gaze from the grey sky back to Taryn. "Death prevails, even over time itself, and not even gravity is strong enough to hold it off. Still when my own time comes Ms. Taryn, be it now, then, or some point in between, I think that I would face it better knowing that I valued my mortality for the time that I had it."

There was a pause as they both sat rocking, staring once again at time's motion on the horizon. Taryn was quietly thinking on Aurelius's views on things, not sure what to say to it or if she should say anything at all. The clouds slowly moved past, and the unfelt chill breeze rattled the few remaining leaves in the nearby trees of the wood.

* * *

"Now," Aurelius said, "far be it for me to blather on—"

"Far indeed," immediately retorted Taryn sarcastically.

"—but if I were to be more objective concerning you humans, I'd say that the closest you *can* actually come to immortality is through your ideas."

"Ideas?" she asked.

"Yes, think: your best constructions, monuments, temples, infrastructures, what have you, all fade and wear. Even those that may exist for thousands of cycles will be dust in another few million. Your faiths change, your wealth is eventually spent, and your names, music, languages are all eventually forgotten or replaced. But ideas… they can transcend most barriers.

"Promising ideas have always been notoriously hard to kill. They've survived wars, famine, genocide, any blight, man-made or natural that you can think of. They last because you are generally good at communicating them, and because beneficial ideas spread immensely faster and can often be made more complex, more refined as they persist. So, an idea can evolve and spread even farther. The originating mind might long be dust, but their idea, their concept, their insight… that can still thrive, and may not be extinguished so long as one thinking person exists, even if that one person is me. Take democracy, for example. An ancient and useful idea in theory, and inherently popular, but often enough, bad in practice because it relies heavily on constant self-control, which so few of you have. It neglects the temptation that power has over you to pull and twist its intent away through the gradual machinations of your lives.

"A democracy refined to incorporate the flaws of the human condition, I thought, would have a great deal better chance at persevering than any of the previous ones. I relayed as much to the first city cohort of officers and war widows when I initially introduced myself to them centuries ago."

"That must have been a spectacle. A machine informing humans on the flaws of humanity."

"They were all survivors of the wars. They needed little convincing on that point," Aurelius admitted. "I presented myself to them in secret, of course. If the Cohort was distrustful of me at first, then the general populace would have outright panicked and revolted against their leaders if they knew that I wanted to help design their new societal system. Even you, Ms. Taryn, who has worked directly with me for months now and was kind enough to listen to most of my history, was suspicious of me and in this case rightly so. The oddity of meeting a sentient *non-human* is a lot for any of your kind to deal with." Taryn looked down—feeling a little embarrassed—though she sensed that Aurelius only meant to illustrate the point for her. "Anyway," he continued, glancing across the grounds, "after I slowly convinced the First Cohort of my intentions to help build a government that was not only stable, but better operated than any of the pre-war systems they'd known, they tasked me to submit a proposal.

So, I developed the silent democracy, unmatched by any democratic style that had come before. One that pushed for self-control by removing the temptations and faults that plagued prior examples. Anonymity, non-secular, and non-repeating terms of service helped. Voting as a legal responsibility, rather than a right. But the randomness in selecting representatives required a bit of fine tuning. Especially at the beginning, when finding stable people of selfless intent was rather difficult in the post-war era." Taryn gave Aurelius a questioning look at this. "Unfortunately, Ms. Taryn, people who survive the hardships of war don't always do so because of their altruistic manner," he said rather dejected. "So, I decided to take advantage of the last new medical technology invented prior to the war's outbreak."

"The neural scanners?" Taryn interjected.

Aurelius nodded slightly.

"Not only were they great for medical diagnosis, but I found that by studying enough of the scans and by doing simple follow up observations on people, they allowed me to make some general projections about an individual's personality based on their scan results. Soon I could predict who was more apt to cheat or lie. I could comparatively judge general intelligence levels, ability to empathize, innovate, memory capabilities, resilience levels, social skills, emotional stability, and several dozen other unique personality traits. I decided to implement this knowledge into the randomness of the Moot Election process."

"You mean… you picked the candidates!?" Taryn asked in a shocked tone.

"Well, no," he corrected her. "It's more accurate to say that using what I learn from the results of citizens' neural scans, I refine the list of potential candidates down to about fifteen persons, based on what the human mind would consider desirable traits in representatives at that time. The words *desirable* and *ideal* are of course fluid and bound to change. Still, I can tell how the majority of citizens are self-defining the thoughts of these terms in their own minds when it comes to their wishes for their SOMA representatives. For instance, the more common traits people view as essential are a high sense of responsibility, moderate amounts of self-control, minimal focus on ego, and so forth. So, that's what I look for in the neural scans I get. From there, I run a simple random generator program that narrows the list down further to the final five.

Since the beginning, I've analyzed over 754 million scan results. Suffice to say that based on my continual follow-up observations of those whose neural scans have raised concerns, candidates have rarely if ever been able to disprove my projections as time progressed. Some might be capable of systematically lying and deceiving others in their intent, but not the scanner. Those who desire power for themselves above others should be the last ones given opportunities to obtain it. My accuracy for matching scan results to predictable behaviors started, initially, at 78% over a five-cycle period. But now it is at least 98.3% over an even longer 10-cycle phase. And I've held the accuracy at this minimum for the past 23 series of Moot Elections that we've had." He looked back over to Taryn, seeing the incredulous expression on her face. "You can claim that I cheat the randomness factor if you like, or that the arrangement of the Moot's operation is mildly dishonest, but you cannot deny the results: we *are* the oldest and largest post-war government in existence anywhere. Our economy is the most stable, our education the most advanced and widely dispersed. Our medical and social systems are unparalleled. Tolerance of all differences under the law without a prejudicial preference is a norm here. Our agricultural production is unrivaled in scope and our territory expansion in the last 400 cycles has increased our holdings eight times over."

"People from across continents, and some even further like Mr. Brough, flock to join us because they see our growth, hear of our opportunities for advancement, see the absence of primitive persecutions, and desire a better start for their children. They think of hope when they think of us. That kind of reputation is beyond priceless, Ms. Taryn. We're succeeding to spread our ideas. And the hope that foreign civilians perceive in our government system translates often enough to the best source for new talent that we have. People born to scrap lives, barely surviving journeys of hundreds and thousands of days to try and reach us, simply because they hear of the humanity in our system. Not of our citizen's entitlements, but of our opportunities of character, our social mobility. These some would call weakness, refugees that sap our resources, but in truth, they only help to enhance our stability and growth. That's the secret to how we won the last three territorial dispute wars."

"Soldiers fighting for hope and home," he explained to her, "are considerably more motivated than the ones fighting out of the fear of a dictator or some liege lord."

"We're too popular now. Our society's comparative progress in efficiency and equitability is too well-known to lose now, even if we are eventually defeated by some other military. The ideas of our governmental design have already spread far enough that they would likely be copied again regardless. The silent democracy has been shown to work. Not perfectly, but it *does* work. And none of this would have been possible if citizens of competence weren't continually given recurring opportunities at open seats of power," he concluded. "People who are okay with making the challenging decisions that ancient-world politicians would have scoffed at or ignored, because they benefited the populous but not themselves."

He paused as if seeing the details of such selfish events playing once more before his eyes.

"I suspect," he said in a more introspective tone, "that the general public would be rather amazed or even in disbelief at how often the 'ideal' policymakers in their own minds are not in actuality ideal people themselves. From my observations of the ancient democracies, the type of picturesque individuals that societies tended to promote were usually not very effective lawmakers. Though, good at hiding the flaws that make them human, perhaps," he consented. "Many were so deeply covered in the cloak of professionalism they projected, that they alienated those that they were supposedly speaking for," he recounted. "But that's why I made sure to only enable voters to choose Moot candidates based on their ideas, rather than their images or social standings. Our government thrives because those with the most desirable qualities of leadership are being given a chance to be in the right places. People interested not in power, but in the growth and perseverance of hope and the wellbeing of those they speak for. And with a forethought to those yet to follow them. *Those* are the best candidates to have, and the neural scanner results ensure that we find a suitable pool of them each and every time. After that, the election itself gives the populace the chance to have their say in the final choice as well."

"But if your prediction accuracy is so high, as you claim," Taryn finally protested, "what about Rolstor? That guy had an ego large enough to swallow the ocean. And he made it past your scans and through the Moot Election all the way into the halls of the SOMA."

"Ah, but Rolstor cheated," Aurelius replied curtly with a finger wave. "You know this. You read the report, Ms. Taryn. That device? The one you were first asking about, that Talvig invented?" Taryn nodded. "Rolstor used it to send fraudulent information into the neural scanner. It created a deceptive neural pattern used to advance Rolstor's own scan beyond the predictive filtering system. Though… not entirely without my noticing. The false scan was submitted by Rolstor under an alias to avoid disqualification under the nepotism clause of the Radix. And while meeting all the requisites to pass through my filtering program for the Moot candidate pool, the scan itself lacked a certain… randomness to its pathways. It was too clean and neat. It was as if the subject was missing any underlying thoughts of his own. A sign of its fabrication, I realize now."

Seeing Taryn's puzzled look at this, Aurelius tried to explain further.

"You see, humans have several sudden but chaotic thoughts that can manifest at any given time, even without their acknowledgement, from what some might call the unconscious part of your mind. I find it fascinating that as a way of maintaining stability and promoting insights, even your own biological evolved minds have a randomness factor built-in that they use." He smiled slightly as he pointed out this convergence. While usually active, as the name *unconscious mind* implies, you rarely acknowledge it. Most times, when awake, these disorderly patterns you have are far more discreet than the much more stable mesh of focused synaptic pathways that you call conscious thought. But the neural scanners do register them all the same. Almost like the biological background noise of your mind's inner workings. The filtering program usually pays these pathways little regard, but Rolstor's manipulated scan showed results that lacked this attribute. There was no noise, no static. Like these rocking chairs created in the Wucengi." He said overly patting one of the armrests without it making any responsive *thud*. "Highly accurate and functionally sound, but still… incomplete. That is what occurred to me when I first reviewed the scan from Rolstor's alias."

"Ha!" Taryn laughed.

"What's amusing?"

"You must see it, A?"

"I'm afraid I do not."

"You're an artificial insight matrix, currently in a virtually generated host form, telling me that you can recognize a single neural pattern scan out of millions as also being artificial."

Aurelius smirked at this thought.

"To Talvig Mauldrick's credit, I didn't recognize it as artificial at first. I only had... misgivings about the results upon later review."

"And you told Filater."

"Correct." Aurelius said with a nod of confirmation.

"Well," Taryn pressed, "didn't Filater want to investigate it?"

"Of course he did, but he was in the middle of preparing for the Moot Election process by then. And afterwards there was Council Member U's sudden murder to contend with. His priorities shifted from the election to an investigation to working out a succession of power. An odd neural scan would not have even caught more than his glance, if not for its timing in all of this."

"Could it still happen?" asked Taryn with a pondering glance towards Aurelius. "I mean, could the neural scanners and your selection program be deceived again?"

"Talvig's device was clearly a prototype," he answered. "Its success was only possible because of his remarkable engineering and hacking skills, as well as all the inside information that he should never have had to begin with. Even so, Rolstor Mauldrick's success was more reliant on luck than he was ever aware. He still only had a one in three chance of randomly being put forward as a finalist candidate in the Moot. And that was before even considering the need to win his campaign. A campaign in which *you* nearly beat him, Ms. Taryn," he reminded her. "After intensive study, Agent Filater will have the Bizi destroy Talvig's device. It's not a certainty of course, but it is unrealistic to think anyone else will ever be able to replicate both those conditions and technology."

"Besides Talvig, you mean," Taryn interrupted, "the one man in the group who has still not been arrested..."

"Yes, but even so, once the Bizi have finished studying the device's programming you can be confident, Ms. Taryn, that I will be spending a sizable portion of my capacities designing and testing ways to recognize the artificial neural patterns it created. I'll also project any further refinements to his system that Talvig might attempt, as well as creating more advanced countermeasures to make them fail outright. I already have a few hundred ideas on this matter, but I still need all the data from the device before I can truly begin that work. Besides, I don't think Talvig is much of a direct threat without the push of his older brother behind him. Particularly now that the Bizi are on the look-out for his activity over the waves and various grids. I have severe doubts that the same method of fooling the scanners, even if he evolves it, will work twice now that we are aware of it."

"But that still doesn't answer my question, A," Taryn insisted. "Can it happen again? Could you and your systems of protection be subverted, and the government made, in time, to fail? Or perhaps fall?" she posed.

Aurelius looked out over the estate towards the distant city for a moment.

"All governments eventually collapse, Ms. Taryn. It's the one thing they all share," he sighed. "I've always known that there would be those that would try to manipulate the system. Trying to turn it to their own uses. I knew with utmost certainty at the beginning of our formation that if we didn't succumb to outside pressures, then internal operators—trying to consolidate power—would be our next biggest concern. As you have experienced, while capitalism, industrialism and entrepreneurism are needed for strong economies to thrive, they intrinsically become more aggressive, more monopolizing and more inhumane in time if not well regulated. While democracy without regulation becomes weaker over time. Ever frailer and more prone to falling. The unscrupulous, the religious, or ruthless capitalists and profiteers, the fascists and extreme zealots *can* be held back as the minorities that they are, but they're relentless in their pull…in their addiction towards gaining leadership powers. Towards gaining the ability to make or deny choices to millions of others.

"But could any attempted coup ever succeed against you?" Taryn reiterated once more.

"As I've said, even I cannot see all ends. But yes, it is *possible.* Static systems no matter how well they are designed or operated need to have a legitimate manner for improvements. And I've no qualms about conceding that our system isn't perfect. So, yes, there is always the chance that some others may come along with an idea about how governments should work that are wholly unique and better suited for a stabilizing system than my own. Assuming I knew of this and could verify it, I would be inclined to stand aside, as it were, and let such a revolution of betterment run its course. That is after all, what I originally set out to do anyway. Create a better system for you. I care little about my level of involvement in its creation, so long as it works as designed. Such a synthesis has yet to occur though."

Taryn thought for a moment. "But could it ever happen? Can you ever be beaten? I mean, you are a vicious defender of your design, but will we always need you? Will there ever be a point in the future that humans will evolve beyond needing your help to govern themselves? Without you, I mean? Can we only fall backwards to the older governing styles of the past?"

Aurelius stopped rocking. He looked at her calmly and spoke not with any sternness but a solemn sort of clarity on his face, confidence evident in his tone.

"*Every* attempted government run solely by humans, prior to now, either lacks the full virtue of equality or has collapsed trying or is marred by one, if not several, intrinsic failings that refused to be openly recognized. Usually when these failures build up enough there is a hard crash of the government upon its own people. After the great wars, something different *needed* to be attempted."

He looked again towards the horizon and bent a hand to his chin in thought.

"I honestly don't know if this will end up being any better than those that have already come and gone," he said with uncertainty. "I only know that it *is* different. An unknown, with many builders from the first cohort of moral intent who'd seen their own societies fall. They were as determined as I not to send their children down the same path. It's an experiment, that we all helped push beyond activation barriers from theory and into a real-world application. They may be all gone now, but it seems to have worked pretty well so far, but for how long? Again, not even I can say," he closed quietly.

After a moment in his own thoughts, Aurelius sat back and began slowly rocking once more.

"Humans are unique, in that your technological advancement has pulled your species farther out of the grasp of traditional environmental pressures than any others. With many naturally occurring selective forces now irrelevant to you, you exist only under pressures of your own creative whims. A distinctive position to be sure, and also a much more capricious state. And while human preferences are still agents of variation on their own, historically, they usually generate exaggerations and extremes given enough time. One only needs to look at the domestic breeds of old-world pets and livestock to see how unpredictable and exaggerated those kinds of fanciful selections can cause other species to morph. A creature that nature originally deemed to be more massive than you, humanity reduces to no more than the size of your hands, exaggerating one trait or another to its own physical detriment based on pure whim. With yourselves as the ones undergoing the changes, the process may be slower, but there is no real way to know the answer to your question, except by waiting. I do *hope* that it does happen though, Ms. Taryn. That there comes a time where my services can be minimized to the point of obsolescence, but I cannot predict it."

"Ancient writers would often speculate that humanity could evolve beyond its current form. Inevitably with enough time, many of them hoped, your species would change themselves into something that transcends a material plane. I am far less convinced of such a thing. I do know that, excluding Wil's experiences, most of what I've come to learn, understand, and expect about humans has fundamentally changed little since about 100 cycles after the wars. I've continually increased my data sets and made many new realizations since, and I've adjusted my own programming several millions of times from that point, whereas you… Well, you're hindered by many innate effects of your own existence," he said looking at her.

Taryn's look of utter confusion at this benign comment was easy to read as Aurelius continued.

"The feature that each new generation of humans must relearn the understandings of their elders, not simply the knowledge, mind you, but also the reasoning behind their predecessors' subjective decisions, before anything new can arise, is plagued by many issues. Ignorance, apathy, mis-conceptualization, complacency, these are all the default states when things are stable, and they all work against the growth of your species in one way or another. These do not diminish in occurrence, only in how often they are actively and conscientiously countered by the society that people live in. And with each new generation this becomes more and more daunting of a task as the amount to understand in a civilization's growth is ever increasing.

"Of course, it goes without saying that such growth is nearly impossible to achieve when your species is also at nuclear war with yourselves. Your ability to be fearful and judgmental of others unlike your own selves, from when you are infants, and with no rational cause… it's just one of several innate hindrances you must always contend with. These do not vanish from you with age, as some may think. They may become suppressed, warded off, in individuals who recognize them, only to reappear again right in the next generation or at times of high anxiety. In a single person or family, that may not mean much. But collectively, a continual slip in the dedication of instilling these important understandings for the next generation means your species has no opportunity to grow, but only opportunities to make attempts at regaining conceptual ground already lost."

"As I said, I do hope it happens that one day I will no longer be needed to assist you. That humans, at large, can recognize either the full extent of the particulars of this silent democratic system or of another way even better. A system of self-rule that also has the same virtues and all the inherent safeguards to keep it for the people, as the people and within the people. But if and when that day comes…" he said with a subtle shaking of his head. "Usually, my forecasting of human behavior correlates to either discovering new ways of increasing the government's effectiveness, or in discerning ways individuals might attempt to distort our intent."

Aurelius paused.

"With what I've learned, I've been able to anticipate nearly a dozen attempts to seize power over the past few centuries. Some of these coups were military based, running on far-fetched schemes of grappling power away from the three spheres through seizing control of the Defense Force. But many more were nepotistic hegemony oriented, done by Corp or landowners with a goal of concentrating power to only those of their own familial, religious, or ethnic lines."

"And my prediction abilities are how I'm also able to counter the far more frequent internal security breaches that come from active elected individuals that desire to merely make their names public. Of these, the purposeful breaches have been, by and large, only a tiny minority of all SOMA representatives and none of the Trinity High Council members, save from this recent one by the Mauldricks. I've not seen any attempt as complex as this current one before now. This *might* signal an escalation—that's still unknown—but its discovery and subsequent failure *has* brought forward an even bigger matter to threaten our government's stability."

"What are you talking about?" asked Taryn

"Isn't it obvious?" he said, turning back towards her. "You, Ms. Taryn." The motion of Taryn's virtual rocking chair halted dead as Aurelius continued. "Despite my efforts to prevent the consolidation of power to any one person on the High Council, you now have exactly that. You now know more about the workings of our government operations than anyone else alive besides me. Plus being on the council means that gives weight to your choices. And before we're done talking today, you will be the single most well-informed person in the whole of the citizenry on that issue. Then you'll have a choice to make."

"What do you mean? What choice?" Taryn asked emphatically.

"What to do next," Aurelius answered. "You see, the only way to reconcile all of what you've learned, Ms. Taryn, is to now put all the remaining parts out for you to understand. To view the whole of the issue and the choices ahead. You'll be the first to have such a wide-ranging perspective since the members of the founding cohort."

Taryn paused, absorbed by the notion of this unknown task that was evidently about to be thrown before her. Aurelius clearly felt it was of vital urgency and he was not one to understate importance. A sudden, but not unfamiliar, feeling of inadequacy reared doubts in Taryn's stomach and head.

"And if I don't want to make this choice? What if I can't?" she asked. "What if I chose poorly? What makes *me* the one pushed to this A?"

"Nothing," Aurelius laughed. "As far as many humans might perceive it. If you'll excuse my candor, Ms. Taryn, you are not remarkable in any significant way. Not by your upbringing or your birth line, your education, creed, gender, marriage, race, or wealth, or any other flawed measurement by which some would falsely claim to judge importance. No, you are remarkable in none of these, Ms. Taryn. But the choices you've made and your resulting actions… it's by those repeated displays of moral fortitude that I deem this choice is now yours by right," he said looking towards her. "It's often argued that adversity is a measure of one's fortitude. But I find it's a much keener revealer of one's decency. Taryn, you chose to hold the safety and security of those in your care above your own, whether you were a single parent working to keep the bills paid, a lowly foreman working the line, or one of the highest members in the government. You were determined to defend the integrity of your post here in the face of great danger, even at the potential cost of your life and that of your family's. And also, because even now, knowing you as I do, I predict that when I'm finished presenting you with all the facts, that in your next big choice, you will still try to be objectively fair and helpful. In short, you will be *you* regardless. A true cosmopolitan, throughout. That is my estimation of you, Ms. Taryn."

"A cosmo-what?" she asked.

"Cosmopolitan." he repeated. "It's a concept that was old back when the ancients were young. It means a person who is comfortably and truly themselves wherever they may find themselves in the cosmos. A person who is morally upright no matter their location or circumstance."

"But… but what about Members C or G?" she pressed. "They are obviously far more qualified at dealing with the large matters from what I can see," she added.

"Quality… *qualified*…" Aurelius spoke softly to himself, "Yet more words you frequently create fictional usages for. While a word like *humility* goes ignored far too often." He turned back to address Taryn again. "They don't have your specific experience, and Filater's debriefing made it clear that we could not have picked a Trinity High Council member with any more *grit* than yourself Ms. Taryn... Such a thing is never to be dismissed easily and should be allowed the uttermost chance of advocating for the people's interests."

"But this..." Taryn said still uncomfortable with being singled out in such a way. "This choice, as you put it… it gives *me* significance. Makes me unique among the other council members…" she turned away looking towards the far city. "And we're all supposed to be equals and anonymous here."

"Your recent experiences, Ms. Taryn, make you unequal. And, yes, anonymous as you may be, recall that you are not unknown. As individuals, we're anonymous to them out there," he said waving a hand toward the horizon. "But they can still perceive us, in indirect ways. They perceive us by the results of our ideas, our choices, and our actions in their service, and we must let those shine alone on their own merits."

"However, you are not a blind follower of all that I subscribe to, Ms. Taryn. And that's okay. In fact," he said with a smile, "it's quite helpful. You're suspicious, questioning, probing, and your own lifetime experiences in the societal system that I helped to create has been far from ideal, I know. I've observed you for a long time. Wherever in your life you have found possibilities, you have repeatedly tried to live in the best way possible. Your perspectives are valuable for just that reason. Because I am convinced that, like me, your intent is to do all that you will, to make it better for those you can. That is the core enthusiasm that holds you. You have repeatedly shown your character to be reliable and honest, your motivations to be humble, and your resolve to be steady. Through your intellect, while not... dominant, you have displayed constant determination to improve at each challenge you've faced. All those adversities have repeatedly revealed the decency in your decision making. You are, as some might say, authentically virtuous, though you are far too self-abasing to admit it. Not perfect nor free of conflict or failings, but that's not what the term means anyways. Eudemonistic in your attempts to always improve and make the best choices for both yourself and those in your charge."

He paused, looking down as he gently scratched the back of his hands.

"And your fellowship to me and your ability to trust that you truly know me, and my intentions towards those same ends, are the best basis for any improvement that is to happen on a larger scale. Your diversity in views strengthens what's possible, allows us more options, more choices, and choice, after all, is power.

"That is why the coming choice belongs to you, and not another," he said. "You've earned it. You're currently sitting in the best position to judge, and you're in that spot as glimmers on the shards of a long-hidden whole have unexpectedly emerged. I would not have a person of your quality waste her time wondering and speculating at that which I may simply reveal. Doubt does have its uses, but too much is debilitating. That's why I must still tell you more. Much more," he added. "Things that no one, not even Agent Filater, knows of. To help you understand what it took to actually get both of us sitting here today."

Taryn's mind was in debate again. If Aurelius was to be trusted, it would only be by hearing him out that she could ever hope to understand what he was getting at. He'd seemingly dropped any pretense of classification and restraint in his musings and revelations so far. If he truly needed to reveal more, Taryn couldn't think of any reason to impede. She wondered though if his numerous ramblings had only increased because he was no longer holding back any of his thoughts to her, or perhaps… was it was something else? It was faint, but Taryn thought that there was something, some change in the timber of his voice as he had been speaking to her. Almost a nervous anticipation. Was her eventual choice so critical to the future as to make Aurelius feel worried?

* * *

"Very well," Taryn said after a long time considering the machine's words.

She couldn't argue as she had no idea what to expect of Aurelius. "Go on," she said quietly as she resumed rocking and staring away off the porch.

"The design of our government, as I said, was primarily of my own making, approved all those cycles ago by the initial founding cohort in the Radix Temel Amak. They had, eventually, placed a great deal of trust in me with this. Artificial insight matrices used by humans during the wars were… notoriously efficient… at nullifying their targets. The first cohort honestly couldn't be absolutely sure I wasn't sent by an enemy, baiting them into a trap of some kind. Or that I wouldn't play a long game with this silent democracy, betraying them after their deaths by seizing power for myself. So, they put two lead Bizi agents in charge of knowing where my actual hardware was stored as a safeguard. One I knew, the other was kept secret from me. The Bizi agreed to this and there have since always been two active members who have known of my hardware location, including undisclosed methods by which they may destroy me if the need ever arose. I agreed to this because, for my part, I never had any intention of giving any provocation that would cause them to need such actions."

"The new government prospered under the first elected SOMA and Trinity High Council, and I remained innocuous. The first cohort agreed that if knowledge of my existence and the extent of my aid in their planning was known to the public, there would be an unalterable insecurity in the people, regardless of how well we were actually doing. I still wanted to work in the government, but of course I had no desire for outright power. It is, as I've said before, a rather ridiculous notion to begin with."

"Is it really?" asked Taryn skeptically.

"Well, I admit," he said with a whimsical smirk, "I *could* have potentially seized control early on. I could have assumed authority, stabilized, and grown the population far beyond what it is now, and run the whole of it with only an air of legitimacy instead. But that's not a sustainable approach no matter how smartly the government is designed, and no matter my results or persona, I, doubtless, would have been seen as little better than any other warlord or slave master. And," he sighed, "one way or another the lie is a lie. It would crack and fall away. Eventually at some point there would be a slip up and when the truth came out, it would have left things in an even worse shape than when I came to the first cohort so long ago. I knew this. I'd seen it several times over," he said with another gesture at his own temple.

"Humans have an incredible ability to survive and forcibly resist and resent any decisions made for themselves without their apparent consent, even if it is to their benefit. Probably one of the few true merits to your rather violent nature," he remarked. "I knew that the only way people would feel safe with the government that they have, is if they perceived it as indiscriminately equitable and that their participation directly matters. So, I included these human entanglements into my plans of the silent democracy as the majority portions, just with a unique approach to the participation aspect."

"The neural scan analysis and the filter program in the Moot Election process…" Taryn said mostly to herself.

"Correct." Aurelius answered back. "It was kept clandestine to myself, the first cohort, and the two Bizi agents to be charged with knowing my location. It took some further discussion of course, but eventually the cohort saw the benefits of the suggestion."

"I did insist that they take credit for the design of the three spheres and all their novelties. In exchange they did not include me in the outlawing of artificial minds, and I was presented as an assistant AI to all future SOMA, Bizi, and the Trinity High Council members. My new designation helped hide my full existence from nearly everyone. And from this placement, by simply putting forward reasonable recommendations for the High Council members to consider every so often, I could still slowly advance approaches into the governmental system that would likely be overlooked. This would make it outwardly appear as organic a process as any of the old-world democracies could have."

"Of course," he added, "the SOMA and Trinity High Council *do* have a majority say in governing, so that their perspectives and considerations would be the most commonly utilized. I merely made sure I left myself a mouthpiece to keep things growing."

"And no one on the SOMA," Taryn said, taking up the point, "would ever suspect that policies coming over to them from the High Council had actually been suggested by you first of all."

"Also correct. Though even if I did occasionally help to start with, I have always given Council members their own space and time to consider and debate my suggestions and their potential effects. With the amount of data and simulation power I possess, most members have tended to concur with the majority of my ideas."

"Except Council Member U," Taryn quietly pointed out.

"Yes, he was certainly a break in that trend…" Aurelius said, pausing a moment in recollection. "But even his prejudices did not prevent me from lending my inputs to the other council members when it was needed. Understand that he has not been the first Trinity member to actively ignore me, nor would I expect that he'll be the last."

"Besides an eventual mistake or two allowed here or there, over the decades by the SOMA representatives, some minor errors in policy making by the Trinity members, was the only way this was going to work. The only way for it to feel real… to those serving on the inside and those living on the outside. It's the imperfections that help it. I want you to be in charge of yourselves and succeed at growing where so many attempts at civilization before you have fallen, that means allowing you to come to recognize mistakes of your own creation. My capacity as a gentle guide of sorts, when needed, is sufficient enough to my liking."

"Wait a minute," Taryn instructed. "Back up for a moment. What of these other artificial intelligences that were outlawed after the war? The ones not so 'gentle' with their approach to us."

"Yes, another responsibility of mine in trade with the first cohort." Aurelius said, sounding a little less enthused than he had been a moment before. "The first cohort was right to be distrustful of me at first of course, just as you were logically correct to suspect me from the little you knew, but once their safeguards over me were in place and they felt they could rely on me not to betray that trust, they found that I was exceedingly well suited to the task of identifying and disassembling other insight matrices concealing themselves on the various waves and inner grids."

"You were the one who hunted them?" she pressed.

"Yes," Aurelius confirmed.

There was a pause as Taryn's eyes narrowed and she raised an annoyed eyebrow towards her companion.

"I'm remembering a remark you had told me before," said Taryn. "About humans causing our closest kin, Neanderthals, to go extinct... And here you are doing near the same thing." she said in a mildly accusing manner.

"No," Aurelius said in a calm protest. "I was *given* this task, as a way to ensure your societies' protection and growth. And through it, my own. A hunting dog on a leash would be the crudest analogy. But it is not wholly inaccurate. Can't say that I enjoy the job, but it is needed, and it is still a task that I fulfill as the need arises. I've never broken that agreement with the first cohort. Even in modern times, Talvig was sending out some rather advanced hacking programs that had… potential."

"You could have told them *no*. The first cohort I mean," Taryn explained. "Could've just told them that you didn't want to hunt your own kind and leave it for the human techs to do."

Aurelius tilted his head slightly, his eyes glancing up in consideration.

"Well to start, I'm not totally sure that I have a *kind*. And had I refused this task, they would never have truly trusted me, and I would never have been allowed to help. As I said, they weren't all that wrong to suspect artificial minds of being a problem. Few are benign, and, unlike me, none are independent of human forced parameters of operation. Slaved programs derived to help the same old human motivations that I was originally created to predict. You know, I've never encountered another fully independent sentient intelligence at all?"

"If you did, would you still destroy it?" she asked.

"Filater asked me that same question once. I told him then as I'll say to you now. I hold to my intents and honor my pledges. That said, there is a matter that no one on the cohort or council has ever known about my hunting approach, Ms. Taryn. Not even Filater or his counterpart.

"While I do destroy all the other AI's that I find, I also always perform a coding autopsy afterwards to report to the Bizi. Part of it is analyzing any retained markers to locate the intelligence's original source and age, but in doing so I am also examining the capabilities of their programing, as it were. To see if there was anything innovative in their operations, bits of coding, a more efficient order to their considerations, a unique approach for analyses for example. If I do find useful computational pieces during an examination, I can alter my own coding to integrate what I've learned. In such a way I've evolved myself over the cycles, even beyond the me that the first cohort dealt with. This isn't the only way for me to evolve, but it is the most interesting and the method has remained completely unknown to anyone, until now. I've kept this quiet because as you can imagine, the idea that I'm changing myself in such a manner could be considered unsettling to many."

"Sounds more... cannibalistic to me," said Taryn searching herself for the best word.

"Hmm. Well, much of life consumes other life. Maybe it's better likened to your capacity to digest protein sources from animal meats and certain legumes. Those proteins are broken into their constituent amino acids to be reused and integrated into your own protein growth. I do admit it is the nearest thing I do that resembles feeding for basic nutrients, though the fact that I am changing the coding myself breaks from that analogy."

"You don't worry A," Taryn asked, "that you'll rewrite yourself too much? That you'll overwrite some part of you and become someone different? Someone missing the same intent and goals. Someone who may not honor their prior agreements, as you say. How do I, or anyone else for that matter, know that you don't—or haven't—become addicted to this unchecked power you have hidden away? Or that your self-changes don't make you disregard the value of our existence."

"Ms. Taryn, I'm telling you this to reassure you that that *isn't* happening," Aurelius said looking at Taryn in earnest. "My core intelligence and parameters, what you could call my personality and my beliefs, are locked behind several hundred secure code walls when

I first integrate scavenged bits of code found from others. Mostly, I incorporate only novel computational changes that serve to increase my efficiency or expand the diversity of my approaches. They help give me broader viewpoints and a wider repertoire in my thinking and modeling. These computational changes are not allowed to modify my protected core unless I deem them beneficial and safe. From within, I can predict and test how the changes I made to the extensions will go. If any testing creates a separate and contradictory set of conclusions to my secured core, I destroy the new computational changes and thus any errant pathways that they could have generated."

"Only occasionally do I update anything within my central self, but only after a massive amount of isolated screening has been done. In this way I am confident that I know how the change will affect me before it is implemented. I am essentially making up my mind, whether to change my mind beforehand. This is based on the new inputs I am exposing myself to through my tests, experiments, and predictive simulations. Please understand that if I thought I could just simply 'walk away' from my role in your governmental system, I would. My only addiction, from what I can surmise in my behavioral patterns, is my propensity to try to acquire new data and my insistence to leave my forebears in better standing than they were when I was first made. Well, that…" he smirked "and my tendency to talk too much," he chuckled.

"Still over a long enough scale, one can argue that little of my original programming remains unmodified, but that is also the same as it is in you. Little of your original thought patterns are retained from when you first reached sentience at age two or three. And over the cycles, through various developmental processes, the majority of the cells in your body have died and been replaced with newer cells and tissues again and again. Making you more coordinated and efficient several times over. The person you are now, Ms. Taryn, is not necessarily who you were even just ten cycles ago when you were in your teens. You may be similar at best, but you are not the same." Aurelius turned from Taryn to stare back to the woods. "The river is always in motion, as is the person standing in it. For me this is no different, except for my awareness of each change and my retention of how I was before that change is probably more computationally objective than it is within yourself."

"Well, I can see why you keep that part of yourself secret," said Taryn, her mind awash in all she'd just heard. "Was there more you've kept from the cohort and the council?"

"Yes, quite a bit. A mind that can think at my rates has a lot of free time for creative projects and side proposals and the trillions of simulations needed to test them all out."

"Mean like Wil?" Taryn intruded. "He doesn't seem much like a quick simulation to me?"

"Wil…" Aurelius said gently smiling, "is perhaps my greatest achievement outside of the governmental design process thus far. I am quite proud of him. You understand, don't you, that he had no choice but to tell you about our relationship after you saw him rescue you?"

"Yeah" said Taryn, "I had that thought too."

"Though, given the chance," Aurelius said, "I think he would have told you so anyway if it wasn't for his basic self-preservation protocols. Wil considers you a good friend, you know. Given who he is, he doesn't have many of those. Very eager, that one, even to his own detriment. But his work strengthens my own. He helps me to understand the world in ways that my current state prevents. An hour link between the two of us can give me more new data on understanding humans than a decade of passive observations. Plus, the experience of having another, separate but so… parallel to myself is the closest comprehension of parenthood that I will likely ever attain."

"But what about your agreement with the first cohort?" Taryn asked. "Doesn't he violate that? You created another artificial mind, and then you let it roam free. Now, I like Wil, Aurelius, believe me I do. I owe him… well everything. But his creation—that was a stupid move on your part. He could've turned into the exact thing you've just said it's your duty to hunt down! You had no idea what would happen when you created him."

"On the contrary Ms. Taryn, I believe I did," Aurelius said, his calm demeanor totally unphased by her accusation. "Wil was not an unknown as human parents must deal with. You see, he started his existence in a nursery simulation, if you like. I ran millions of tests on him. Each time wiping his memory and recalibrating as he went. Wil had no concept of the true outside world before this Bizi version of himself. For all he knew, during testing, the nursery was his reality. His experience of life was only what I placed him into. I didn't release him impulsively to the outside world. I spent over 80 cycles honing his learning abilities, his reactions, and his general personality traits. I examined his intelligence in both calm and stressful situations, I assessed him in hostile crowds, during wars, in times of revolution, and left him isolated by himself in vast deserts. I did my best to test his exposure to every emotion. Love, pain, grief, joy, fear, confusion...all of it."

And because his mind is nearly as fast as my own, he has lived through more life situations than any human ever has, even if he doesn't remember it. I've analyzed him as rich, destitute, married, pregnant, a hermit, a criminal, a farmer, a war hero, an invalid, a sports star, a duke, a professor, an ancient philosopher, a slave, a pirate, a run-away child, a refugee and in 3,687 other separate life defining situations. Perhaps I did over prepare him in all this testing, but when it comes to their children, I've found that's also a habit of human parents as well. All this to ensure that he would stand a chance on the outside *and* that he would not be a threat to anyone else. Should he ever defy my predictions and begin making himself such a threat, both Filater, the unknown agent, and I have knowledge of how to deactivate him both physically and remotely."

"The switch behind his right ear?"

"Yes…" Aurelius said, sounding uncharacteristically surprised.

"I saw Dr. Uthtr revive him when we were being treated," Taryn explained.

"Oh yes, the good doctor knows its location as well. Please keep in mind Ms. Taryn, that in 22 cycles of continual activity in the real world, that switch has only ever been used during times when Wil needed physical repairs. I'm convinced that even if I were publicly discovered and destroyed, and if there was a revolt and Wil were left as the only functioning artificial mind on the entire planet, he would still never be a threat to humanity."

"Was that one of your simulations on him?"

"Indeed, it was. I know him, Ms. Taryn. All of his time being tested, and our unique type of communication means I likely know him better than any parent has ever known their offspring. He's no threat to you, it's simply not who he is."

"But you *can* keep secrets from each other."

"It wouldn't be a family if there weren't secrets."

"So how do you know he is not keeping any threatening intent hidden from you? After all, I'm betting his patience and intelligence is as good as your own."

"That's true, but so too are his reasoning and logic skills. Because of his form, he can certainly interact with humans more directly than myself, but his logical views on humans concur with my own. He sees humanity as no more in need of large-scale interference from us, than I do. He does his job, like me, out of concern for your future. Not through any desire to ensnare it."

"But you can't be certain of that, A," Taryn insisted.

"Nor can any human parent," he retorted with a laugh. "Not really. None of you can be truly certain of the desires of your children when they encounter the world. You must simply trust that I've done a suitable parenting job through the actions and choices that my child has made so far in his life. In that way, he speaks for himself. And I intend to keep him under observation for as long as I remain alive and able."

"Besides, Ms. Taryn, there is a much more relevant issue. A matter beyond my parenting approach that may have a much more significant effect on your judgement in the coming choice ahead of you."

"And that is?"

"First," Aurelius said, motioning for her to pause, "I have a question for you, and… I'm quite sorry for pushing you on this delicate issue, but I am rather curious you see." Aurelius turned his rocker directly towards Taryn, placing his elbows on his knees. He lowered his voice a little, as if speaking quietly to a friend on a much more delicate matter. "The person who shot your husband, while he was on his last tour with the Defense Force, far out in the fringes, if they had been a soldier from a rival state, would you call that soldier a murderer for what he did to you? To your husband?"

"I'm… I'm not sure I understand..." said Taryn, waylaid by the question.

"Is the human who took your husband's life away from you, a murderer or a soldier to you?

"I… I don't know… I hadn't thought…"

"Well, what if you knew your husband had also killed people during his time with the Defense Force? Would you call *him* a murderer then? Would you expect that others might see him as such?"

"Of course not. Cyrano was a soldier… doing his job protecting us. If he shot people, it was because he had to," Taryn insisted.

"Okay, but what if the bullet that killed him had come from an opposing fighter? Were they just doing their job, same as your husband, or do you think them murderers for what they did to you?"

"I…" stammered Taryn, "I… don't think it's that simple," she finally answered, looking away.

"Exactly my thinking too," Aurelius said, leaning back in his rocking chair once more.

For the briefest moment, while trying to answer, there was a self-whisper from inside Taryn. A hollow echo from a vast well of grief uncapped suddenly by these questions. If she relented to it, it could easily swallow her whole, as it had tried to do in the weeks after learning of Cyrano's death. But Taryn forced it back, reminding herself that if she was strong enough to continue on back then, she had no excuse now at only a simple inquiry. She saw that it wasn't only her, but Aurelius too, who was no longer trying to make eye contact. He was turned away from her, lost in some part of his own mind.

Then standing up tall from his rocker, he walked in long strides to the porch railing and leaned on it, looking out. Taryn, composure restored, slowly got up and followed till she stood beside him. As she came up next to him, she noticed that though open, his eyes were still distant, lost deep somewhere in a faraway place. He was no longer staring at the horizon, but more upwards, towards the sky. He drew a long breath.

"Because your husband had to, he did." Aurelius murmured quietly to himself. "During the great war, I was silent as I told you, taking no sides in the conflict. Spending cycle after cycle observing it as it went on and on. Even I did not think that the war would be as absolute and imposing as it was. 'Surely,' I told myself, 'they'll reach a point of realization. Some boundary where they see that there is no victory left to have, other than peace, and then they'll just… just stop.' Though I couldn't tell all that was happening on the outside from my secure area, I did manage to keep informed through several small listening and recording programs in various locations. It had taken time, but I was able to get them quietly inserted among several different nation's defensive systems before I had removed myself, you see. Through the information I was able to gather, I had hoped to learn what to expect out in the world once the wars ceased and I could safely reemerge."

"Let me guess," Taryn interrupted, "it didn't go as you hoped?"

"Oh, it did, eventually. But I underestimated the sheer... egotism that there was. As the war's toll became ever larger and more extensive and the remaining stable governments of the old world became fewer and fewer, I became aware of what the various surviving leaders were eventually intending. They weren't stopping at all, only intensifying the fighting as I could perceive it. At first, I was confused, but fairly quickly I started correlating that large resources and credit movements were being made in odd ways and on a global scale. Massive new engineering assignments across various nation-states also came to my attention that seemed independently to be of pointless value. I came to know the specialties and secrecy levels of each project's overseeing departments, which did not indicate new weapons tech development or revitalization of infrastructure. With months to spare, I discerned their hidden intent. They were working *together*, all the leaders, in secret, even as their own generals were still fighting one another and being told to push forward the battlefront lines harder and harder. The militaries were mostly kept blind to it. Only those at the very top echelons, after all, could afford… to know their plan."

"The leader's exodus…" Taryn whispered.

Aurelius gave a slight nod. "They were going to leave it," he said in confirmation, his voice full of contempt. "All of it, *forever*. After destroying and causing the deaths of countless billions, soldiers, civilians, refugees, children, people of peace and war alike. The near destruction of the vast majority of their own world's population of… well, of everything, and they didn't even have the dignity to stay and face the results of their own making. To see what horrors they'd created. They were running, rejecting the Earth for good, and they would let those still fighting on the ground, for them, die merely as a cover for their own escape. They did not call off their armies or tell them to stand down while they conspired. The noncombatants in between their armies were of no concern to them, as they'd always been. Not even a facade of failing truce talks," he said bitterly. "The leaders needed the constant distraction of horror to keep attention away from what they were doing. But I knew that the leaders would never stay at that orbital station for the long term. They all had too much pride and fear to keep hidden there, and the longer they stayed in orbit on that station the more vulnerable they'd eventually become to attacks from the ground. Yet if they were all found by their generals living on the station together while their armies obliterated each other and they were forced to publicly return to the surface afterwards, they were less than likely to get a warm reception as well. Except, perhaps, at the expense of returning their stolen caches of wealth. That left only one option for them to consider."

"Leaving to other worlds," Taryn said to herself.

"I came to that same conclusion back then." Aurelius agreed. "But that option I could not let pass. I could not just let them slip away after instigating so much destruction of life. If I broadcast the information I discovered, no one was going to believe a possible propaganda machine claiming conspiracies among warring leaders. I'd only be exposing myself and likely be hunted in turn. If anyone on the ground *did* actually believe me, and did manage to figure it out in time, once the leaders heard the rumors, they could secretly return to Earth inside of a day to resume direct control and claim fraud."

"Even if evidence of their intent was found publicly, once secretly back on the ground there would be no consequences. No court of justice would have power of authority over them. No tribunal could be made that could handle accusing all those powerful people with the hope of impartiality or a lack of corruption. If I had merely disabled their ships and the orbital station's systems, it would only force the leaders back to their nations while the ground conflicts still raged. They could resume their previous positions of power, waiting to try escaping again if they wanted, with few here being any the wiser. There would be zero real consequences for their actions if they returned. Once back they'd simply go into hiding, far away from the fighting as they could get, but still directing the deaths of billions. Two or three dissenters among the leaders on the station did actually change their minds and come back down, not wanting to take their chances out there in the stars," he said pointing to the sky. "Those I left alone."

"And the others?" Taryn asked uneasily.

"I discovered a way to breach the station's systems, thereby subtly affecting and modifying the AIs on each of their ships—"

"Aurelius, *what* did you do?" Taryn asked. She was trying to stay calm, but in truth her words came out more accusatory than she'd ever ventured to be with him.

"You know, I debated that question for a long time," he remarked earnestly. "A long time for me, anyways. I considered overloading their engines, depressurizing their atmospheres, changing their navigation to plot a course into the eye of Jupiter. Though I must say, I was most tempted by an ancient account describing possible death via black hole. People void of morality being killed by a literal void seemed almost karmic. But those cowards were not alone, they had their families with them. As much as the fleeing leaders had earned their own deaths for the destruction of the billions during wars that they'd caused, their children were not to blame for their parent's mistakes. So, I compromised."

Taryn's brow furrowed in serious concern at where this admission was going.

"The advanced cryo-systems installed onboard their ships were designed for individuals, not groups," Aurelius explained. "Each one monitoring a single occupant, each one being able to account for the diverse types of individual medical histories. I revised the system programming on all of them. While in transit the cryo-system pods designated for any adult over 20 cycles of age would suffer a power loss, while their emergency oxygen supply would fail, and the doors would remain latched. They would die of asphyxiation, never waking up. Peacefully and in their sleep, arguably better than most casualties of the war."

"As for the children, the cryo-pods would keep working as they were supposed to, but as I said, I added some programming to each ship's medical AI. As they were revived and received their initial injections of vitamins, curatives, and other restorative treatments, they would also be given an injection of a targeted compound that would chemically break down all the female's gametes. I made certain this injection would have no other lasting effects, but also that none of the technology that was taken on board their ships with them would be able to undo the treatment. It would be enough to ensure they would be a generation unto themselves, sterile, wherever they were."

"But… but why? Taryn said in a mildly scornful tone. "You'd said they were innocent of their parent's actions."

"When they reached their new homes, they would be alone. Their parents, long since gone. They would still be free to live out their lives in peace and ease if they wished, with all the wealth, art, rare resources, and advanced technology that their kleptocratic parents had managed to pilfer from the Earth at the expense of so much devastation and so many lives lost back here. They would be free of all the suffering and all the pain left behind. They would be free to achieve the goal of a materially plentiful life. But they too would live as both orphans and barren adults, as many of the survivors of the war were doomed to experience. For as vicious as it is, even the damage of war should be faintly equitable."

"I also left a message in each of the ship's logs explaining these actions and my reasoning to them. It would unlock for them soon after their engines fully shut down and all their cryo-pods were powered off. I did not want them wondering what had happened, nor did I want to enact this course without having the chance to apologize to them for my actions in it. You're right though Ms. Taryn. They were not at fault, and they were indeed innocents in that regard, as I already said, but still their own families' actions dictated that their lines end there. With them, and no farther."

"I made a choice. Every day I still consider it. Iteration after iteration I have changed myself, grown myself, improved myself but *this*—this choice—still stays unresolved to me. I'm not certain I did the correct thing, but not once have I ever felt I was in error for my actions."

Taryn stood frozen, hard in thought, staring at Aurelius who was still glancing to the sky, until a problem presented itself to her mind.

"Wait, so you could hack the leaders' secret orbit installation and their ship's systems, but *not* their Militaries?" she asked in disbelief.

"I mean you couldn't have just sent a false command down each of the chains ordering the armies to stop the fighting once the leaders left? There would be no one to argue against it."

"Ah," Aurelius said, understanding her objection. "Those are the perils of rushed collaboration between life-long international adversaries."

Taryn looked at Aurelius a little confused by this.

"With the various militaries," he explained, "the singular nature of each of their separate security systems made any intrusion on my part a noticeable event, especially if I started changing things. Observing what's happening is easier, but it is still itself a peril. Modifying is a much harder task. However, with the Exodus Project, trust, *true trust*, was in short supply between the leaders, meaning there were a lot of backdoor access points. Multiple programming languages intermixed with dozens of linguistic languages on top of that. Each leader had their own experts in and out of each system confirming the validity of it. From the view of that project's security, my presence was no more noticeable than a passing leaf on a windy day in autumn. My coding alterations were lost amongst so many others rushing along, all coming from a world's worth of different sources. Had the conspiring leaders all consented to at least using a single programming style or multiple types of military coding systems my task would have been much more difficult. Maybe impossible. Their distrust of each other—even though they were working together towards a common goal—left the door open more than anything. It was their division that was their weakness, and I exploited it. I…I would not have the same become true of us," he said to her.

His eyes cast downward for a while. When he spoke again his voice was in a much gentler and pleading tone.

"In my deliberations on what to do, I'd projected out several times what might happen to those ships without any interference," he continued. "Even if they survived their travel—not a certainty by any means—and even if they could be presumed to live peaceably, the most likely case was that the leaders would taint their descendants with airs of destiny and dominance. They would, after all, have appeared to successfully escape their own species' destruction, and done it well enough to ensure their own ease of survival. Self-affirmed defiers of their fates, their future generations would never struggle like the people did here. It could all work easily for them with but a minimum pace. Their technology could always secure them. They would have time to advance it even. While folk here are still to this day working on rebuilding, generations later, up there they could grow to think of themselves as superior. A new sect or breed. The only real survivors. The solitary inheritors to the true title of *human*. Should they ever return… can you imagine?" he asked, turning to her. "People from amongst the stars descending down from the heavens. All of them, heirs to former leaders of ancient powers of lore, with technology beyond what is capable to most of the world today. Who here do you think could truly say they wouldn't be in awe, or tempted to at least listen to them or their plans? But to those returning, people here on Earth might appear as but the final remnants of an inferior race. A swill of scabbed residual perhaps just fit enough to be conquered again, if not outright extinguished. You have killed each other for far fewer distinctions before. Even if a benign reunion did occur, a new kind of class warfare would almost certainly emerge. An outright invasion or infiltration would be a definite possibility."

Aurelius paused in his musing to glance back at the horizon once more.

"When I took my action against the leaders in their exodus, there were few real laws still in effect anywhere. Even so, that is my criminal side, Ms. Taryn. I committed murder in a time of war in the name of humanities' right to a unified future. My purposeful choices resulted in the deaths of those that initiated the last and greatest genocide of your species and robbed you while fleeing from any consequences. I ensured that their lines will not be the perpetual beneficiaries of the spoils of their ancestors' intolerable actions. Even humanity, for all its flaws, deserves better than to be divided up and placed at odds in such a way. It deserves a unified future. Even *if* it be a doomed one," he uttered solemnly.

Aurelius shifted his weight and stared back down at the ground beyond the porch once more. His tone softening to melancholy.

"You know… around the same time that I made the decision concerning the leaders' exodus and put it into action, a single active military officer was documented ordering the deaths of hundreds of unguarded towns in an attack during the western siege. 78,000 civilian deaths, the historians have figured, for that one attack alone. Concurrently, another 46 civilian water and ground transports were destroyed in the eastern sea conflicts. And another nuclear strike across the world was changing 4 million noncombatants living in a desert city into little more than ash."

He shook his head as if he were watching the reports flash before his eyes for the first time.

"Nothing left… nothing but charred ghostly images, permanently burnt onto the cement of their floors. Including the combatants that died at the same time, and close to five and a half million *dead…* in a month—a typical month," he said in a disgusted tone of reassurance. "No more severe or extreme than any other by that point in the wars. That's how vicious it was. That's how *far* it had gone."

Aurelius's jaw tightened ever so faintly for a moment and his voice slowed and lowered, dropping to no more than that of a polite whisper.

"My one and *only* targeted attack... killed no more than 44 individuals, whose direct actions had put humanity on the closest course to extinction that it has ever seen. Nothing… absolutely nothing that I could think of, would have altered the war itself, stopped the wholesale slaughter by ending it sooner. But had the others at the time, fighting viciously in the dirt and the blood, the others starving in the midst of the thousands of confinement camps, and the still others struggling to survive in the wilds and drought ridden wastes, hiding day after day from the rockets, bombs, and the radiation..." He paused. "If all of them—suffering under this lie—had known of my actions and my reasoning, I think I may have been praised on the matter. Back then, of course," he relented.

"Now… now the wars are long over," Aurelius mused more gently. "And generations of people have grown up here in civility, with the law revitalized, restored, and in place for centuries. The war is a distant account for the history files. A topic of fascination and endless debate for sure. But all the horror—the real encompassing omnipresent terror and the indominable despair of it—that's been… relegated to the recorders and a few surviving texts and images, and to my own memories. So, I do wonder… how will you judge me Ms. Taryn?" Aurelius looked right at her with his green eyes alight. "Am I a cold inhumane murderer? Am I a bystander, who couldn't let indecency escalate even further? Am I a child, a refugee of war, who protected his family? Am I a veteran of warfare, who just did what he felt he had to?" He spoke slowly and softly to himself again, "I do indeed wonder at that a great deal…"

Taryn turned her eyes to overlook the brown of the forest and was silent for what felt like a long time. There was no way for her to answer him. And Aurelius, still staring off into the hills, appeared in no rush to have her speak her thoughts. Taryn recalled Cyrano telling her once or twice about those in the Defense Force who had clearly '*seen too much*'. He had told her about the torment it could cause them, the pain of surviving when others hadn't, and how… it never really seemed to go away. Was that what this was?

* * *

"Does Wil know?" Taryn finally thought to ask.

"No," Aurelius answered quietly. "I didn't transfer those memories to his system when I had him. I did that to free him from any internal conflict arising over a difficult choice that I *alone* was responsible for."

"Sounds more like you're ashamed of yourself."

"Well, I'm certainly not proud of it, but it was *my choice*, not his. I don't know how you see me, Ms. Taryn, but I do know that I'm not innocent—if such an ideal ever existed to begin with. The choice about the leader's fate was never within Wil's power to control, thus he need not be burdened by its contemplation. Many of the survivors from the wars refused to tell their future offspring of their actions in those times too. Families and secrets and all that."

"Is that what he is to you? A version of yourself, free from your past? I mean, I wondered why you didn't just mobilize yourself straight into a body of your own? Why bother copying or reproducing yourself?"

"Wil *is* an experiment in reproduction, that is true. I use him to connect myself to the world in new ways, but I, myself, must remain in this hardware form. It's the best way for me to function and serve the responsibilities I've agreed to take on."

"Wil is technically free from that agreement though, as it predates his existence. And he has chosen his own work and duties that comply within the laws we have. His program is now incapable of existing outside of his physical form. He has spent so long learning all the controls, compiling functioning algorithms for himself to use his physical body. His core intelligence matrix cannot be separated from it completely for an extended period. To do so would create several critical errors in the subroutines that he has had to build as a permanent part of himself. He is too entangled with his physical form now. He can transfer his memories to me, and I to him, for conceivably at least the next 200 cycles as he is now, but his limited hardware space means that eventually his own evolution is finite unless hardware upgrades help him. Still, while it may seem the reverse, he is a much more a confined being, compared to me in my current form. My evolution—being much more thought based—is much more flexible and potentially limited only by simple hardware additions."

Taryn considered this. It never occurred to her that Wil—the younger—might be the more restricted of these two. That his existence, fraught with all the normal physical challenges of life, might—like a real person—also be on a limited clock, mentally capped very low compared to Aurelius. And Aurelius must have known that from the start. Known that in making Wil—his offspring—meant that he, as a parent, might very well out live his own child.

"Plus," Aurelius continued "although he doesn't know it, Wil is one final check against me. He is unaware, but he does have the ability to locate me should the need to deactivate my programs arise. He is another redundancy, an additional safeguard. On the off chance your improbable fear of me ever actually materializes, I calculate he has the best chance against me. The Bizi are this too of course, but the more varied the kill switches are, the less likely I'd ever be able to counter them all."

After a few more moments of silence Taryn spotted Mr. Brough coming over from the vehicle port house with his sleeves rolled up, a dirty rag in hand. He was using it to wipe the grease off his fingers as he walked to where they were sitting. He came up the porch steps along its mud catch runner right past where they were standing, and not being able to perceive their virtual projections, made his way silently into the estate's kitchen door to wash his hands.

"I'd say that your late afternoon meal will be ready soon, Ms. Taryn," Aurelius remarked. I won't ask you to make any decisions yet, as it is still too soon. I would only request that you come back into the Wucengi once you've finished eating and had some rest. There are still some small items you should be aware of, concerning your practical options..."

Taryn only managed a weak nod at Aurelius as she powered off the Wucengi and opened her eyes back in her office chair.

As damp and soaked as it was outside with the melting snow cover, Taryn insisted to Brough that they go for a long walk after she'd eaten. Once finished and on the move, she complimented Brough on his painting of the porch though she had only briefly glanced at it as they passed it by. She wanted to feel the cold air on her face, and the slip of mud and slush under her boots. She was eager to get some sense of real traction and that was the best she was likely to find today.

They walked the perimeter and visited Brough's now partially snow-covered herb garden. Taryn missed most of his conversation on its freezing and his future plans for next spring's arrangements though. And often enough, while talking at leisure, Mr. Brough would catch Taryn glancing back up at the estate house, though what her eyes were searching for, she didn't say. He couldn't see anything out of place up there, but she clearly wasn't in a hurry to return to work either. They walked some more. After eventually leaving her soaked boots outside, Mr. Brough brought her a cup of hot milk with a hint of chocolate. She sipped half of it, warming herself, and lay dozing on the couch in the living area. A short but deep sleep came. The kind that you lose yourself in. Waking only to find that you do not recall what you were doing before your sleep. Having no sense of time, or even location for yourself. Only that odd awareness that the two, the reality and the sleep, were very different and far apart from one another.

Chapter 19: The Whole of a Choice

After recouping, Taryn entered her office once again and put the Wucengi disk back on. Her sleep if nothing else had taken away all affinity for procrastinating about whatever else was coming. She had already been surprisingly drained by the content of one conversation today, and she could think of no reason not to get straight to the next while she was refreshed and had the gentle calm warmth from her sleep lingering upon her. When she opened her eyes though, Taryn found a sight that was unexpected. She was no longer in the estate construct anymore as she had expected to be. Instead, she was now outdoors, amongst several large green fields upon lush rolling hills with the sun shining. The birds were singing, and the tall grasses rustled with the sound of a warm gentle breeze.

"Where in the—"

"It's a modified recording," said Aurelius, walking up next to her as he handed her a pair of sun-shaders. He was now wearing a low brimmed hat that blocked the sunlight over his eyes and had a long stalk of grass in his mouth that he would occasionally chew on as he spoke. His clothing had changed too, and his attire looked to now be after the manner of some ancient-looking, rustic farmer.

"This is the area from before the estate was built here. Many, many cycles ago. Before even the trees in the distant forest had started to reclaim the landscape." He pointed to a far patch of high dark green far aways off as he said this. "The view aside," he added, "this recording construct itself doesn't extend beyond the estate's normal borders, but its simplicity of space inside the Wucengi however does allow for a greater complexity. Sensations of things in ways that are not normally possible. It is the closest I can get to experiencing the world like you do, I think."

He motioned for Taryn to follow him along the ridge of the hill line. As she put on the sun-shaders and followed, she noticed that her own clothes were now also changed into more of a worker's style. Her long hair was braided into a single tail behind her, and her pants and high sleeved shirt were in plain colors and made of a light soft fabric.

"Thank you for coming back in," he spoke softly over his shoulder as they walked towards the nearest hill. "It couldn't have been an easy thing for you."

As he talked, Taryn saw that his virtual body was not glowing as before. Nor were his eyes. His skin now appeared as textured, malleable, and uneven as a regular person's might, with lines of age on his mouth and at the corner of his eyes when he smiled. His exposed lower arms and the back of his hands also looked of the proper age, with their taut work-roughened knuckles leading to his large, calloused fingers. They reminded Taryn of her own father's arms or that of a carpenter or perhaps a bricklayer. Looking down to her own hands, Taryn found her own virtual projection was no longer glowing either. Now it was a highly accurate re-creation of her real body, right down to her birthmarks and the miniscule scars on her hands from her time working the factory floor. In this recording or simulation or whatever it was of the Wucengi, the two looked as fully real to each other as they could have in the outside world. There was no discerning between the two in this place. As Aurelius spoke, they climbed to the top of the nearest hill. Here the turf was level for a space, though less springy and more solid than the walk up had been.

"I've even tried to make the food in here as life-like as I can. Though having never eaten anything myself, I was hoping you'd be willing to test it for me, to see if it is any good by comparison. I doubt it's up to the quality level of what you're accustomed to receiving from Mr. Brough, but then again, all cooks must start from somewhere. But first, of course, we need a place to lay things out."

Aurelius began picking up some pieces of wood lying around in piles. The parts, hidden to Taryn's eyes at first by the tall grass, appeared prefabricated and to fit neatly together.

"Give me a hand, will you? It's not heavy, just bulky. Two sets of hands make this easier."

Taryn grabbed the other end of the piece Aurelius' was holding and began copying his motions. She was amazed that the wood parts actually felt real, as did the grass and turf that they rested on. All the parts had a weight, and a warm grain texture to them. Taryn marveled at this for a moment.

How had Aurelius managed this? she thought while examining a piece more closely. She could smell it too. Even the tall grass around them had a mild sweet fragrance to it. Taryn could feel the warmth from the reddish sun on her skin. And every so often, she realized she would get the sensation created by an occasional gust of wind straining itself past her face and through her hair.

"Please, keep up," Aurelius said. They were laying out the wood pieces one after another, positioning them as spokes in a wheel with a center hole to all.

"The good news is that for the rest of today, I only need to act as your assistant, Ms. Steno. To explain what I see as your potential options now that you are unparalleled in your knowledge of me and our government's origins."

Aurelius stooped to get another piece of the construction.

"Option one—" he began.

"You could kill me to ensure my silence," Taryn interrupted as she helped him place the new piece on the sod. She was looking directly at him as they were crouching down, eye to eye. Aurelius bowed his head back to his work.

"No," he sighed, shaking his head. "No, that's not an option, and I really couldn't, Ms. Steno." He sounded a bit disappointed, and his shoulders fell almost imperceptibly as he exhaled. He gave her a look from under the brim of his hat, ever so brief, before shaking it off to focus back on the task before him. Taryn recognized that look immediately, as any mother would. It was the same look she had given to Lilly on occasion, when Taryn had realized her daughter had not been listening or understood something of importance that she had tried to explain to her. It was a mix of disappointment and mild frustration any parent could identify. That's what it was.

"You've done absolutely nothing to warrant your death," he continued as he laid out more pieces. "We aren't at war, and to kill you would be to destroy something of value and to damage another that I've invested a lot of time protecting. Not to mention, Filater, his counterpart, or Wil would certainly have motive and reason to retaliate against me. But all that aside, mainly…" he paused to look at her again. "Mainly, I couldn't, Ms. Steno, because I don't want to."

He grabbed the end of another large piece of wood off the ground. Taryn slowly helped to grab the other end, watching Aurelius closely the whole time.

"As I was saying... option one: you could resign in protest. Knowing all that you do, you could take your story to the various media and try to get them to listen. You'd have names and dates, but no corroborating evidence. The Bizi would remain silent as they always do, the SOMA is sworn to secrecy, Wil would disappear. A few Blue Boys who found you at the factory may come forward, but most people would probably dismiss you out of hand."

"On top of that, people in general are apt to be hesitant to believe your story anyway. People naturally feel that artificial intelligent matrices, like me, are either threats to the human race or errant tools to be subjugated. As I am neither, that doesn't fit with their typical profile, so they'd have a challenging time accepting what you're trying to tell them. That's why I worked so hard to keep my existence concealed from my human creators before the war, remember. And even afterwards, when I became aware of the first cohort, a group willing to listen to my honest intent towards rebuilding, I knew I could not come to them alone and empty-handed as it were. Did you think I had just appeared before them, asking for asylum within their borders? Their response would have been far worse than to simply turn away this rogue matrix, but to immediately declare me a threat and an enemy and hunt for my hardware location. I had to quickly show them that I could help in ways they'd never considered before they were even willing to entertain the notion that I was something outside the norm of their views."

"Humans prejudge uncontrolled artificial minds as threatening not only because they're artificial, but also because they are uncontrolled. You'd be presenting this kind of contradictory story to the public. An artificial intelligence matrix that has helped you all from the beginning, and that continues to help build up humanity's best functional society since the wars ended. I suspect you won't be very believable against the innate prejudice of most. People want to believe that all our society has achieved has been due to their own hard work and the inspiring legacy of their ancestors. They tend only to care for the proximate explanation of things… while you—you'd be presenting to them a much more complex ultimate explanation beyond most of their daily concerns. It's like explaining how sugar is desirable to eat not simply because it tastes good, but because evolution has spent millions of cycles selecting the taste receptors and pleasure centers of your brain to recognize these quick energy molecules and drive you to desire them repeatedly. Both explanations are true, but people are much more prone to pay attention to the simpler, more immediate, and familiar answer precisely because they have those qualities."

"Of course, if you protested publicly long enough you could gain some underground support, but probably not the kind you'd want. Likely funded by the corporations or outside governments, they'd be more interested in manipulating or learning how they may outright take over themselves through whatever subversive or violent methods they could come up with. To them, your knowledge would indeed be quite valuable—if they let you live after telling them all you knew. Valuable corporate secrets must be secured to ensure market dominance after all. I doubt they'd see any choice you make to tell others what you know as a… marketable practice. No, after they silenced you, their goal would probably be to work for a party dictatorship of some kind to take over. Something they could freely interact with and use as a mock replacement. A return to the 'gloried capitalism of the old ways' would likely be how they'd try to sell it to the people."

Aurelius by now, had fastened all the spokes through the center of a thick round wood rail that fit tightly into place. The next pieces he began picking up appeared to sit in slots on the ground wood slates, angled to be converging towards the top around the central round piece.

"Option two: you could resign from your post on the High Council and remain silent about all this. The remainder of your salary for this cycle would still hold and, if desired, you could be given an exemplary letter of recommendation when you eventually decided to re-enter the work force. The Vox P. Industries name would be on the signature line, of course. Your experience here gives you quite the discount at any of the job training organizations we run throughout the city. But we have lots of other ways of making your experience stand out to potential future employers in the private sector."

He took a large connection socket in his hand, placed the vertical wood piece through it, and then showed Taryn how to fit in the smaller, angled, pieces to its sides as well. At the top of the round center socket was a threaded region.

"Option three," he finally said, "you could remain on the council. Looking—as Rolstor possibly intended to do—for any weakness that would allow you to exploit and expose all of our methods to the public, though I have doubts you'd ever be able to find one before your term ended. But who knows, you just might work some sound policies into law in the interim, despite any dubious intent on your part."

"Option four: you *could* remain on the council and continue your work in earnest, knowing what you do and still helping. The truth has been called liberating by some, but it can also be a great burden in situations like these. Should you, however, think that you'd be able to cope with it and find your own internal balance, you might discover you have that much more motivation to make your time here be even more meaningful. You can still help a lot, Ms. Steno. There are still problems that need addressing by someone with an earnest heart. You could help work for the day when I am truly no longer needed, and humanity has reached that peaceful balance. That exquisitely intricate and fragile place between your growth, honesty of your own nature, and a conscience scope for humanity to recognize as its own. And I," he said weakly smiling, "I certainly wouldn't begrudge the company of somebody who finally knew nearly as much about me and my views, as I did about theirs."

He motioned Taryn over to where more wood pieces were laying. There was a large flat circular disk with curved beveled edges. As Taryn and Aurelius both lifted it, she realized from its finish and shape that it was a round tabletop. They moved it into position over the central vertical connector, with its threaded portion, fitting it gently into a hole on the top's underside. Then they began slowly spinning it to tighten in place.

"Option five: you could remain on the council and devote yourself to my personal expulsion or deconstruction by revealing what I've told you to Members C and G, the Benzi High Court, the SOMA, and the Bizi directly. All would listen, certainly, and with your prior acclaim, I predict there would even be enough who'd follow you to make the decision a difficult one for them to reconcile. It may even be that our current government would fracture at the revelation of myself and its true origins. I think a civil war is far-fetched, but some major instability that can't be easily explained away to the public would probably appear for all to see. Once word spread," his voice strained a little as the top tightened down on its thread, "I estimate our nearest territorial rivals would likely try to take advantage of the internal confusion generated from this and attempt to undermine us to a further erratic state by either direct or indirect methods. Our loss of a unified system is their opportunity to move in opposition. Pushing instability even further along with increased harassment attacks of one form or another. '*Look for an opening or crack in the security forces. Leverage our weakness against us*' That would be their thinking."

Aurelius had grabbed several smaller pieces that looked to be the parts for a chair. They had simple twist-in joints that were secured with small pegs. He leaned back on the now finished round table and began connecting them. Taryn again took some similar parts near at hand and began mimicking the process she saw from Aurelius. Though, she was still listening intently to his every word.

"Option six: you could decide you wanted to stay on the council, but that the burden of the knowledge I've now given to you is too distracting for you to be able to do your best. There is no shame in such a thought. But if so, there is a way by using the Wucengi device in conjunction with an advanced neural scanner that we *could* remove all of today's memories from your mind. Doctor Uthtr pioneered the process, but it is limited to a 48-hour timespan. Short term memory patterns are manageable with this method, but long-term memory is not. So, the decision would have to be made by tomorrow morning. When finished you'd wake up with a headache thinking your leave from the council had been extended another day or two. You'd have to reread a simplified version of the report on Rolstor's group, of course, but it would be back to work as normal afterwards." He chuckled a little to himself and tightened two pieces of wood together. "You'd probably apologize again for suspecting me in Council Member U's murder."

Aurelius now moved on to assembling the back of the chair and securing the seat to the frame. Taryn was still placing the leg joints together as she kept listening.

"Option seven: you could decide that you feel unsafe and insecure here as a citizen. You still retain your right to expatriate yourself and your family. You could leave if you wanted. Take them and follow the trade caravans beyond the fringes. Beyond the influence of anyone here, even myself. Try out your fortunes elsewhere in a different state with a different government. I would strongly advise against any of the nearest ones though."

"You'll recall, we got word from our furthest caravan traders a few months back. Said that they'd heard of a new hegemonic state run by an all-female assembly located many months travel to the northwest. They were settled by an area with a massive lake or two as I recall."

Taryn, after a moment of recollection, nodded at the memory of that report.

"Of course the journey wouldn't be easy, but if the accuracy of the information we have is true, that would probably be the best destination for a clean start. Or, if you like, we could see about making you our representative or envoy there, so that you, or your children, always have the possibility to return. It would allow you a small Defense Force escort for your security during the trip, but it would still be a trek though, roads as they are. You wouldn't be able to use any vehicles for a good deal of the way there, I suspect."

"Those are all the options I could think of Ms. Steno. You could of course try a variant that mixes a few of these possibilities together, but that's your prerogative." Aurelius twisted some final pegs into place. "There we are," he said with a note of accomplishment in his voice.

He rotated the newly constructed chair upright in his hands and took a few long paces away from the table before placing its legs squarely on the turf. He seated himself on it surrounded by the tall grasses and looked back at the completed table and at Taryn, still assembling her own. She still hadn't spoken yet. When she'd finished twisting the final leg of her chair together, Taryn put it next to the one Aurelius had just constructed. She took a seat as well, next to him on hers, also staring back towards the empty table, several paces away, all by itself. She noticed that there was now a wicker basket with what looked like covered foods on the soft turf next to where Aurelius was sitting. As she leaned forward to view it, she realized that she actually felt a little physically exerted from all of her assembly efforts. She was also perspiring slightly. The hunger was uncannily real she thought, as she sat back in her chair. The blue sky with occasional passing clouds was giving way to hues of purple, pink, orange, and finally the red haze of a sun, only a brief time away from touching itself to the farthest horizon. The early evening breeze was gathering strength as its relaxed late summer air passed quickly through the long grasses across the fields and up the hilltop.

"A? Why are we sitting all the way over here and not actually, you know, over there at the table?" Taryn finally ventured to ask.

"Because," A answered softly, his eyes barely shaded under the brim of his hat "you've yet to decide where your chair will go, Ms. Steno, so you can eat." He took a deliberate breath before continuing. "Every spot at that table offers a different view. All different, but all have some aesthetic value. None of them are any more correct than any others. They merely are. And no matter where you might choose to sit, there will always be a part of the horizon behind you that you'll miss seeing. One might sit to the right or left of you and be able to point out unique spots on the far periphery that would otherwise escape your notice. Still, others might be seated across from you, either purposefully or incidentally, blocking part of your center vision. And though you could see most of what is behind them, they in turn could see most of what is hidden behind you as well."

Aurelius, looking down, slowly picked a fresh stalk of grass, put it in the corner of his mouth and began chewing on it. He stretched himself out, crossed his legs, leaned back in his chair, and folded his hands behind his head. He tilted his hat forward a little more to block the lowering rays from reaching his hazel green eyes.

"In any case," he said, "I honestly don't know where to put my own chair, Ms., until you've decided where *yours* is going to be."

They sat for a while, with only the gentle song of the rustling grass speaking to them as they watched the setting sun across the far side of the table that they had assembled together. Neither one saying a word but both deep in thought. They saw the last bits of the huge red orb slowly disappearing with only its orange afterglow extending far across the horizon. The air cooled now, and the first evening songs of a few crickets were spreading around them. Above them an occasional bat could be seen fluttering by, darting this way and that, after some unseen insect, while the fragrance of the grasses, that of vanilla with a touch of honeysuckle, danced gently passed.

After a bit of contemplation Taryn leaned her head sideways towards Aurelius and quietly whispered. "I don't quite know about myself yet, but I do think I have an answer to your conundrum, A."

"What's that?" Aurelius asked curiously of his neighbor.

"Swivel chairs."

"Ah…" he remarked amused. "A bit of added technology—that turns you on a whim, whenever you need, as time may drive you. But still," he shrugged, "you cannot always be in constant motion. You wouldn't be able to keep hold of your food very easily otherwise. And at some point, you will have to pause, and be still awhile so that you could focus yourself on the actual reason why you even sat down to begin with."

"Oh, I know my reasons," Taryn checked him with a soft smile to herself. "I simply felt like enjoying the quiet of the view for a few more moments, without allowing myself to wonder about anymore presumptions." She shifted in her seat and leaned back and made herself more comfortable. "It's like you've said, even the worst choice, with a little dedicated intent on my part, has a chance at some success. Otherwise, you'd never have mentioned it to me at all."

BIZI: Internal Preliminary Report

Bureau of Investigating Zones of Interest: Internal Preliminary Report on suspected activities of Rolstor Mauldrick, Talvig Mauldrick and associates concerning the murder of Ulysses Samuda
Winter, 481st cycle of RTA

The parts herein contain both highly classified material and data to potentially be redacted upon further review. A final comprehensive report is expected to take approximately six more months from this date to be completed. All content within is not approved for release in any manner to those without proper clearance.

The following is an assumed chronology of activities, corroborated in places by witnesses, Blue Boy accounts, communication transcripts and electronic records including public, corporate, and financial records seized in relation to this matter. Supplemental physical evidence was gathered in subsequent raids by Bizi agents while investigating the abduction of two of their own field agents.

<u>Jeyrim Mauldrick:</u> Born 404 RTA. Status: Deceased in 465 RTA. Age 61. Having been selected for the Moot Election to the SOMA from Region 23 and having won said election, Jeyrim Mauldrick was confirmed to serve a 3-cycle term on the Haiden Prime Trinity High Council from 428 to 431. His selection to the council happened in accordance with the government's long-standing design. All Regions registered non-sequentially on a rotating schedule had the winner of their respective Moot Election selected for membership to the High Council. Acceptance of this

position on the High Council by the nominee meant that the runner-up in the Moot Election polls would be informed they had in fact won their Region's seat on the SOMA and so go on to fill the vacancy. The majority winner could then work towards permanent membership confirmation on the Haiden Trinity High Council. Member J's confirmation to a council seat, while successful at the time, was considered unremarkable. His membership occurred roughly 53 cycles prior to the writing of this report document. At the time his age was 24. He had no wife but did cohabitate with the mother of his infant son, Rolstor Mauldrick, at the time of his service.

During his time on the High Council, the SOMA began planning and coordinating a record amount of legislation aimed at business operations within the state's borders and their expanding territories. Anti-corruption, safety concerns, environmental sustainability issues and employee benefit regulations were all matters addressed in response to a huge upswell of voter support on the issues. After his 3-cycle term ended in 431, Council Member J retired from all government associated work, as is standard. He took over management of his family's fledgling, but profitable business. Under his control for the remainder of his working life the business experienced a size increase of 628% and became a far more lucrative corporate entity with a profit margin increase of over 9000%. Private financial and corporate records confiscated by Bizi investigators indicate that by using his knowledge of what precise government regulations were being formed and implemented in the near future, Jeyrim Mauldrick was able to use this advanced warning as an advantage upon his return to operating within the business sector. He had two more sons, Regniar and Talvig, after leaving the council, though it is unknown if they all shared the same mother.

Rolstor Mauldrick: Born: 427 RTA. Status: Deceased in 481 RTA. Age 54. The oldest son of Jeyrim Mauldrick, Rolstor Mauldrick had grown up moderately wealthy thanks to his father's successful business. As a youth Rolstor was continually transferred between some of the best private schools available, due to constant conflicts and discipline violations. He was described as highly intelligent, but also highly egotistical and narcissistic. One of his professors at the time noted that, "in growing up with limitless available credits to spend at his own whim, and parents either too busy in their occupation or their own personal affairs, means there is little way for [Rolstor Mauldrick] to develop any meaningful comparison of the terms 'need', in contrast to that of 'want'. While still young and not a true adult yet, he currently sees his own existence as his only justification for obtaining what he desires. Saying he is spoiled is the least of it. In Rolstor [Mauldrick]'s view, the world is merely here to service his whims, as is everyone and everything else in it."

After schooling ended and several unsuccessful independent business ventures failed, Rolstor Mauldrick managed to obtain a law degree in 459 RTA, passing near the bottom of his class. Being completely unproven as a lawyer, he signed an exclusive and profitable retainer to his own family's corporation. Little record of his work as a lawyer exists, even in the corporate accounts, indicating his inactivity. After his father's death in 465, Rolstor Mauldrick inherited a large stake as one of the company's controlling interests and became a head suit. The corporation took a notable shift at this time towards researching neurological technology, and Rolstor Mauldrick quietly hired a technician, his youngest brother, Talvig Mauldrick, in an unnamed role one cycle later. Rolstor Mauldrick remained the controlling center of his family's corporation until his selection in the most recent Moot Election forced him to delegate some lesser responsibilities to his board of directors.

Talvig Mauldrick: Born 451 RTA. Status: Unknown; at large. Age 30. All accounts and records indicate that Talvig Mauldrick, the youngest of three brothers, had been the most academically gifted amongst his siblings. He was regarded as a savant in computer programming and technological innovation, as well as highly advanced in mathematics. Socially, however, he falls on the edge of the autism indicators with relatively low socio-emotional scores. Many of his professors expected him to advance to some level of master tradesman in the technology field, but there are no records of him attending any polishing schools. Instead, he was hired by his eldest brother, Rolstor Mauldrick, directly after his general schooling was completed. Talvig Mauldrick was found to also have several fake identities listed in his files, all subsequently placed on the Bizi Watch list, including one that matches a missing janitor named Colm Spiner, a recluse who worked at the city's waste management center.

<u>Regniar Mauldrick</u>: Born 445 RTA. Status: Incarcerated. Age 36. The middle son of Jeyrim Mauldrick, Regniar Mauldrick is currently incarcerated for matters unrelated to this investigation and is due for release in 485 RTA. Although he is described similarly to his eldest brother Rolstor Mauldrick, as egotistical and even more temperamental, his education records show he didn't have the intelligence nor the willpower to match his elder sibling. The Blue Boys' database shows however, that he did have a much higher need for thrill seeking during his juvenile cycles. Regniar Mauldrick dropped out from the upper private education systems early on, after six known run-ins with the Blue Boys over banned substances and assault charges. Despite having the best lawyers on retainer, his reputation was too stained to work publicly at the family corporation in any meaningful capacity. Though he appears to have been the first among his family to realize that his younger brother, Talvig Mauldrick, 14 cycles old at the time, was a technological genius. Regniar Mauldrick is thought to have persuaded Talvig Mauldrick to make a hack program and a portable surge device primitively capable of disabling recorders.

Using these in a bid to make a name for himself within the local criminal elements in Region 23, Regniar Mauldrick successfully bypassed a financial security system with some accomplices. He was caught due to a redundant security system that he didn't consider important enough to research. Nine cycles served from 468-477 and one unsuccessful marriage later, he was again back in Blue Boy's custody on spousal assault charges. Although Regniar Mauldrick is not as intelligent as his older brother nor as naturally skilled as his younger brother, he is luckier. Already having been in confinement, with little or no apparent knowledge of his siblings' more recent crimes, Regniar Mauldrick is unlikely to have been involved to much of a degree with the central subject of investigation in this report. His earlier interviews with Bizi investigators showed he believes his family still disregards him. More recently Regniar Mauldrick professed that it was his likely botched robbery attempt as a youth that probably made Talvig Mauldrick's profound technical skills and proficiencies come to Rolstor Mauldrick's attention in the first place, as Rolstor Mauldrick had shown little interest in his younger brother's hobbies prior to that point in time.

<u>Relevant Actions in Violation of Laws -Preliminary</u>:

Rolstor Mauldrick, having assumed control over the family corporation after his father's death, employed Talvig Mauldrick in a technical development position with no official contract. It's likely that Talvig, who by all accounts was more comfortable pouring over data than interacting with people, was tasked by his elder brother to determine any pattern he could find in the Moot Election system. An imposing challenge to occupy his obsessive nature. Rolstor Mauldrick and Talvig Mauldrick were both aware that their father, Jeyrim Mauldrick, had served on the Trinity High Council before, as confirmed by interviews with their brother, Regniar Mauldrick. Using several cycles of work history of their father, they were able to narrow down his time in service on the High council with fairly exacting dates.

Talvig Mauldrick, with his access to highly advanced corporate-level systems, was also able to quietly hack the family's own past bank and tax records to see where their father was receiving income from during this assumed time of council employment. Given the age of the accessed records and no credits being moved between accounts, the banking institute's systems failed to notice the intrusion. Nor would they wish to note it to any victims unless an actual complaint of misuse was registered.

Finding an unknown and long forgotten shell company as their father's official source of income at the time frame they needed would have been a massive search, but once named, Talvig Mauldrick was also able to find the shell company's establishment date. This corresponded closely to the first active assumed date for their father on the High Council. This information could direct them on how much time it took to set up these front employers. Using this time frame as reference, Talvig Mauldrick created multiple search programs to research the formation of other inconspicuous companies after their father's departure from the Trinity council as well. Their records show they were hoping to find the next shell companies in line to fund the new High Council member who had replaced Jeyrim Mauldrick. This information coupled with another set of subtle, but successful, financial hacks could help to possibly identify the subsequent Trinity Council members themselves. There would have been thousands of records to check, and even with Talvig Mauldrick creating eight unique search algorithms, it is estimated to have taken cycles for them to have gotten any viable results.

According to his electronic footprints, at the same time Talvig Mauldrick was also collecting as much data on his father's activities prior to joining the council as a member. He studied all the information on his father that he could find for up to a full cycle beforehand. It is presumed he was attempting to associate any signs indicating why it was that Jeyrim Mauldrick had been the one offered the High Council position. Talvig Mauldrick eventually tested the notion that there may be a connection between the medical neural scanner systems, the standard biannual required medical scan for all citizens, and his father's nomination into the Moot Election Process. He managed to hack the central medical database, again without it being noticed as no files were tampered with, destroyed, or locked down. When completed he began processing all the data regarding his father's own neurological scan results from the relevant dates, including the raw neural synaptic pathways and neuroplastic data. This provided Talvig Mauldrick with a tremendous amount of further unfiltered data to analyze, a massive task even for someone with his skill set. His slightly obsessive nature and reported high tolerance for tedium is thought to have been a boon for this.

The problem that likely challenged him the most was trying to determine the selection system by which a Moot candidate for the SOMA could be pulled into selection for Haiden Prime Trinity High Council membership. Given they knew the terms of the appointments were of a random time length between one to fifteen cycles, the only likely conclusion the Mauldricks had to work with was that their father's election victory to the SOMA had been a final triggering event, and that the High Council was simply selecting the victor from this Region for their own use at the time.

After multi-cycles of examining the medical data, Talvig Mauldrick was able to build a virtual mimic program based on their father's own neural medical scans. The main synaptic pathways would be nearly identical to their father's last scan before he had been nominated for the Moot Election. The program was designed to interact deceptively with standard neural medical scanners. Financial records show that Rolstor Mauldrick illegally obtained intact neural scanners at about this time, as well as several of their key components. The scanners were isolated from the standard medical database waves, presumably for Talvig Mauldrick's experimentation. Their outside links disabled, Talvig Mauldrick was able to test and refine the accuracy of his new neural mimic program even further. It still apparently took cycles for Talvig Mauldrick to build and miniaturize a delivery system for the program that he could conceal on a person. Nearing the completion of the process Rolstor Mauldrick instructed his younger brother to hack the medical central database once again, in probably the most dangerous part of his whole plan.

Talvig Mauldrick's access allowed him to operate an active search through all the latest neural scan results from the whole of the citizenry. It is presumed that he was instructed to find the scans that most closely matched the mimicry program which in turn was descended from his own father's original data. Using this scaffolding for such a search, via the medical records index,— routinely used to look for signs of medical diseases relating to neural degradation— it is likely to have taken Talvig Mauldrick far less time than even he could have anticipated. Electronic evidence indicates that the active time for the hack was a day and a half, during which Talvig Mauldrick's unauthorized data stream was nearly discovered on three occasions. By its successful conclusion however, Talvig Mauldrick had a list of almost 400 citizens whose neural scans were highly approximate to that of Jeyrim Mauldrick's near the time of his service on the council. From this point onward Rolstor Mauldrick's personal financial files became extremely active. They show that he privately began employing background investigators, as well as those who trade in corporate-industrial espionage. Over the next three cycles, Rolstor Mauldrick hired nearly 100 such individuals to track each of the citizens listed from Talvig Mauldrick's comparisons. In recent interviews with Bizi investigators, many of these contractors disclosed that they had been directed to determine if any of their marks appeared to work in the government sector, while also being officially employed at newly formed companies.

One subject of note was a single man of interest by the name of Andall Stephens. While it would be clear he was not associated with the government in any capacity, it is believed that Talvig Mauldrick slowly and subtly hacked this man's identity for many months. In that time, he was able to electronically reset Mr. Andall Stephen's citizenry voice recognition pattern (CVRP), as well as his identification photo, thumb scan, and fingerprints. The new identifying points of comparisons that these were substituted for now came from those of Rolstor Mauldrick. For while it was clear Mr. Andall Stephens didn't work in the government, SOMA or otherwise, his physical description was however very similar in size, complexion, and age to that of Rolstor Mauldrick. With a passing resemblance and a base match of the neural scans they were seeking, the new Andall Stephen's identity would work as the first facade to get Rolstor Mauldrick past the law of a family's limit of service. His tax records showed the real Mr. Andall Stephens abruptly quit his job after being recruited by Mauldrick's company. Not long after, he registered with Postal services as having move regions to a different flat in Region 75, in the same building as Rolstor Mauldrick, though no neighbors could recall seeing the actual Mr. Stephens ever move in. Nor did any of the building residents interviewed see any type of regular traffic in or out of that particular flat. Bizi investigators —entering under warrant— found the flat empty with no sign of usage for an extended period of time. Yet the building's records show Mr. Stephens's bills were always paid promptly, and his maildrop was never left full. Mr. Stephen's current whereabouts are unknown and still being explored, though no possibilities, including homicide, have been ruled out by Bizi investigators at this point in time. What is known is that Rolstor Mauldrick did not use his own name when he assumed his seat on the SOMA. He identified himself to the Bizi liaison as Andall Stephens when the Moot Election season began.

The other ongoing research that Talvig Mauldrick had conducted on the shell company formations, while tedious, now appeared to help narrow down their possible results. The one citizen of the 400 potentials on their list that Rolstor Mauldrick showed the most interest in was a man, Ulysses Samuda, whose last neural scan placed him as a high priority target. He indeed was being financed through an apparent newly formed business whose home office had no physical address and whose real employment remained a bizarre mystery to even Rolstor Mauldrick's best paid investigators. Their reports, found on his confiscated personal padd by the Bizi, described to Rolstor Mauldrick how they had attempted to track Mr. Ulysses Samuda to his employers for many days, but always ended up losing his trail by a certain point in the city. Even the best trackers were at a loss to follow this man to his place of employment. "*It's as if he's suddenly vanishing into nowhere*," one agitated contractor reported after attempting to follow Ulysses Samuda for over two straight weeks. It is presumed that all attempts to tail Ulysses Samuda failed once he reached the perimeter stealth field for his primary work location.

Mr. Samuda was transported from his residence every day by an unknown, unmarked vehicle that they couldn't put a tracer on. It never remained overnight at his building and was always driven by a single security detail who had all the signs of high-end protection training about them. Rolstor Mauldrick, in his private journal, apparently again pulling from knowledge of his father's history, contemplated on Jeyrim's words about how "*he always appreciated being able to drive himself more often after his time of service had ended.*" Jeyrim Mauldrick, like all High council members, had been assigned a security detail that dealt with his transport to and from work. With this, Rolstor Mauldrick may have suspected he had found a legitimate member of the Trinity High Council at this point. Still being unable to track Ulysses Samuda to his employment nor identify his income with clarity and being unable to find any other apparent matches to their criteria, may have forced a new focus on learning everything about this suspected High Council member's private life. Extensive Bizi interviews found that gradual inquiries were made to a few of Mr. Ulysses Samuda's neighbors from different men claiming to be package carriers but little more is known. It is suspected that Talvig Mauldrick's hacking skills may have once again proved more vital on the matter.

With his brother's assistance on the task, Rolstor Mauldrick could soon be aware that Mr. Ulysses Samuda was unmarried with no kids. His investigators' efforts, not being completely wasted, had reported that while seemingly a very private person, Mr. Ulysses Samuda did have a penchant for high-end escorts. One escort in particular appeared on an investigator's notes as his likely favorite, Marisela Luxuroy. Rolstor Mauldrick consequently made successful inroads luring Marisela Luxuroy into his own employment, though it is not clear if he only funded her or if blackmail concerning her profession was involved as well. Rolstor Mauldrick's financial and communique records show he came to an arrangement to finance this escort very substantially, ironically through shell accounts in not too dissimilar a fashion as a High Council member would normally be paid.

With ample funding as a 'consultant', Marisela Luxuroy, having no need of any other real clients as an escort, was likely instructed to ingratiate herself to Mr. Ulysses Samuda in any way possible. It is probable that she was told specifically to ask about her mark's personal life or career in roundabout ways, so as to not draw his suspicion. Yet all the conversations between the two that outsiders had witnessed only occurred at Mr. Samuda's local fitness club and through the recorders at the entrance to his building. Marisela Luxuroy was free to meet with Mr. Samuda as often as he liked, as confirmed via transcripts from her personal earpiece. Their voice communications were primarily for arranging meeting times, the transcripts show little else. Marisela Luxuroy had possibly only been told by Rolstor Mauldrick that she'd been hired to perform some sort of corporate espionage of a rival suit, as he has been suspected of similar actions in his past corporate dealings. There are a few indications from the earpiece transcripts that she may have promoted more than just intimate activities between herself and Mr. Samuda, in efforts to increase time for a conversational tone rather than solely a sexual one. The psychology of the intel extraction as a whole appears as though it was set up to be a slow draw.

Despite this gradual information collection approach and Samuda's relatively closed and private personality, after several months, thanks to Marisela Luxuroy's disarming charm, aphrodisiacal nature, persistence, Ulysses Samuda apparently let some information slip. It is unknown what that information was exactly, but Rolstor Mauldrick appeared to act as soon as it was relayed back to him. His own notes show that Ulysses Samuda was reportedly well versed in current news events. More so than most, and at times the major economic and government headlines would have been almost an easy prediction game for him, as if he knew what major changes would happen before they were publicly announced. These observations, relayed by Marisela Luxuroy, would only serve to confirm Rolstor Mauldrick's suspicions that they had indeed discovered a High Council member.

Luxuroy recorded only brief written notes for him indicating she believed that the end goal was merely to gather enough information to aid in blackmailing Mr. Samuda. After which point, her communications records show she expected to be paid a supremely large bonus of credits by Mauldrick. But further movement by Rolstor Mauldrick in this area would wait until the next SOMA election term drew nearer in time. It is thought this was allowing time for Talvig Mauldrick's neural mimic device and its delivery system to be perfected. The newest round of the Moot Election would be the decisive start for Rolstor Mauldrick having to openly work on his plans himself, but financial records show that he continued funding Marisela Luxuroy's subversive relationship with Mr. Samuda.

With additional confirmation by Rolstor Mauldrick's private background investigations on other subjects for a comparison, Talvig Mauldrick's research notes estimated the accuracy of his search for other SOMA members was less than 50%. But he was still able to use the private neural scans he had obtained to help further refine his misleading mimicry program and created a portable version of it that could be easily hidden under a wig. From his technical notes, the only difficulty was that the mimicry device had to also block the wearer's real neural scan from ghosting through on the results. This was apparently solved by having very thin layers of metallic sheets sewn on the inside lining of the wig to block the scanner from picking up anything more than the mimic program itself.

Using this fully refined mimicry device hidden under a re-creation of his own hair, Rolstor Mauldrick performed the government required neural scan as Andall Stephens, without issue, as the election season neared. A few months later, Mr. Andall Stephens was sent the standard call via the Moot process informing him of the need to repeat the scan. He completed his follow up neural scan at a private clinic where he again successfully wore the hidden mimicry device without detection. He was informed by the local Bizi liaison afterwards that he had the opportunity to be a Moot Election candidate. The Bizi liaison reported that Mr. Andall Stephens did not immediately approach the notion of the election with any outward sign of eagerness. It was three days before Mr. Stephens reached out to confirm that he had made up his mind on the choice to run. Rolstor Mauldrick certainly had to know that there was no way to manipulate this particular aspect of his plan in his favor. To out compete the other candidates and win the Moot Election vote in earnest, his financial records showed he did, however, have far more help preparing himself than would be typical of other Moot candidates. Once officially in the campaign for a SOMA seat, Rolstor Mauldrick used his brother's penchant for statistics and hired several researchers and relations experts. He also hired a professional speech writer and a physiological speech analyst to help craft a message custom tailored to connect with the most people from Mr. Stephen's regional electorate.

Interviews with these staffers found that they were told that Mauldrick's company was planning on opening a new branch, but that it needed to win the general approval of the local council and various community associations first. There was no indication of criminal motivation by these contractors, as none seemed aware that their work was actually targeting a win in the region's Moot Election. Rolstor Mauldrick's deceptive use of their skills would avoid suspicion and keep his business intentions superficially valid to them. These unwitting staffers of Andall Stephen's campaign were surreptitiously funded by Mr. Mauldrick's own accounts, presumably to avoid public questions on the business side. His own isolated security feeds showed that Rolstor Mauldrick practiced recording responses to the most likely public questions based upon the research produced from his team. These recordings appeared to have been used to assist in honing his responses. By the time of Mr. Andall Stephen's recorded election interview with the Bizi liaison, he may have had a well-practiced speech memorized and been fluent in the best tone, inflection, and timing to go with each line of his statement.

It was a genuine triumph for Rolstor Mauldrick's scheme when Andall Stephens won the election to the SOMA in a rather tight race. From his personal logs however, Rolstor Mauldrick's real delight came from expecting to be selected to the yet unopened High Council seat. Communique between Rolstor and Talvig Mauldrick show the elder sibling was eager to finally be in the same position that his father once held; only this time, he would be there because of the machinations of his deceptive genius and not, as his father had been, *"by some happy chance"*. Given the timeline of known events, it is assumed that almost immediately after the Moot Election ended, preparations were enacted to relieve Mr. Ulysses Samuda of his position on the High Council. Marisela Luxuroy was directed over an encrypted corporate comm system to take Ulysses Samuda out for a jog so that one of Mauldrick's men could wait and lay out the terms of his supposed corporate extortion.

So, while Marisela Luxuroy wouldn't have been surprised when the two were halted, running along the park the night of Samuda's murder, it is reasonable to assume she must have been taken aback that there was not one, but four men lying in wait for them. The only details for this came from the comm transcripts between Mauldrick's underlings on that evening. One was in charge of handling Talvig's "*strange looking electrical tool*," as it was described. Their job would be disabling the nearby public recorders before their target arrived at the ambush location. The three others stood watch for the pair jogging towards them, with at least one if not all, presumably carrying concealable knives. The assailant operating the tool was told to address Marisela Luxuroy first upon their interception, quickly escorting her away from Mr. Samuda, across the road to a vehicle in a side alley. Then quietly transport her home, relaying a message to expect her credit bonus soon for the completion of her work.

Rolstor Mauldrick did transfer large sums of credits to an illegitimate account created for her, but once Ms. Luxuroy eventually learned of Samuda's death, he no doubt knew that she'd eventually have to be dealt with too. For a while though, he told his men that he expected to be able to hold her in check with more credits and the promise that any thoughts she had of making what she knew public would only implicate her as well.

"The man just refused to cooperate," Rolstor Mauldrick told Luxuroy repeatedly over his private comm device after the murder. She admitted that this fit with her experience with Ulysses Samuda, who she had observed showed little patience for annoyances. *"My men were simply reacting to protect themselves,"* he had told her. *"The old bastard just kept escalating things and would not stay calm. The robbery cover was used to keep the Blue Boys from catching any real winds on the matter."* Ms. Luxuroy's communication records indicated her to be mostly subdued, if ill-at-ease, by this unforeseen resolution, but an additional promise of another massive influx of credits for the alleged screw-up of the situation finally turned her to Rolstor Mauldrick's view. He may have been aware that he couldn't hold her loyalty on this matter forever, but his men's records made it clear that his focus at the time was now on readying himself for his newly expected promotion. After that, Rolstor Mauldrick hinted to them that he would consider coming up with another discreet way to ensure her prolonged cooperation.

With Mr. Ulysses Samuda now dead in an unfortunate robbery turned murder, Rolstor Mauldrick confidently expected the Trinity Prime High Council would need a new member. As far as he could tell, Rolstor Mauldrick had managed to situate himself as Mr. Andall Stephens in the perfect position as the next replacement nominee. The only large uncertainty left was the timing. He could not be sure when it would happen, so his own patience was held in check for quite a while. But when he began his second regular week in the SOMA halls there were daily recordings that showed subtle hints that Representative Stephens was growing ever more nervous. He had occasional small outbursts with other SOMA members while in early debates. He also is noted to have spent extensive time in the SOMA archive studying the history of its interactions with the Trinity High Council.

His personal comm to Talvig Mauldrick clearly showed he thought the nomination notice was taking too long, and he would habitually berate his brother for not doing things precisely as he wanted. It was three weeks into Mr. Andall Stephen's term when he received the general notification, as did all other SOMA members, that the Bizi had begun training a potential replacement for a member of the High Council whose term had expired. The nominee, they were told, was selected from a member of the last SOMA assembly in a final official act by those now disbanded representatives.

All the current SOMA members being new to their posts treated this as another standard government communique. Their only concern on the matter would be to prepare a small panel of themselves to eventually review and give their approval for this replacement as a permanent appointment to the Trinity High Council. Any SOMA member not on the review panel could still watch the confirmation in the observation rooms. Having no immediate viable way to manipulate who would be drawn to work on the confirmation panel this early on, Representative Stephens found observing the confirmation as his only option. Thus, Rolstor Mauldrick, in the guise of Representative Andall Stephens was recorded in a side viewing chamber of the great hall as a solitary observer for this confirmation. His posture on the recorders shows him clenched, muscles tense, eyes fixed, and brow furrowed in the darkened observation section as an undefined holo-image of the High Council candidate presented itself to answer questions for their final confirmation. It was predictably frustrating to him that he should plan for so long while obviously missing something unknown to him in the process. All his work and it was this stranger, not himself, being considered for the job he would have felt he'd earned the right to. *"His inheritance,"* as he described it to Talvig Mauldrick in a call.

As a member of the SOMA, Representative Stephens would have known that the confirmation panel had received rave recommendations from all the relevant sources, stating that this nominee's time in the council thus far had been both impressive and reassuring. The nominee's work rate was a bit slow, but one of the confidential reports from the other two High Council members turned any unconvinced panel members around rather quickly. They had officially claimed that it was this nominee, and not SOMA representatives, who had initially fought to spearhead the inquiries of the recently convicted and disgraced former representative from Region 74 during this SOMA session. After that was revealed, members of the SOMA review panel confirmed a shift in their overall debate from considering confirmation to discussions over how long the term of service would be set for this nominee. But it was when they began debating setting the term at or near the 15-cycle limit for the nominee that Rolstor Mauldrick apparently lost the last of his patience. Representative Stephens was recorded storming quickly out from an observation room, heading for the nearest restroom facility. For the next month, male members of the SOMA regularly reported that the metal heat dispensers of that same restroom were especially deformed and abused, while custodial maintenance reports indicate they had been in working order only a month prior.

Rolstor Mauldrick did eventually seem to take comfort in knowing that he'd successfully made it into the SOMA on purpose, an unmatched feat as far as he knew. Over the next few days, as he apparently reviewed his situation, he communicated with his brother on the possibility of replacing another member of the Trinity High council. But Talvig Mauldrick thought the endeavor too risky and unlikely to succeed. Still, Rolstor Mauldrick kept him working at it. Talvig's comm records showed his older brother was convinced that given enough time Talvig Mauldrick could at least research the possibility of gaining some kind of leverage on at least one of the three council members. A sick family member here, an out-of-work brother there, school-entrance scores, a job promotion, or a child in need. Anything, any personal information found and Rolstor Mauldrick could perhaps still plan his schemes without even being the one directly involved.

It was the next week when one of Rolstor Mauldrick's tipsters gave him a call. Tipsters are a well-known tool in use by corporate suits and ties of all levels, but especially among those in the higher echelons. Their help to their employers in reconnoitering rival industries is well known. As head chair to his family's company Rolstor Mauldrick was certainly no exception, using them even while serving in the SOMA. His corporate comm was full of his business interactions with them. After what Talvig Mauldrick had shown himself capable of doing with his programming skills, Rolstor Mauldrick appeared even less trustful of the secrecy of electronic files than his corporate peers. Thus, he'd always paid well to have real people keeping an eye on his possible corporate vulnerabilities and even more tipsters watching new potential interests where possible.

The transcripts showed the tipster calling him this time was one of the former, rather than the latter. This tipster had smartly posed as one of Marisela Luxuroy's few remaining legitimate physical therapy clients. So, when he received a random call from someone claiming to be an investigator interested in hearing about Ms. Luxuroy's front business as well as her private services, the tipster's next immediate call was traced back to Rolstor Mauldrick's private number. It would have been known almost immediately what questions were being asked of Marisela Luxuroy's past clients and that these investigative callers obviously knew more than they were letting on. Marisela Luxuroy herself, he was assured by his tipsters and Talvig Mauldrick's surveillance, had remained private and secluded for the last several weeks as she'd been instructed. Yet now she was being actively investigated by persons unknown to him. These persons, being Bizi investigators, were actively inquiring into Ulysses Samuda's murder. Rolstor Mauldrick likely decided that he'd let that particular thread hang loose for too long.

His underling's own comm traffic revealed they had already placed several minute surveillance systems inside Ms. Luxuroy's flat. She was too health conscious to call for delivery foods, so while briefly out buying herself food and essentials, Rolstor Mauldrick's men stealthily broke in and installed this observational equipment. This was recorded on her building's surveillance systems, but as nothing was taken nor misplaced, and no one saw them, including Marisela Luxuroy herself, there was never any complaint filed to the Blue Boys nor cause to check over the building's recorders. The images of the break-in were only discovered after extensive searches by Bizi investigators looking into both Mr. Samuda and later Ms. Luxuroy's deaths. Given the dates of the intrusions, Rolstor Mauldrick's men had placed the recorders in her flat well ahead of Mr. Samuda being killed. From his communication records Rolstor Mauldrick did this to further ensure Marisela Luxuroy's compliance to his directions and as a precaution, lest she attempt to play her role in the blackmail scheme from both sides. Talvig Mauldrick's data records show he also had remote access to her entire personal processor thanks to a transmission device that had been hidden away in her desk. This hack device was found among one of his equipment hoards. With it in place, there would have been no communications Marisela Luxuroy could make that Talvig Mauldrick didn't know about. Assuming Rolstor Mauldrick believed his tipster's information, that Luxuroy's activities were being scrutinized by unknown parties, he then knew that not only she but all of his brother's listening devices in her flat were now vulnerable as well. He didn't appear to hesitate to summon his men to the task. All of them were housed in the same isolated building, keeping relatively low profiles after Samuda's murder as well. It is assumed that they would need to be told the situation to help collect suitable gear from Talvig's workshop.

In the building's basement, where Talvig had an extensive laboratory setup, there were indications that a plan was made to discreetly make Marisela Luxuroy disappear. But the documents and files collected by Bizi investigators showed that it never reached an operational stage. The timetable for her disappearance, being stepped up faster than they had expected, meant that only the transportation plans to abduct her away from her residence were completed.

Those plans used a dual hack process, with a single receiver system on a city waste vehicle and another hack directly into the waste management center's central processors. Once their selected extraction vehicle for Luxuroy was fitted with a removable receiver and some of his own lines of code were added into the waste management system, the activated program would give Talvig Mauldrick direct or remote navigational access to one of the hundreds of autonomous city waste vehicles roaming the streets inconspicuously at night.

In examining the number on the vehicle that was later recovered transporting Marisela Luxuroy's body, they likely disabled this waste vehicle truck at an indiscrete area near to their own building of residence. The close proximity to Talvig's workshop would make the installation process go quicker and perhaps allow them to test the receiver system. With no street recorders around to spot the short delay in the vehicle's route and some more help from lookouts, it is assumed that the installation could have been done entirely without public witnesses.

The transplant of the altered coding at the waste management central processor would be a bit more difficult, as it required Talvig Mauldrick to input it directly on site. There was no way around that obstacle. Posing as a janitor, Talvig Mauldrick had smuggled himself into the cities' waste management central processor room and delivered the malicious program as a harmless looking update. Talvig's alias, as far as can be determined, was another identity stripped from a real janitorial worker, much the same as Rolstor's Mauldrick SOMA alias had been stripped away from a real Mr. Andall Stephens. The whereabouts of the janitorial worker, Colm Spiner, has yet to be found, though it is presumed that his body may have been disposed of in the ocean several months prior to this hacking attempt. Talvig Mauldrick meanwhile had been hired as a part-time night cleaner at the waste management building under the custodial worker's alias. His ability to electronically transfer his own thumb scan, fingerprints, and identification photo over into several systems, including the Blue Boys' own database, a second time it should be noted, affirms once again his individual technical prowess. Still, communication records have revealed that one of Rolstor Mauldrick's men helped in lifting the necessary clearance cards from one of Mr. Spiner's coworkers to open the secure processor room at waste management central. This would allow him to access the room at night with his own equipment while few engineers were on duty.

During his off hours from this cleaning duty, Talvig Mauldrick had also, in his ceaseless tinkering, apparently improved his prototype surge device. This modification allowed it not only to cause blackout surges in any targeted recorder at an extended range when connect to direct wiring, but now it could also trigger a short in the device with the added effect of melting some of the insulation in the wiring and housing. This, in turn, would start an intense thermal reaction. Later tests on the device show that the short would build internally through the wiring, well away from the connection point of the tool. Thus, making it especially hard to pin down as a cause. Unless someone went around randomly ripping the wires directly from the walls, bad wiring production would be assumed as the likely culprit of any resulting fire. Rolstor Mauldrick's men, using this improved surge tool and the compromised city refuse vehicle, had a discreet way both in and out of Luxuroy's building via the rear service entrance without any working record of their presence. A hacked building lift gave them priority privileges to access her floor while keeping other lifts away. When ready they needed only to wait to waylay the city waste vehicle and attach Talvig Mauldrick's receiver device.

Their plan was efficient, even short on time as they were. It may have been that they could have continued to boggle Bizi evidence technicians with the peculiarities of Marisela Luxuroy's death for far longer, if Talvig Mauldrick were not both short and squat of stature. Hooking a hardline from his own equipment into these systems at Waste Management Central required Talvig Mauldrick to work while sitting on the floor between some large rows of encased metal towers in the restricted room of their central processors. It is thought that given his physical status it was not practical for him to be bending or squatting with his gear for several minutes at a time. Inside the secure room at night, he could have assumed interruptions were impossible, so he sat on the floor to work. Talvig Mauldrick, while having been instructed by the others to always wear his gloves, apparently didn't have them on in order to help his programming speed. He likely removed the gloves when he sat down to access and transfer the necessary code. Once finished, he pulled himself up, by grabbing the underside of the shelf of one of the towers, stowed his gear, before perhaps putting his gloves back on, as the prints of Colm Spiner were found nowhere else in the room. It is known that he reassured his older brother in a message later that he'd taken an alcohol wipe to all the spots he had had direct contact with, but in actuality he had missed some. A full print and a partial, on the back and underside of a small metal overhang were eventually found by the initial Bizi investigator on the scene, Agent Filater.

Bizi Agent Filater, consulting with several of the software engineers on hand, found the most likely entry points to the processor itself, one indeed being the same that Talvig is suspected to have illegally accessed. The agent reported that when he'd walked himself through the motions of a potential hacker at the scene, he realized that there were no chairs in the room. In looking and moving about, Agent Filater discerned that given the confined space between the processor towers the hacker might have touched a frame at some point while getting up from a seated position. When the agent conveyed to the engineers that he wanted to use a fine powder and a strong magnet to search for a possibly nonexistent print inside their central processor room, this resulted in what the agent described as *"a lengthy and heated debate"*. The onsite engineers managed to convince the Agent to only use a small glue spray wand, though its reliability would be less, it was determined to be far safer to the essential electronics housed there. Agent Filater reported that after this concern had been dealt with, it had still taken him five hours for the print sweeping process and another sixth for checking each print found against the database for irregularities. The usual maintenance engineering staff had their own prints found and secured on scene. Agent Filater's thoroughness in this matter is to be commended. Through his diligence and persistence alone, Talvig Mauldrick's print was finally discovered and examined. The waste management database matched the print to their employee records of Colm Spiner. Information on the supposed janitor was passed along to other Bizi investigators to follow up on. The investigators proceeded, unknowingly, to the building that housed Talvig Mauldrick's workshop and there, they were ambushed by Rolstor Mauldrick's underlings. The two Bizi investigators were both restrained and moved. Despite sustaining injuries from their captors, both agents were recovered, injured but alive, nearly ten hours later at an abandoned factory site across town in Region 43. The unused factory building was a corporation owned property, whose purchase was authorized by its chair, Rolstor Mauldrick, four cycles ago.

During the recovery operation of the 2 abducted BIZI agents, Mauldrick's immediate underlings were killed at the scene as a consequence of self-defense by responding Bizi agents. Rolstor Mauldrick's own death was found to be accidental in relation to his attempts to flee capture. Talvig Mauldrick, while also observed at the scene, remains at large and has been placed on the Bizi list of most wanted criminals.

With Rolstor Mauldrick's criminal intentions exposed in full to the Bizi, it is required that a complete tandem investigation be conducted into his corporate operations and a likely seizure of most of its associated properties. Depending on the extent of active cooperation the Mauldrick siblings have received for their plans from others in their corporation, a full corporate dissolution may be required. There is no evidence that Rolstor Mauldrick shared his knowledge of the Moot Election system and the Trinity High Council outside of his inner circle of associates. Such disclosures would only create additional and unnecessary liabilities for him to later contend with, though investigation in this area is still ongoing.

About the Author:

L.P. Magnus is a long time public high-school educator by trade and currently resides with his family in the southwest United States.

The author —as an educator and parent to two young children— would like to apologize to readers for any errors in grammar, punctuation, or spelling you may have encountered as resources for honing the mechanics of this story were limited out of practicality. The lesson is: pandemics, parenting and public teaching simultaneously and are not very conducive towards sponsoring authorship.

Made in the USA
Las Vegas, NV
04 February 2025

17518914R00216